A WOMAN'S POWER

"Ah, Maddy, Maddy," he said, moving closer to her. "You ought to give me a chance."

"To do what?" she countered.

He smiled. "Come on, Maddy. But I'm always the one who starts the kissing. For once, I'd like *you* to take the initiative."

A sudden, reckless impulse caught her. He wasn't immune to her, any more than she could ignore him. The desire she read in his eyes was not the sort of thing a man can push away whenever he wanted. This, she knew, was a woman's power over a man. *Her* power. She wanted to test that power, to make him acknowledge it. She walked toward him.

"You say you're a man of your word," she said.

"I am."

"Put your hands behind your back. Promise me you'll keep them there." Bemused, he obeyed.

Going up on tiptoe, she slowly eased her arms around his neck. The reaction of his body was instantaneous, and profound. Because he couldn't touch her, she felt safe. And more reckless than ever. The planes of his face had gone taut with desire. She knew he longed to touch her, to crush her to him. And he couldn't. Bound by his own word, he couldn't. She could do anything she wanted to him, anything at all, and he could only stand here and let her. It was a heady thought. It thrilled her to an astonishing degree.

UNTAMED HEARTS

Wendy Haley

ZEBRA BOOKS
KENSINGTON PUBLISHING CORP.

To Mom and Dad
for always being there.

ZEBRA BOOKS are published by

Kensington Publishing Corp.
850 Third Avenue
New York, NY 10022

Zebra and the Z logo Reg. U.S. Pat. & TM Off.

First Printing: October, 1996
10 9 8 7 6 5 4 3 2 1

Printed in the United States of America

Prologue

Cofield, Texas
1868

"Good heavens, Maddy. What have you gotten us into now?"

Madeline Saylor glanced at her older sister. Blanche's fragile, heart-shaped face had gone pale with dismay as she surveyed what was to be their new home.

"What's the matter, dear?" Maddy asked, although she already knew.

"It's . . . it just seems so, well, uncivilized."

With a sigh, Madeline looked out over the town of Cofield, Texas. It had sprung up in the West Texas hills like a great, sprawling mushroom—faster, it seemed, than paint and good taste could keep up. Yes, it was a crude little town compared to the gentle civility of Virginia. But the War had taken that life away, and Cofield held something infinitely precious: hope.

"Take a deep breath, Blanche," she said.

With a startled glance, Blanche obeyed. Maddy, too, filled her lungs. The air was tinged with sunshine and wood smoke, with a definite underlying aroma of cattle.

"That's the smell of the future," Maddy said. "Tallwood is the past, and like everything else we once owned, gone. But we Saylors have always carried everything we need here," she tapped her head, "and here." She touched the green-sprigged fabric of her bodice.

Tears glinted in Blanche's hazel eyes. "So why don't we get started?"

"Why don't we, indeed?" Maddy's heart swelled with pride.

Leaving their trunks with the man who ran the stagecoach office, they walked into Cofield. Stores lined the expanse of dirt that passed for a main thoroughfare. Most of the buildings were two stories, obviously with living space above. The street was crowded with wagons, buggies, and mounted men, and a haze of dust hung in the air.

"Don't worry," Maddy said as Blanche sneezed. "It's the smell of vitality. We can be part of that, and build a whole new life for ourselves."

Maddy caught a glimpse of their reflection in a store window: two tall women, one wearing green-sprigged ivory, the other pale blue, both Saylors to their toes. Oh, Blanche's hair was a shade or two lighter than her own dark gold, and there was a gentleness about Blanche that Maddy had always admired but never possessed herself.

People stopped to stare. Some even came out of their establishments to watch the Saylor sisters' dignified progress down the street. Maddy lifted her chin a notch higher, greeting everyone with a jaunty nod.

Then an empty storefront caught her attention, and she stopped to peer in the window. Cobwebs hung in the corners, and a thick layer of dust covered the floors and the few tables that occupied the room.

"What do you think?" Blanche asked.

"I—"

"Kin I help you ladies?" a man asked.

Maddy turned, and found herself looking at a grizzled little man who barely came up to her chin. But his blue gaze was straight and unwavering, and his hands had seen plenty of labor. An honest man, in her estimation.

"Perhaps you can, sir," she said. "Can you tell us who owns this property?"

"I do," he said. "Why?"

Ah, she thought. A blunt man. Good.

"My name is Madeline Tallwood Saylor, and this is my sister, Mrs. Blakely. We are seeking to lease a property that can be used as a business downstairs, with living quarters for us."

Surprise flickered in his eyes. "I'm Bill Smith. I own and run the general store right across the street. Came over when I saw you lookin'."

"Pleased to meet you, Mr. Smith." Maddy held out her hand.

He glanced down at her dainty white glove, then wiped his palm on his shirt before taking it. "Ma'am."

"My sister and I are seamstresses," she said. "We've come to Cofield to start a dressmaking business."

"That so? Most ladies hereabouts go to Preston for their fancy duds."

It sounded almost like a challenge. Maddy liked the gleam of humor in his eyes. "Don't you think they would prefer to do business right here in Cofield?" she countered.

"Might. Depends."

"Ah." Maddy snapped her parasol closed and rested the tip on the boardwalk. "My sister and I designed and sewed the gowns we're wearing."

He scratched his chin, an audible scrape of fingernails on day-old whiskers as he looked them over. "Real nice," he said after a moment. "I wondered why y'all got so dressed up to look at an empty store."

"Advertisement, Mr. Smith," Maddy said.

His mouth twitched. "All right, Mrs.—"

"Miss Saylor."

"Miss Saylor. Where y'all from?"

Delicately, Blanche flicked dust off her sleeve. "We're from Virginia, sir."

He grunted. "War was hard on ever'body."

"Indeed it was."

He slanted a glance at Blanche, and his eyes softened for a moment. "Your man?"

"He was killed at Bull Run," she said quietly.

Bill Jones crossed his arms over his chest and studied them for a moment. Then he nodded. "Rent is twelve dollars a month, plus a dollar a month if you want the furniture. There's the front store and a small room for storage in the back. Two rooms upstairs for livin'. Stairs outside in the back."

"Twelve dollars!" Blanche fanned herself. "Really, Mr. Smith."

"Prime location," he protested.

Maddy nodded. "But we will also help your business, for the gentlemen can tend to spend time at your store while their wives are being fitted."

"You cain't be sure of that," he said.

"True. But you seem to be a sensible man, with a head for business. So you know as well as I that there are no guarantees. One must go with instinct, and take one's chances."

He grunted. "I've always trusted my gut."

"Good," she said. "Now, Mr. Smith, this space has obviously been empty for a long time. Wouldn't anything that drew customers to this location be good for you?"

"I s'pose," he admitted. Grudgingly.

Maddy made a quick tally of their resources; quick, because there was so very little. A mere forty-seven dollars was all that remained the Carpetbaggers' acquisition of the family home. Every cent counted. "I suggest a rent of eight dollars a month, and you throw in the furniture for free."

"Ten."

"My sister makes the best pecan pie in the South," she added.

"That ain't fair, Miss Saylor," he complained. "Not fair a'tall."

Maddy smiled.

He heaved a sigh. "All right, eight it is. You drive one h—

heck of a hard bargain. Now, I got one more question for you. Are y'all related to Derek Saylor?"

With a defiant lift of her chin, Maddy met Jones's gaze squarely. The Saylors had never justified themselves to anyone, and she wasn't about to start now; Derek was hers, she loved him, and there was nothing else that needed to be said.

The Carpetbaggers had taken everything they owned, but no one could take the Saylor pride. If Bill Jones intended to renege on their bargain because Derek was considered a criminal, let him.

"Yes," she said. "Derek Saylor is our brother."

"He's a wanted man."

"Yes," she said. "He is. Does that bother you?"

Bill Jones scratched his cheek again. "Nope. Jest wanted to know."

"Ah." Maddy inclined her head, touched by his willingness to judge her solely on her own merits. She'd found such open-mindedness rare. "Thank you, Mr. Smith."

"Now, when do you all want to move in?"

"Today," Maddy said. "Now. Our dressmaking supplies are being held at the stage office, so if you could tell us where we might hire someone to help us carry—"

"I'll fetch 'em with my wagon if one of y'all will watch my store while I'm gone."

"Why, that's very nice of you," Blanche said. "But we wouldn't want to impose—"

"Ladies, you ain't strangers any more. You're neighbors. Cofield might seem a mite raw and woolly at times, but us folks do help one another out."

Maddy smiled. "Then we accept, and thank you."

He strode across the street. Still smiling, Maddy turned to her sister. Blanche's eyes were shining.

"I think we're going to like it here, Maddy," she said. "I really do."

One

John Ballard leaned against the rough boards of a storefront and watched the dressmaker's shop across the street. Two tall, blond women came out and stood talking on the boardwalk. One was pretty and sweet-looking, with hair the color of ripe corn. The other had hair that seemed to catch the light like spun bronze, and a figure to make a man's blood run hot through his veins.

He drew a slow, deep breath, almost tasting her perfume on the air. Now that was a woman! Her face held the promise of temper and passion, and he had the feeling a man could get burned alive from her loving. Dangerous, yes, but surely worth every moment . . .

"Hey, mister."

Ripped rudely out of his reverie, John turned to see a young boy standing behind him. A very dirty boy, whose trousers were at least a foot too short for him.

"Is there something I can do for you, son?"

"Name's Tommy. Tommy Elliott. You're the Pinkerton man the stagecoach office was expectin', ain't you?"

John sighed, mentally dismissing his plan to pass himself off as one of the itinerant cowboys who frequented towns like this. "How did you know?"

"I heerd you talkin'. I hear most everythin' goes on in this here town."

Smiling a bit grimly, John crossed his arms over his chest. "And?"

"I expect you're lookin' for Derek Saylor."

"Why do you think that?"

The boy gave him a withering look. "Because you're watchin' Blanche and Maddy Saylor, that's why."

John couldn't help but be amused. He half-turned so he could watch the women and the boy at the same time. "Does Derek come to visit them?"

"If'n he has, no one's seen him. Now look, mister. Them two," Tommy thrust one dirty thumb toward the women, "is ladies. The real kind. They come from some highfalutin Virginia family, but they don't put on no airs. And tough. The war cleaned 'em out and they came here to start over with nothin' but a couple of nickels to rub together. They done all right, even though some of the other ladies turn their noses up at doin' business with an outlaw's sisters."

With a lift of one dark eyebrow, John asked, "Is there anything else you might be able to tell me?"

"Depends."

John pulled a shiny new half-dollar out of his pocket and spun it into the air. The boy snatched it with a flick of his thin hand. "What do you want to know?"

"Which is which?"

Tommy glanced across the street. "The one with the yaller hair is Blanche. Sweet as an angel, Blanche is. The other's Maddy . . . uh, Madeline. Maddy's real smart, better with money than most men. That's what ole Bill says, anyways."

"Ole Bill?"

"He runs the general store across the street. I tell you, he thinks right much of them Saylor sisters. He thinks you're botherin' them . . ." the boy drew his finger across his throat in an expressive gesture.

Thoroughly amused now, John tossed another half-dollar to the boy. It disappeared as quickly as the first.

"Thanks, mister," Tommy said. "Anythin' else I can do for you, jest let me know."

A moment later, he was gone. John turned back around to

watch the women. *Ladies,* the boy had called them. Certainly they dressed the part. His gaze traveled Madeline's curvaceous body, more than enticing in a blue satin gown. By damn, he thought. That is one hell of a woman!

"Whoa, John," he muttered. "You're working."

Blanche Saylor turned away, a basket over her arm, and walked toward the west end of town. Madeline went back into the shop. On a wild, powerful impulse, John started across the street.

Even as his feet took him toward the shop—and Maddy—he wondered what the hell he was going to say to Derek Saylor's sister.

Then one corner of his mouth went up in a smile. As his Pa had always said, honesty was the best policy.

A beam of golden sunlight slanted through the shop window, laying warmth across Maddy's shoulders as she sewed. Six months had passed since she and Blanche had come to Cofield, and spring had crept up on them.

Cofield hadn't become home yet; the stigma of being Derek Saylor's sisters put a barrier between them and the townsfolk. But she and Blanche had managed to gain enough business to keep them fed, and their happiness had always been their own.

The door opened, and Bill Smith stuck his grizzled head into the room. "Happy birthday, Maddy."

"Why, thank you," she said, cautiously. "You're not going to ask me how old I am, are you?"

"Why would I do that?"

"Because almost everyone else has."

He grunted. His head disappeared, and for a moment she thought he'd gone. Then he looked in again. "I already know how old you are. Blanche told Maisie Phelps, and Tommy Elliott overheard them. He went and told ever'body in town. Now, Maddy, there ain't no need to be embarrassed; pretty woman like you cain't hardly be called a spinster, even at twenty-five."

It took a great deal of self-control for Maddy to keep from laughing. "You are too kind."

"Don't mention it." He ducked out again.

"Good Gad," Maddy muttered, lifting her needle.

A faint sound brought her attention back to the doorway. She turned, thinking it might be Bill Smith come back to offer more words of consolation about her spinsterhood. Truly, he was a dear, but . . .

Her thoughts went spinning away when she saw the tall, broad-shouldered figure in the doorway. It was only a silhouette against the bright spring sunlight, but the sight sent her blood racing through her veins. Then her needle slipped, stabbing deep into her finger.

"Ouch!" she hissed.

The stranger moved quickly; before she had a chance to react, he'd crouched beside her. "Are you all right?" he asked.

His voice was deep, and had a dark, smoky quality that sent shock waves racing along her nerves. This had never happened before; men simply didn't affect Maddy Saylor. But this one did. And a Yankee, by his accent. For Heaven's sake!

"I-It's nothing," she protested.

John didn't know why he took her hand. The sight of blood on her pale skin did something strange to his insides, and he could no more have kept from touching her than he could have flown.

Instinct, he supposed. Pure, gut instinct.

"Your eyes are exactly the color of a summer storm," he said, surprising himself. Of all the things he'd expected to say to her, that was surely the last.

Maddy's nostrils flared with surprise. His eyes were even bolder than his words, and sent her pulse soaring even higher. She had to do something about this!

"Indeed, sir," she said, drawing on all the cool Saylor dignity at her command. "You're being very forward."

Coolness had no effect on him. "Not forward," he said, his voice shockingly intimate. "Just honest."

She found herself staring into his eyes. Cat's eyes, she thought. Greeny-gold, startling against the sun-browned skin of his face. Laugh lines radiated from the corners of his eyes and bracketed his mouth. Of its own accord, her gaze lingered on his lips. Well cut and sensual.

Suddenly, she realized she'd been staring. And he knew it. Amusement turned his eyes more gold than green for a moment. She dropped her gaze to her hand, which he still held. A bright bead of blood marked her index finger.

"Excuse me," she said, removing her hand from his grasp.

Without thinking, she put her injured finger in her mouth. And froze as she saw something hot flare in his eyes. She should have been frightened. But it only sparked an answering heat deep in her, a rush of molten weakness she'd never experienced before.

She didn't like it. And she certainly didn't trust it.

Setting the fabric aside, she rose from the chair. She felt better once she'd put some distance between herself and the stranger.

"What can I do for you, sir? Are you here to pick up something for your wife, perhaps?"

He got to his feet, moving with feline grace and economy of movement. Her traitorous gaze traveled his long, lean frame before she got herself under control again. His smile lines deepened.

"I'm not married," he said. "I'm looking for Madeline Saylor."

"I'm Miss Saylor."

He cocked his head to study her, and she saw a scar, startlingly white against his skin, running along the edge of his lean jaw and down the side of his neck. She resisted the urge to ask how he'd gotten it.

"My name is John Ballard," he said. "I work for the Pinkerton Detective Agency."

Every muscle in her body tensed. "Yes?"

"I'd like to ask you some questions about your brother."

"Why?"

John blinked. He hadn't expected that blunt response to his question. It said much for her mettle—and intelligence. His interest sharpened. "Because your brother stole a large amount of gold from Polk Stagecoach Lines, and they'd like to have it back."

"My brother is not a thief."

"Your loyalty is admirable, Miss Saylor, but a number of honest people swore that it was your brother who robbed those stagecoaches."

"I don't doubt their honesty," she replied. "I just know they're wrong."

"You're awful sure of yourself."

She met his gaze levelly. "I'm sure because Derek himself told me he didn't do it, and a Saylor never lies. It's a matter of honor."

John inclined his head, acknowledging the sentiment, if not his belief in Derek's truthfulness. "And it's a matter of honor for me to bring him in to face trial, and to see that the Polk Company's gold is returned."

"Then we seem to be at opposite positions on this issue," Maddy said.

He crossed his arms over his chest and propped one lean hip on her worktable. "If he's innocent, why doesn't he give himself up and trust a judge to hear him out?"

"The judge is a Yankee."

"I'm a Yankee."

"I knew that the moment you opened your mouth, sir," Maddy replied with elaborate sweetness. "And I'm trying very hard to overlook it."

A tremendous wash of emotion went through John as he comprehended her resentment. North and South, still at odds. The war had cost them all; he'd lost more than he thought he could survive. And until now, he'd thought he'd pushed those feelings so deep they'd never trouble him again. But this beautiful, fiery-eyed Rebel had just opened that door a crack, and that was a very dangerous thing.

"Are you saying that a Yankee judge won't give justice to a Reb?"

Maddy lifted her chin defiantly. "As you say, seven honest people swear they saw him. And I say that a Yankee judge is going to listen to those people, ignore the possibility that they've made a mistake, and find my brother guilty."

"Your point being that Yankees are incapable of understanding a point of honor."

"Since you said it, I cannot help but agree," she replied.

Maddy tilted her head back to look more fully at him. She'd angered him. It seemed as though a veil had been stripped from his eyes, that closed cynicism falling away to reveal something deep and dark and dangerous.

"Everyone has the capacity to abandon honor," he said.

"Not a Saylor," she retorted. "We'd just as soon cut our hearts out."

John closed his hands into fists. She'd pushed him hard, right enough, and he realized he'd revealed more of himself to her than he had to anyone else. She hadn't earned it. His past belonged only to him, as did his pain. Ruthlessly, he pushed it all back inside and slammed the door.

Maddy watched his eyes change. It seemed as though he'd drawn a shutter over them, hiding everything inside. A thrill of alarm curled up her spine; John Ballard was a man who kept his head, a man who couldn't be manipulated or goaded into making a mistake. A dangerous man. More so, she thought, because he had a curious, unwelcome effect on her insides.

"Actually, I'm not quite a Yankee," he said, under control again. "I'm from Montana."

"Then I'll have to condemn you on your own merits."

"I suppose you will," he said.

"Now that we've agreed on that, I really do have work to do—"

"Not so fast," he said. A cynical, sensual smile curved the corners of his mouth as he surveyed her with a bold gaze. "We haven't talked about Derek yet. I find him a fascinating character. Almost a legend. Some people seemed to think him a hero—"

"He is."

"In the South," he corrected. "The North considered him the Devil himself."

She tossed her head. "Pshaw. The Yankees were just mad because he broke out of their prison and then led them a fine dance for two years." Pride quickened her breath and her temper. "He made fools out of them. With less than a dozen men under his command, he hit the enemy hard, and he hit them often. When the Cause asked him to serve, he served well. Yes, we consider him a hero."

"And now he robs stagecoaches."

"That isn't true."

"I intend to catch him, Maddy."

She drew her breath in sharply. His words had been a threat, but her name had been spoken like a caress. Heat and anger coiled through her body, a treacherous mingling that frightened her for a moment. Then she lifted her chin, denying it.

"Have at it, Mr. Ballard," she said. "And may God have mercy on your soul."

His dark brows went up. "Sympathy for the enemy?"

"It's all I have to give you."

He walked slowly toward her. Maddy had to tilt her head back to look at him as he got closer. Not many men were taller than she; this man, however, made her feel small and disturbingly vulnerable.

"Are you sure about that, Maddy?" he asked softly.

"Only my friends have the right to call me Maddy," she snapped.

With his forefinger, he traced the satin curve of her cheek, sending reaction catapulting through her. She wanted to draw away, but her body didn't seem to work. Her gaze drifted to the scar upon his throat. She could see the play of muscle beneath the skin, the strong, rapid beat of his pulse.

"Formality between us would be a lie," he murmured. "And wasn't it you who told me the Saylors never lie?"

She ought to be angry. But all she felt was heat, a molten warmth that slid lazily through her veins to pool deep inside her body.

"Leave me alone," she whispered, afraid of her own weakness.

His hand spread out over her cheek, a gesture rife with possession. That, too, was blatant in his eyes. "I can't, Maddy. You see, I'm not the first agent who was sent here to find your brother. The other fellow chased Derek east and west, north and south, and never got close enough to breathe his dust."

"So?"

"Derek Saylor is the man the Yankees called the Gray Ghost." Humor glinted in his eyes. "The polite ones, anyway. I've studied his tactics, and decided not to play his game. He's too good to be hunted. No, I'm going to wait him out. He'll make a mistake, sooner or later, and I'm a patient man."

He moved still closer, until his chest nearly touched hers. Maddy could feel the heat of his body even through her clothes. Her pulse throbbed, a hammer-beat of dread and anticipation in her ears.

She had to get hold of herself. He was deliberately playing havoc with her senses, and she had to stop him. She took a step backward.

He followed. She retreated again, and again he closed the distance between them. A moment later she found her back pressed against the wall. He stopped when a scant inch separated them, and for a moment it seemed that he filled her whole world.

"Do you know why I'm so sure he'll make a mistake, Maddy?" he asked softly.

A dozen generations of Saylor pride kept Maddy's head high and her gaze steady. "I have no doubt that you'll tell me."

"You're right."

John propped his hands on either side of her head, trapping her against the wall. As he stared into her stormy, defiant eyes, he felt a desire so strong he had to grit his teeth to control it. He'd never met a woman with such fire, such strength, or such stubbornness.

"A wise man would have gone straight to Mexico after robbing that train," he said. "But not Derek. You see, he isn't about to abandon his sisters. Not that I blame him. I've only just met you, and I'm having one hell of a time tearing myself away."

It was outrageous. *He* was outrageous. She'd never been spoken to like this in her entire life. "That is quite enough, sir. If you don't leave at once, I'll—"

"Scream for ole Bill to shoot me?" Still, his voice and eyes caressed her.

"I can shoot you myself," she said.

John was thoroughly enjoying himself. He'd gotten her good and mad now, and he liked the fireworks in her eyes. "Are you sure you won't tell me where Derek is?"

"Quite. Even if I knew, which I don't. Now release me."

"I'm not holding you, Maddy."

But he was, he was. With his desire-filled eyes, with his nearness, he held her. His gaze dropped to her mouth. She knew he was going to kiss her, and she had the sudden, shocking urge to know what he'd taste like.

"Maddy? Blanche called, her voice high and breathless. "Maddy, is anything the matter?"

John Ballard held Maddy's eyes for a moment longer. She could see disappointment and frustrated desire in his eyes. Her breath went out in a sigh.

Then he straightened, releasing her from the prison of his gaze. He stepped away from her and turned toward Blanche.

She stood just inside the doorway, her blue eyes gentle as ever, but her right hand hidden among the packages she held. Maddy shook her head slightly, denying the question in her sister's eyes.

"Blanche, this is Mr. Ballard," she said. "He's a Pinkerton agent. He came to tell us he's been sent to bring Derek to justice."

Suddenly he grinned, a startling flash of pure, reckless humor that set Maddy's heart racing. Good Lord, she thought. He has dimples! Very masculine ones, of course, but dimples nonetheless.

"Good afternoon, ladies," he said, his gaze lingering on Maddy several moments longer than was proper. "It's been a pleasure. I look forward to our next meeting."

She looked at him from beneath her lashes. "Is that a threat?"

"Only a promise, Maddy."

Blanche gasped. He swept her a perfect bow, then headed toward the door. Maddy knew he wasn't finished; a moment later, he stopped.

The room was so quiet she could hear the rasp of dust beneath his boots as he turned to her again.

"There's just one thought I'd like to leave with you," he said. "Polk's raised the reward for your brother to ten thousand dollars. Dead or alive. Think about the kind of men who'll be looking for that reward. I, at least, would like to bring Derek in alive. You might think about whether he's better off with those others or with me."

Then he was gone.

"Dead or alive," Blanche said. "Oh, dear."

She dropped her packages onto the table, revealing the revolver in her right hand. Casually, she dropped it into her sewing basket.

"What should we do about this, Maddy?"

"I don't know yet, dear. But I do know we'll have to be very careful. Mr. Ballard is a very intelligent man."

"If only we could find out who really robbed that stage."

"If only," Maddy agreed. Shaking out the dress she'd been working on, she held it up for inspection. "This is the one Mrs. Privett asked for. What do you think?"

Blanche cocked her head to one side. "I think you were right to insist on that extra tuck in the bodice. Emily is rather generous in the bosom. What will we do if they do catch Derek and send him to prison?"

"I don't think it would be that much harder for us to break him out of Leavenworth than it was to break him out of that Yankee prisoner-of-war camp. I simply can't allow my baby brother to spend the rest of his life in prison for something he didn't do. And that's if they don't hang him."

"Oh, dear," Blanche said again.

"Besides," Maddy smiled at her older sister, who was so gentle and so very strong, "you said you enjoyed wearing trousers."

"I did. I felt delightfully free without hoops and corsets, and it was so much fun just to leap on the back of a horse and ride like the wind."

"With Yankee bullets flying all around?"

"Ladies are taught to take inconveniences in stride," Blanche murmured.

Maddy laughed in delight. Impulsively, she swept her sister up in a quick, hard hug.

Released, Blanche smoothed an errant curl back into place. "Now, about this Mr. Ballard—"

"There's nothing to be said," Maddy replied, too casually.

"I've never seen you look at a man the way you looked at him."

"Do you mean in pure, unadulterated fury?"

"That wasn't fury, Maddy, and you know it." Blanche picked up Mrs. Privett's dress and ran her finger over one neatly stitched seam. "You were attracted to him. I could see it in your face, and so could he."

Maddy felt her cheeks go hot. "He came here to hunt our brother."

"And now he's hunting you."

"Nonsense. He's playing a game, that's all. He thinks that if he frightens me enough, I'll take him right where he wants to go: to Derek."

"I don't think Mr. Ballard plays games."

Maddy made a sharp, impatient gesture with her hand; she'd had enough of John Ballard for one day. "I don't play, either."

"I'm worried," Blanche said. "He was right about the reward. I saw the new 'WANTED' poster outside Sheriff Cooper's jail today. Two men were looking at it, and they had the coldest, meanest eyes I've ever seen on a human being."

Fear darkened her eyes, and the sight made Maddy's heart twist in pain. Blanche should never have been exposed to the ugliness of the world. She should be safe and secure, with a loving family all around her. Instead, she'd lost her parents, husband, home, and unborn child; she'd suffered fear and cold and the privations of hunger.

"I'll take care of it, I promise," Maddy said.

Blanche managed a shaky smile. "You always do."

"Good. Now do me a favor and get Mrs. Bartleton's ivory silk gown from upstairs? She's due at three for a fitting."

"Of course, dear." Blanche hurried toward the back door.

Alone, Maddy allowed herself a moment of weakness. Bowing her head, she covered her face with her hands. In the self-imposed dimness, she wondered how she'd ever be able to keep the reckless promise she'd made.

Ten thousand dollars, she thought. Dead or alive.

Oh, Derek.

TWO

"More tea, Maddy?" Blanche lifted the silver teapot that was one of the few things they'd managed to save from Tallwood's gracious collection.

Maddy glanced up, straight into her own distorted reflection in the teapot's curved side. "Thank you, yes."

She cupped her hands around the hot porcelain cup, her mind twisting and turning as she sought some way out of this mess. For all of them.

If only John Ballard hadn't come. Those greenish-gold eyes of his saw too much. She felt as though he'd gotten a glimpse into her soul yesterday, and she into his. It was not a comfortable feeling. And not just because he'd use it against her. A bonfire blazed inside him, controlled but not quite contained, and it would burn her up if she wasn't careful. It wasn't simple passion, that fire; it contained anger and pain, and would be highly dangerous to the unwary. A prudent woman would run the other way.

But Maddy was a Saylor, and prudence was not her way. The danger itself held a powerful lure; she wanted to meet it, fight it, tame it.

She knew she was at a disadvantage; she was inexperienced in the ways of men, and she was certain that John Ballard had more than a little experience with women.

Maddy didn't like being at a disadvantage. She'd have to find a way to counter it. For one thing was certain: John Ballard wasn't about to go away.

"It was awfully kind of Mr. Jones to put the stove in for us this winter, wasn't it?" Blanche asked. "It's nice to be able to cook for ourselves."

"Mmm-hmm."

"We've been very frugal," Blanche continued. "I think we almost have enough to buy our own mounts. I'm starting to feel like we're taking advantage, borrowing Bill Smith's wagon the way we do."

"Mmm-hmmm."

John Ballard, Maddy thought. There were many secrets in his eyes. He would try to tear her secrets from her, but he'd never reveal any of his own.

"And Zeke Mayhew's bull needs a new dress for the barn raising," Blanche said. "Do you think that pink taffeta will do?"

"Pink is fine," Maddy said. Then she blinked. "Who?"

"You haven't been listening to a word I've said."

Maddy sighed. "You're right, Blanche. I've been thinking."

"Sometimes it's best to stop thinking and let your feelings take over."

Maddy was possessed of a sudden, swift memory of John Ballard's bold eyes and sensual, cynical mouth. Determinedly, she scrubbed it out of existence. "Not in this case, I'm afraid."

With a sigh, Blanche rose and began tidying the room. It was painfully clean already, but Blanche always cleaned when she was worried about something. Maddy's heart contracted. They'd done the best they could with curtains and rag rugs, but the touches of prettiness only emphasized how little there was: a table, two chairs, a battered sideboard, and an uphol-stered armchair.

"Maddy?"

"Hmmm?"

"What were you and Mr. Ballard doing when I interrupted yesterday?"

The question took Maddy by surprise. Enough so that she couldn't stop the heat from rushing into her cheeks. *He was going to kiss me. And I was going to let him.* She would have cut her tongue out before saying that aloud, however.

But she'd already paused long enough to reveal herself to Blanche. The smile on her sister's face caused Maddy's cheeks to flame still more.

"I don't want to talk about it," Maddy snapped.

"You can't ignore this, Maddy. And you can't make it go away simply by wishing."

Maddy sighed. "I don't know why everyone thinks you're so delicate and sweet. You're the most tenacious human being I've ever come across—"

"And you're the most stubborn," Blanche retorted. "Now, about John Ballard."

"I hate him."

The corners of Blanche's mouth turned up. "But you were going to let him kiss you, weren't you?"

Maddy opened her mouth to deny it. But the lie, tempting though it was, stuck in her throat. The Saylors never lied—even when it hurt.

"All right," she admitted. "I was a bit . . . fascinated by him. But more like one would be fascinated with a rattlesnake."

"Ah. Good."

"Good!"

"I'd begun to wonder if you were going to go through life completely unaffected by men," Blanche said. "It's nice to know you're no more immune than the rest of us."

"Blanche—"

"It's perfectly normal, Maddy. After all, he's a handsome fellow. He has just enough of the rogue in him to make him interesting, but there is kindness in his eyes—"

"Kindness!"

"Didn't you see?" Blanche grinned. "But I suppose you were looking for . . . other things."

"Like a place to stick a knife," Maddy said through clenched teeth.

"Ah, Maddy."

"Ah, yourself," Maddy retorted. "You're too nice, Blanche. You see niceness in people when it isn't deserved. You always have. John Ballard is many things, I'm sure, but I doubt there's much kindness in him."

"I know what I know, Maddy."

"And I know that John Ballard is nothing but trouble," Maddy said with perhaps too much force. "And I intend to stay well away from him."

Blanche's lashes fluttered downward, hiding a sudden flash of humor in her eyes. "Of course, dear. That's the only wise thing to do."

"Now let's think about the important thing: what we're going to do about Derek."

Turning, Blanche started cleaning again. "I wish this would all be over. I just want us all to be safe and free and happy. Lord knows we've seen enough of the other side of life."

Suddenly, Maddy caught hold of the idea she'd been wrestling with all morning. She rose too quickly, sending her chair scraping back across the floor.

"We *will* be safe and free and happy," she said, iron determination in her heart. "But first, our baby brother is going to be needing our help again."

"What do you mean?" Blanche asked.

"Now that the reward for Derek has gone up, what do you want to bet there'll be another robbery?"

A line appeared between Blanche's golden brows. "I don't understand."

"This train robber has already gotten Derek blamed for his crime. This is the perfect time for him to do still more hold-ups—and have our brother hang for it. That is, if someone doesn't shoot him first. Then the real thief can live like a king on the stolen gold, and no one will even look for him."

"And?" Blanche prompted.

"I thought you and I could add some spice to the stew, so to speak."

"Oh. Well. I see what you mean." Blanche took a deep breath and let it out in a sigh. Then she smiled. "Dear me, I suppose I'll just have to find those trousers again."

Maddy angled her parasol to block the unrelenting Texas sun as she stepped out onto the sidewalk. She wore a white muslin gown, which Blanche had embroidered with tiny pink rosebuds around the hem and neckline.

"You look as cool and fresh as a lemon sorbet," Blanche murmured.

"I certainly feel like ice inside," Maddy replied. She smiled at her sister, thinking that Blanche looked very young and fragile in pale blue.

She lifted her face, sensing something different. Cofield had changed. An aura of danger seemed to hang in the air now, a strained sense of waiting lurking beneath the everyday hustle-bustle of the thriving little town.

"Maddy, could you hold this basket for a moment?" Blanche asked. "My bonnet has come undone."

Absently, Maddy took the heavy sewing basket from her sister. Blanche turned to look at her reflection in the store window as she tied the ribbons of her dainty straw bonnet.

"There," she said, reaching to take the basket back. "I don't know why it's so important for me to have every button, bow, and grommet in place when things are bad. But for some reason, it makes me feel better."

"You're just like Mother," Maddy said. "Remember how she'd make everything and everyone work together while Papa would rush about, shouting at the top of his lungs and getting absolutely nothing done?"

"Yes. And no one ever paid a bit of attention to his roaring, for everyone knew what a soft heart he had underneath all the bluster."

Maddy swallowed against the sudden tightness in her throat. Father had died of fever during the War, and mother had pined away to follow him a few months later. Now she and Blanche and Derek were all that was left of the proud Saylor heritage.

"We'd better go," she said. "We don't want to be late for Mrs. Terrell's fitting."

They started walking toward the west end of town, where the Terrells lived. Maddy saw two hard-eyed men come out of the saloon and start down the boardwalk toward them. She knew the type. Predators, both. Burned to leather by wind and sun, their eyes leached of emotion by all the violence they'd seen.

The men stopped to let them pass. Maddy felt those snake-cold gazes on her, and her skin crawled with dread.

"Bounty hunters," she murmured when she was sure they were out of earshot. "Are those the two you saw yesterday?"

Blanche shook her head.

"So we have four so far," Maddy said. "Not nearly as bad as when Derek had a whole Yankee company hunting him."

"They had the eyes of wolves," Blanche whispered. "I'm afraid, Maddy. What if they find him?"

"They won't find him," Maddy replied. Firmly, as though to convince herself.

Then she caught sight of Derek's 'WANTED' poster on the wall outside the sheriff's office, and her heart shriveled into a cold knot. It hurt to see Derek—handsome, dashing, honorable Derek—a wanted man.

Ten thousand dollars. Dead or alive.

With a hiss of indrawn breath, she ripped the poster off the wall and crumpled it in her hands. Her parasol bounced unheeded along the sidewalk.

A shadow fell across her, startling her into looking up. Zachary Marsh stood in front of her, dangling her parasol from one stocky finger. His four tall sons flanked him, blocking the sidewalk.

She'd never liked the Marshes, any of them. Zachary owned the largest ranch in the area, the Star M, and used his money to bully the townsfolk whenever possible. His sons, Alf, Warren, Gordon, and Vince, had their father's ruddy, blond looks, but none of his force. They'd been vocal in their disapproval of Maddy and Blanche living in Cofield.

Odds were he hadn't come to offer support in her time of trouble.

"Well, Maddy," Zachary said. "I always said you Saylors would bring trouble to town."

She raised one eyebrow. "That's true, Mr. Marsh. You always said it. Repeatedly."

"Yep. Now we got bounty hunters, Pinkerton men, and who knows what-all walkin' our streets. We don't like it."

"We're in agreement there," Blanche said. "We don't like it either."

Vince hooked his thumbs in his belt. He looked Maddy over slowly, and his eyes were an insult. "It'd be best for ever'body if you and yore sister left town. Leave the decent folks alone."

"Oh?" Maddy studied him from beneath her lashes. "What would you know about decent folks? Everyone knows you spend most of your time in the saloon drinking and wenching. And, may I add, to the sorrow of the poor ladies upon whom you bestow your attention?"

His face turned brick red. Maddy counted to ten to see if he'd think of a retort, then returned her gaze to Zachary. "Is that all, Mr. Marsh?"

"We want you out of here," he growled. "And we're not alone. Plenty of other folks ain't impressed by yore fancy manners. Trash is as trash does, and yore brother ain't nothin' but a common thief."

"Really?" she asked. "The stagecoach company thinks he's well worth a ten-thousand-dollar reward. Hardly a *common* thief. Now, if you'll excuse us, we have an appointment."

Zachary dropped the parasol to the sidewalk. Grinning at Maddy with a mouthful of big, square teeth, he stepped squarely on the dainty thing, crushing it beneath his boots.

Maddy opened her mouth to say something scathing. But someone grasped her arms from behind, startling her into silence. Before she could do more than gasp in surprise, she found herself lifted effortlessly, then gently set aside.

John Ballard stepped forward to take his place at her side. A thrill raced through her, anticipation and dread and desire all rolled into one.

He'd come for trouble. His eyes looked more gold than green in the stark sunlight, and she could see the coiled readiness lurking beneath his outwardly casual stance. He looked lazily feral, like a mountain lion that knows it can kill with a single swipe of its paw.

"Lookin' fer trouble, son?" Zachary asked.

John smiled at Zachary Marsh. A wicked light came into his eyes, and Maddy's heart began to pound.

"You've broken the lady's parasol," he said.

Zachary's eyes narrowed. "Seems that I did."

Men! Maddy thought in exasperation. "Mr. Ballard—"

"Shut up, Maddy," he said, quite pleasantly. He didn't look away from Zachary. "You owe the lady an apology for breaking her parasol."

"Think so?"

Still smiling, John shifted his balance slightly. "Yes, I do. Now, about the apology—"

"The lady and her parasol can go straight to hell," Zachary snarled.

John moved so fast that Maddy didn't actually see his fist connect with Zachary's face. She just heard a horrible crunch of bone, and saw blood spurt from Zachary's nose.

"He broke my nose!" Zachary howled, reeling away.

"Git him!" Alf shouted.

"Get out of here, Maddy." John shoved her behind him as the four men lunged forward.

Maddy, of course, had no intention of leaving. No Saylor ever ran from a fight, especially one so one-sided.

The Marsh boys descended on John *en masse,* stupidly interfering with each other. John sidestepped, graceful as a dancer, letting Alf and Warren stumble past him.

Maddy lifted her skirts as she gave Warren a push that sent him staggering into his brother. Both fell. As they flailed to their feet, Maddy took Blanche by the arm and drew her into the street, away from the melee.

"Shouldn't we do more?" Blanche asked.

"Not quite yet," Maddy replied, wincing as Vince's fist connected solidly with John's cheek. "Mr. Ballard seems to be enjoying himself just now, and I'd hate to spoil his fun."

"I will never understand men," Blanche said. "Even Papa and Derek, love them as I do, could be completely unreasonable . . . and unmanageable. But then, I suppose that's what makes them interesting."

Maddy couldn't take her gaze from John Ballard. He held his own very well, she thought as he sent Gordon flying backward with a solid blow to the jaw. Cursing, Vince grabbed him from behind. John jabbed his elbow into the other mans diaphragm, then grasped him by the collar and slung him into his brothers, bringing all four down in a heap.

"Bastard!" Warren snarled, leaping up to catch John with a wild roundhouse swing.

John's head snapped back, and blood streamed from a cut above his brow. But it didn't slow him at all. Ducking his head, he bulled straight into Warren's solar plexus, slamming him into the wall behind him.

"Oh, good show," Blanche breathed.

The fight spilled into the street. Maddy thought John fought superbly and with reasonable fairness, considering that he was outnumbered four to one. She winced as he sank his hands into Gordon's hair and slammed his head into the hitching post. Gordon sprawled flat on his back, his face slack. Three to one, Maddy amended.

Her nostrils flared. Actually, if she'd liked him more, she might have thought John Ballard was rather . . . magnificent. Something wild and reckless coiled through her veins, hotter than the Texas sun.

Alf bent, grabbed a handful of dust, and flung it straight

into John's eyes. The other two brothers leaped on him, bringing him down.

"Maddy!" Blanche cried.

But Maddy had already started to move. Snatching up the tin bucket that hung on a nearby horse trough, she waded into the fight. She swung the bucket, hard, and connected with Warren Marsh's head.

The bucket rang like a gong. Warren's eyes lost focus. A heartbeat later, he fell over onto his side. Maddy drew the bucket back for another swing.

Someone caught it from behind and ripped it from her hand. She whirled to find Zachary looming over her, his face bloody, his eyes savage. Out of the corner of her eye, she saw John Ballard surge out from beneath his attackers and leap toward her. Then her focus narrowed to Zachary's murderous eyes, and the big hands that were reaching for her throat.

"Damned uppity female," he snarled.

Blanche appeared behind him. She smacked her parasol down on his head, snapping the delicate wood handle. With a growl, he swung toward her. His head was sunk low between his shoulders as he lunged forward. He caught her with a backhanded swipe that sent her plunging hard to the ground.

Time seemed to stand still. Maddy's ears rang as she watched Zachary draw his foot back, ready to kick Blanche's motionless body.

"Blanche!" Maddy screamed. "Blanche!"

Three

Maddy flung herself forward, but she knew it would be too late. "No!" she cried.

A shadow seemed to pass between Blanche and the man who threatened her. Zachary Marsh reeled backward, his nose again spurting blood, and landed on his back in the street. Maddy gaped in astonishment at the lean, sunbrowned man who'd knocked him down.

Then Blanche began to stir, and Maddy forgot everything else in her haste to reach her sister. Dropping to her knees, she pulled Blanche into her arms.

"Blanche, are you hurt?" she demanded, pulling her sister into her arms.

"I'm fine," Blanche said, struggling to rise. "Really, Maddy, I'm fine. Let me . . . Look out!"

Maddy ducked. Gordon Marsh came flying past, his long blond hair fanned out around his face. He landed with a grunt. A moment later he rose, shaking his head as if to clear it. Maddy scrambled to retrieve the tin bucket.

A tremendous explosion split the air, dropping a blanket of shocked stillness over them all. Maddy's ears rang. She saw Sheriff Cooper standing a short distance away, smoke sifting from the scattergun he held in both hands.

"Time to break it up, folks," he said.

Maddy became aware of the crowd that had gathered on both sides of the street. Then a warm hand cupped her chin, drawing her head around. She found herself looking into John Ballard's eyes, and felt as though she'd fallen off a cliff.

"Are you all right?" he asked.

She wasn't, but it had nothing to do with the fight. Her gaze roved over his face, tallying the damage he'd taken in her behalf. Oh, Lord, now she was beholden. She had the sick, sinking feeling that he'd take payment in full.

"I seem to be in better shape than you are," she said.

"This?" He reached up to touch the cut over his eye. "Ouch. It's nothing."

"S'cuse me, folks," the sheriff said. "But I'd like to know what the hell—pardon my French, ladies—is going on out here?"

Gordon Marsh scrambled to his feet. "That feller attacked us, Sheriff," he growled, pointing at John.

"That so?" The sheriff's grizzled brows rose. "All five of you?"

A laugh rippled through the watching townsfolk, and all the Marshes—the ones still conscious, that is—turned brick red. The sheriff raised a wintry gaze to the boardwalk, and his mustache took on a belligerent air.

"Don't you folks have anythin' to do today?" he growled.

The watchers quickly went about their business.

Cooper turned back to John. "Did you throw the first punch?"

"Yes."

"Why?"

John brushed some of the dust from his shirt. "They broke Miss Saylor's parasol, and I thought they should apologize."

"Ah." Sheriff Cooper then turned his flat grey gaze on Maddy. "Did he break your parasol, Maddy?"

"He did."

"On purpose?"

"He was very rude," she said.

"Rude," the sheriff echoed. His attention shifted to the lean, dark man who'd rescued Blanche. "And what was yore part in this, mister?"

Blanche moved to stand beside her savior. A splotch of red marked her cheek where Zachary Marsh had struck her. "He, too, objected to Mr. Marsh's rudeness."

The sheriff grunted. "What's yore name, mister?"

"Hank Vann." His ice-pale gaze lingered for a moment on Blanche's cheek, then rose to her eyes. "I'm a bounty hunter."

Her lashes fluttered downward for a moment. Then she lifted her chin and looked directly into his eyes. "Thank you, Mr. Vann."

He inclined his head. Maddy saw surprise flicker across his hard face, then something that looked like self-deprecation. She almost smiled; Blanche had that effect on people. Especially men. In her company, they found things in themselves they'd forgotten they had.

The sheriff cleared his throat, pulling her attention away. He favored each of the men with a level stare for a moment. Then he relaxed his grip on the scattergun.

"Here's the way I look at it," he said. "The fight seemed to come out even, even though it were five to two."

"Now just a minute—" Gordon began.

"You want to count the ladies?" Sheriff Cooper inquired. "I'm sure folks'd get a lot of entertainment out of that, 'specially since they was gettin' the best of the hoo-haw . . ."

"No," Vince growled.

"Now," the sheriff continued, "I shorely dislike rudeness, especially toward ladies. So I'm gonna fine you each twenty dollars an' the cost of two new parasols. Now git Warren and your pa on their feet and haul yore sorry asses—pardon my French, ladies—out of town."

Gordon swiped his sleeve across his face, smearing blood and dust into a comical mask. "We ain't finished with this."

"In my town, you are," Sheriff Cooper said. He shifted his grip on the shotgun. "Git."

Gordon, Alf, and Vince collected their brethren and limped

off toward their horses, which were tethered outside the saloon. Maddy heaved a sigh of relief.

"Thank you for intervening, Sheriff," she said.

Reaching out, he took the bucket from her. He held it up and turned it so they could all see the impression of Warren's head in the metal.

"Somethin' you learned in Virginia?" he inquired.

"Southern ladies are taught to deal with a wide variety of situations," Maddy said.

"I bet," the sheriff said. "Maddy, about Derek—"

"I don't know where he is, Sheriff."

"I ain't doubting that. But if you could get a message to him, mebbe convince him to give himself up . . . Well, don't you think he'd be safer in jail?"

Maddy looked into the man's level, honest eyes. Then she turned to Hank Vann. "Mr. Vann, what is your opinion of my brother's safety in Sheriff Cooper's jail?"

He smiled. "Ten thousand dollars is a lot of money, Miss Saylor."

"Enough to tempt a man to break a prisoner out of jail?"

"Enough to take this town apart board by board, and leave nothing but ash behind."

Blanche gasped. He turned to look at her, his pale gaze boring into hers. All of a sudden she swayed, her face going very pale. The bounty hunter swept her into his arms.

"Got to get her out of this sun," he said.

"I-I don't know what came over me," Blanche murmured. "I just feel so . . . dizzy."

Maddy turned to lead him back toward the dress shop. Inwardly, she wondered. Blanche might look fragile and soft, but a warrior's heart beat beneath that vulnerable-looking exterior. And Blanche had never fainted in her life.

Then John Ballard fell into step beside her, and rational thought flew right out of her head.

"What about you, Maddy?" he asked. "Feeling a little faint yourself?"

"I never feel faint," she said.

"A pity," he murmured.

He slanted her a grin, and her nerves quivered in reaction. Why, of all the men in the world, did this one affect her so? "You really ought to go to Dr. Brennan's office and get that cut looked at."

"Can't you?"

She blinked. "Can't I what?"

"Look at my cut."

Maddy didn't want to get that close to him. No. Not at all. "But it might need stitches," she protested.

"You're a seamstress, Maddy."

She opened her mouth, then closed it again. He had her. He'd done battle for her honor, and now she was honor-bound to see to his wounds.

Her heart thrummed as she led the way upstairs to the apartment she shared with her sister. Hank Vann turned sideways to ease Blanche through the doorway, then gently set her in the armchair. The two men seemed to overfill the room.

"How are you feeling, Blanche?" Maddy asked.

"I'm fine now. I suppose all the excitement just rushed to my head." She fanned herself with one small, white hand. "It's stifling in here. Goodness, I need some fresh air. Mr. Vann, would you mind?"

He was at her side in an instant, steadying her as she rose to her feet. Maddy felt her mouth drop open. So that was Blanche's game! If she hadn't seen it with her own eyes, she wouldn't have believed it.

Blanche and . . . the bounty hunter? It boggled the mind.

Stunned, she watched Blanche and Hank Vann leave. Her sister's soft, lilting laugh drifted up on the quiet air.

Then she looked at John Ballard, and found him grinning at her as though he'd read her mind. But something darker lurked beneath the humor flashing in his eyes, something that watched and waited like a cat waiting to pounce.

Only then did she realize what was going through *his* mind: they were alone.

And he, drat him, knew exactly what *she* was thinking; he didn't exactly smile, but the creases bracketing his mouth deepened suspiciously. She turned a shade too swiftly, and went to get the pitcher and washbasin from the bedroom.

When she returned, she found him already seated at the table. Waiting. "Is this where you want me?" he asked.

She wanted him anywhere but here, but knew that saying so would only bring one of those cynical smiles. And she was at enough of a disadvantage as it was.

With a clean, soft rag, she gently cleaned the blood and dust from his face. He smelled of musk and leather and man. Her nostrils flared. She had the feeling that scent had somehow imprinted itself on her soul; had he come up to her in darkness, she still would have known him.

"Your hand is shaking," he said.

Furious that she'd let her feelings show, she pulled the cloth away from his face. "It's . . . just reaction, I suppose."

"Reaction to what?"

She blinked. "To the fight, of course."

"Sure?"

"Of course." Her voice held more heat than she would have liked, which made her even angrier. "Now, if you would just sit quietly and let me work, I'll take care of that cut."

John settled back, content with the results of the conversation. As she started washing the cut again, he let his gaze drift around the room. The stark severity of the place surprised him; it didn't look as if Derek Saylor's sisters were enjoying any of his ill-gotten gains.

His attention drifted back to Maddy. Damn, but she was one beautiful woman! Her hair had loosened during the fight, and a riot of shining bronze curls framed her face. His gaze moved lower. Her breasts swelled the front of her dress, and the sweet, feminine curve of her hips was pure enticement.

He drew a deep breath, inhaling Maddy and lilac. The

woman stirred him far more than did the perfume, stirred him far more than was safe for either of them. He wanted to stroke her, to feel that white, silken skin heat beneath his hands. There was much passion in those stormy blue eyes, a fire so hot a man could be burned alive.

His body responded to the almost unbearable picture his imagination had painted. He had to shift position to ease the discomfort of his jeans.

"Did I hurt you?" she asked.

If only she knew, he thought. "It's all right."

Maddy hesitated for a moment. Then she looked into his eyes, and her heart felt as though it might beat its way right out of her chest. For she saw desire there, a need as raw and primitive as a Texas thunderstorm. Untamed. Unreasonable. And very, very dangerous.

She wanted to run away. From him, from herself. But Maddy Saylor had never run from anything, and she wasn't going to start now. She shifted her attention back to the cut.

"It doesn't need stitching," she said, her tone all business. "But it will likely leave a scar."

He shrugged. Although she tried not to, she glanced at the thready white line that ran down his neck.

"I got that in the war," he said.

Maddy took her hands from him. He'd been her enemy during the war, and now her enemy again because of Derek. She'd known this from the beginning. But he'd done her a service today; enemy or no, she owed him her gratitude.

"I must thank you for defending us," she said.

"Must?" he repeated. "Then I must also thank you for bouncing that bucket off that fellow's skull."

"I couldn't stand there and do nothing."

"Sure you could. But you didn't."

He reached out and grasped her wrist. Alarm sizzled along Maddy's nerves. The desire in his eyes, in his touch, was a trap. And her treacherous body responded, rivulets of heat coiling along her limbs.

For a moment, she found herself leaning toward him. Then self-preservation took over, and she stepped away from the table.

John smiled. He'd felt the leap of pulse in her wrist before she'd pulled away, and he'd seen the wave of reaction in her eyes.

"You don't have to play the lady with me," he said.

Her eyes narrowed. "But I *am* a lady."

"Ah, Maddy, you don't know what you're missing. You ought to loosen up a little, enjoy life."

"Loosen up?"

"Mmm-hmmm. Don't be so stiff."

It stung her. She told herself she was a fool for letting him get to her, but she couldn't help it. "Perhaps I'm stiff because I just don't like *you*."

His brows went up. "Oh? Well, I heard you're twenty-five years old and have never been married, and that you don't have a beau. So you apparently don't like anybody."

She turned hot, then cold, then hot again. And all through it, he just gazed at her with those cynical cat's eyes. For once, she regretted being a lady. She'd like to stomp her feet and scream at the top of her lungs, and let him know exactly what she thought of him.

"I think it's a shame," he murmured, rising slowly to his feet.

Taken aback, she stared at him. "What . . . ?"

"You're beautiful. Beautiful and passionate, and you were made for a man's loving."

She opened her mouth to retort, but her brain refused to work. Perhaps it was shock—or perhaps it was the way his gaze dropped to her open mouth and stayed there, and the frighteningly intense hunger that swept like wildfire through his eyes.

Of its own accord, her gaze drifted downward along the clean, strong line of his throat. A wisp of dark hair was visible in the open neckline of his blue shirt. The sight hit her in the pit of her stomach, a pure, visceral female reaction that both confused and infuriated her.

Her attention wandered lower, taking in the powerful curve of his chest, the whipcord-lean waist and the strength of his legs. He was aroused, blatantly so. The sight of the thick bulge brought the blood rushing to her cheeks.

Even in the midst of her shock and outrage, some hidden part of her responded, reveling in the extent of his desire for her. This was a woman's power over a man. She had never felt this before; it was heady and wild, as reckless as the passion in his eyes.

Then reason rushed back in a stinging tide, and she found her voice again. "Get out."

"Now that wasn't ladylike, Maddy. It wasn't even polite."

"Polite!" she gasped, lost in a blinding flare of temper. *"Polite!* You're lucky I don't—"

"What?" he asked, his voice turning silky. "Exactly what is it you would like to do to me?"

Maddy took a deep breath, astonished by the violence of her emotions. No one had ever affected her like this. No one had ever brought her to the brink of screaming like a . . . a . . . shrew. This had gone far enough. Silently, she raised her chin to a haughty angle and pointed toward the door.

Instead of leaving, he caught her outstretched hand and pulled her against him. A firestorm of reaction swept through her; it seemed as though the layers of clothing burned away, leaving her skin—and sensation. She could feel his manhood hard against her body, and the sheer male aggression of him stunned her.

Her head went back as her shocked gaze met his. He'd dropped all pretense of civility; she was looking at primitive male instinct. Unreasonable. Uncontrollable.

"Maddy," he growled.

His mouth descended on hers, all heat and possessiveness. For a moment she was paralyzed with astonishment; then instinct took over. But it wasn't the instinct to escape that claimed her. No, it was desire. A wild rush of sweet, hot need washed through her as he parted her lips, sliding his tongue into the heat of her mouth.

She moaned softly when his lips left hers. But he only raised his head enough to look into her eyes.

"You see, Maddy?" he murmured. "Just because you're a lady doesn't mean you can't be a woman."

Maddy wanted to look away. If she could just look away, she could stop this. But his gaze imprisoned her, and she didn't have the strength to break free.

"Say my name," he said.

She shook her head, knowing there was danger here.

He moved lower, until his lips hovered just above hers. Against her will, against all reason, she opened her mouth in an invitation as old as time. Vaguely, she registered disbelief at her own behavior.

"Say it," he said again.

Maddy had no strength to resist the demand in his voice, no strength to resist the demand in herself.

"John," she whispered. Because he needed it. And so did she.

His eyes darkened, molten gold turning still hotter. She knew she'd moved him, shaken him, perhaps as much as he'd shaken her. He nipped at her bottom lip, then ran the tip of his tongue over the sweet flesh. Maddy opened her mouth, inviting him in. But he resisted, biting softly at one corner of her mouth, then the other.

"John," she sighed.

He caught the exhalation in his mouth. Then he tilted his head, fitting his mouth more fully to hers. She felt his hand slide up her back and into her hair to cup the back of her head. He tasted of heat and passion and sheer, male possessiveness.

And she loved it. She'd never known this part of herself, this wild creature that reveled in a mans touch, a man's desire.

No, she thought hazily, *this* man's. No one else had ever stirred her with this unbearable need.

She ought to be afraid. In some small corner of her mind, perhaps she was. But not now. Now, she only knew his touch, the heat of his lips, the tempestuous sensations racing through her body as he plundered her mouth.

"Maddy," Blanche called from outside.

Her sister's voice shattered the mood like a dash of ice water. Gasping, Maddy tore herself from John Ballard's embrace. She stood staring at him, her mind reeling. How had this happened? Oh, Lord, how was she going to keep it from happening again?

"Oh," she said, reaching up to touch her lips with shaking fingers. "You—"

"And you," he finished for her.

"Maddy," Blanche called again. This time, her voice came from right outside the doorway. A moment later, she stepped inside.

Her eyes seemed overbright, and Maddy was relieved to see that she didn't notice the tension in the room. "So, you seem to be finished," she said. "How is the cut, Mr. Ballard?"

"How can it be other than fine, with such expert care? But you can call me John." He glanced at Maddy, mischief in his eyes. "Even Maddy has relented."

Maddy's cheeks flamed. She snatched the washbasin off the table, sloshing pink-tinted water everywhere. Blanche hurried to help.

"There," she said, tossing the soaked rag back into the washbasin. "Maddy, have you spoken to John about the barn raising tomorrow?"

Maddy stared at her uncomprehendingly. "What?"

Blanche smiled up at John. "Tomorrow, at Zeke and Dolly Mayhew's ranch. I hope you'll come."

Maddy's mouth dropped open in astonishment at her sister's perfidy. She couldn't believe it, she simply couldn't believe it!

"I wouldn't miss it for the world," he said. A wolf might have envied his smile. "Thank you very much."

Four

Maddy sat on the wagon seat beside Bill Smith. Her parasol was white and frilled, with delicate blue ribbons to match her dress. She glanced over her shoulder at Blanche, who perched serenely on a keg in the back of the wagon. Her pale yellow dress gleamed like butter in the sunlight.

As though sensing Maddy's stare, she glanced up and smiled. Maddy returned her gaze to the road ahead.

"Y'all sure are quiet today," Bill said.

"Maddy is angry with me," Blanche replied.

"What fer?"

"Treason," Maddy said.

Bill turned to look at her. "Huh?"

"I invited two men to the barn raising," Blanche murmured.

"So what's wrong with that?"

Maddy lifted her chin a notch higher. "One is a bounty hunter, and the other is a Pinkerton agent. Both are after our brother."

Bill's eyebrows soared so high they disappeared beneath the brim of his hat. "Ain't they the two fellers who got in a fight with the Marsh boys yesterday?"

"They defended our honor," Blanche said.

"We said thank you," Maddy pointed out. "You didn't have to invite them to the barn raising."

The wagon hit a bump, sending Blanche bouncing a foot above her seat. Her expression didn't change, nor did the angle of her parasol.

"I heered one of 'em broke that bastard Zachary's nose." Approval lay plain on Bill's seamed face. "Half the town's been wantin' to do that fer years."

"That was the Pinkerton agent," Blanche said.

"Who busted a bucket on Warren's head?"

Blanche smiled. "That was Maddy."

Bill let out a guffaw, startling the horses into a trot that sent Maddy jouncing along the seat like a Mexican jumping bean. Fortunately, the horses slowed before she actually landed in Bill's lap. She sent a silent prayer of thanks heavenward that she and Blanche had decided to abandon their hoops like the rest of the ladies. Life in Texas didn't lend itself to hoops.

"Whoops," Bill growled. "Fool horses. Sorry about that."

Maddy glanced over her shoulder at Blanche, who'd been bounced onto the wagon bed. Her bonnet hung down over one eye. The two sisters gazed at each other for a long, frozen moment. Maddy was the first to start laughing.

"Oh, dear," Blanche gasped, wiping tears from her face. "That was a truly unique experience, Bill. Remind me to bring a pillow the next time I ride with you."

Maddy's laughter died as she caught sight of a plume of dust on the road behind them. "Someone's following us. Coming fast."

"Hmmph." Bill pulled his rifle from beneath the seat and laid it across his knees. "Prob'ly jest someone in a hurry to git to the Mayhews. But there's so damn much riffraff runnin' around these days that it pays to be sure."

Maddy laid her hand on her reticule—and the little derringer pistol concealed inside. She knew Blanche was doing the same.

She could see the shape of a mounted man inside the dust cloud. He rode well. Coming from a Saylor, who'd been on horseback almost before she could walk, that was a compliment.

Her eyes narrowed. Something about the set of the man's shoulders seemed familiar. Suddenly, her stomach did a wild flip-flop, and mingled dread and anticipation tingled along her veins.

John Ballard.

With a sigh, she took her hand off her reticule. "Temptation, get thee behind me," she muttered.

Suddenly she smiled, her sense of the absurd taking over her ill humor. Really, she didn't want to shoot John Ballard. He might be the most infuriating man she'd ever met, but she was in control of her emotions. Maddy Saylor was *always* in control.

And what of the kiss? a treacherous corner of her mind whispered. That torrid, tempestuous kiss that had seared her to her soul?

He'd caught her by surprise, that was all. She'd been vulnerable after the fight, and he'd taken advantage of the situation. Never again. She knew his ploys now.

"Why, it's Mr. Ballard," Blanche said. "He must want to ride along with us." Turning her attention to Bill Jones, she explained, "He's the one who broke Zachary Marsh's nose."

Bill grunted, then slipped the rifle back under the seat. Maddy felt as though her doom were approaching as the hoofbeats grew louder and louder.

She shouldn't look. She didn't want to look. But an unexpected and unwilling impulse pulled her head around. Even as she did it, she knew it was a mistake.

He'd dressed for the barn raising. His shirt had faded from blue to almost white from hundreds of washings, and the wind plastered it to the hard muscles of his chest. A pair of battered jeans rode easily on his hips. His Stetson carved a wedge of shadow across his eyes, hiding them from view. But Maddy knew he could see her; one of those devastating dimples appeared in his cheek when he realized she was watching him.

It took an effort of will to pull her gaze away. Or maybe self-preservation, she thought with a slash of sour humor. Always in control, was she?

"Hello, John," Blanche called with a gaiety that made Maddy want to strangle her.

" 'Morning, Blanche," he replied, slowing his mount so that he rode beside Maddy. He nodded to the man who drove the wagon, then settled his gaze on Maddy.

She wore blue a shade lighter and brighter than her eyes. The contrast made her pupils look like the depths of a storm-swept sea—secretive, sensual, and brimming with invitation. He knew she didn't realize she had that come-hither look in her eyes; that in itself stirred him more than any open flirtation could. He wanted to kiss her all over again. Hell, he wanted to do a lot more than kiss her.

He'd spent the night tossing and turning, haunted by dreams. Erotic, explicit, tormenting dreams of Maddy naked, her skin like satin beneath his hands, crying his name as he buried himself in her sweet, hot depths. He'd suffered. Oh, he'd suffered.

And this morning she looked at him as if she'd never seen him before in her life.

Stubborn, smoldering, irresistible Maddy.

He smiled at her. "Good morning, Maddy."

"Good morning," she replied. Coolly, thank goodness. "This is our friend, Mr. Smith—"

"Call me Bill," the older man growled. "Own the general store on Main Street."

"I'm John Ballard. Pinkerton agent."

"Lookin' fer Derek Saylor?" Bill asked.

John smiled. "Isn't everybody?"

"Hmph. Not me. I set too high a store on these two ladies to be huntin' their brother."

Maddy blinked back unexpected tears of gratitude. Bill—rough-edged, gruff, sometimes unshaven Bill—had the heart of a gentleman.

"How dear," Blanche murmured.

But John could only look at Maddy, and the sudden sheen

in her eyes. Damn. He wished they'd met some other way. Any other way.

"It's not that easy a choice for me," he said, speaking to the other man but wanting Maddy to understand. "No matter how much I admire these ladies, I have a job to do. Anything else, and I'm abandoning my own honor."

"Put thataway," Bill growled. "I cain't fault you."

"What about you, Maddy?" John asked. "Can you fault me?"

She met his gaze squarely. "I understand honor, Mr. Ballard. But Derek is my brother. I'm on his side, and I will not step over that line."

John leaned to one side. Taking her hand, he raised it to his lips. "I understood that from the beginning."

She could feel the heat of his mouth through the fabric of her glove. Sensation spread out from that outwardly-innocent contact point, flowing in a molten tide through her body. Her breath grew shallow.

And suddenly, she was afraid. By her own reactions, she made herself vulnerable. She knew it; he knew it. Plenty of women had no doubt fallen to his blandishments.

For some reason, that thought stiffened her spine as no other could. She was *not* some foolish, lonely woman ripe for the plucking by some bold-eyed, sweet-talking male. There was much more at stake than a simple flirtation; Derek's life was the prize of this particular game. And so was she. If he could, John Ballard would take everything. Everything.

She would rather have faced a dozen Yankee soldiers out for blood.

"Are you having fun, Maddy?" Blanche asked.

"Not really." Maddy surveyed the enormous side of beef over which she'd been given sovereignty. It sizzled gently over a bed of coals, and she hadn't the faintest idea of when it might be considered cooked. "Did Hank Vann come?"

"No." Blanche's smile faltered for a moment. Then she recovered. "But I must say that John Ballard knows how to handle a hammer."

Of its own volition, Maddy's gaze went to the barn. John knelt on the roof, nailing boards together with precise, efficient movements. Sweat soaked his shirt, turning the fabric nearly transparent and showing the ridges of muscle in his back and shoulders. He'd rolled the sleeves up above his elbows, revealing brown, sinewy forearms that rippled every time he moved.

He rose to his feet, then leaped across a four-foot gap to another part of the roof. He moved with all the tightly coiled grace of a mountain lion, and Maddy's pulse stuttered.

She tore her gaze away. "Blanche, have you noticed that the other women are working right along with the men, while I'm stuck watching a cow that obviously doesn't need my help, and you're in charge of the water bucket?"

"They obviously think we're too delicate."

They looked at each other and nodded. Turning in unison, they headed toward their hostess.

"Dolly," Maddy said.

Mrs. Mayhew dropped the board she was carrying and turned. Tall, broad-shouldered, and broad-hipped, Dolly had a wealth of salt-and-pepper curls and warm brown eyes. Sweat trickled through the sawdust on her face.

"Hoo-ee, it's one scorcher of a day, ain't it?" she gasped, swiping at the mess on her face.

"A scorcher," Maddy agreed. "Now tell us why Blanche and I are assigned to nonsense tasks when the rest of you are working here at the barn?"

"They ain't nonsense tasks," Dolly protested.

Maddy raised her brows. "Dolly, this might be our first barn raising, but we're not stupid. I know nothing about cooking that great chunk of beef. And I doubt that twenty-odd men, who've been working hard all day, are going to be particular as to how their meat has been cooked."

Dolly snorted. "Shoot. If 'n it were still on the hoof, they'd chase it down and eat it."

"Exactly my point," Maddy said.

"All right, here's the way of it," Dolly said. "You two are, well, delicate. We cain't expect a purty little pony to do draft horse work."

Maddy's mouth dropped open in astonishment. "We're as tall as you are, Dolly Mayhew!"

"It's not that," the older woman explained. "It's just . . . the ribbons and things, and the dainty little white gloves——"

"We should be coddled just because we were foolish enough to come overdressed for the occasion?" Maddy asked. "We came here to help our neighbors, not to play fancy ladies in the shade."

"What about them duds?"

Maddy shrugged. "What about yours?"

Dolly glanced down at her faded gingham dress. Then she chuckled. "Sorry fer the misunderstandin'. If you wouldn't mind, jest grab some of them boards over there and haul 'em on over to the men."

"Thank you," Blanche said.

Dolly picked up her board and trotted away. Maddy led Blanche toward the pile of lumber their hostess had pointed out. The smell of fresh-cut wood stung their nostrils.

"I noticed you didn't tell Dolly that we brought a change of clothes," Blanche said.

"I think that would have shocked her more than us asking for some real work," Maddy replied. "And if no one else changes, we won't, either."

A sudden glow bloomed in Blanche's face, and Maddy turned to see Hank Vann standing nearby. Maddy didn't find him a handsome man; his features were too sharp, his jaw a shade too long. But those hawk's eyes of his turned gentle when he looked at Blanche—gentle and just a bit surprised, as though he was astonished to find such a thing as gentleness in himself.

Then he turned and strode away. A moment later he disappeared into the knot of people working on the barn.

Almost afraid of what she'd see, Maddy turned to look at her sister. Blanche's face held such a look of naked yearning that Maddy's heart contracted with pain.

"Oh, Blanche," she whispered.

"I couldn't help it, Maddy. It just happened."

Maddy bent and picked up one end of a long board. Blanche hurried to pick up the other. They didn't say anything as they delivered their load to the barn and started back for more.

"Darcy was a good husband to me," Blanche said. "But he's gone."

"Blanche—"

"Hank probably hasn't been a nice person; there are shadows in his eyes that frighten me. But the moment I looked at him, I saw something . . . felt something I thought was gone forever. Maddy, I know he's hunting our brother. I know he may only be interested in me because of the reward. But . . ." She took a deep breath. "You've never been with a man. You've never experienced the pleasure of being touched, being loved, when it's the right man."

Maddy shook her head, beset by a sudden, visceral memory of the way she'd all but gone up in flames when John touched her. His kiss had rocked her to her soul, and forever changed how she thought of herself.

"When Hank looks at me," Blanche continued, "I feel beautiful. I feel desired. I'm willing to take the risk of being hurt as long as there's the slightest chance it might be real for him, too. And perhaps I can make him want something more than the reward."

"I understand," Maddy whispered, her throat tight with sudden emotion.

"You do?" Blanche's mouth softened. "Oh, I see."

Maddy felt her cheeks grow hot, and tilted her head so her bonnet hid her face. "I meant that I understand the way *you* feel. You weren't made to spend your life alone. You'll be a good wife to whoever you marry, and a good mother to your children. I, on the other hand, am very happy being alone."

"Maddy dear, do you remember our Greek studies?"

"Yes."

"Do you remember what Papa said about *hubris?"*

'The pride that goeth before the fall', Maddy thought. "I remember very well, Blanche. And you might as well not say the rest. I'm fine. And I know exactly what I'm doing."

Blanche smiled, a secretive, knowing sort of smile. "Of course, dear. You always do."

"Thank you very much." After a moment, Maddy asked, "How will you deal with Hank as far as Derek is concerned?"

"We've agreed not to talk about Derek. Either of us."

"You've . . ." With a sharp exhalation, Maddy picked up another board. "Blanche Saylor, are you telling me that you and this . . . this man have already agreed to see each other—"

"—and that we've established a workable solution to our mutual problem? Yes."

"Fire and damnation!"

Blanche gasped. "Maddy!"

"Excuse me," Maddy snarled. "I meant hellfire and damnation!"

She stalked off, easily hefting the board with strength born of outrage. Hank Vann wanted Derek, dead or alive. Blanche was sorely misleading herself if she didn't think that fact would hang over their relationship like a dark, bloated cloud.

"Hey, Maddy!"

She knew that voice, registered it in the sudden racing of her pulse. It had a lazy air of sensuality to it that played havoc with her nerves. She wanted to ignore it, and him. But her eyes didn't obey her.

He stood on the edge of the roof above her, one boot planted on the top rung of a ladder. His hands were propped on his hips, drawing her gaze to the jeans that clung so casually and disturbingly to him.

"What do you want?"

"The board."

"What?"

"The board," he said again. Amusement sparkled in his eyes and softened the hard cut of his mouth.

Maddy had forgotten the board. Silently berating herself for letting John Ballard scramble her senses again, she heaved the board upward. He plucked it from her grasp as if it weighed nothing.

"Hand me that tin of nails, would you?" he asked. "There, to your left."

The impulse to tell him to get his own dratted nails was strong. But Maddy had insisted on helping, so help she would. Tucking the heavy tin in the crook of her left arm, she started up the ladder.

"You know," John said, "your eyes look like summer stormclouds when you're mad," John said.

"I am not mad."

"Sure you are. You're mad about the kiss."

"If you mean I was insane to have allowed you—"

"Participated, Maddy. You were, as I recall, a rather enthusiastic partner."

If she'd had the strength, she would have hurled the nails at him. "If you were a gentleman—"

"But I'm not," he said, a touch of anger coming into his eyes now. "I'm a Yankee. Now, Maddy, about the kiss."

Maddy glanced around. With all these people around, one would have thought *someone* would have interrupted by now. At least she was nearly up to the roof; a moment more, and she could escape.

"Maddy," John hissed.

The intensity of his voice surprised her. She tilted her head back to look at him. Unfortunately, her gaze began at his feet and had to travel upward along his body before reaching his face. Long, lean, and aggressively male, he set her pulse to racing and turned her knees weak.

She hated it. And she hated him for causing it.

Silently, she lifted the tin of nails and set it down on the roof. If she could have flown to get away from him, she would have.

"Now, about that kiss," John growled.

"I don't want to talk about it."

"I do."

He stood above her, arrogant and infuriating, his hands planted on his hips. As though he expected her to obey simply because he ordered it.

Maddy's eyes narrowed. John Ballard had a great deal to learn, particularly about Saylor women. She studied him for a moment from beneath her lashes. Then she smiled.

"Mr. Ballard, you can go straight to the devil," she said.

"Why you little . . ." With a smooth, swift movement, he reached down and grabbed for her.

Maddy dodged. But her foot slipped off the rung, and she lost her balance completely. Her fingertips slid over smooth, sunwarmed wood, but she couldn't quite get a grip.

A heartbeat later, she found herself falling.

Five

Someone screamed. The sound seemed to crystallize in the air around Maddy as she started to topple. She closed her eyes, already anticipating the moment when she'd hit the ground.

Then something warm and iron-hard clamped around her wrist, stopping her fall. Astonished, she looked up to see John crouched at the very edge of the roof, his face taut with strain as he strove to keep from sliding off as he held her. Maddy could hear sawdust scraping beneath his boots.

"Don't move," he gritted.

Maddy couldn't have moved if she'd wanted to; her arm was one solid mass of agony. John gathered himself, a coiling of muscles she could see even through the fabric of his shirt.

Then, with a steady pull, he drew her up. Sweat broke out on his forehead, and all the tendons in his neck stood out. She felt the edge of the roof bump against her side, then her hip. A moment later, she lay safely upon the boards. Her breath went in with a huge sigh, and only then did she realize she'd forgotten to breathe. John dropped to his knees beside her, panting with effort.

"All right?" he asked.

"Yes. You?"

He nodded, but a shadow of pain darkened his eyes. Maddy knew his arm had to hurt much worse than hers did. "John, your arm . . ."

Her voice trailed away when she saw his eyes darken still

further. But not with pain. Desire flared in those green-gold depths, hotter than the lemon-yellow sun overhead. Then his long, dark lashes swept downward, and she knew he wanted to kiss her.

She couldn't. He couldn't. Just now her nerves were singing with reaction to him; she was capable, at this moment, of responding to him with unseemly passion.

Oh, Lord, she thought. The best thing to do would be to put some distance between them. She had to get away from the passion in his eyes, and the molten pulse-beat of desire within her own veins.

She gathered her feet beneath her, and found herself sliding toward the edge of the roof again. John slipped his good arm around her waist and pulled her back. She raised her hands in protest, only to find them resting on his chest. Without thought, she spread her fingers over the hard swell of his muscles. He was firm and warm, and it was all she could do to keep her hands from straying.

"Thattaboy," Bill Smith called from below. "That was one hell of a catch. What're you gonna do with her now?"

Blushing furiously, Maddy glanced over her shoulder to see almost everyone gathered below, watching. She tried to move away from John, but his arm tightened around her waist.

"Bill, are you saying she's mine now?" he called.

"Hoo-eee," Dolly shouted, her broad, good-natured face red with merriment. "Yours! Jest try layin' *that* claim, and you're gonna see if a man kin live without his hide. 'Cause that gal looks like she's ready to tear yore skin off in little tiny strips."

"Might be worth it," John said.

The crowd laughed uproariously. A wicked light came into John's eyes, and Maddy nearly launched herself off the roof again. "Don't you dare," she hissed.

"What do you think I have in mind, Maddy?"

"Whatever it is, forget it this instant."

He grinned at her. Slowly, still keeping his arm around her, he drew her to her feet. "Stop teasing the lady," he said. "You're making her blush.,

"But ain't she purty, all red and shiny like that?" Bill hollered.

"That she is, my friend," John said, grinning at Maddy. "That she is." Lowering his voice, he whispered, "It's a damn good thing we had an audience. Or else we'd have settled the kissing issue right here and now."

"Perhaps not the way you intended," she retorted.

"Want to bet?"

Her lashes fluttered downward. "I never gamble."

The dimple creased his cheek. For some strange reason, the sight of that tiny indentation played havoc with Maddy's insides, and she was possessed by the sudden, shocking urge to kiss it.

"Shall I carry you down?" he whispered.

"Definitely not."

"Why? Too risky?"

"Too foolish," she retorted. "Now let me go."

"I'm not holding you, Maddy."

Too late, she realized it was true. She hadn't noticed him dropping his arm; his mere presence had enveloped her, anchoring her to him. She felt stripped bare, exposed by her own weakness.

"But it's all right," he said, mischief in his eyes. "If you're good, I'll hold you again later."

Surely, no one had ever descended a ladder as fast as Maddy did then. She turned to look up at him. He stood much as he had a few minutes ago, his hands propped on his hips, his eyes bold. Something wild and reckless swept through her. Saylor blood, Saylor temper. They didn't take well to humiliation.

She looked straight into John Ballard's eyes. And then she smiled.

"You can try," she said.

His eyes widened in astonishment at her audacity. Before he could recover, she turned and stalked away.

Hah! she thought. There wasn't a Yankee born who could get the best of a Saylor.

"Well, we did it," Maddy said, looking out the Mayhews' bedroom window at the nearly-completed barn. The unpainted wood shimmered in the light of the just-risen moon. "I didn't think it was possible."

"Well, to quote our hostess, we-all worked like hogs," Blanche said, leaning over to peer at herself in the tiny, battered mirror on the wall. "I really like Dolly. She has a good heart. Do you know she miscarried six babies in addition to the ones that lived?"

"How terrible," Maddy murmured. "And she still has such joy in her eyes."

"She said that life takes endurance, but that it takes courage to keep one's laughter." Blanche stared at herself a moment longer, but her gaze had lost focus.

"Maddy . . . will we ever find a real home again?"

"Home is where we make it."

"But it isn't, not really," Blanche said. "We haven't been accepted here. Oh, there are people like Bill and Dolly who judge us on our own merits, but we've never managed to really fit in. We're too—"

"Prissy?" Maddy finished for her. "But you know that's not true."

"Well, they seem to think so," Blanche countered. "Which is why we were given those ridiculous jobs at first."

"This is a different world from the one we came from. We have to earn our place here—if we want one. Do you want one, Blanche?"

She pushed an errant golden curl back from her forehead. "I want . . . something. We've been drifting since the war. Not only from place to place, but in our hearts."

"And you think Hank Vann might be your anchor?" Maddy sighed. "Oh, Blanche."

The line of Blanche's chin firmed, and for a moment she looked just like their stubborn father. "Perhaps, perhaps not. But I'm willing to give it a chance."

Maddy rose; this was not the time to argue. She smoothed the skirt of her gingham dress. "The music has started. Why don't we go enjoy our neighbors, and perhaps induce them to enjoy us?"

She linked arms with her sister, drawing her into the outer room. Dolly's house had no hallway; every room let to another, and each had at least two doors. For all its awkwardness and the obviously made-by-hand furnishings, the house had a cluttered hominess that Maddy found very appealing. Sort of like Dolly herself, she thought.

Outside, the air had cooled with the dying sun, and a welcome breeze riffled along the ground. The air smelled of wood smoke and sawdust, with a hint of sage for flavoring. Maddy felt her nostrils flare.

"Maddy!" the urgent whisper came from the shadows at the east side of the house. "Blanche!"

Maddy knew that whisper. Derek! For a moment, disbelief froze her mind. Had he gone mad, to come here like this? She exchanged one incredulous glance with her sister, then grabbed Blanche's hand and hauled her toward the spot from which the summons had come.

A tall shadow appeared in front of her. Reaching out, she grasped a handful of fabric.

"Derek, you're insane!" she hissed.

"Always, dear sister," he replied. "Come this way. We have to talk."

He led them to a clump of trees behind the house. Maddy was all but quivering with concern, and the moment they were hidden, she rounded on her brother.

"What are you doing here?" she demanded. "To take such a risk . . ." She let her voice trail away as she saw the greasy black mess that had once been hair as blond as her own. "What did you do to your hair?"

"Soot," he said cheerfully. "Had to have a disguise, and this was the best I could do on short notice."

Blanche flung her arms around him, gaining herself a swipe of black across her cheek. Maddy, however, put her hands on her hips and studied her brother from beneath lowered brows.

"You are out of your mind," she said. "Do you know how many people are looking for—"

"I knew you'd be upset by the 'WANTED' poster," he replied. His eyes were midway in color between Blanche's soft blue and Maddy's indigo, and possessed more devilment than any man should have. "I had to make sure you were all right."

"Upset . . ." Maddy took a deep breath. "Derek, of all the people in the world, you ought to know that Blanche and I are hardly the sort to be sent into a tizzy over anything, let alone a piece of paper."

"I must say I'm flattered," he said. "Ten thousand dollars. Most impressive. Not many men are worth that much to themselves, let alone anyone else."

"This isn't funny, Derek," Blanche said. "There are a lot of men who'd kill you for that amount of money."

"Of course," he replied, smiling that crooked grin that had melted the heart of every woman he met. "But then, there are a lot of men who'd kill me for nothing. But they've got to catch me first. And that's the trick."

"This isn't a matter for jesting," Maddy said.

But Derek just kept smiling, and she knew she couldn't reach him. Derek had inherited their father's looks, charm, and wildness. To him, this was all a game, a wonderful, dangerous game he had every confidence he would win. And even death was something to be met cheerfully, with a smile.

But to his sisters, this was deadly serious. For they would be the ones to bear the pain of losing him. Still, until he found something more important than recklessness, they would simply have to love him . . . and try to keep him alive.

Maddy sighed. "Where are you . . . No, don't tell me. Then I can continue to tell people that I don't know where you're hiding."

"That might be for the best," he agreed. "But if you need me, you can get a message to me at Miss Penny's in Gatesburg."

"Miss Penny's . . . House of Pleasure?" Blanche asked.

A hint of red came into Derek's cheeks. "It's not what you think," he protested.

"And what are we thinking, brother dear?" Maddy asked.

"The worst," he retorted. "Penny is a . . . friend of mine."

"I see," Blanche murmured.

He cleared his throat. "Now, I don't want you two doing anything rash. You've put your lives in danger too many times for my sake. This time, let it be."

"Let it be?" Maddy echoed. "And how are we to do that, pray tell?"

"You stay here. No midnight rides hell-for-leather just to confuse the enemy, no fighting, no—"

"So," Maddy said, her eyes narrowing. "You want us to just stand here and let them hunt you down like some wild animal . . . and for something you didn't do?"

"Yes, Maddy. That's exactly what I want."

With a sharp, angry movement, she whirled away from him. "We will not abandon you."

"Now, see here, Maddy—"

"She's right," Blanche said. "We love you, Derek. We've pulled through harder things than this, but only together." Her mouth turned up at the corners. "Besides, it's too late. We've already been in a fight."

"Damn it—"

"It was a very ladylike fight," Blanche continued. "We even let a Pinkerton agent and a bounty hunter defend our honor, although Maddy did have to knock one fellow unconscious with a bucket."

Derek opened his mouth, but no sound came out.

"And everyone already knows we're the key to finding you, so it's impossible for us to remain uninvolved," Maddy said, adding, "even if we wanted to, which we do not."

That seemed to release Derek from his paralysis. He crossed his arms over his chest. "I forbid it."

Unmoved, Maddy studied him. "Perhaps your . . . friend may be biddable, Derek. But your sisters are not."

"If Mother were here—"

"She would pinch your ear right off for having had anything to do with Miss Penny's House of Pleasure," Maddy said.

"Well—"

"And she would have proceeded to do what was needed," Blanche added. "No matter what she had to do. Mother was completely ruthless when it came to defending her children, as you very well know."

Derek flung his arms wide, capitulating. "Do you realize that I've never won an argument with the women in my family?"

"Cheer up," Maddy said. "No one else has, either."

"Hellfire and damnation," he growled.

"Precisely," Maddy replied. "Now, get out of here before someone sees you. The Pinkerton agent and one of the bounty hunters are here, and they'd like nothing better than to get their hands on you."

He grimaced. "Promise me—"

"No," she said.

They stood facing each other, fists clenched, jaws thrust forward in identical lines of stubbornness. A faint sound drifted in on the breeze, a whisper of noise that wasn't quite natural.

"Go," Maddy hissed.

Derek melted into the darkness as though he were part of it. Maddy and Blanche picked their skirts up and walked silently in the opposite direction. Keeping the trees between them and the sound, they moved out into the open.

"Who?" Blanche whispered, the barest breath of sound.

Maddy chopped at the air with the edge of her hand, cautioning silence. "Well, Blanche, what do you think of your first barn raising?"

"Oh, I liked it. I'd begun to think that Texas entertainment was the cowboys' weekly Saturday night brawls."

"Well, dear, the night's not over yet," Maddy replied. She could now track the soft footsteps following them. Whoever it was, he knew something about sneaking about. "Did you hear that Emily Gaines took a broom to her husband for mooning at the girls at the saloon?"

"She didn't," Blanche gasped. "Really?"

The soft noises came closer. Maddy's nostrils flared as she realized there were two sets of footsteps. "Just look at that moon," she said. "Isn't it the most beautiful thing you've ever seen?"

"They didn't have a moon in Virginia?" John Ballard's voice drifted out of the darkness like rich velvet.

"Oh!" Blanche gasped. "I didn't know anyone else was out here."

John stepped out of a patch of shadow cast by the corncrib. He'd changed his clothes. He wore stark black and white: black trousers, white shirt, black string tie. He'd combed his hair straight back from his forehead, but waves piled up upon his collar.

He needs a haircut, Maddy thought, possessed by the impulse to run her hands through those thick curls. She stood very still, pinned by his gaze. He was devastatingly handsome, as comfortable as a cat in the darkness. Her breathing became shallow, and for a moment she wished she could change into some winged night creature, and escape.

"You're both exceptionally beautiful tonight," he said, bowing. "Much too beautiful to be wandering way out here by yourselves."

Maddy opened her mouth to reply. But before she could think of anything to say, Hank Vann seemed to materialize out of the darkness behind Blanche. Awareness of him washed across Blanche's face, making her seem to glow.

Without thought, Maddy reached toward her sister. But Hank Vann now dominated Blanche's world, a lean dark shadow come to warm himself at her fire.

"Blanche," he murmured.

"Hank."

The four of them stood still and silent as the breeze swirled around them. Then the high, pure notes of a violin rose to dominate the night. As though released by the music, Hank Vann held his hand out to Blanche.

"Let's go dance," he murmured.

Without a word, Blanche laid her hand in his. Together, they turned and headed for the barn. Her soft mauve skirts swirled around his black-clad legs as they walked.

"Maddy," John said.

John's breath stirred the hair at her temples. She felt no surprise at finding him this close; like this afternoon, his presence enveloped her, surrounded her, constrained her. A sense of inevitability settled on her soul, as though Fate had just taken her future out of her hands.

He laid his hands on her shoulders. His touch was gentle, and should have been undemanding. But his fingers curved over her flesh with undeniable possessiveness. Her body came to life beneath his touch, her blood surging faster through her veins, her breath deepening. It was as though her skin yearned for his touch, her breasts swelling and becoming strangely over-sensitive beneath her clothes. Shockingly, she wanted John to touch them. Would she burst into flame, then? Surely, Surely.

This, she knew, was what Blanche had missed, and had found again with Hank Vann. This . . . helpless, terrible, exquisite reaction, this weakening of limbs and resolve, this demand deep in her body that had become an ache.

And it was weakness. Maddy was the one who'd held the

Saylors together, and who had to get them through this latest crisis.

With an effort of will, she took a step away from him. Her shoulders felt empty without the warmth of his hands, but she pushed the feeling of loss aside. The loss of Derek would be greater.

"I haven't had a thing to eat yet," she said. "If you'll excuse me—"

"You're not getting rid of me that easily," John said. "I'm not about to miss your reaction to your first bite of real honest-to-God Texas Longhorn."

"I'm not sure I want to eat a Longhorn," she replied.

"Think of it as a character-building experience. After all, where else are you going to find a cow that's meaner cooked than on the hoof?"

Maddy stared at him in astonishment. He laughed, his teeth flashing white against his tanned skin. Taking her hand, he tucked it in the crook of his arm. "Come on, Maddy. I want a piece of Mrs. Sanderson's famous peach cake while there's still some left. Three layers high, and so rich it would tempt an angel."

"Which you certainly are not."

"Never claimed to be." He grinned at her, and that dimple appeared in his cheek again. "But I'm willing to be reformed."

"I'm only a dressmaker, not a worker of miracles," she retorted.

"Too bad," he said. "It's going to take a miracle to keep people from assuming we've been kissing out behind the house."

Maddy drew her breath in sharply as her face began to flame. After that scene on the barn roof today, the others would no doubt think exactly that.

John put his hand over hers, his palm hot against her skin. "Don't worry about a thing, Maddy. I'll sneak us in so unobtrusively that no one will know we weren't there."

Maddy was suspicious, of course; far too much mischief

lurked in his eyes for comfort. But she knew she had no choice. He wasn't about to let her go, and she had no intention of making a scene. She'd already been branded a spinster, and desperate. Better to extricate herself quietly.

The townspeople had gathered in the open field beside the barn. The full moon hung like a beacon overhead, pouring a gentle silver shimmer over everything.

Everyone seemed to be watching the couples spinning to a lively reel on the close-cut grass. John drew Maddy to a stop at the edge of the crowd. To Maddy's relief, no one seemed to notice their arrival.

"Unobtrusive, as I said," John whispered. "I'm a man who keeps his promises."

"Or threats?" Maddy asked.

"Yes," he agreed. "Always."

No humor lightened his eyes. Suddenly chilled, Maddy turned her attention to the musicians. She was surprised to see that Jake Lattimore, the butcher, was the fiddler. His face shone with heat and pleasure, and his thick, stubby hands moved with astonishing finesse as he made his instrument sing. With him stood Arthur Afton, playing guitar, and banker Darius Taylor, whose harmonica wailed a sweet duet with the fiddle.

"Not the sort of thing high-bred Virginia ladies are used to," John said.

Maddy glanced at him from the corner of her eye. "You have no idea what we are used to," she retorted.

"You might be right." He smiled at her. "Dance?"

"Certainly not."

He took her by the hand and pulled her toward the spot that had been set aside for dancing. With a twirl that sent her skirts flying, he spun her in among the other couples. For a moment, she was too astonished to move. But he caught her by the hand and swung her into the rhythm of the dance.

Trapped again, Maddy thought. He'd tricked her neatly. But

the music was lively, the breeze was cool, and she hadn't danced in a very long time.

She spun away from him, swinging around another partner, then spun back into his grasp. "Is this, too, what you call unobtrusive?"

"No," he replied. "But I wanted to dance with you, and I didn't like your answer when I asked."

"So you took?"

"Yes."

"Some people . . ." She paused as he whirled her at arm's length, then brought her back. ". . . Some people take no for an answer."

"I'm not one of them."

The dance ended. Maddy found herself standing in the circle of his arm, her gaze locked to his. For a moment the world seemed to fade away. Then she remembered who she was and where she was, and stepped back.

Before she could escape completely, however, John caught her by the wrist. His touch was no longer gentle, and his eyes held the same hardness they'd had when he'd spoken about promises—and threats. Alarmed by the sudden change in him, Maddy lifted her gaze to his.

"I know Derek was here," he said.

Six

Maddy's blood ran cold in her veins. She was aware that the music had started again, but only peripherally. If John hadn't taken her hands and forced her to move, she might have stood there through the entire song.

He led her away from the other dancers. She lifted her face to the breeze, letting the coolness seep into her. Slowly, her mind began functioning again. Tilting her head back, she met his gaze levelly.

"What do you plan to do about it?" she asked.

John's eyes narrowed. He didn't think he'd ever been so annoyed at anyone. Another woman might have played coy or cried, or most likely of all, lied. But not Maddy. No, she looked him straight in the eye and asked him, baldly and boldly, what he planned to do.

But by damn, he admired her. And yes, he wished he were the focus of that unshakeable loyalty and fiery courage. He wondered if Derek Saylor knew how lucky he was.

He was suddenly gripped by a blinding-hot urge to pull her close, to crush his mouth down on hers and make her call his name again. It was the primitive, powerful male urge to possess a woman on every level. To dominate her, to make her his.

His spirit clamored for it, so strongly that he had to clench his hands into fists to keep from touching her. For it wouldn't work. Maddy couldn't be dominated. She was too strong, too stubborn.

Simply, Maddy had to be won.

And how was he to do that? he asked himself, looking down into her storm-blue eyes. He was the man who'd vowed to bring her brother to justice, and she would never allow herself to fall for him. She'd readied herself for battle; he could see it in her eyes and the determined set of her jaw.

Well, he wasn't about to accommodate. He knew Maddy enough now that to engage her like this, when she was prepared, was tantamount to bashing his head against a brick wall. No. He'd beguile her instead, throw her off balance.

Under control now, but only marginally, he reached out and ran his fingertips along the satin curve of her cheek. He watched her eyes darken, her lips part in unconscious reaction. And there it was: her weakness, her Achilles heel. Passion, the great force that had brought prideful men and women down from the beginning of time.

It was his downfall where she was concerned; and it was also hers.

"That vaunted Saylor honesty is a problem sometimes, isn't it?" he asked.

"You have no idea," she replied.

He let his hand drift down her neck to her shoulder, then down the length of her arm. Finally, he circled her wrist in a grasp that was as gentle as it was determined.

"Let's get something to eat," he said. "I'm starving."

Maddy blinked, once again surprised by his sudden change of mood. She'd expected an argument. Instead, he'd taken a complete turn, and she wasn't sure how to respond.

"I—"

"Just come, Maddy." A wicked light came into his eyes. "Don't worry. I intend to continue our discussion. But not on an empty stomach; I'll need my strength if I'm to continue fencing with you."

"Why don't you just leave me alone?"

"Ah, that wouldn't do," he replied, his voice caressing. "That wouldn't do at all."

Still holding her firmly by the hand, he towed her to the

table where Dolly Mayhew presided over the food. She beamed at them like a fond mother hen over chicks that have just done something good.

"Hello, Mrs. Mayhew," he said.

"It's about time you let that poor gal eat," she replied with a grin that fairly split her face. "Now, jest let me find a clean plate . . . Ah, here's one. Y'all don't mind sharing, right?"

"Right," John said.

Maddy watched Dolly heap the plate with beans, corn, tomatoes, and fried potatoes, then covered them with a slab of hard grey beef the size of a washboard.

"Gravy?" Dolly asked.

"I don't think—" Maddy began.

"Got to have gravy," the older woman said, dipping a huge ladleful of dark brown liquid over the beef. "Here you are."

"Thank you, ma'am," John said.

He balanced the plate in one hand as he led Maddy to a bench made of a board set across two nail kegs. With a studied flourish, he indicated the makeshift seat. Maddy eased herself down as the board creaked a protest.

John sat down and put the plate on the seat between them. He sawed off a small bite of Longhorn and offered it to Maddy.

Her stomach recoiled. "I don't want it."

"Eat. You don't want to insult our hosts."

John watched her contemplate denial, then close her eyes and open her mouth. He took a moment to study the delectable picture she presented: lush red lips, the edges of straight, pearly teeth and a tantalizing glimpse of the sweet, wet flesh beyond. It was almost more than he could bear. The fork shook as his hand began to tremble, and it was all he could do not to kiss her then and there.

"Maddy."

She opened her eyes a slit, and found John staring at her, an all-too-easily-read expression on his face.

"If you know what's good for you," he said hoarsely, "you'll take this fork from my hand."

She took the fork. "Lecher. Can't you think about anything else?"

"Apparently, not when I'm with you." John crossed his legs; his body had echoed the sensuous turn of his mind.

Maddy put the beef in her mouth and chewed. And chewed. But her teeth had little effect on the fibrous mass, and she finally gave up and swallowed the thing whole.

"So that was Longhorn," she said.

"Would you like more?"

"No."

He smiled. "So, let's talk about Derek."

She studied him calmly. "Why didn't you go after him?"

"Because Hank Vann was there."

"And you don't want to share," she said.

"I told you, Maddy. I'd like to take your brother in alive. Let someone like Hank Vann see him, and that's unlikely."

"Don't you think he'd have some care for Blanche's feelings?"

He chopped at the air with the edge of his hand. "Haven't you heard of Hank Vann, Maddy?"

"No," she replied; trying in vain to quell the sudden churning of her stomach. "Should I?"

"He's been bounty hunting for about ten years now, and he's good at it. Very good. That kind of business hardens a man. Hank has earned himself the reputation of a man who'll stop at nothing to get that reward."

"And what about you?" she retorted.

"I'm not after the money."

"Perhaps not. But Derek would be imprisoned just the same, wouldn't he?"

"Maddy—"

"My brother didn't rob those stages."

John raked his hair back with one hand. "Maddy, I don't want to debate that with you. Guilt or innocence is the law's decision, not mine."

"And you're only doing your job?"

"Yes," he said, although he had the distinct feeling he'd just stepped into a trap.

"Right or wrong."

John's temper began to smolder. "I'm willing to listen, Maddy. Do you have some kind of proof, other than your admirable sisterly loyalty?"

"No," she said.

"Then I have to take him in."

Maddy got to her feet. "No. You have to find him first. And you can stop your flirting ways right now. I'm not some simpering fool who'd betray her brother for some attention from a man. You'll never get to Derek through me."

After raking him with a smoldering look of disdain, she turned and walked away.

She should have known he'd come after her. She really should have known. But it wasn't until his hand clamped on her arm that she realized the trouble she was in, and by that time, he'd drawn her into the privacy of the darkness behind the barn.

He pulled her close, molding her against the solid wall of his chest. Alarm and anticipation ran through her body. But pride brought her chin up and stiffened her spine, and she levered her arms to create some space between them.

"You want Derek," she said. "Not me."

John was tired of sparring, tired of holding himself back when he desired her more than any woman he'd ever known.

"Look into my eyes, Maddy," he said. "Tell me what you see."

Flames, she thought. She saw passion's fire raging in those green-gold depths, desire hotter than anything she'd ever known. Desire hot enough to consume her totally. She feared it, even as something deeply feminine in her reveled in it.

"I see . . ." she began, wanting to lie. Wanting to deny what was in him. And in her. "I see . . ."

"You'd like to lie."

"I'd like to be left alone," she retorted, stung that he'd read her so easily.

"No, you wouldn't," he murmured.

He spread his hands over her waist, then ran them in a long, slow caress along her sides. Heat blossomed, coiled through her in a lazy tide, and set up a molten ache between her legs. His thumbs brushed the sides of her breasts oh, so lightly.

She should have been shocked. But a strange lassitude had gripped her, sending her eyelids fluttering downward in an invitation as old as time. He caressed her upper arms, his fingers curving possessively over her flesh. And again brushed her breasts as he ran his hands down to her wrists. Her nipples pouted into swollen points, and a sigh escaped her.

"You see, Maddy?" he whispered. "This is what's real between us. Nothing else. Nothing more."

She knew she ought to deny him. But her rational mind had drifted off on a cloud of sensation, and she was helpless to bring it back. His gaze caught hers, holding it as he drew her hands up and around his neck.

Her mouth opened, inviting him without her bidding. He nibbled on her upper lip, then gently sucked on the lower. Sensation sharpened, grew more insistent, and Maddy daringly thrust her tongue into the moist heat of his mouth. Their breaths mingled on a shared gasp.

Fitting his mouth to hers, he kissed her deeply, with such driving passion that her whole body thrilled in response. His tongue played with hers, slick and hot. She craved his touch, her body aching for the heat of his hands.

He ran his hands down her sides and back again. His thumbs caressed the swell where her breasts met her ribs, and she arched her back in mindless invitation. And then he claimed her aching breasts at last, cupping the swollen flesh, circling the taut nipples in a caress that made her gasp. She'd never known anything could be so exquisite, so compelling.

"I wonder if you know what you're doing to me," he muttered against her mouth.

She didn't want to talk. She only wanted to feel. So she bit at his mouth, urging him closer, deeper. He obeyed, as driven and mindless as she. He continued to caress her breasts, rolling her nipples between his fingers until she whimpered in sheer, unbridled pleasure.

John struggled to keep the few shreds of control left to him. But oh, God, she smelled of lilac and woman and desire, and it was all he could do to keep from taking her right here. He had to stop this before he lost what wits he still had.

"Maddy," he said.

"Mmmm?"

"We've got to go somewhere else."

That got through the haze of pleasure fogging her brain. "What?"

"We can't do this here. Too many people—"

"Oh! Oh, my God!"

She sprang away from him, her cheeks flaming. She couldn't believe this had happened . . . But it had. It wasn't his fault; he was just being a man. *She* should have known better. This was awful. She'd revealed her deepest weakness to her brother's enemy, and she knew he'd use it. Over and over, he'd use it. She felt as though she'd stepped off solid ground and into quicksand.

Drawing herself up, she faced him with what dignity she could muster. "I . . . shouldn't have allowed that to happen. I led you on, and I had no right to. I assure you it won't happen again."

He leaned back against the barn and studied her. "That was quite a speech, Maddy."

"I meant every word."

"That doesn't matter."

Maddy's head came up in surprise. "What?"

"You don't know much about men and women, Maddy. So I'm going to give you your first lesson tonight. Passion is a powerful thing, and passion like this is downright irresistible.

It's kind of like touching a match to dry tinder; once lit, that fire's going to burn until all the fuel is gone."

"How flattering."

"It's true," he growled. "And if you think otherwise, then you're just lying to yourself."

Her temper flared, because he might be right. But she welcomed the heat of anger, for it overshadowed the desire thrumming through her veins.

"I wish I'd never met you," she said, her voice intense for all that it was a whisper.

He smiled at her, his long, lean body infuriatingly relaxed, his eyes bold as they raked her from head to toe. She tried not to blush again and failed as her memory conjured the memory of his hands on her, the way he'd tasted, the way he'd felt.

His eyes seemed to take that memory from her and reflect it back twofold. He knew her. He'd roused her passion and her response, and he wasn't about to forget it.

"It's too late, Maddy," he replied. "You'd better get used to having me around."

She stood there trembling. His gaze dropped to her mouth, and her body reacted instantly. Sweet, hot arousal spun through her, setting up a chain reaction that seemed to end in her very soul. If he kissed her now, she'd respond. If he touched her now, she'd respond.

It was weak, so weak. She'd always thought herself above human frailties, protected by her Saylor pride, her wits, and her stubbornness.

Then John Ballard had walked into her life. Arrogant, too sure of himself and of her, he'd shattered her composure, shaken her certainties . . . and taught her the exquisite risks of pleasure. Maddy Saylor would never be the same.

She turned and ran. Not from John.

From herself.

Seven

Maddy stared up at the ceiling of her quiet bedroom, listening to Blanche's soft breathing in the bed beside her. She hadn't slept at all. The first silvery light of dawn stained the window; the time for sleeping was lost to her now.

If she'd thought to escape John Ballard, she'd been wrong. He'd invaded the privacy of her home, and most especially, her mind. Even now, her breasts tightened at the memory of his touch, as though he'd been imprinted somehow in her flesh.

She shifted restlessly, her hips flexing in response to the sudden liquid warmth between her legs. The Saylors had never been a cautious lot, but this reckless desire frightened her as much as it compelled her.

"Maddy?" Blanche whispered.

"I thought you were sleeping."

"Couldn't." Blanche plumped her pillow up against the headboard so she could sit up. "It's John, isn't it?"

"It's everything. John and Derek and Hank Vann, too," Maddy said. "This is a mess, Blanche."

"You like him."

"Who?"

"John Ballard. Your lips were swollen when you came back to the dance floor last night."

"Good God!" Maddy cried in consternation.

Blanche laughed. "My lips were swollen, too. Oh, don't worry, no one else noticed. But you really are swearing an awful lot lately, dear."

"I have a lot to swear about."

Maddy fell silent for a moment, struggling with herself. She hated to admit her attraction to John Ballard to herself, let alone anyone else. But she and Blanche had been sisters and best friends all their lives, and this was too close to her heart not to be shared.

"Blanche, this thing between men and women—"

"You mean kissing, touching, making love?"

"Yes. Is it nice?"

"Nice?" Blanche took a deep breath. "Oh, Maddy, *nice* isn't the word. Being loved by the right man is like nothing else on earth. It's like being caught up in a thunderstorm, lightning crashing all around, your body soaring with the wind."

Maddy crossed her arms over her breasts, overwhelmed with the picture her sister's words had evoked. Yes, it would be that way with John Ballard; just his kiss had shaken her to her soul.

But it wasn't real, not to him. To him, it was a game. Make love to Maddy, get his hands on Derek. He would take her to the heights . . . and then he would betray her.

"Aren't you frightened, Blanche?"

"Of what?"

"Of loving Hank, and then finding out he was just using you to get to Derek?"

"Hank isn't doing that," Blanche said.

"How do you know?"

"I just know."

Maddy sat up and lit the lamp, needing to look into her sister's eyes. Blanche seemed so serene, so at peace with herself and Hank. *I just know.* It was a woman's surety, a woman's faith. Pure. Simple. Powerful. Maddy didn't understand it; her own feelings were complex and confused, and there was nothing in this situation she could trust.

"*How* do you know?" she demanded, frustration edging her voice. "How can you be sure?"

"There's no certainty in life, Maddy dear. Once, I had certainty. I was so sure I would be married to Darcy forever, and we'd raise a dozen children. But Darcy was killed in the war, and I lost the baby we'd started." A bright sheen of tears turned her eyes silver for a moment. "I've got to make a new life for myself now."

"And what about Derek?"

"I have faith," Blanche said softly. "In Derek, and in you. No one can catch Derek, and you'll find a way to prove his innocence."

Maddy pressed the heels of her hands against her eyes, overwhelmed for a moment with the weight of her responsibility. Memories came flooding back: her mother's face, wasted by illness and overwork but lovely still, framed against the pillow by her thick, dark hair.

Mother had asked to talk to Maddy alone. She'd struggled against encroaching death, clinging to Maddy's hand as though it were her only lifeline to this world.

'Maddy', she'd whispered, 'I cannot . . . fight any longer. You must take over now. Blanche is too sweet; she hasn't the ruthlessness to survive the times to come. And Derek is a reckless, wild boy. Like your father, he's not . . . practical. You're the only one with the strength to pull the Saylors through. Promise me you'll watch over them.'

'I promise', Maddy had said. 'You can count on me, Mother. I will never let them down.'

And then her mother's eyes closed one last time. Her hand went limp, and Maddy gently set it back on the bed.

Maddy had accepted the responsibility willingly. But just now, it was a very heavy one. Then, as though lightning had struck her mind, she remembered the sign she'd seen tacked to the livery stable wall, and she straightened.

"Time to get up, Blanche," she said, flinging the covers aside.

"What is it?"

"There's a sale at the livery stable this morning. I think it's time we bought our own horses."

* * *

John mingled with the crowd of men who'd gathered at the corral behind the livery stable. Lucius Browning, owner of the Twin Pines Ranch, had brought a number of horses in for sale. In Cofield, it was an event. Half the town had come out, if not to buy, to watch.

"Plannin' to buy?"

The voice came from behind him, but John knew before turning that it belonged to Hank Vann. He studied the other man for a moment. Vann had a hard-edged look to him, but his gaze was direct, and John could read no dishonesty there.

"No," he replied. "I've got my mount. But there are a few good-looking animals there."

Hank turned to watch the town banker bid successfully on a handsome black gelding for his wife. "Well, that one sure don't know horses from his own ass. That gelding's got a hot eye, and that woman ain't goin' to be able to handle him."

John ran a practiced eye over the gelding and the woman, then nodded agreement. "Blanche Saylor is a fine woman."

"Blanche Saylor's none of your business," Vann growled.

"She's Maddy's sister."

"That makes her your business?"

"Yes."

John watched Vann digest that. After a moment, he nodded. "Just make sure you stay on your side of the fence, Ballard."

"I'm content where I am," John replied.

He was surprised to see the bounty hunter smile. "Those Saylor women are one hell of a handful, ain't they?"

"I've never seen the like," John said. "What about Derek?"

"Well . . ." Hank ran his hand over his jaw. "I figure I'll just cross that bridge when I come to it." His eyes hardened. "But I'll be the first there, don't you worry."

"I wasn't worried," John replied.

They stared at each other for a moment, measuring the risk and the challenge. Then Hank's gaze shifted to a spot behind

John, and his expression changed. "Speak of the devil. Or the angels."

John turned. Maddy and Blanche strolled toward the corral. Blanche sported a brown riding habit; Maddy wore a green one as deep and rich as a pine forest.

"Damn me for a fool," Hank muttered. "But I've gone soft on that yellow-haired woman."

John had already turned to follow Maddy. Hank fell into step beside him. Intent as two hunting wolves, they followed the women. To John's surprise, Maddy and Blanche walked right up to Lucius.

"My sister and I are interested in purchasing two mounts, Mr. Browning."

Hank started forward, but John put one hand out to stop him. They could intervene later if necessary; right now, it looked as though Maddy had all her armor on, and wouldn't appreciate interference.

Lucius smiled. "Well, now, ladies. I'll jest pick you out something pretty." He led them over to a bay mare with a white blaze on her forehead. "Now this is the nicest little filly you'll ever ride—"

"Except that she's cow-hocked," Maddy said.

"Ah. Yes." Lucius cleared his throat. "How about this here chestnut gelding? He's a fine-looking animal."

Maddy glanced past the chestnut. A tall bay gelding stood quietly at the edge of the corral, staring back at the spectators. He wasn't a pretty animal, but he was deep-chested and sturdy, and had a hint of Arabian delicacy to his head.

She walked toward him, and his nostrils flared as he caught her scent. His black mane and tail fanned out in the breeze, and he lifted one black-stockinged leg to paw at the ground.

"Watch out, Maddy," the sheriff called. "Lucius had some trouble with that one."

No wonder, she thought. Mr. Browning was a scoundrel and a liar, and this horse had nothing but honesty in his eyes. She laid one hand on his neck. He allowed her touch, his soft brown eyes perusing her face as though to memorize her.

"I'd like to ride him," she said.

"I ain't got no ladies' saddles," Lucius said.

"That isn't a problem," Maddy replied.

She waited while Lucius slapped a saddle on the bay's back. The horse shifted restlessly, obviously not liking the man. Maddy rubbed his forehead, soothing him and getting him used to her touch. Then she mounted sideways, curving her knee around the saddle horn.

"Come on, boy," she murmured.

John hung his elbows on the top rail of the corral and watched her ride. She could sit a horse, that was for sure. Damn, she looked like a queen. Empress Maddy, come to live among the common folk.

She slid the bay into a lope, and something unique happened. John leaned forward in fascination. Somehow, woman and horse had merged. They moved as though they'd been locked together since birth, their movements natural, as graceful as a swallow arrowing through a twilight sky.

John's heart gave a strange lurch as he watched her. The sunlight struck bronze sparks on her hair and turned her eyes midnight blue. Even the bay had taken on a new quality, his coat gleaming like fine brandy in the sun, his tail rippling like a banner behind him.

Maddy drew the horse to a stop and dismounted. He nibbled at her hair as she turned to Lucius. "He'll do, Mr. Browning. Now, as to price . . ."

"Twenty dollars," Lucius said.

John started forward, ready to protest the absurd price. Then he heard Maddy laugh.

"Really, Mr. Browning," she said. "That is most amusing. Ten."

Lucius Browning's jaw fell with an almost audible click. Then he closed his mouth and sized Maddy up with a jaundiced eye. "Now, ma'am, I couldn't let a fine piece of horse-flesh like this go fer less'n . . . seventeen."

"Goodness, Mr. Browning. We're simply not talking on the same level here. Not propitious, considering the fact that we came here to buy two mounts. Perhaps it would be better for us to wait until some other—"

"Fifteen," he growled.

"Twelve."

Lucius's eyes grew wide. "Ma'am, you cain't . . . Fourteen."

"If you throw in the saddle and bridle," Maddy said.

"Done," he said. "You drive a hard bargain, miss. Now about yore sister's horse—"

"Blanche is quite capable of choosing her own mount."

"Right." Lucius glanced at Maddy hopefully. "She capable of dickerin' fer herself, too?"

Maddy smiled. "Oh, no, Mr. Browning. I'll do all the negotiating."

He grunted. "I might as well shoot myself now," he muttered, storming off toward Blanche.

Turning toward the bay, Maddy stroked his velvet nose. "We're a pair now, boy. What shall I call you?"

He snuffled at her hands, and she laughed with delight at having a horse again. "I know," she said. "I'll call you Ali Baba in honor of the heritage I see in your face."

John walked up behind her. The scent of lilac drifted on the air. He didn't think he'd ever smell lilacs again and not think of Maddy. He could just see the curve where her jaw met her neck, and it was all he could do not to kiss that tender spot.

"Hello, Maddy," he said

His voice swept over her like a wild tropical wind. Her pulse stuttered, and her hands trembled on the reins for a moment. Then she steadied herself and turned to face him.

He stood between her and the sun. As she tilted her head back to look at him, it seemed to her that he filled all the world. She wished she could see his face, to know whether humor or cynicism lit his eyes today. Or something else. She wondered if the memory of that tempestuous kiss haunted him as it did her.

"Good morning," she said, proud that her voice didn't quiver like her insides.

"Why do you need a horse?"

She lifted one shoulder, let it fall. "We have to go to outlying ranches for fittings and things. And although Bill Smith has been more than generous with his wagon, we don't feel we can impose forever."

John's gaze drifted to the full swell of her breasts. He remembered—oh, how he remembered—their sweet weight in his hands, the way her nipples hardened in response to his touch. He wondered how she'd taste.

"Why this sudden, driving need not to impose on Mr. Smith?" he asked.

"It isn't sudden," Maddy replied. "We've only now managed to save up enough money."

"I see."

"Good."

Her tone was cold, but John could see her pulse throbbing in her throat. Whatever her voice held, she was definitely not cold. From that glorious bronze hair to her toes, and every delectable inch in between, Maddy Saylor burned with passion.

"You've made a good choice," he said, nodding at the bay behind her.

"You thought I'd become enamored of that pretty, cow-hocked mare, didn't you?"

"Lucius certainly did."

She tossed her head. "He's a shrewd character. But he should be shrewd enough to hide the duplicity in his eyes."

"What do you see in *my* eyes, Maddy?"

The question took her by surprise. He moved to one side, and now she could see him. It felt as though her stomach dropped straight down to her toes; not only did the memory of shared desire fill his eyes, but also the promise of more.

Spurred by remembering the darkness he'd revealed once before, she lifted her chin. "I see desire. I see ambition. And I see the pain of memories you've chosen not to face."

John drew his breath in sharply, shocked by her observation. Somehow, without knowing he'd done it, he had revealed the black despair in his own soul. It shook him, this realization that he'd been so transparent. He had to distract her, to make her forget somehow that she'd ever seen it.

"Women tend to see what they want in a man," he said, rejecting his own vulnerability. "And you're no different from the rest."

Maddy glared at him with narrowed eyes. "Go away," she said.

That damnable dimple appeared. "You're being rude, Maddy. I'm trying to be nice."

"You don't try to be nice," she retorted. "You just try—"

"To kiss you?" The dimple grew deeper. "But Maddy, you're eminently kissable. Irresistibly so."

"Go away," she said again.

"Would it make you happy if I apologized for taking . . . liberties?"

"It would if I thought you meant it."

John could see her pupils dilate, and his reaction was instantaneous and male. He took a step closer. "How could I regret a kiss like that?"

"I'd rather talk about horses."

"No."

"Why did you come here?" she demanded. "Why can't you leave me alone?"

"Because I can't," he said simply.

He raised his hand, and for a moment Maddy thought he was about to caress her. She stilled, inside and out, mesmerized.

But he reached past her to stroke the bay's forehead. Maddy saw the horse accept his touch, and a shiver ran quicksilver up her spine. She would rather Ali Baba hadn't liked him; then she might have justification for her own conflict.

"He likes you," she said.

"So would you, if you gave yourself a chance."

She opened her mouth to answer him, but speech failed her as his gaze dropped to her lips. He wanted to kiss her again; she could see it in his eyes, feel it in the heightening of her own senses. Some small, sane part of her brain gave thanks that they weren't alone.

For she didn't think she could deny him. Her body roused just at the thought of his touch—that strange, sweet lassitude flowing like honey along her limbs.

Treacherously, Blanche's words shot through her memory: making love with him would be like being caught up in a thunderstorm, lightning crashing all around, her body soaring with the wind.

John saw her eyes change, saw arousal pooling in those storm-blue depths. The sight hit him hard, sinking deep. She stirred him in a way he didn't understand. With a look, a gesture, with that proud, defiant lift of her head, she seemed to touch his very soul.

"Sheriff!" Saul Roggins, the deputy, pushed his way through the crowd. "We got news come in on the telegraph."

Sheriff Cooper strode forward to take the paper from the deputy's hand. Foreboding drifted down like a great, dark bird to settle on Maddy's shoulders.

The sheriff read the note, and then his pale gaze lifted to Maddy's. He cleared his throat.

"Seems Derek Saylor robbed hisself another stage yesterday."

Eight

"It's not true," Maddy said into the sudden silence.

She looked into her neighbors' faces one by one. They didn't believe her. Of course, they didn't believe her.

Derek had been branded a thief. So had Blanche and she. Like their brother, unfairly and without a hearing. They'd tried so hard to make a life for themselves here. She drew her breath in deeply, and was surprised that it hurt.

"My brother is not a thief," she said.

Her voice quivered, and she was humiliated by her own weakness. She'd known this would happen. She'd expected it. It shouldn't hurt. It shouldn't matter. But now, looking into the faces of her neighbors, she realized that it did matter. She cared what they thought of her, of Blanche and of Derek. Sudden, unexpected tears stung her eyes.

"Now, Maddy," Sheriff Cooper said. "Don't git yoreself into a swivet. It ain't—"

Whirling, she mounted Ali and rode into the stable. And straight through, ducking to clear the doorway opening onto the street. As soon as they were clear, she urged the bay into a gallop. Dust boiled up in clouds from beneath the horse's hooves as they headed out of town.

The bay seemed to understand her need to put distance between her and Cofield. She welcomed the speed, reveled in the rake of the wind through her hair and the smooth coiling of the horse's muscles beneath her. It felt almost like freedom.

"Good boy," she crooned. "Thank you."

Ali's ears flicked back to acknowledge her voice, then forward again as he settled into a distance-eating lope. She wished she could ride thus forever.

But of course, she had to go back. Acceptance or no, her stand would have to be made in Cofield. This thing with Derek must be fixed here and now, or they'd all be fugitives for the rest of their lives. A Saylor never ran from a fight.

Out of the corner of her eye, she caught a flicker of movement. Startled, she glanced up to see a mounted man crest the top of a nearby slope. Her nostrils flared. She knew that rider, knew him down to her soul.

John Ballard.

"Not now," she muttered. "Oh, please, not now."

But of course, there was no escape. From the moment she'd laid eyes on him, he'd pushed his way into her life until he'd invaded her very dreams. And now this, her moment of weakness and desperation. It infuriated her.

John came toward her, taking his mount down the slope at a pace that sent dirt and stones sliding down ahead of him. Even in her anger, she couldn't help but admire the skill with which he kept the horse on its feet. And that made her even more furious. How could she keep hating him when he was so damnably much man?

Then a wild impulse came over her, primitive and powerful. With a flick of her reins, she urged Ali back into a gallop.

"Maddy," John called. "Stop!"

Maddy didn't stop. Couldn't stop. She heard him coming after her, and leaned forward over the bay's neck to urge him to still greater speed. His mane whipped back against her face, and she welcomed the sting against her skin. A shadow caught up with hers.

"Go away!" she shouted.

John urged his mount beside hers, wondering for a moment if she'd lost her wits. The wind had flung her bonnet to hang by its ribbons against her back, and had whipped her hair into a glorious bronze aureole around her shoulders. His heart gave a bounce, then settled into a tight rhythm that matched the pounding of the horses' hooves. By God, she was beautiful!

He moved up beside her, leaning over to grasp her reins with one strong, sun-browned hand. The horses lurched to a halt.

"What the devil's wrong with you?" he demanded.

She turned to him, her eyes storm-swept and furious. Then she cut at him with the ends of her reins, catching him a stinging lash across the forearm. Driven by a hair-trigger reaction to the unexpected physical attack, he snatched her off her mount and imprisoned her securely across his thighs.

"Let me go!" she hissed.

He shook his head. "I don't think you can be trusted not to run away."

"I'll do as I damn well please!"

John struggled with his temper, tempted beyond words to put her over his knee and give her a wallop. But he could see in her eyes that she expected him to; she'd damn well goaded him into it. And that wallop was bound to turn into one hell of a fight.

"You're swearing, Maddy," he said. "That's not ladylike. Nor is hitting."

"Then leave me alone," she snapped.

More goading. She was well and truly in a swivet, as Sheriff Cooper would have said. He shifted his grip from her shoulders to her waist. Damn, he liked the feel of her. Those curves pressed against him in just the right places. And her breathing caused a fascinating movement in her breasts.

And suddenly, fighting was the last thing he wanted to do with her. His forearm brushed the swell of her breast, sending arousal sweeping along his veins.

"Why did you run from me like that?"

"I told you already," she retorted. "I wanted to be left alone."

"But I don't want to leave you alone," he replied, his gaze drifting inexorably back to her breasts.

Maddy was becoming increasingly aware of the saddle horn pressing against her hip. As the pressure worsened, she shifted in an effort to find a more comfortable position.

"Uncomfortable?" John asked. "Here."

He pulled her closer against him. Maddy's jaw dropped as she realized that he was aroused. Very aroused. She could feel him against her thigh, hard, urgent, demanding. Realizing at last the danger she was in, she sat very still.

"I could take your word that you won't run again," John said.

She nodded. "I'd be happy—"

"But I don't want to," he continued. "I'd rather keep you right where you are."

"You're a—"

"A man who's got a beautiful woman right where he wants her." The dimple appeared. "Although you're as unmanageable as you are beautiful—"

"Will you let me finish a sentence?"

"No," he said.

He claimed her mouth with all the aggression she'd stirred in him with her beauty and defiance. Her back was stiff and resentful beneath his hands, but her mouth was warm and honeysweet, and he wanted to drown himself in her. He slid one hand into the riotous wealth of her hair. The skin at the nape of her neck was hot to the touch, and as smooth as satin.

Maddy stirred beneath the invasion of his tongue. She should scream, fight, claw him with her nails. But her body had become one huge heartbeat, and it obeyed only him. Maddy herself was trapped in a silken web of desire, wit and will and caution suspended in a soaring tidal wave of heat.

She gasped as he caressed her throat, his thumb drifting beneath the collar of her blouse. Her skin tingled, anticipating more. He drank her gasp, taking it into the wet heat of his mouth. That, too, aroused her unbearably There was something raw and almost savage about his passion today, something that stirred her to her soul.

A breath of wind sifted over the skin of her chest, and she realized with a shock that he'd undone her buttons. She gasped as his hand covered her breast with only the thin shield of her chemise between them. He skimmed the edges of the chemise with his fingertips, leaving fire in his wake. She opened her eyes once as she felt him tug at the ribbons, but closed them again as he freed her breasts.

He lifted his head, and the loss of his kiss felt like abandonment. She cried out softly.

"Shhh," he soothed. "I only want to look at you."

John held her still, his hands on her ribs. Her breasts were full and high, a bounty of white flesh topped with enticing dusky-pink nipples. He claimed those sweet mounds, one hand for each, sliding his palms along the silken skin.

Her nipples were already erect and swollen, waiting for him when he lowered his head to taste them. He ran his tongue around the aureolas, savoring the differing textures of her skin. Then he teased the taut nub at the center. She moaned softly, and it was the sweetest sound he'd ever heard.

He wanted her. He wanted her now. She'd roused him to a fever pitch—heart, mind and body raging with the need to make her his.

"Maddy," he whispered, letting his breath flow across her nipple, eliciting another of those soft moans.

Maddy didn't know what had come over her. Some sort of madness had gripped her, turning her into a wanton. She looked down at him, there at her breast. His hair fanned out across her chest, adding more sensation still to the havoc he was wreaking with his mouth. Pleasure rivered throughout her body and settled between her legs, that now-familiar liquid ache that bordered on pain.

She was shocked at the extent of her desire. She wanted his touch, needed his touch, more than anything she'd ever experienced. And what came after this . . . this incredible sensation?

But she knew, she knew: thunder and lightning, and her body soaring with the wind.

It would trap her. It would trap Derek.

That thought stabbed crystal-clear through the haze of passion. She couldn't. *They* couldn't. With an effort of will that made her shake, she fought the urgings of her body. She closed them off, one by one. Saylor pride, Saylor honor.

It hurt. Oh, it hurt. But she did it.

John felt her withdrawal, and it was like a knife in his guts. He'd never been so close to forcing a woman in his life. He closed his eyes for a moment, trying to get his careening emotions under control. He ached for her. Mind and body and soul, he ached to possess her.

He could seduce her. He could kiss her now and make her forget Derek, forget her anger, her caution, and even her damned suspicions. But afterward, he knew he'd look into her eyes and see the dimming of her spirit, and that he couldn't do. He wanted Maddy. All those things that made her Maddy—good and bad, seductive and infuriating, defiant and passionate.

He was a fool, of course.

With a sigh, he lifted his head and looked at her. "What's the matter?"

"I can't do this," she whispered.

He gently clasped her throat. Her breasts rose and fell in an unquiet rhythm, and those rosy nipples were distended with need. Admiration raced through him, a tribute to her willpower and her pride, and it made him want her that much more.

"This is magic," he said. "Some people live their whole lives without experiencing it. There's nothing shameful in it, nothing to be afraid of."

His words sparked heat in her veins. She pushed it away determinedly. "We are who we are," she replied. "There is no place in our lives for magic."

"Are you so sure, Maddy?"

She wanted to be. "Yes."

"Then why does your body say otherwise?"

Maddy drew her clothing together. Strangely, she didn't feel embarrassment. Perhaps that had been burned out of her by the enormity of her passion. And his.

She could see regret darken his eyes when she covered herself. Instead of distressing her, it sent a thrill coiling through her.

"I wish you wouldn't look at me like that," she said.

The dimple came back. "I can't help it. I'm surprised you don't burst into flame right here and now."

Maddy ducked her head. Not from embarrassment, but to hide her reaction to his words. Simply, he'd stirred her again; it was a heady thing to be desired so much—even for the wrong reason. She found herself wishing he'd wanted her for herself, and not just to reach Derek.

"I . . . I must get back to town," she said.

He tilted her face up, forcing her to look at him. His eyes smoldered with frustrated passion, a frustration she shared down to her soul. She tried to turn from it, but he held her in place.

"You've got to face this, Maddy."

Pride ran hot through her veins, the pride of a woman who'd faced everything from war to death to the loss of the world into which she'd been born. Maddy Saylor would not be thought a coward over a simple weakness of the flesh.

Lifting her chin, she met his eyes squarely. "I *am* facing it," she said, her voice as calm as her gaze. "Derek stands between us like a wall, John Ballard. And as long as his freedom is the price of my actions, he will always stand between us. It would be better for us both if you left me alone."

"As I told you last night, I can't." A deep resolve hardened his eyes. "And even if I could, I wouldn't."

"Then beware," she said.

They stared into each other's eyes, a look of shared desire and challenge that all but set the air aflame. There was no going back now, Maddy realized. He'd set out to have her,

Derek or no Derek, and he would stop at nothing to reach that goal.

It thrilled her at the most basic of levels. Pure female instinct curved her mouth upward. She saw reaction hit his eyes, and knew he understood. He smiled at her, a predatory grin that promised as much or more than it threatened.

"We'd better get back," he said.

"Yes, we should." And to up the ante, she added, "Mr. Ballard."

Laughter sparked in his eyes. He had the feeling she'd lead him a wild dance, and that he'd enjoy it very much. But he intended to win. "You're quite a woman, Maddy Saylor."

"I?" She let her lashes drift downward. "I'm just a poor, displaced Southern lady trying to make her way in the world."

"In a pig's eye," he retorted amiably.

"Indeed," she agreed.

Nine

Maddy glanced at John out of the corner of her eye as they rode into town. Strangely, she was glad to have him with her. He seemed so strong and solid, a buttress against the disapproval she was bound to face. Maddy Saylor, outlaw's sister. Perhaps all Cofield now thought what Zachary Marsh had said the other day: the Saylors had no place with decent folk.

Condemnation. Judgment. Rejection. Maddy was prepared for it all. She just wished it didn't hurt so much.

"What's the matter?" John asked.

She glanced at him, and her gaze became entangled in his. He was remembering . . . what had happened between them. It lay in his eyes and the sudden tightening of his face. Maddy looked away. She didn't want to think about it right now; if she did, then she'd want him to go away. And right now, his presence was more comforting than it ought to be. Either that, or she had less strength than she'd like.

"Yoo-hoo, Maddy!"

She turned toward the voice, and saw Prissy Taylor, the banker's daughter, strolling down the sidewalk just ahead. The girl waved, her gaze drifting from Maddy to John and back again.

"Hello, Prissy," Maddy called, touched by the unexpected gesture.

But then Prissy's mother came out of a nearby shop and joined the girl. There was no friendliness in the older woman's face. Her mouth was set in a grim line of disapproval, and she grabbed her daughter's arm and hauled her away.

"Don't let her bother you," John said. "She's a nasty old biddy."

Maddy stared at him. "How would you know?"

"Everyone knows. She looks down her nose at nearly everybody, so you're in good company."

Maddy rode in silence for a moment, digesting that. Then they passed the bank, where a knot of men had gathered outside the doorway. One man tipped his hat as she rode past; the others glanced the other way to avoid speaking to her.

"Bastards," John growled.

"It doesn't matter," she said.

John looked at her and saw the fierce, high angle at which she carried her head. A prideful woman, was Maddy Saylor. But he knew it did matter. Inside, where no one could see, she was hurting.

"Don't worry about them, either," he said. "They're sheep. They don't have the courage to think for themselves, and someone sure forgot to teach them some manners."

"Manners!" Maddy had to laugh.

"Aren't you the one who hates rudeness above all things? Hell, I had to fight one battle over that already."

The fierceness in his voice surprised her. She hadn't expected protectiveness. She wasn't the sort of woman who elicited protectiveness from men; that seemed to be reserved for softer, less independent women.

"This will pass," she said, turning the dun onto the alley that led to the stable. "And if it does not, there are other towns."

"You'd leave?"

"If we had to. Blanche and I have learned to leave things behind when we have to."

John didn't like the heaviness in her eyes. She'd left behind a great many things that were precious to her; he knew more than most how hurtful that could be, for he'd had his share of loss. But some losses were too great; unlike her, he'd learned not to have friends, or even want them.

Until now, he'd been content. He'd pushed his emotions deep inside and thought himself safe from them. Until now. Maddy had swept through him like a summer storm, and nothing seemed safe anymore.

His gaze drifted along the graceful line of her neck, the lush swell of her breasts, and the proud, straight sweep of her back. She was so beautiful she took his breath away—regal and elegant, with a passion hot enough to make a man's blood burn.

He didn't like it. He wanted her to stay where he'd put her to begin with: as a means to an end in getting Derek Saylor. It annoyed him that he couldn't make that happen.

"His name is Ali Baba," she said.

John blinked, trying vainly to integrate her words into his thoughts, and failing. "Who?" he demanded finally.

"The horse. His name is Ali Baba."

John watched the bay's ears flick back to acknowledge her voice, then flick forward again. Then he looked at the woman, and his heart gave a curious, disturbing lurch.

He denied it. He refused to look at it, or to accept it. Glancing at her from the corner of his eye, he said something he knew he would come to regret.

"Don't you think it a coincidence that you named him after a thief?"

Maddy stared at him, completely shocked. His momentary gentleness had put her off guard enough for this sudden harshness to hurt. It angered her that she'd allowed herself to become beguiled by his charm and left herself open for him to hurt her this way.

Without a word, she turned forward. Her back was ramrod-straight as she rode into the livery stable.

Maddy sat in the darkened shop and watched the street outside. John Ballard rode past, looking hard and predatory as he headed toward the edge of town. Hunting Derek. She let the curtain fall back into place.

Now was the time.

"Blanche," she called softly.

A trapdoor opened in the ceiling, letting a flood of lamplight into the room. Blanche's trouser-clad legs appeared in the opening, swinging as she levered herself straight, then dropped lightly to the floor.

Maddy rose and faced her. They looked much alike in men's garb, although Blanche's slimmer figure was more suited to shirt and trousers. Still, at night and on horseback, they would look enough like Derek to be his twin.

"Here we go again, sister," Blanche said, a grin tugging at her mouth. "By the way, I told Bill Smith—in front of several people—that we planned to ride early in the morning, and not to look for us until sometime in the afternoon. That way, we have all night to—"

"Wreak havoc?" Maddy finished for her.

"We have never wreaked havoc, as you very well know," Blanche said. "Well, there was that Yankee ammunition cache that was just begging to be blown up."

"And don't forget that encampment with all those lovely tents that burned so nicely," Maddy added.

Blanche smiled. "Perhaps just a little havoc, then. But now we have no war, only bounty hunters, and I suppose it wouldn't be nice to do more than lead them around in circles."

"Quite," Maddy agreed.

"And how is Mr. Haverty?"

"Our livery stable owner is in his cups, as always," Maddy said. "He'll never know our mounts are gone. John just left, so we'll be out from under his watchful eye."

"And Hank has been gone all day," Blanche said. Suddenly she laughed. "You know, it must be awfully crowded out there with all those men swanning around looking for Derek."

Maddy settled her Stetson at a jaunty angle. "Well, if they

want Derek Saylor, we'll just have to give them one. Or two, or three."

Arm in arm, they walked to the back door. But once Maddy unlocked it, all thought of playing ended. Maddy felt it in herself, saw it in Blanche. They might laugh in the privacy of their home, but this was serious business, with Derek's life at stake.

They slipped through the dark streets, moving swiftly and silently. Maddy knew that close up, she and Blanche couldn't pass for men. But they'd learned years ago to use every patch of shadow, every post and pillar, to blur the issue of identity should anyone see them. They'd even learned to walk like men, with an aggressive stride and a slight swagger of the shoulders.

It had served them in good stead. They'd fooled the Yankees, and they'd fool their brother's hunters now. The Gray Ghost would regain his uncanny abilities to be in several places at once, and no one would suspect his sisters of being anything but useless, pampered ladies.

The smell of stable drifted on the night air, a scent as familiar to Maddy as her own perfume. She and Blanche crossed the street, then quietly slipped into the stable. Mr. Haverty's snores rolled through the building in a slow cadence.

"Hsst," Blanche whispered, pointing to the wall on which their tack hung.

Maddy nodded. She and Blanche had learned long ago how to read each other without speech, and fell quickly into their old ways of working together.

Ali Baba whickered softly as Maddy slipped into his stall. She quieted him with a hand on his flank, whispering the need for silence. She led him out of his stall so that Blanche could saddle him, then went to fetch Blanche's mount.

A few minutes later, they rode quietly out of the stable and headed for the edge of town. Ahead, the moonlight silvered the wrinkled bulge of the hills. They seemed so peaceful just now. But Maddy knew there was little peace for the Saylors; there hadn't been for a very long time.

"Ready?" Maddy asked.

"Ready," Blanche said.

They rode in silence for several miles. But Maddy knew that Blanche was thinking hard about something; her pretty face was pensive beneath the brim of her hat.

"What is it, dear?" Maddy asked.

Blanche let her breath out with a sigh. "Oh, I'm just being silly, I suppose. It's just that I'm a bit tired of fighting all the time. Not that it hasn't been fun, but there are times when I'd like to just sit in my own little house and know that the world was safe and right."

"The world stopped being right when the first shot was fired at Fort Sumter," Maddy said. "Then everything got caught in a whirlwind, and us along with it."

"Yes, but . . . Don't you want to be loved, Maddy? Wouldn't you like a husband and children?"

Those words brought a rush of thoughts to Maddy, visions of things she knew were impossible. But oh, they were treacherous, lovely thoughts: a child running toward her, dark hair blowing in the wind, laughter sparkling in startling green-gold eyes just like her father's. And John Ballard, his smile at last without cynicism, bending over her in the warm glow of the fireplace, his hands hot as he pulled her up for a kiss.

Seductive. Treacherous. She pushed those thoughts away sternly. They were fantasy, an illusion that would cost her much if she let it blur reality. For John Ballard didn't love her. He was a predator, pure and simple, and he would use her any way he could in order to accomplish his goal. He would bring Derek in, uncaring of guilt or innocence, his only interest fulfilling his job. The consequences didn't matter. Derek didn't matter. *She* didn't matter.

"I don't think marriage and children are for me," Maddy said. "So I'll be fierce old Aunt Maddy to your children, and enjoy myself very much."

"That would be a waste," Blanche said. "You'd make a fine mother."

Maddy lifted her shoulders and let them fall in a shrug of indifference she didn't feel. "You know men don't like independent, opinionated women, and you know I can't pretend to be other than what I am."

"I don't think John Ballard minds that you're strong," Blanche said.

"He doesn't mind because he has one thing in mind: finding Derek. And if I let my guard down with that man for one moment, he'll take everything I hold dear."

"You underestimate yourself, dear sister."

"I understand reality," Maddy retorted. "Now, back to the business at hand. We've got to split up, and make sure we're seen. Where would you like to go first?"

Blanche cocked her head to one side. "Mmmmm. I thought I might ride toward Preston. There are several large ranches outside town there, and someone is bound to spot Derek Saylor riding through."

"Good. I'll head toward Palatine, and try to make myself seen on the way. That will put us at least ten miles apart, and only God knows how far from Derek." Maddy smiled. "You do realize, sister mine, that we've each chosen towns in which there are saloons and bawdy houses."

Blanche smiled. "We do know our brother," she agreed. "Be careful, Maddy."

"You, too."

They parted then, Maddy turning north toward Palatine, and Blanche southeast. Maddy was worried about her sister. Truly, she told herself, it ought to be safe; they'd done this sort of thing often enough during the war. But they'd been familiar with the territory—every tree, every house, every dip in the roads.

But they didn't know this land, and some of their opponents did. Still, there was nothing to do but try.

She rode for an hour, then another, without seeing anyone. The hills lay stark and very beautiful under the moonlight, every fold and crevice holding pockets of indigo shadow. A wild place, Maddy thought, but one could come to love it.

But the weather soon changed. Black banks of clouds piled up on the horizon, swallowing the moon. Lightning flared on the underbelly of the clouds, and she knew it would rain soon. The storm lay between her and Palatine, and she wasn't sure whether to go on or not.

Then she spotted the flicker of a campfire in a fold of a nearby ridge. She reached out to stroke Ali Baba's neck.

"It might be tricky here, my friend," she said. "Are you ready?"

His ears flicked back to acknowledge her voice, if not her words. If that fire up ahead belonged to a bounty hunter, as she suspected, tonight would be a true test of Ali's mettle.

She angled her way up the slope just above the fire, where slabs of rock protected her from being seen. Once at the top, she dismounted and retrieved her field glasses from the saddlebag. Propping her elbows on one of the sheltering rocks, she peered down at the camp.

The scene jumped into focus. Three men sat around a small campfire, mere silhouettes at this distance and angle. One more lay wrapped in a blanket at the edge of the light. Even as she watched, the others turned in for the night.

"Well, well, well," she murmured. "It's time for Derek Saylor to make an appearance."

She mounted and turned Ali downhill. As they worked their way toward the camp, a trickle of anticipation ran up her spine. It was part fear, part excitement. The Saylors had all been cursed with a wild recklessness that had bedeviled generations of the family.

Rain began to fall as she neared the camp. It muffled Ali's hoofbeats, and she decided to take him right in with her. The bounty hunters' mounts were tied at one side of the circle of firelight, and she decided to put herself downwind.

The other horses jostled a bit when Ali and Maddy slipped among them. That, combined with the approaching storm, was bound to set them off soon. Maddy leaned over and cut the rope that secured the animals. They pulled away, eyes showing white in the fitful light.

Maddy drew her pistol and fired it into the air. The horses spooked, neighing shrilly as they stampeded right through the camp. Shouting, the men leaped to their feet, guns drawn, only to add to the confusion.

There was so much noise that she didn't even try to muffle her passage as she turned Ali back the way they'd come.

"Here we go, boy," she said.

She urged the horse up to the top of the ridge, placing herself where she was sure to be seen. The shouting in the camp increased. She grinned then, and swept her hat off so that the lightning flashed on her hair. Hair just the color of Derek's, of course.

Suddenly she pulled Ali's reins, urging him to rear. As the horse pawed at the air, she lifted her voice in a wild Rebel yell.

As though reading her mind, Ali came down on all fours. He kicked his heels disdainfully at the bounty hunters, then spun and headed down the hill.

The chaos behind them faded, and Maddy knew the men had regained control of their mounts. A moment later, she saw two of them on her trail, legs flapping as they spurred their horses into a gallop.

To her right, a stretch of bare rock glittered silver in the lurid illumination of a lightning flash. All she had to do was head across that rock, slide into a fold between the hills, and she'd lose her pursuers.

A prudent woman would have. A prudent *man* would have. But prudence had never been a Saylor trait. Maddy turned Ali in the opposite direction, toward some open ground she spotted in a break between two hills.

The bay ran with long-legged economy of movement, settling into a lope that would tax the fastest of pursuers. A gunshot cracked behind her, but the bullet went whining uselessly off into the distance. At this speed, and in this light, the bounty hunters couldn't have hit the side of a barn. The shooting was only to make them feel better about losing.

Big, fat drops of rain pelted her face, driven by the wind and the rush of Ali's movement. Above her, the storm muttered and roared. For this moment, she belonged to the night, as wild as the hills, as free as the wind.

Maddy laughed in the sheer delight of it. This was what drew Derek, the draw of a freedom that washed through one's soul like the tide. Dangerous, yes, but that sweet, seductive rush was worth a bit of danger.

She emerged from between the hills and entered the stretch of flat ground. Ali flicked his ears back, begging the question. Maddy let him have his head. He slid into a smooth, ground-eating gallop, leaving the bounty hunters cursing in her wake.

One dropped back as his mount tired. Another mile later, the second fell behind. Ahead, another section of hills piled like a great, wrinkled skin upon the land. It was time to lose her pursuers entirely. She slowed Ali to a walk on the uneven ground, directing him up along the rocky shoulder of a hill where their trail would be blurred.

Lightning crawled across the sky, for a moment lighting the hills as bright as day. During that brief illumination, Maddy spotted something that set her heart to pounding. For coming down the slope of a nearby hill was a horse and rider. The lightning turned the animal's coat platinum, nearly blending it with the ground around it. But Maddy had seen enough. She'd know that horse anywhere. And its rider.

John Ballard.

He'd seen her, of course. Perhaps he'd heard the commotion at the bounty hunters' camp, and had pinpointed its cause. Either way, he'd come for her.

With a flick of her reins, she urged Ali back into a lope. This was going to be very tricky; not only did she have to stay ahead of John, she had to make sure he didn't get a good look at her, for he was bound to recognize her horse.

So she ran a race against time and visibility, using every fold of terrain, every patch and pocket of shadow in order to obscure her identity. She would have lost another pursuer. But not John; he matched her move for move, trick for trick, always staying close enough so she couldn't slip away.

Maddy stroked Ali's neck, feeling the surge of his muscles beneath her hand. He had a long stride and a brave heart, but John's dun looked fresher, and she'd judged him an animal with staying power. The bay would never be able to stay ahead on a straight run.

So, she thought, it was time for misdirection, the Gray Ghost's specialty. She changed direction, moving in a subtle circle until they were headed back the way she'd come.

She shot a glance over her shoulder. John had gained on her; if her ploy didn't work, this contest would soon be over. She needed time, a few precious moments when she couldn't be seen, so she and Ali could slip away.

"For Derek," she said, bending low over the horse's neck. "Come on, boy, bring us through."

The bay's stride lengthened still further. The wind slashed into her face, and raked at her clothing. Lightning stabbed at the ground a short distance away, and for a moment the hills stood starkly revealed.

She spotted the bounty hunters huddled in a group, hats pulled low, slickers whipping in the wind. She hurtled down the slope toward them at a reckless pace, knowing the storm drowned out all lesser sounds.

They reached level ground amid a spray of mud and stones. Ali slipped for a moment, but kept himself upright with an agile lurch of his muscles. Maddy leaned forward, crooning encouragement to the animal, and set him straight toward the bounty hunters.

Just as she reached them, lightning flared again. She couldn't have done better had she requested it. She caught a glimpse of four astonished faces, pallid in the searing light. With a whoop, she sailed Ali right over them. Then the rain-filled darkness clapped down around them like a shroud, and she was away.

A few moments later, she heard gunshots behind her. She knew John was in no danger; these shots were the bounty hunters' delayed reaction to her startling appearance.

But the shooting was sure to make John veer off her trail. Not forever, she knew. But long enough.

Suddenly, as though Heaven itself were on her side, the sky seemed to open up. Rain came slashing down in torrents. The dry land soaked up as much as it could hold, then shed water like a snake sloughing its skin.

Maddy had gained what she needed. She turned Ali southwest, and slid into the fold between two hills. Behind her, the rain washed the hoofprints away almost as soon as they were made. She smiled, taking her hat off to let the rain sluice through her hair.

"Take that, arrogant Mr. Ballard," she said.

Ten

Sunlight splashed across Maddy's eyes, waking her from a deep sleep. Automatically, her fingers closed on Ali's reins, which she'd wrapped around her hand to keep him from wandering off during the night.

The storm had driven her to spend the night in this rocky cleft she'd found tucked under the lee of a hill. She opened her eyes to see Ali's forequarters bisecting the opening.

"Good morning, boy," she said.

He whickered at her. With a groan, she unfolded herself from the rather uncomfortable curl in which she'd slept, and went out to greet the morning.

The sunlight was even more unyielding, glinting harshly off the puddles of water dotting the rocks. Soon, however, those pockets of moisture evaporated into the air. Ali whickered again, tossing his head as though asking her to hurry.

"You're right," she said. "But I've got to take time to return to town as Maddy, instead of Derek."

She'd taken her tack and saddlebags into the cleft with her to protect them from the rain. Fetching them, she pulled out the riding habit she'd brought just in case this very thing happened. Changing clothes hurriedly, she pulled the pins out of her tightly-wrapped hair before winding it into a loose braid down her back.

The temperature rose swiftly. Maddy welcomed the heat of the sun as she rode back to town, for it dried her hair and drove the last lingering chill of the night from her flesh. There was a spring in Ali's step that telegraphed his delight in heading back to his stable. Maddy wished she felt the same. But just now, Cofield didn't much feel like home.

Perhaps nowhere would. Perhaps she and Blanche and Derek would drift forever like tumbleweeds, pushed hither and yon by the winds of adversity. It didn't sit well; the Saylors had always been people of the land.

Cofield shimmered in the heat distortion upon the horizon. Ali whickered happily. Maddy stroked his neck, enjoying the sun-warmed feel of his hide beneath her gloves.

"Are you ready for some hay?" she asked, watching his ears flick backward. "And then a little later, some nice grain?"

He tossed his head, and she laughed at that parody of a nod. There were times when she thought horses truly did understand what people said, and that their frequent obtuseness came from stubbornness, not stupidity.

No one seemed to notice her as she rode into town. In fact, the few people she met pretended she didn't exist, which suited her just fine. She took Ali to the stable, unsaddled him, and began grooming him while he munched hay contentedly.

"You are a fine horse," she murmured. "A fine horse."

His skin twitched as she ran the brush over his flanks. She'd always enjoyed this task. Serenity came with the smooth, rhythmic movement of her hands and the warmth of the animal. Surprisingly contented after the night she'd spent, she began to hum under her breath.

" 'Morning, Maddy."

John's deep voice brought her whirling to face him. He stood leaning on one side of the stall opening, his mouth curved in a smile, his eyes watchful.

"Good morning," she said.

"I was here at seven. Ali Baba was already gone."

"I like to ride early," she said.

"How early?"

"Early."

"I see." He crossed his arms over his chest. "Did you know that Derek was seen near Peyote Flats last night?"

"Oh?" Maddy asked, all innocence.

"And I stumbled across him outside Palatine last night."

Maddy turned back to Ali and ran the brush over his hindquarters. "I find that astonishing, considering the fact that those towns are rather far apart."

"He's the Gray Ghost, remember? He flits from place to place faster than any man ought to be able to. That was his specialty during the war."

"I suppose it was," Maddy murmured.

"Well, he's damned lucky I wanted to bring him back alive; I had plenty of chances to shoot him last night."

"Why didn't you?"

The question startled him. "I didn't come here to kill him, Maddy, just bring him in."

"I'm glad to hear that you refrained."

John studied her. Her movements were slow and fluid, and didn't betray any agitation. She bent slightly to run the brush over the horse's flank, and he couldn't help but admire the graceful line of her back and waist. In fact, she looked downright delectable this morning. Delectable, and distracting.

"Where did you go?" he asked, forcing his mind back onto the original subject.

"When?"

He scowled. She knew very well what he was talking about. It was always games with her, games within games within games.

"Did you meet Derek this morning?"

Setting the brush aside, Maddy turned to look at him. She'd obviously annoyed him. Good. She'd meant to. He was too great a threat to Derek; not one man in fifty could have kept up with her last night, and she was almost as good as her brother.

"Where I go and what I do is none of your business," she said, her voice sweet, her eyes not.

"But Maddy, it is my business," he said. "After all, I want you to be safe."

"You want Derek," she retorted. "And you're not going to get him."

He smiled again, and that dratted dimple set her pulse to racing. She hated the fact that he had this effect on her. It wasn't safe, not safe at all.

"I could have had him last night," he said. "Dead, of course. But I'll take him alive. It's just a matter of time."

Maddy studied him from beneath her lashes. He had good reason to be arrogant about his abilities. But she couldn't resist the chance to puncture that overinflated ego just a little.

"Did it ever occur to you," she said, "that if you were in pistol range, so was Derek?"

John blinked. "What's that got to do with anything?"

"My brother is the best shot I've ever seen. If he'd wanted you dead, you'd be lying out there in the hills."

"How do you know we were in the hills?" he asked, narrowing his eyes.

Maddy wasn't about to let him throw her. She gave Ali one last swipe of the brush, then poured a few inches of grain into his feed bucket. "It was a reasonable assumption, don't you think, considering that there are hills all around Cofield?"

"Maybe."

"Maybe, my eye. You know very well that's the case. Now, if you'll excuse me, I'd like to go freshen up."

She put the brush away. When she turned around again, however, he hadn't moved from the doorway. And he didn't look as though he intended to. Leaving would entail squeezing past him, a procedure that would put her in too close proximity.

"Are you planning to stand there all day?"

With a cynical bow, he stepped aside. She swept past him, nose in the air. Just when she was sure she'd gained her freedom, he reached out and caught her arm.

"Just a second, Maddy."

His palm was hot, and her heart was beating too fast for comfort. "Let go of me."

He ignored her, drawing her toward him until he could curve his arm around her waist. Slowly, inexorably, he drew her toward him, fitting her against his hard body. "You smell like sunshine," he murmured, burying his face in her hair.

"Stop it," she gasped.

"Why do you keep fighting it? Don't you know how special this is?"

"It's insane, is what it is," she said, levering her arms between them in a vain attempt to break free.

John knew he should let her go. She was trouble, pure and simple. He knew she'd been out to see Derek; she knew he knew. And she'd stood there and defied him, not caring in the least what he thought about it.

But none of that mattered. The only important thing was Maddy, how she smelled, the sun-washed cleanness of her hair, the softness of her in his arms. She felt the same; he could see it in the slight blush of color in her cheeks and the throb of the pulsepoint in her throat.

He touched his tongue to that spot, feeling her instant response in the increased speed of her pulse beneath the skin. Slowly, he ran his tongue up along her throat to the curve of her jaw; upward still, to the luscious double curve of her mouth. He paused there for a moment, his breath mingling with hers.

Then her lips parted. It was an automatic response, and not a welcome one to her; he could see a brief flash of rebelliousness in her eyes in the moment before desire took control. He didn't care. He only wanted to kiss her.

Which he did. Thoroughly, if not quite gently. He reveled in her response, the heat of her, the way her tongue darted forward to tease his. So much woman, he thought. Surely worth every bit of trouble she was bound to be.

Maddy fell into a well of sensation. He toyed with her mouth, nibbling at her lips, exploring the edges of her teeth and the too-sensitive flesh inside her lips, then slipping his tongue deep. She couldn't help but respond.

He made a sound deep in his throat, an irrepressibly male sound that sent riptides of desire shooting through her body. His hands spread out over her back, possessing her, fitting her tightly to the muscled hardness of his chest. He was aroused, his manhood pressing tightly against her belly. This, too, excited her, and it was all she could do to keep from rubbing herself against him.

Suddenly he lifted her, bearing her back into Ali's stall. She closed her eyes, too deeply buried in sensuality to protest. A moment later she found herself pressed up against the rough boards of the stall. She shivered in reaction as his hands spread out over her ribs, his palms hot through the fabric of her riding habit.

"You see?" he whispered. "It's magic between us, Maddy."

Yes, it was. Oh, yes, it was. Maddy slid her hands up the ridged hardness of his back to his hair. Digging her fingers in, she brought his mouth down to hers.

He swept in like a conqueror, all heat and arrogance and possession. She accepted him, welcomed him, for this was what she needed. A sigh escaped her as he cupped her breasts, his thumbs stroking her nipples into aching points through the fabric.

He lifted his head enough so that he could look at her. Their breaths mingled, as did their gazes. Still holding her locked with his eyes, he thrust one leg between hers. A sort of madness possessed her then, and she moaned with a need as sharp as it was mysterious to her.

John slid his hand down her body slowly, oh, so slowly, until it rested on her mound. She arched against his hard thigh, undone by the sensations caused by his touch. He slipped his fingers between her legs, caressing her just where she ached the most. At the same moment, he claimed her lips in a wild kiss, delving deep into the honeyed sweetness of her mouth. His tongue moved in the same rhythm as his fingers, and

Maddy found herself swept away on a tidal wave of desire. The ache grew stronger, deeper, until she was certain she felt it in her soul.

"That's it," he whispered. "Let it happen."

Maddy had no idea what he was talking about. She only knew that her body had been taken over somehow, and that it needed something only he could give. She gasped and clung, arching up against those caressing fingers.

Then the world seemed to explode. A violent storm of sensation caught her, a pulsing tide of pleasure that sent wave after wave coursing through her body. She cried out, and he caught the sound with his mouth.

Slowly, she relaxed against him. He tilted her face up, and she trembled at the sight of his glittering eyes. Arousal lay in those green-gold depths, desire withheld so long it might have become dangerous. And with it, she saw triumph. She wished she knew what that meant, but her brain didn't seem to be working quite right yet.

"Was that your first time to experience a woman's pleasure?" he asked.

She couldn't lie, couldn't deny him an answer. Meeting his gaze, she nodded.

"There's more, you know," he said. "And I plan to show you all of it, Maddy. Everything."

"I—"

"I'm going to worship you with my eyes, my hands, my mouth. I'll show you pleasure you've never dreamed of."

Reason came flooding back into her mind, and with it, horror. She'd been weak. Weak and stupid. And she'd just given him a tremendous weapon to use against her. Now she understood the triumph she'd seen in his eyes.

He thought he had her. She, Maddy Tallwood Saylor, had fallen for his blandishments and caresses, and was his to claim whenever he liked. Well, he had another thing coming.

"Let me go," she said. Calmly. Coolly. As if her insides weren't quivering.

His eyes narrowed. But he did take his hands from her and step back a pace. Maddy took a deep breath.

"This was my fault," she said. "I . . . lost control, and I should never have let things go so far. It was ill-advised and very wrong, and it won't happen again."

John crossed his arms over his chest and studied her. Her eyes had become remote, closed to him. Ah, he thought, she'd regained her rational, sensible self, and was now regretting her response. Well, nothing about her had ever been ordinary, and she'd never played by other women's rules. That was what had attracted him to her in the first place.

She hadn't won. She wasn't going to win. Because this thing between them was too strong for either of them to resist, and their joining was as certain as the sun coming up the next morning. She was a stubborn, determined woman, and it would take time and patience to bring her to his bed.

And until he caught Derek Saylor, he had nothing but time on his hands.

"Come on," he said. "I'll walk you home."

"I'd rather you didn't."

He grinned at her. "I want to."

Apparently, she was to be spared no humiliation. She smoothed her rumpled riding habit, but was nearly undone by the flicker of desire in his eyes. It wouldn't take much for that spark to flare into open passion, and that was one blaze she didn't think she could handle. She had to get out of this stable before he touched her again.

So she inclined her head, acquiescing. One side of his mouth went up in an ironic smile, and he held out his arm. Her hand trembled just a bit as she tucked it into the crook of his arm, a weakness she sternly stilled.

He led her out into the street. Mr. Taylor, who owned the bank, happened to be walking past, his wife on his arm. Never one to insult a customer, he tipped his hat. His wife, however, merely put her nose in the air and sailed on past.

"My dear," the banker protested.

"I will not acknowledge that woman," Mrs. Taylor snapped. "Her brother is a common thief."

Maddy's temper flared. Taking her hand from John's arm, she lengthened her stride and blocked the Taylors from continuing.

"I heard what you said, Mrs. Taylor," she said. "I'll have you know that my family is descended from Robert the Bruce and several kings of England. Now, my brother might be labeled a thief, but he is hardly common."

"Just one moment—"

"And I'll have you know, too, that my family owned one of the largest plantations in Virginia before the war, and at one time we could have bought and sold your husband's bank several times over."

"Now, see here, young lady," Mrs. Taylor sputtered.

Maddy lifted her chin disdainfully. "What I see is a socially inept woman who seeks to raise her status by denigrating others. Where I come from, that sort of behavior wouldn't be tolerated. And I don't intend to tolerate it now."

Mrs. Taylor's mouth opened, but nothing came out. Finally, she closed her mouth with an almost audible snap, and gave her husband's arm a jerk.

The banker had turned an unbecoming shade of magenta. But it was laughter Maddy saw in his eyes, not anger. She suspected that it had been a very long time since his wife had been incapable of speech, and that he appreciated it immensely. His jowls and belly shook as he tried to control his mirth.

Mrs. Taylor glared at Maddy for a moment, then grabbed her husband's arm and hauled him away. Maddy stood victorious on the field of battle. She felt wonderful.

"You ought to see your face," John said, laughter dancing in his eyes. "Remind me never to get into a battle of words with you."

"Wills, you mean."

"That is a battle I always win, Maddy."

"You've never fought with a Saylor."

"And you've never fought with a Ballard."

Their gazes met and warred. Neither gave an inch. Finally, John held out his arm again, and Maddy took it.

It was not a truce.

He walked her to the shop, where Blanche stood talking to Dolly Mayhew. As soon as Maddy walked in, Blanche gestured for her to join them.

"Maddy, Dolly needs our help," she said.

The older woman nodded. "See, I'm supposed to go to Janet Taylor's shindig next week, and I ain't got nothin' to wear but split skirts and worn gingham. I'd sort of like to make a splash, if you know what I mean."

"I know what you mean," Maddy said, mentally assessing the woman's tall, spare frame. "Blanche, what do you think about that gorgeous green silk that came day before yesterday?"

"I think it will be perfect. Now, Dolly, you just come into the back for a moment, and I'll get you measured. You're going to look like an empress when we're finished with you."

Dolly touched her wiry hair. "Just make me look like a woman, and I'll be tickled," she said.

Blanche drew the older woman into the back room. Maddy, overly aware of John standing just behind her, turned to face him. "Go away," she said. "I have work to do."

"You have a miracle to perform," he retorted. "I'll leave you to it. But first . . ."

With a swift, leonine movement that caught her completely off guard, he swept her against him and gave her a kiss so hot and passionate that it staggered her. She gave no thought to resistance. Her hands automatically went to his hair, where she hung on for dear life as he possessed her mouth. Her defenses crumbled.

Then as suddenly as he'd grabbed her, he released her. "See you soon," he said.

He walked out of the shop, leaving her staring after him. She reached up with shaking hands to touch her mouth.

Oh, Lord, she thought. Oh, Lord.

* * *

Maddy held up the beginnings of Dolly's gown to examine her stitching. She and Blanche were working late, lace curtains shielding the interior of the dress shop from the street outside.

"How was your little . . . jaunt last night?" Blanche asked.

"John Ballard nearly caught me," Maddy replied. "Or rather, caught Derek. If it hadn't been for that storm, I don't know what would have happened."

"Maddy, is there something you'd like to talk about? Something . . . about John?"

Yes. Tell me how to stop feeling things for him I've never felt for a man. Tell me how to keep from going up in flames every time he touches me.

"No," she said. Shaking out the fabric, she held it up again. Light spilled like a waterfall over the rich silk. "I think this is going to be one of the prettiest we've ever made, don't you?"

"Dolly will be the most striking woman there, and that nasty Janet Taylor will be so green with envy that she'll match that gown."

Blanche sewed in silence for a while, but Maddy knew her sister had more to say. Gentle Blanche might be, but there was no one on God's green earth more tenacious, not even Mother. Hank Vann was in for a surprise—once the rose petals dropped from his eyes.

"There's something special between you and John, isn't there?" Blanche asked.

"Well—"

"Don't even think about lying, Maddy. I know you, too well, and I saw the way you looked at each other today. It was a wonder the shop didn't burst into flames."

Warmth spread through Maddy's body as her traitorous mind called up the memory of John's caresses, the wonderful, astonishing release he'd given her. She didn't know what had come over her this morning. To allow him to . . . Her lashes

drifted downward, an unconscious response to the desire coursing like hot honey through her veins. It seemed as though
some madness had gripped her, making her thrill to that searing heat his touch had brought. There had to be some way to
control her reactions, to contain them. There had to he some
way to protect herself . . . from him, and from her own burgeoning desire.

A crash startled her out of her musings, and she lifted her
head to listen. "Where . . . ? she asked.

"The saloon," Blanche replied.

"Saturday night."

"And the saloon is filled with the cowboys from that trail
drive that came in this morning," Blanche said, shaking her
head. "Take them, add the bounty hunters and the cowboys in
from the ranches all around, add far too much whiskey and
far too few, er, ladies to go around, and trouble was inevitable.
I fear that Dr. Brennan will be spending the night sewing cuts
and binding broken heads."

Maddy smiled. "As Papa used to say, a man must have a
grand bash occasionally or life ceases to have any real mean-
ing."

The voices grew louder.

"It sounds as though the fight has moved into the street,"
Maddy said, cocking her head to one side. "They seem to be
having a very good time, don't they?"

"Indeed they do," Blanche agreed. "We should be hearing
Sheriff Cooper's scattergun soon. Shall I use the white or ivory
lace?" She held up the shirtwaist she was working on.

"Ivory," Maddy said. "Sheriff Cooper is wise enough to let
them wear one another out before interfering. They've got to
have some fun or they'll just tear up the jail."

A few high-pitched yips echoed in the street, followed by
shots as one of the cowboys emptied his pistol at the sky.
Maddy wasn't worried; it wasn't the first time something like
this had happened in Cofield. A few broken chairs, a few broken bones, perhaps, and half the male population left with

pounding hangovers—she and Blanche had become accustomed to it.

"Now, Maddy, exactly what is your plan—"

More shots rang out, and the whine of a ricochet showed that they hadn't been directed toward the sky. Hoofbeats pounded down the street toward the dress shop. A moment later, Maddy heard a loud crash of breaking glass from across the street.

"The light," she said.

Blanche turned the lamp off. Now in darkness, Maddy moved to the window. The street seemed to be full of mounted men. Even as she watched, one took aim at Bill Smith's storefront window and shot it out.

"Oh, Lord," she muttered.

Another window shattered, and the men whooped in drunken delight. They started shooting wildly.

"Look out!" Maddy cried, seeing one man wheel his mount toward her.

She and Blanche hit the floor just as their own window burst inward. Glass sprayed the room. Maddy glanced at Blanche to make sure her sister was all right.

"I do believe it's time for Sheriff Cooper," she said, picking a sliver of glass from her sleeve.

As though prompted by her words, a shotgun blast shattered the night. But this time, silence didn't fall; a flurry of gunfire answered.

Maddy rose to her feet. Flattening herself against the wall, she peered out into the street. Sheriff Cooper had taken cover behind one of the barrels outside Bill's general store. A few dozen yards down the street, three men were likewise barricaded behind a horse trough.

Blanche took a post on the opposite side of the window. "What do you think, Maddy?"

"I wish they were farther apart," Maddy replied. "At this distance, they might actually have a chance of hitting one another."

She stiffened as she saw John Ballard easing along the wall of a nearby store. On the other side of the street, Hank Vann moved like a shadow. But even shadows needed some kind of cover to remain unseen, and the moonlight was just too bright.

"Uh-oh," she muttered. "Blanche—"

"Yes."

Blanche moved silently toward the storeroom. A shot rang out from the rooftop above. Splinters sprayed out from the wall behind Sheriff Cooper. He rolled out from behind the barrel and ran for a new hiding spot.

But the man on the rooftop fired again, hitting Sheriff Cooper in the leg. He sprawled heavily in the street. John Ballard sprinted to him, hauling him up by brute force. Bullets smacked into the dust all around them. Hank Vann ran out to cover them.

"Here," Blanche said, thrusting a rifle into Maddy's hands.

Knocking the last remaining shards of glass from the window frame, she pulled the weapon to her shoulder and took aim. Her shot smacked into the horse trough an inch above one of the men's heads. She levered another round into the chamber and fired again. Blanche, her own rifle cradled on her shoulder, took up a position on the other side of the window again.

John and Hank Vann fired at the man on the roof above as they dragged the sheriff back toward safety.

"Cover them," Maddy said.

She and Blanche kept up a steady barrage of shots, gouging chunks of wood from the watering trough. Pinned, the three cowboys could only hug the scant safety of their wooden haven.

"I didn't think . . ." Blanche ejected an empty cartridge from her rifle. ". . . You'd be much interested in saving John's hide."

"I'm saving Sheriff Cooper's hide," Maddy pointed out. Then she added, "Besides, if anyone shoots John Ballard, it's going to be me."

Bill Smith appeared in the glassless window of his store.

He held an enormous Sharps rifle to his shoulder, and aimed toward the man on the roof. Fire and thunder belched from the barrel, almost knocking him off his feet. The man on the roof returned fire, and Bill dove out of sight again.

John and Hank dragged the sheriff into the shelter of the general store. With them safe, Maddy took the opportunity to reload. Blanche did the same.

One of the cowboys, taking advantage of the lull, rolled out from behind the trough and sprinted toward his horse. Maddy fired at his feet, carefully aiming an inch behind his heels. He sped up considerably. Leaping on his mount, he spurred away down the street.

"Just like old times, eh, Maddy?" Blanche asked.

"Indeed it is," she replied. "Thank goodness Papa was partial to repeating rifles."

Blanche laughed. "Daddy simply liked guns."

"That he did. And—" Maddy broke off, spotting a stir of motion behind the trough. "I think the other two are going to bolt now. Which one do you want?"

"The one with the blue bandanna," Blanche said. "I've always been partial to blue . . . There they go!"

The two cowboys pelted toward their horses. Puffs of dust spurted up just behind their feet as Maddy and Blanche began to fire again.

"It would be so easy . . ." Blanche murmured.

"This isn't war, dear," Maddy replied, sending a last shot after her rapidly-retreating target. "It isn't our place to deal with those men permanently. Although the fellow on the roof bothers me. Those other men fired in the heat of battle, but he sneaked up there with clear intent—"

She drew her breath in sharply as John Ballard appeared in the doorway of the general store. A bullet cracked into the doorjamb beside him. He rolled to one side, bringing his gun up as his knees hit the sidewalk. Then he fired once, twice.

A man cried out in pain. Maddy heard a thump as he fell from the rooftop.

"Apparently you don't need to be bothered about him any longer," Blanche said. "Now, sister dear, what are we going to say to our neighbors?"

"I haven't the slightest idea," Maddy said. "Even if I were a liar, it would take one whopping big tale to try to make them think all those shots came from somewhere other than inside our store."

She dreaded this. Most of all, she dreaded facing John Ballard. He saw too much with those cynical cat's-eyes, and tonight she'd tipped her hand badly. He was as tenacious as any Saylor; he wasn't about to let this go until he'd unearthed the truth. And the truth would put Derek's head into a noose.

Maddy watched John Ballard straighten and slide his gun back into the holster. Then his gaze fastened on the dressmaking shop. For a moment, his eyes seemed to catch the moonlight and cast it back.

"I should have shot him while I had the chance," she said, more to herself than to her sister.

Blanche didn't ask who. She only smiled.

Maddy sighed. Tucking the rifle into the crook of her arm, she stepped out into the street.

Eleven

John straightened, his gaze riveted to Maddy as she walked across the street. She cradled a Henry repeating rifle in her arms, and looked right at home with it. Judging from the number and accuracy of the shots that had come from the dressmaking shop, both Saylor sisters were more than acquainted with firearms.

"I'll be damned," Hank Vann muttered behind him. "I'll be triple goddamned."

John glanced at the other man. "Are you thinking what I'm thinking?"

"I hope not," Vann replied. " 'Cause that means I'm not crazy out of my mind."

John let his breath out in a hiss of frustration. He'd been acting crazy since he'd set eyes on Maddy Saylor, and things weren't getting any better. Damn her to hell, he thought. She'd stirred him up all over again, and in a way he didn't like. Didn't like at all.

Derek had become a legend during the war. And why not? He sometimes seemed to have the uncanny ability to be in two places at once. The Gray Ghost. All the while, Maddy and Blanche stayed home like the genteel ladies they were. Or did they?

John ground his teeth as cold fury swept through him. He'd seen Maddy ride. He'd seen her shoot. And he didn't think there were many things she wouldn't dare.

He was only peripherally aware of Blanche; Maddy held all

his attention. In the moonlight, her eyes looked as deep and secretive as a nighttime sea. Those secrets were real, he knew. Just how deep they ran, well, he'd just have to find out.

People started coming out of nearby houses. That, too, infuriated John; he wanted Maddy to himself, and he wanted answers.

"I'll go check that fella who was on the roof," Hank said.

He strode to Blanche. Snatching the rifle from her, he put one hand on the small of her back and took her with him.

Apparently Hank, too, wanted some answers, John thought, watching Maddy walk toward him. If he hadn't seen that shooting for himself, he might have thought butter wouldn't melt in her mouth. Lady-of-the-Manor Maddy. She'd played with those cowboys, deliberately aiming just behind their feet to make them run faster. Damn. He knew men who'd give their right arms to be able to shoot like that.

"Is Sheriff Cooper all right?" she called.

Bill Jones appeared in the doorway behind John. "Sure. Bullet went right through the muscle, is all. He's madder than a rattlesnake with his tail in a fire, though." His grizzled brows went up. "Where the hell did y'all learn to shoot like that?"

Maddy shot a glance toward John, wondering what was going on behind those gold-green eyes of his. "It wasn't anything, really."

"Not anything!" Bill exploded. "Hell, woman. They ain't a man in this here town goin' to believe that."

"Well . . ." Maddy glanced at John again, wishing she knew how he was taking all this. "Papa believed that a lady should learn how to play the piano, speak French, and shoot straight to protect her honor."

Bill hooted with laughter. "Well, this here's one feller who ain't plannin' to lay one fingernail on Saylor honor, that's fer sure."

A murmur of agreement rose from the crowd. Sheriff Cooper pushed Bill aside and hobbled out onto the sidewalk. Blood dribbled from the wound in his thigh.

"Sheriff, you shouldn't be walking on that," Maddy exclaimed. "You must get to the doctor—"

"I'll git to him soon enough," the sheriff growled. "Anybody hurt?"

"Just the man on the roof," John replied. "Hank's gone to see about him."

"I hope he's still breathin'," Sheriff Cooper said, with a wince. "I got some unfinished business with that feller." His sharp gaze fastened on Maddy. "That a Henry rifle you got there, Miss Saylor?"

"It is," she replied.

"I always admired them Henrys," he said. "Twenty rounds a minute—"

"Closer to twenty-four," Maddy said.

Then she glanced at John again, and she stiffened, realizing her mistake. Only an expert could get twenty-four rounds a minute from the Henry rifles, and John knew it. He was smiling, the self-satisfied grin of a cat who's just caught a nice, fat mouse. Slowly, he crossed his arms over his chest.

Maddy needed a distraction, any distraction. "Sheriff, you're bleeding badly," she said. "You really ought to get to Dr. Brennan."

The sheriff grunted. He started walking, cursed, then cursed again when Bill rushed to help him.

"I don't need yore danged help," the sheriff growled.

"If you pass out, we're gonna have to carry you," Bill replied. "And remember, the doc likes his bottle on Saturday nights. If you ain't watchin', he might just turn you into a gelding by accident."

That stopped Sheriff Cooper's protest. Maddy didn't know whether to be shocked or amused. Then she glanced at John, and decided that extreme caution should rule the day just now. Everyone else had turned back into their houses; she was now alone with John. Very alone.

"I wonder where Blanche and Mr. Vann have gone," she said, hoping to distract him.

"I expect he has as many questions as I do," John replied. "We're going to have a talk, you and I."

"This is hardly the time—"

"Now, Maddy."

She tilted her head back to look at him. Rage flared fox-fire-bright in his eyes. A more docile woman might have been afraid. But Maddy's temper flared to match his, and all thought of caution was lost in a wild sweep of anger.

"Don't you *dare* tell me what to do," she said.

John pulled the rifle from her grasp, resisting the urge to fling it up into the night sky. Damn, but she was an infuriating baggage!

"We're going to talk, Maddy," he said. "You can do it the easy way or the hard way, but you will do it."

Her eyes narrowed in a fine, hot rush of temper. Who was he to act the injured party? So he wanted to argue, did he? Well, she had some anger of her own to get out.

"For some reason, Mr. Ballard, you seem to think you have some special claim on my time. Well, you're wrong. I have no intention—"

Her breath went out in a gasp as he swept her up into his arms. Then she breathed in again, and fury took over. She had never, never been so angry in her life. If she'd had a weapon . . . She snatched at her rifle, which he held tightly against her knees as he carried her.

"Won't work, Maddy," he said.

She thought he was taking her into the shop. But when he strode into the alley beside it, she knew he was headed for the tiny quarters she shared with Blanche. A tiny, cold trickle of fear slid rapier-sharp through the shield of her anger.

"Where are you going?" she demanded, although she already knew.

"To a place where we can talk," he replied. His calm eyes belied the note of savagery in his voice.

She held herself away from him with braced arms as he mounted the stairs. "I can walk."

"I don't trust you not to run away."

"I never run," she retorted, drawing on all the dignity at her command.

He stopped, and for a moment she was sure she could feel his heart beating in his chest. Her own heartbeat rose to match his, as though her body were automatically tuning itself to his. She lifted her chin defiantly, although that warning thread of alarm still stitched along her veins.

John stood with her in his arms, unmoving, his gaze locked to hers. He could see the pulse throbbing in her temple, a sure sign that she wasn't nearly as composed as she wanted him to think. She was a delicious weight in his arms. Curved and ripe and as lush as a banquet even with arrogance in her eyes. He shifted his hand so that his fingers lay spread on her ribs just beneath her breast. Her eyes changed, darkening as though a mist had passed through them.

Magic, John thought. Pure magic. Only time would tell if it were good or bad.

"If you knew what I was thinking now, you'd run," he said. "You'd run as far and as fast as you could." He took a deep breath, trying to ease the sudden tightness in his chest. "And you still wouldn't be safe."

"I should have let them shoot you," she whispered.

"Yes," he agreed, "you should have."

He climbed the rest of the stairs. Setting her on her feet, he kept one arm tightly around her waist as he tried the knob. It was locked, of course.

"Open it," he said.

"No."

With a muttered curse, he kicked the door open so hard it banged on the wall behind it. Taking a firm hold of her arm, he hauled her inside, kicking the door closed behind him.

"Let me go," Maddy said, her voice as calm as her insides were panicked.

His gaze bored into hers for a moment. Then he relaxed his hand, releasing her. She moved away to the opposite side of the room, painfully aware that had he not agreed to release her, she would have been helpless to break his grip.

It made her furious; from the moment she'd met him, he'd set her world to spinning. She'd always been able to keep everything in order. She'd felt in control of her own destiny. Now, it seemed as though everything had turned to chaos. And John Ballard stood at the center, cause and focus of the storm. In this moment, she hated him for it, hated herself for not having the strength to keep him from mattering.

"How dare you?" she hissed.

He smiled at her. "One thing you ought to know about me, Maddy," he said. "I dare anything."

She took a deep breath, startled both by the savagery in his voice and by her reaction to it. She'd never seen him like this. She'd never seen *anyone* like this. Papa had always been easy to manage, and so had Derek. But John seemed to fill the room with his presence, larger than life and not in the least manageable.

A thrill raced up her spine, fury and dread and a bright, treacherous thread of desire. For this contest between them was one that would take all her wits and courage to win. If she *could* win.

"Now," he said, "tell me about the guns."

"The guns were my father's," she replied. "It's the only legacy we took from Tallwood."

"Tallwood's your home?"

"Was," she said, her throat tightening as it always did when she thought about that. "Saylors had owned Tallwood for a hundred and fifty years. After the war . . ." She shrugged to shift attention from the sudden tears that had sprung to her eyes. "Blanche and I managed to hold on for two years. But the Carpetbaggers got the taxes raised so high we couldn't meet them, and then seized our home. But they didn't get Papa's guns."

John saw her eyes soften from anger to sorrow. His heart

made that curious lurch again. But he hardened himself to it, determined not to let Maddy distract him again.

"Where did you learn to ride and shoot?"

"Papa. He had us on horseback almost as soon as we could walk. And as for guns, well, we Saylors have always had a talent for them."

"Did you help your brother during the war?"

Maddy studied him intently. Until now, she hadn't realized just how badly she and Blanche had exposed themselves by becoming involved in the fight. No dust settled on John Ballard. She had to divert him from the dangerous path he was treading. And the only way to do that was to tell the truth. A partial truth, that is.

"Of course we did," she said, watching surprise dawn in his eyes. So, she thought, he'd expected her to lie. She felt a grim sort of satisfaction. "We gave him food, shelter, and supplies whenever he needed them. And we prayed for him."

John cocked his head to one side, wondering at her sudden show of cooperation. Unlike Maddy. Very. "What about the Yankees? What did they do?"

"The Yankees destroyed our lives," she replied, her voice as stark as her words. " 'Twas a high price to pay for men's politics. My sister and I won't pay it again."

His brows went down; she wasn't the only one who'd paid that price. His life, too, had been shattered, and he hadn't had anyone to help him put it back together. "Which means?"

"It means," she said, pulling in a deep breath, "that you can go straight to Hades with your questions. I will never tell you anything that can be used against my brother."

John's eyes narrowed. It was a direct challenge, and hit him like sparks to tinder.

"That was a mistake, Maddy," he said softly.

He started toward her, walking with a soft, sure-footed gait that sent ripples of alarm shooting through her. She shifted to the right, hoping to have a chance to dart past him and out the door, but he moved to block her. She glanced around the room, searching for some way out of her predicament. Oh, Lord, she couldn't let him touch her again. She'd already learned the danger of that very well.

"I'll scream," she warned.

John smiled. "Do you think that would stop me?"

"You are—"

"Very, very tired of playing games," he finished for her.

He stalked her with a casualness that only partially masked the hot male aggression in his eyes. Maddy felt true fear. Not of him, of herself. For even now, despite the dictates of her mind and of prudence, her body thrilled to the sight of him. He was angry. He was arrogant. But a molten thread of promise coiled through the dark intent in his eyes, and everything that made her a woman responded to it.

With an effort, she pulled her rationality over her like a cloak. This wouldn't do. She couldn't let John touch her; if he did, he'd know the full extent of her weakness. And he'd use it to take Derek from her.

Slowly, she edged toward the sewing basket in which Papa's big Colt was hidden. John came after her, and she knew time was running out fast. She leaped for the basket. Snatching the Colt, she raised it, centering the sights on John's heart.

"That's quite far enough," she said.

John stared down the barrel of the big .44. It didn't waver in the least. And after that display outside tonight, he had no doubt that Maddy could hit what she aimed at.

His nostrils flared, and he was possessed by a wave of fury so powerful it shook him to his toes. She'd swept into his life like a tornado, and she'd torn the curtains he'd drawn to keep the past at bay, leaving him raw and aching. Just now, he didn't give a damn whether she shot him or not.

"Go ahead," he said. "Shoot."

He kept walking. Her finger tightened on the trigger, and for a moment he thought he'd misjudged her. Then her eyes changed hue, becoming as dark and fathomless as a stormswept sky, and he knew he'd won.

When he stopped, the barrel of the gun was pressed to his chest. He looked straight into the turbulent depths of her eyes and smiled.

"You see, Maddy?" he said. "You don't want to shoot me nearly as much as you think you do."

"Yes, I do," she replied, her eyes narrowing. "I was just taught not to shoot people who aren't shooting back."

"You don't believe that any more than I do," he murmured.

The soft, intensely masculine timbre of his voice sent a ripple of reaction sliding through her veins She fought for logic, for the rationality that usually served her so well. She fought for her anger, for that was her only protection.

But rationality and anger had gone spinning away, leaving only the memory of how John's face had tightened when he'd freed her breasts to his gaze, the raging desire that had turned his eyes molten and sent a wash of response through her. And the pleasure . . . the urgings of a need so powerful that her body ached with it. Only with him. Only for him. It had shattered her notions of who she was and what she wanted.

"Why were you so sure I wouldn't shoot you?" she whispered.

He took the gun from her and set it aside. "You saved my life. I doubt you'd be willing to take it now."

"I didn't save your life. I was—"

"Saving Sheriff Cooper," he finished for her.

"Yes."

Suddenly he smiled at her. The sight of that grin sent her pulse pounding, and every beat had his name on it.

"No," she said.

He stroked her cheek, a touch both gentle and full of promise. His thumb strayed to the corner of her mouth, and it took an effort of will not to part her lips. Then he slid his hand into her hair, winding his fingers deeply into her chignon.

Captured. Claimed. She couldn't get away now, from him or from herself. And she didn't care, for his eyes held a sensuality hot enough to burn her. This was a woman's power, she realized. To take a strong man, a hard man, and light a fire in him hot enough to consume them both . . . it was both terrifying and incredibly seductive.

Some tiny, far-off corner of her mind cried out for her to stop, to think, but the voice of caution was lost in the warm-honey flow of desire purling through her body.

If he touched her, she'd go up in flames.

Of course he would touch her; she could see the intent in his eyes. He would set her blood on fire, he would turn her core molten and her limbs weak.

And she wanted him to. She couldn't have stopped him now any more than she could have pulled the moon down from the sky.

Her body felt as though it had turned liquid as he slid his arm around her waist and pulled her against him. Slowly, slowly, but oh, so thoroughly, fitting her to him as though he intended to keep her there forever. She felt as though they'd merged somehow—muscle, bone, heart, and soul dissolving in passion's blazing heat.

"Maddy," he whispered.

She'd passed beyond speech. Stunned by the emotions he was making her feel, she clung to him. He framed her face between his hands and simply looked at her. Her breathing grew shallow, and her pulse began to race. She felt naked, stripped of all her defenses. And he knew, he knew. Arousal and triumph pooled in his eyes.

And then he kissed her. It began gently, a feathering of his mouth across hers that brought every nerve ending to a quivering alert. She sighed as his tongue rubbed against hers, then delved deep as he tasted more of her.

"Why do you have to do this to me?" she whispered, her mouth against his.

"Do you think I have any more control over this than you do?" he replied, biting softly at her lips, then kissing his way along her cheek to her temple. "Whenever I touch you, it's like being dipped in fire. Everything else burns away but you."

"If you . . . ah," she gasped as he slid his tongue into her ear with devastating effect, "wouldn't keep coming around me—"

"No choice there, either."

"This is insane."

"True," he murmured, his hands spreading possessively across her back.

She shivered as he began to suck her earlobe. Truly, she'd never known, never imagined that there could be so many places on her body that could give her such tingling pleasure.

"Why are you doing this to me?" she whispered.

"Because you're beautiful," he said. "And I want to."

Maddy started to say something in protest, but he laid his hand over her mouth.

"Shhh," he murmured. "Don't fight this so hard, Maddy."

"I always fight," she said, almost unaware of what she was saying.

"There are things too big to fight."

She drew her breath in with a sigh, then let it out again slowly, as though it might hurt.

John wanted to kiss her, touch her, taste her—everything at once, and all together. She'd touched him somewhere in his soul, in a spot so secret and deep he hadn't been aware of it himself.

He didn't understand it. But he did know that he'd die if he didn't keep touching her. Slowly, he maneuvered her backward until she was pressed up against the wall. Linking his fingers with hers, he planted his hands on either side of her head. It was a most effective—and arousing—position. Her mouth was swollen and eager, her breasts lifted high by the elevation of her arms. She was beautiful, passionate, the most woman he'd ever met in his life.

To his surprise, he found himself shaking. He'd never been so close to losing control with a woman. "I want to taste you," he said in a whisper as fierce as his passion.

Her gaze lifted to his, and for a moment she looked soft

and vulnerable. The sight sent him over the edge. With a muttered exclamation, he claimed her mouth. She tasted of heat and woman. And he was lost. If she didn't share this searing, uncontrollable passion, then he'd have nothing. Never, never, could he allow her to see the power she held over him.

"Do you want to run?" he whispered.

It took Maddy a moment to find her voice. She felt shattered by the intensity of what he was making her feel. "Yes," she replied, the admission torn from her by the storm raging in her soul.

He gazed into her eyes for a long moment. Then he released his grip on her hands. Freed, she let her arms drop to her sides.

But she wasn't free; perhaps she never would be quite free again. She tried to step away from him, but her body refused to obey. It had been bound somehow to this man who seemed able to take her very will away from her.

"Run now, Maddy," he said. "Run while you have the chance."

She couldn't. It had nothing to do with Saylor pride. No, it was simply the fact that she couldn't make herself do it. She could only stand before him, trapped by something that was stronger than wisdom and caution and even self-preservation.

"I can't," she whispered.

It was a devastating revelation. Practical, logical Maddy didn't do things like this—didn't feel things like this. She felt as though she'd been stripped naked, her every weakness exposed.

John ran his fingertip along the curve of her cheek. He knew how high a price the world could exact from those who fought it. And Maddy had fought. Hard, uncompromisingly, against any odds. Looking into her eyes like this, when her spirit lay exposed to him, he realized she'd never regretted the cost.

But she'd regret making love with John Ballard tonight. He sighed. Derek stood between them, a silent and invisible chaperon. John wanted her. Heart, mind, and soul, he wanted to possess Maddy completely.

He could seduce her. Hell, she all but went up in flames when he touched her. But in having her, he'd lose her. She'd hate him for seducing her, and she'd hate herself more for allowing it to happen. Now, faced with the decision, he found himself unwilling to take the chance.

"Maddy, Maddy," he whispered. "Haven't you ever let yourself go?"

Her lashes drifted downward. "I've done the things I've needed to do," she replied. "Honor, duty, necessity. It's the same for you, as you have so often told me."

"We're back to Derek," he said.

"Always."

"Damn your brother to bloody hell," he growled. "This is between you and me."

"Do you think it can be that simple?"

"Ask your sister that."

Maddy pulled her hands away. She didn't know why he'd allowed her this reprieve, but he had. "Blanche is more trusting than I."

"You weren't always so mistrustful."

"The War changed many people," she replied. "I lost my mother, father, many friends, my home, and my way of life. Everything I'd been brought up to expect had been shattered. And acquaintance with Carpetbaggers didn't make me a trusting person."

"Do you think you're the only one who lost?" he asked, his voice tight with pain.

Surprised by the harshness of his tone, Maddy tilted her head back to look more fully at him. That burning darkness had come into his eyes again, the shadow of something so big and hurtful that it filled all his soul. She drew her breath in with a hiss.

"What happened?"

John couldn't answer; he was bound inside himself by

memories of battle, the thunder of artillery, the screams of dying men, the hot wetness of blood on his hands and the light of life fading from his brother's eyes.

He couldn't give her this. This was his, to be forgotten if possible, to be borne somehow if it couldn't. With a muttered oath, he let her go.

"I'm not interested in playing this game with you," he said.

"Game? What game?" she demanded.

"This . . . thing between us. You're the one making it into a contest, with Derek as the prize."

"Isn't it?"

"No."

"But it is," she said. "It is defined by your desire to destroy my brother, and mine to save him. And rest assured that I will win this contest."

"We'll see," he murmured.

He cupped her cheek in his hand, letting his thumb stray close to her mouth. Maddy's eyelids drifted downward as though she were expecting him to kiss her. He wanted to. But damn her to hell, he had no choice but to play her game. She'd find out soon enough that she'd taken on more than she could handle.

"Good night," he murmured, his breath fanning warm across her lips.

And then he was gone.

Twelve

Maddy spent most of the next day working on Dolly Mayhew's gown. She'd gotten the bodice mostly put together, and had put many tiny tucks in the bosom to give Dolly a more feminine curve to her figure. She was determined to make Dolly look absolutely beautiful.

Finally, her eyes grew so tired she could hardly focus, so she set the gown aside. She glanced at the clock.

"Good heavens!" she gasped. "It's nearly six o'clock! Where has the day gone?"

And where had Blanche gone? Maddy stiffened, realizing that she hadn't seen her sister since early afternoon. It wasn't like Blanche to disappear when there was work to be done.

She rose, stretching to get the kinks out of her back, and stepped outside into the sunshine. The smell of beef wafted down from the hotel, as did the sounds of revelry from the saloon. Maddy strolled along the sidewalk toward Bill Smith's store. If anyone might know where Blanche had gone, Bill would.

"Howdy, Miz Saylor!"

Maddy turned toward the voice, and found herself face-to-face with Virgil Sawyer, foreman of the Double D Ranch. Virgil had been one of those snubbing her yesterday, and so his sudden friendliness was quite a surprise.

"Hello, Mr. Sawyer," she replied, raising one brow questioningly.

"That was some fine shootin' last night," he said.

"Thank you."

He smiled at her, his sun-browned face creasing into wrinkles. "Folks around here appreciate good shootin'. They been sayin' you Saylor ladies ought to be right handy to have around"

"Well, that's nice, I'm sure," Maddy said, even more confused than before. "But I thought we were rather more useful as dressmakers."

"Frippery, ma'am, if you don't mind me sayin'. We Texans tend to admire more practical things."

"I'm glad to hear it," Maddy said.

"Jest wanted you to know," Virgil said, tipping his hat. He walked away, whistling under his breath.

Maddy watched him go, then shook her head and continued on. Truly, Cofield was an astonishing place, she thought. Had she and Blanche known that acceptance could be won by shooting up the town, they would have done so long ago.

"Yoo-hoo, Maddy!"

The caller's voice was feminine this time. Maddy looked up to see Prissy Taylor, the banker's daughter.

"Hello, Prissy," she called.

Prissy climbed up onto the sidewalk and swished her skirts to remove the dust they'd collected in the street. "It surely is hot today, isn't it?"

Maddy nodded.

"I just wanted to tell you how impressed we all were by what you and Blanche did last night. I never knew women could shoot like that."

"The women in our family can," Maddy replied. "Our father taught us."

"Well, that's really something," Prissy said. "Mama says it's most unladylike to shoot guns, but there's nothing unladylike about you and your sister."

Maddy laughed. "Thank you for that, Prissy. Speaking of my sister . . . have you seen her?"

"I saw her about noon, I think. She was talking to Mr. Smith, down at the general store."

"Thank you. Please give my regards to your parents, will you?"

Maddy made her escape then. Not that she didn't appreciate her neighbor's sudden friendliness, but she wanted to find Blanche. She hurried to the general store.

Bill was busily wiping cans and setting them on the shelf behind the counter. He glanced at her over his shoulder, giving her a wink before turning around.

"Hey, Maddy. How's things?"

"Fine. Have you seen Blanche?"

"Last I saw her, she was walking down the street with that Vann feller."

Maddy closed her eyes for a moment. This was what she'd dreaded, and expected. *Oh, Blanche!* she thought. *You are too trusting by far, too reckless with yourself.* "Did you see where they went?"

"Didn't look."

"Blast," Maddy muttered.

"What's the matter?"

"I can't find Blanche anywhere," Maddy said. "And I'm getting very worried about her."

"Vann kin protect her well enough."

She put her hands on her hips. "But who, pray tell, is going to protect her from him?"

"Ahhh, so that's the way it is." With a grimace, Bill raked his hands through his greying hair. "All right, I'll ask around. Quiet-like, so as not to start folks a-talkin'."

"Thank you, Bill."

"You go on home now. It'll look better fer me to do the askin'."

"But—"

"You let ole Bill take care of this. Go on, now."

Maddy knew he was right. It was hard, though, for her to walk back to the apartment as though nothing were wrong.

She slammed the door behind her and went to scrub her face in the washbasin. Truly, she and Blanche had far too much in common with this. Blanche wanted Hank; Maddy wanted John. Both men wanted Derek.

Maddy scrubbed her face until it stung, then straightened and looked at herself in the tiny mirror over the bureau. Her eyes looked huge, with an almost visible aura of excitement hovering in their depths. Her mouth seemed fuller, more expressive. She looked . . . vulnerable.

She looked like a woman in love.

"No," she said, her voice low and intense in the quiet room. "Not him. Not now. Not ever."

Someone tapped lightly at the door, and she hurried to answer it. She found Bill Smith waiting outside. He held his hat in his hands, turning it over and over as though he'd become very nervous.

"What is it?" she demanded.

"I think she went off somewhere with Vann," he said.

"Hellfire and damnation," Maddy swore. "I've got to find her, Bill."

"I don't know where Vann bunks," he said. "But there's a feller who does. Name of Jim Berry. He's at the saloon now."

"Then I'll have to go talk to him."

"You cain't go in there!" Bill yelped, obviously scandalized.

"Of course I can," Maddy replied.

"But there are whores in there," he said, then instantly turned red. "I mean . . ."

"That's all right, Bill. I know about such things."

"But—"

"Not another word." she said. "Thank you for all your help."

"Damn it, Maddy—"

"Good night," she said firmly.

He sputtered for a moment. Then he turned and stomped out, nearly shaking the stairway right off the building. Maddy sighed. It wasn't that she didn't appreciate his concern. But she had to find Blanche—preferably *before* something irrevocable happened—and she didn't care what she had to do.

Neither Papa nor Derek was here to protect Blanche's honor; Maddy would have to see to it herself.

"Ah, Blanche, everything seems so simple to you right now," she murmured, winding her hair into a tight knot at the nape of her neck. "But it won't be. It can't be."

Hiding the pistol beneath her shawl, she slipped down the stairs. Music and laughter rolled down the street from the saloon, but it was still early.

A solid wall of noise assailed her the moment she walked into the saloon. Men stood three deep around the bar, and the reek of smoke and whiskey hung thickly in the room. Other men crowded the tables, watching those who were playing cards. The saloon girls smiled and flirted, their skin flashing pale amid their scanty clothing.

For a moment Maddy stood unnoticed. Then several men turned to stare at her, nudging their neighbors to look as well. The din abated somewhat. Maddy found the situation oddly amusing; she couldn't have been more out of place if she'd grown an extra head.

She turned to the nearest man, who recovered enough to tip his hat. He seemed very young, perhaps still in his teens. "Sir, I wonder if you could help me."

"Ma'am?"

"I'm looking for Mr. Berry."

"Right over there, ma'am," the cowboy said, pointing.

"Thank you."

She was very aware of the stares that followed her as she made her way toward the table. Another woman might have been frightened. Maddy only kept her pistol handy, and relied on cool Southern dignity to see her through.

Jim Berry was a huge man with a bristling black brush of a moustache He held a tiny blonde on his lap while he played poker. The young woman stared challengingly at Maddy, as though expecting her to steal her . . . beau away.

"Mr. Berry?" Maddy asked.

He fixed her with an unblinking stare. His eyes were the color of a muddy stream, and as hard and cold as glass. "That's me. What d'you want, honey?"

"I'm told you might know where Hank Vann is."

One thick brow rose. "Maybe I do. Why do you want to know?"

"May we talk privately?"

The brow went higher. "You want to go upstairs?"

The other men laughed uproariously. Realizing what they thought, Maddy felt her cheeks flame. But she kept her chin up, her gaze straight and steady, and waited for the guffaws to subside.

"Darlin', you can take me anywhere you like," Berry said. With a swipe of one arm, he flung the young woman out of his lap. She sprawled heavily on the floor. He leaned the back of his chair against the wall behind him, balancing it on two legs.

"Come on, honey," Berry said, patting his thighs. "Come set right here and ole Jim will tell you everythin' you want to know."

Maddy bent and laid her hand on the fallen woman's shoulder. "Are you hurt, miss?"

The young woman turned a startled blue gaze on her. "No. Just . . ." She bit her lip, tears clouding her eyes.

Beneath the rouge and powder and the scanty clothes, Maddy caught a glimpse of the girl she'd once been. Many of these women turned to this profession out of desperation—Maddy knew too much about desperation to judge this woman.

"I understand," Maddy murmured.

The young woman's eyes widened. Maddy straightened then, awash in a sudden surge of fury that a woman had been treated so shabbily and not one person had stood up for her.

Maddy leveled a stare at Jim Berry that should have burned him to ash where he sat. "Now, Mr. Berry, about Hank Vann—" she began.

"Aw, honey, you don't need Hank Vann when you can have me," he said. "Any of the gals here can tell you I'm worth spendin' time with. Ain't that right, Maisie?" He glanced at the girl whom he'd treated so badly.

"Sure," she replied, rising to her feet. "If you like goats."

His moustache writhed as his grin turned to a snarl. "You stupid whore. You're not fit to lick my boots——"

"Excuse me," Maddy said, loudly enough to override his voice. "You're being very rude."

"Rude?" he echoed.

"Rude," she said again. "Weren't you taught to treat ladies with respect?"

Laughter rippled around the room again. But Maddy didn't think it was derisive, as it had been before. It didn't seem as though Jim Berry had made himself popular in Cofield.

Berry hooked his thumbs in his belt and stared at Maddy with open insolence. "That ain't no lady. That's a whore."

"Ah," Maddy said. "Apparently you *weren't* taught better."

"What?" he demanded.

"Was I unclear?" Maddy asked.

His eyes turned ugly, and she knew she'd made an enemy. So be it, she thought.

Slowly, Berry let the chair fall onto its front legs. Then he rose. Maddy found herself staring up at six-plus feet of man, and one who obviously had no scruples about hitting women.

"Apologize," she said.

Surprise took some of the annoyance from his eyes. "Apologize?"

"Yes," she said. "Apologize."

Berry scowled. Maddy got a glimpse of a huge, square hand coming straight for her throat. Then someone reached past her, gripping Jim Berry's wrist in a way that made the big man's eyes bulge.

Without looking, Maddy knew that John Ballard had come to her rescue. Again.

"Out of the way, Maddy," he growled.

"John, is this really necessary?" Maddy asked.

"Stay out of it, Maddy," he said, his voice calm.

Jim Berry clamped his free hand on John's wrist. The two men stood almost nose to nose, tendons standing out like wires in their forearms. Maddy thought she heard bones creak. Then beads of sweat broke out on Jim Berry's forehead. Droplets grew, collected into rivulets, and began to stream down the big man's face.

"She yours?" he panted.

"Yes," John said.

"Now just a moment," Maddy yelped.

John shot her a glance that all but froze her blood in her veins. "Shut up, Maddy."

"I will not!"

"Ought to take a buggy whip to that one," Jim Berry gasped. "She's got a tongue sharp enough to skin a rattlesnake."

John smiled, a predatory flash of white teeth that sent a shiver up Maddy's spine. Jim Berry didn't know how dangerous the situation was. Or how serious John was. She watched the corded muscles of his forearms writhe beneath the skin as he tightened his grip still further.

Men, Maddy thought. "John—"

"Not now," he growled.

"See here," she snapped, completely out of patience. "I don't have time for this nonsense. I want to know where Hank Vann is, and I want to know now."

"And?" John prompted.

"And Mr. Berry knows," she said.

She slid the big Colt out from beneath her shawl. The men behind her pressed close, obviously not wanting to miss anything. Well, she wasn't about to let them. Her temper was running high, and she needed to get to Blanche.

"Mr. Berry," she said, her voice low and silken with threat, "if you won't tell me where Hank Vann has gone, I'll just have to shoot you."

"You ain't gonna shoot me," he retorted.

She smiled. It was the same smile she'd used when the Yankees had overrun Tallwood and had plundered it of everything that could be eaten or sold. The Yankees hadn't liked that smile; judging by the way Jim Berry's face paled, he didn't like it, either.

Slowly, she pulled the hammer back. It made an audible click in the silent room, and alarm dawned on the faces of the men surrounding Jim Berry. Then Maddy raised the pistol, and that whole side of the room emptied.

"It's all right, gentlemen," she said. "I generally hit what I aim at and nothing else."

John glanced at Maddy, admiring the sight of a beautiful woman able to handle a gun like the Colt. And she was certainly able to handle it; her grip was firm, her aim secure, and her eyes had the flat look of someone who'd been pushed too far. He had to back her up. Once she got what she needed from Berry, then it was *his* turn. Oh, yes. He wanted his turn.

"If you're going to shoot him, do it and get it over with," John said. He saw a glint of humor in her eyes, and knew she'd play the game right along with him. Damn, but he liked a woman with a quick mind!

"I'm just trying to decide *where* to shoot him," she said, cocking her head to one side.

"Well, hurry up and decide," John growled. "I'm getting tired of holding him for you."

Maddy smiled in pure delight. "Oh, you don't have to hold him. I can hit him running as easily as standing still."

"Hey!" Berry yelped. He looked like a chicken who'd just spotted the cleaver.

"You shouldn't have made her mad," John said. "It would have been much easier had you just told her what she wanted to know."

"Vann camps somewheres east of town. Don't know exactly where, and expect that he likes it thataway. You're goin' to have to try to track him there," Berry said.

"Thank you, Mr. Berry," Maddy said, carefully easing the hammer up again. "You've been most kind."

"Now that the lady is satisfied," John said, "it's my turn."

"John—" Maddy began.

"He shouldn't have threatened you," he said, his voice low and deadly "I'm going to have to kill him for that."

Stepping forward, she put her hand on John's forearm. It felt rock-hard beneath her palm, and once more she was thrilled by the primitive strength of the man. Now, she had to tame it, to gentle it somehow.

"John," she said softly, looking into his eyes. "Let him go."

"He would have hurt you," he growled.

"But he didn't, thanks to you. Now let him go."

"No."

Maddy moved closer. "Please. Do it for me."

Her words didn't have the power to cut through the haze of anger, but her eyes did. He looked into those endless indigo depths, and felt as though his heart were being pulled right out of his body.

"For you," he growled.

He gave Berry a shove that sent him staggering. He slammed into the table, then fell crashing to the floor amid scattered cards and the shards of a broken whiskey bottle.

"If you so much as look cross-eyed at her again, I'll tear your throat out," John said. His tone was matter-of-fact, but his gaze delivered a cold and deadly message.

Berry wiped blood from the corner of his mouth. Hate turned his eyes flat, but he didn't try to get up. "We're gonna cross paths again, Ballard. And then we'll see."

"Any time," John replied. "Any time at all."

Maddy turned toward the door, confident that John would cover her back should anything happen. Truly, he could be a most useful man at times. Then she sighed, chiding herself for that weakness. John Ballard wasn't useful. He was just plain dangerous.

The moment they stepped outside, John grasped her arm. "I'm going with you," he said.

"I didn't say I was going anywhere," Maddy countered.

"Look, Maddy, Bill Smith told me about the problem. That's why I came to the saloon looking for you. Now, with Blanche off alone with Hank Vann, I can't imagine you *not* going to look for her."

"I don't want you to come."

"Too bad," he said with infuriating cheerfulness. "I'll even saddle Ali Baba for you."

"You are an insufferable man."

He pulled her closer, tucking her hand into the crook of his arm. "It's only one of my talents, Maddy. As you get to know me better, you'll find I have many others."

She jerked away from him and strode toward the stable. "I don't have time for this," she snapped.

Of course, he followed her. One might as well try to stop a thunderstorm as keep John Ballard from doing whatever he wanted.

She shot him a glare. "You really shouldn't tempt me so when I'm armed."

"Maddy darling, I said you could shoot me whenever you want to," he murmured. "It would be a small price to pay for the pleasure of your company."

A few minutes later, they rode east out of town. Clouds dotted the sky. The wind tossed them across the moon's face, sending black, winged shadows scudding across the earth.

Maddy spotted a hoofprint that showed a notched shoe, and stopped Ali beside it. "Blanche's chestnut has a notched shoe," she said, pointing to the track.

"You checked?"

"Do you really think I'd just let Hank Vann purchase a horse for my sister without checking?"

John smiled. "I don't know many women who would have."

"Blanche and I aren't your usual sort of women. In my family, we were expected to use our minds."

"I'm learning to appreciate the difference," he said. "So, Miss Saylor, which way do we go?"

Maddy wasn't about to fall into his trap "I thought you'd be able to tell me."

"What if I didn't know how to track?"

She met his gaze directly, and smiled "Then you shouldn't be trying to catch Derek Saylor."

A touch of grimness darkened John's amusement. She knew how to play a game very well, did Maddy Saylor. "What would you have done if I hadn't been here?"

"The intelligent thing, I assure you."

His eyes caught the moonlight, and for a moment they almost seemed to glow. He wanted her. However convoluted his reasons might be, his desire raged hot and high, and her very soul knew it. Responded to it. For she wanted him, too. Beyond caution, beyond pride.

Something that might have been dread, or perhaps anticipation, coursed like quicksilver through her veins.

"Which way?" she asked, her voice too breathless for her liking.

He smiled, and she knew he'd caught that undercurrent in her tone. "That way."

Maddy lifted her head in surprise. Blanche and Hank had left the road and headed northeast. Strange. Either they saw something they wanted to explore, or they were looking for a private spot to . . .

She urged Ali into a lope. The bay settled into a surefooted pace, and John dropped in beside her.

"Blanche is old enough to make her own decisions, Maddy."

She shot him a glance. "Blanche follows her heart She doesn't understand that there are times when the heart can't be trusted."

"Don't you think Hank Vann loves her?"

"Not when he's hunting our brother."

"Perhaps Blanche doesn't agree," he said softly.

"I have to take care of her," she said, forcing the words

from a throat gone tight. "I promised I'd protect her, and protect her I shall."

Her statement hit John hard. He'd said something very like that when he and his brothers had marched off to war, and he'd had that same certainty when he'd said it. They'd been young, all of them. When the war ended, his brothers were dead, and he was no longer young. His youth and his certainties had died with his brothers on the battlefield.

Cocky and arrogant, he'd sworn to protect them. And all he'd been able to do was comfort them when they died.

"Don't make a promise you can't keep," he growled.

Surprised by the harshness of his tone, Maddy turned to look at him. His expression showed nothing, but his eyes held that same dark torment she'd seen before. She didn't know the face of the demon he harbored deep in his soul, but it was a painful one.

"What happened to you?"

"What do you mean?"

"Something or someone hurt you badly," she said. "You can't hide it all the time, you know."

John felt as though he'd been stripped to his soul. He hated it, hated being vulnerable.

Blood everywhere, bullets and minié balls whining overhead. His brothers, one by one, dying in his arms. He'd spent years pushing those memories aside, and didn't want them back.

"I have nothing to hide," he growled. "Unlike you."

Stung, Maddy opened her mouth to retort. But then a gunshot cracked through the quiet night air, silencing her.

John kicked his mount toward Maddy's dun, crowding the other horse into a patch of shadow. To his relief, she didn't argue, nor did she try to resist; in fact, she already had the big Colt out and ready. Even in his haste, he had to admire his always practical, if slightly bloodthirsty, Maddy.

They sat their mounts in the darkness, ears tuned. A moment later another shot cracked, then another.

"Two different rifles," John said. "You'd better stay—"

Maddy kicked the bay's flank, and he shot forward. She watched his muscles bunch beneath the skin as he stretched out into a gallop. Behind her, she heard John curse.

"Stay indeed," she muttered.

She could hear the pounding of hoofbeats behind her, and urged Ali Baba to greater speed. John Ballard was not going to keep her from going to Blanche.

The ground was smoother here, the notched tracks easier to see. They were farther spaced now, indicating that the other horse had gone from a lope to a gallop. Maddy's heart pounded in time with Ali's hooves. She had the same tightness of chest, the same sick twist to her stomach that she'd had the night Derek had been wounded.

"I'm coming, Blanche," she whispered. "I'm coming."

She noticed a dark, irregular stain on a rock ahead. As Ali flashed past, Maddy saw it for what it was.

Blood.

Thirteen

John bent low over his horse's neck as he tried to catch Maddy. The bay's hooves seemed to float over the ground, touching down only occasionally to propel him and his rider forward.

Maddy was beautiful, fiery, magnificent. And she was riding straight into the line of fire without a care for her own safety. His mind conjured up the image of a bullet knocking her out of the saddle, extinguishing all that passion and beauty forever.

His whole being rose up in protest. It wouldn't happen. It couldn't happen. Wheeling his mount, he set off in pursuit.

"Damn you," he muttered. "Stop."

She wasn't going to stop, of course; that headlong determination would carry her straight to hell if that was what was required to help her sister.

A rock outcropping jutted up from the ground ahead. It was the perfect spot from which to ambush someone, and John's instinct for danger clamored wildly. If he could have flown to her, he would have. Instead, he pushed his mount to its limits in an attempt to interpose himself between her and danger.

"Maddy," he called, keeping his voice soft to prevent it from carrying. "Maddy, wait!"

She ignored him. He dug his heels into his horse's flanks, trying for yet a little more speed. A flash spurted out from atop the outcropping, followed by the crack of a rifle. An answering flash appeared in a stand of scrub pines a hundred-odd yards away.

"Blanche!" Maddy called.

"Here!" Blanche's cry came from within the trees.

Maddy turned Ali toward her sister's voice. John, his reflexes honed by his fear for her safety, swung his own mount around. But he knew he wasn't going to catch her; somehow, the bay's stride lengthened further, as though the horse were taking speed and strength from its rider's determination.

Whoever hid in the outcropping must have heard Blanche's cry, for another shot rang out. A plume of white dust rose from the ground a yard behind the galloping bay.

John shifted his reins to his teeth. Pulling his rifle out of the boot, he sighted in at the outcropping. He couldn't see the shooter, but he could damn well keep the bastard pinned down until Maddy got under cover.

"Go," he muttered. "Go!"

As a bullet ripped through the trees, another shot rang out, and reflex took over. Flinging himself toward Maddy, John bore her from the saddle just as a bullet zinged past his ear. He landed hard on his back, shielding her from the ground with his body.

Stars pinwheeled across his vision for a moment. Then he scooped her up and flung her toward the fallen tree that served as cover for Blanche and Hank Vann.

Maddy rolled next to Blanche, turning once to make sure John had joined her. "Are you all right?" she demanded, grabbing her sister's arm. Then she saw the dark red stain covering much of Blanche's right sleeve, and her heart leaped into her throat. "You're bleeding!"

"It's Hank's blood," Blanche said.

Maddy turned to look at the bounty hunter. He'd taken a bullet just above the collarbone; a steadily-widening red stain covered the front of his shirt. Blanche had tried to bind it up, but the blood had seeped through the makeshift bandage. Pain made his eyes glitter, but he'd still managed to keep hold of his pistol.

"Bushwhacked, by God," he said. "The first shot came out of nowhere."

Maddy drew her breath in sharply. "Let me see that."

"It's all right," he protested.

She ripped a strip of fabric from her petticoat. "Of course it is, Mr. Vann. Getting shot isn't anything to worry about for you big, strong men."

Hank's pale gaze drifted to John. "You're a reckless fellow," he said.

"Always have been," John agreed, sighting in on the outcropping again. "Keeps life from getting dull."

"Yeah. Takes a special kind of man to enjoy walking through a nest of rattlesnakes before breakfast every . . . Ouch!"

Maddy eased the folded fabric against his wound. "You could have let Blanche do the shooting, you know," she said.

"So she told me," Hank growled. Beads of sweat dotted his upper lip. "More than once, I'd like to add. But like I told her, as long as I'm alive, it's my job to protect her."

"That's the most ridiculous thing I've ever heard," Maddy retorted.

"Don't worry about her," John said. "She's just mad because she came all the way out here to shoot you, and now she's not going to be able to."

"Shoot me?" Hank's eyes narrowed. "What the hell for?"

"You shouldn't have taken my sister out unchaperoned," Maddy said. "It isn't proper."

Hank looked at John again. "Is she fooling?"

"I'm afraid not," John replied.

A bullet struck the trunk just above his head, then whined off into the trees. Maddy set the Colt down on her knees and reached for her reticule.

"We can't allow him to pin us down like this," she said. "Mr. Vann is going to bleed to death if he doesn't get medical attention."

John nodded. "That's my Maddy. Always practical. How many rounds do you have, my sweet?"

"Enough to keep him pinned down while you work your way behind him."

"Give me thirty seconds to get clear," he said. "Then keep shooting long enough for me to get to that rock."

He eased away from her, moving as silently as a cat. Maddy watched him from the corner of her eye as he entered a wedge of shadow at the far edge of the trees. He seemed to become part of the night, a patch of silent darkness just a little more dense than the rest. A moment later, he disappeared from view.

One in a thousand men could move like that. Derek could. Dread darted cold along her veins and settled in a lump in her stomach. She wondered exactly what John's duties had been during the war. There had been men who'd been the Yankee equivalent of Derek, men who had gone through the South like wolves—cold, silent, deadly.

If he were one of those . . . he might truly be good enough to catch her brother.

Beneath that thought, her mind registered the passing of time. Thirty seconds. Bracing the barrel of the Colt on the trunk in front of her, she fired a shot toward the top of the outcropping.

Hank shifted position to bring his own weapon to bear. He swore under his breath, and Maddy saw that he didn't seem able to lift his arm any longer. But his eyes were still hooded and flat, and showed none of his pain.

"For a minute I thought you'd decided not to cover him," he said.

Maddy glanced at him. "In our family, we do our killing openly."

"Right. Now, this thing about shooting me—"

"Shooting you was definitely on my mind," she said.

"Now, Maddy—" Blanche began.

"My sister is a grown woman," Maddy continued, ignoring Blanche's protest. "But that doesn't mean I won't protect her from anyone and anything that might hurt her."

"I'm not going to hurt her," Hank growled.

"I'm sure you don't intend to," Maddy replied, firing a pair of shots at the rocks.

The bushwhacker returned her fire. Maddy smiled when she saw the flash from the top of the outcropping; she had his position now. She fired steadily until the chamber was empty, paused to reload, then settled in to keep the man pinned down.

She couldn't see any sign of John, although he should have been plainly visible against the almost-bare ground that lay between the trees and the outcropping. If he was out there, he'd somehow become part of the landscape.

Fear lay cold in her heart. Not for Derek this time, or for Blanche. For John. It didn't matter that he was arrogant, infuriating, and dangerous to Derek. She only wanted him to be safe. The thought of him dying, of never seeing him again, never touching him or being touched by him, was simply . . . unbearable.

"No," she whispered. "Oh, no!"

The world seemed suddenly shaky beneath her. Her breath became shallow, and her pulse began to pound heavily in her ears. In all her life, she never would have expected this.

Maddy Saylor had fallen in love.

She glanced at her companions. Blanche was looking at Hank with naked love in her eyes. The emotion was so raw, so powerful that Maddy's throat tightened involuntarily.

The Saylor sisters had fallen. Love had crept into their hearts on treacherous, silent feet, and before they'd known what was happening, had taken hold. It had grown and strengthened and spread, until it had become as much a part of their being as breath and blood and heartbeat.

She hated it. This love she felt had the depth and breadth of the sky, the sea, and the land all together. It was a force beyond anything she'd ever known, and there was nothing she could do to control it.

Love would make her far too vulnerable to John Ballard, drat his tricky soul—and Derek would pay the price. Tears stung her eyes, and she dashed them away with the back of her hand.

Grimly, she took aim and fired. And again. She found herself praying for John's safety, her lips moving in silent echo of what was in her heart. He would claim her soul with his passion and the love she couldn't deny. And then he would put Derek in a cage, and rip her heart out in doing it.

Even knowing that, she wanted only to see him safe again.

"Hellfire and damnation," she muttered.

He had to have reached the rocks by now. Firing would only hinder him, so she eased the gun down to her lap. Silence settled around her like a shroud.

Then she heard hoofbeats. A moment later she saw a horse and rider thunder off toward the north. If she'd had her rifle, she could have dropped the man.

She didn't relax until she saw John drop down from the rocks and stride toward her. A cloud scudded across the moon, dousing his face in shadow. It made him look still more the predator, and reaction raced cold up her spine.

Hastily, she turned to rest her back against the rough bark of the log. If she didn't look at him, she might be able to get her thoughts—and her will—back in working order. She couldn't let him see what was surely exposed in her eyes.

Love, she thought, was the single most dangerous thing in the world.

He entered the trees a few moments later. She didn't hear him; he moved too quietly for that. But she felt him, her body registering his presence as though he'd touched her. Her awareness of anything else faded; he filled her sight, her senses, her being.

He leaped lightly over the log and joined them. Maddy was uncomfortably aware that his gaze was very intent, and focused wholly on her. *Please,* she prayed silently, *don't let him see.* It was all she could do not to cover her face with her hands.

"Looked like you scared him good," Hank said.

John nodded. "I wish I'd gotten a better look at him. But

he ran the moment I got near the rocks, and I didn't see much more than his backside as he leaped on his mount."

"I'd surely like to know who he was," Hank said.

Maddy pushed an errant curl back from her forehead. "Well, Mr. Vann, since you seem to be the one he was after, perhaps you should go through a list of your enemies."

"Too many to count," he said cheerfully. "Could have been almost anybody."

John studied Maddy. Something odd lurked in the back of her eyes. It had the look of a secret to it, and suspicion curled along his veins. Damn. He wished she would stop playing this game; just once, he'd like to look into her eyes and truly know what she felt for him.

"Well, we're not going to find out tonight," he growled. "So we might as well get Hank to a doctor and you ladies safely back into town."

Hank leaned his head back against the log, the first indication of weakness he'd shown. "Horses ran off south," he said. "I doubt my Durango's gonna go far. Chances are Blanche's mount will stay with him."

"I'll go look for them," John said. "I won't be gone long; you keep a hard eye out for trouble."

He claimed his mount and swung lithely into the saddle. Then he urged his horse into a canter and headed south.

Maddy heaved a sigh, then turned to Hank. "Mr. Vann," she said, "what are your intentions toward my sister?"

"I'm in love with her. I plan to marry her."

"When?"

"As soon as she'll have me," he said. "Tomorrow couldn't be soon enough for me."

The flat admission shocked Maddy for a moment. She glanced at her sister. Blanche's skin almost seemed to glow, as though her love shone through flesh and bone for all to see. She reached for Hank's uninjured hand, and they linked fingers as though they never intended to let each other go. The sight brought an uncontrollable tightness to her throat.

Ah, Blanche, Maddy thought, *you've set yourself up for certain heartbreak. And I, and I.*

Maddy understood Blanche's reasoning. Derek was infallible, so no one was going to catch him. Thus, the issue of Derek's freedom wasn't going to come between her and Hank.

She was wrong, of course.

"You got any problem with your sister marrying a bounty hunter?" Hank asked, his gaze direct.

"Do you think I'd object because of your occupation?" Maddy countered.

"Yes."

Another blunt admission. Although Maddy was stung by his assumption of her snobbery, she was glad to have this chance to speak her mind. "Mr. Vann, we don't come from one of those families that judge a man by either birth or occupation. We judge him by what he *is*. And if Blanche loves you, I must take your suit seriously."

Surprise flashed in his pale eyes. Then he smiled, and Maddy caught a glimpse of the man inside. His love shone out, as gentle and pure as a spring rain, and her throat tightened again. She wanted Blanche to have that kind of love; he would treasure her, protect her . . . and perhaps tear her heart out. Maddy had to know which.

"Now, sir," she said, forcing the words out. "What are your intentions toward my brother?"

Blanche drew her breath in sharply. "Maddy—"

"This is an issue that must be faced, Blanche. Neither Derek nor Papa can ask this question, so I must." She returned her attention to Hank, who'd watched their exchange with a gaze that had suddenly changed. "Mr. Vann?"

"What do you want to know?" he countered.

Maddy cocked her head to one side. "If my brother walked into these trees, what would you do?"

"I'd bring him in. Alive, for Blanche's sake."

"And if I told you that Derek has the sort of spirit that will wither away without the sun and wind and the freedom to roam?"

"Then I'd tell you he shouldn't have broken the law," he replied.

Something dark and stricken came into Blanche's eyes. Maddy had to swallow hard to keep from crying; Hank's logic was so akin to John's, so simple, male, and shortsighted.

"You will break my sister's heart," she said. "Perhaps not today. Perhaps not a month from now. But you will. For Blanche loves our brother, and she knows that he wouldn't survive that federal prison. Her spirit would wither along with his, and eventually there'd be nothing left for you."

He studied her for a long time in silence. When he finally spoke, his voice was harsh.

"You want me to stop hunting your brother?"

Maddy opened her mouth to reply, but Blanche gestured sharply, silencing her.

"No," Blanche said. "*I* do."

"Damn." Hank ran his good hand through his hair. "Blanche, if I don't get that reward, I've got nothing to offer you. With that ten thousand, we can buy us some land and—"

"Stop," she whispered. "Please, stop. He's my brother."

"I know that," he said. "I'd do anything in my power to make things be different. But I can't. You've got to understand, Blanche. I grew up hard and poor, and didn't have many choices when it came to my life. I want better than that for you and the children we're going to have. If I don't collect that reward, then I don't have anything to offer you."

Blanche looked at Maddy. Her eyes were calm now, and very sad. "This is what you've been trying to tell me all along, isn't it?"

"I'm sorry," Maddy whispered, her chest taut with pain for herself as well as for her sister. "Oh, Blanche, I'm sorry."

Blanche started to cry, that same soft, pained sound Maddy had heard so often during the war. She almost broke then, losing the shell of composure she'd clung to so tightly. She'd tried so hard to protect Blanche, and had failed so many times in so many ways.

"Hank," Blanche whispered. Reaching out, she took his good hand in both of hers. "I can't marry you."

"Damn it—"

"No," she said, gently pulling her hand from his and rising. "Let me finish while I'm able. I cannot build happiness on the foundation of my brother's ruin. I . . . I truly wish it could be otherwise. I wish we'd met anywhere but here, any time but now."

Lines of pain bracketed Hank Vann's mouth, but they had nothing to do with the bullet that had pierced his body. This wound was far deeper, Maddy knew. Tears stung the back of her eyelids—for him, for Blanche, and for herself.

"Don't do this, Blanche," he said. With a convulsive effort that brought sweat popping out on his upper lip, he tried to get to his feet. "Damn it, if I could get my legs under me, I'd damn well convince you—"

"No," Blanche said, laying her hand on his shoulder to keep him still. "There can be no convincing."

Side by side, she and Maddy faced him. The Saylors always stood together. It had brought them through adversity and joy, gain and loss and everything the world could throw at them.

"I have no choice, Hank," Blanche said. "I'm sorry."

Hearing hoofbeats approaching, Maddy cocked her pistol and moved to where she could see the newcomer. She saw John riding toward her, leading two horses behind him.

He looked as lean and handsome as a panther, and his eyes were deep and mysterious in the moonlight. She wished she could ignore the clamor of her senses. She had to. Hank Vann had offered Blanche true love; John offered only passion, and that was something Maddy could do without.

Can you? a tiny, cynical voice whispered in her mind. *Can you really? Remember how he made you feel. Remember how he tasted when he kissed you.* Ah, it was torment.

His gaze caught hers and held it. Warmth spiraled through

her body, born of the tempestuous desire she read in his eyes. With an effort of will, she forced herself to look away. She found Blanche studying her, those pretty blue eyes again awash with tears.

"Oh, Maddy," she whispered. "I'm sorry."

Maddy found her own eyes stinging for the loss of things she hadn't even known she wanted until now. Her gaze drifted back to John, who still watched her with that all-too-easily-read expression. A poignant wistfulness crept into her soul, and she was suddenly tired, so tired, of duty.

"I suppose we're not destined for happiness," she said.

Blanche took Maddy's hand. "I suppose we aren't. But we shall get through it together, as we've gotten through so many other things."

Maddy's throat was too tight for speech, so she merely squeezed her sister's hand and watched John swing down from his mount. He stood, legs spread, hands jammed on his narrow hips, and surveyed them.

"I've never seen longer faces in my life," he said.

"Bottom just dropped out of the world," Hank growled.

John studied the other man for a moment, noting the restless dissatisfaction in his face, then turned to Maddy. "What's the matter?"

And suddenly, she was blindingly furious. Furious that things had worked out this way, furious that John had to stand there looking so compellingly virile that her heart began to race, and that she wanted him despite honor, duty, and common sense.

"The matter," she replied, her voice as icy as her blood was hot, "is that men in general are fools, and the two biggest ones on God's green earth are standing right here."

Fourteen

John studied the others one by one. Hank's face was seamed with pain and frustration, and Blanche had a steely look of determination beneath a steady wash of tears. Maddy—beautiful, lush, infuriating Maddy—wore an expression of open challenge. Oh, something had happened, all right, he thought. And judging from the look in her eyes, it was destined to cause him a great deal of trouble.

He looked at Hank. "What did you do?"

"Made the wrong choice," Hank growled.

"Maybe I should shoot you myself," John said.

"Maybe you should."

"Gentlemen," Maddy interjected. "May I point out that Mr. Vann is bleeding rather badly, and that he might just die if we don't get him to the doctor?"

"I've been hit worse'n this and did just fine without a doctor," Hank retorted.

Maddy had had enough of men, and these two in particular. Twisting her hair into a tight knot at the back of her head, she fixed them with her best withering stare. "Very well. Since you don't need us, Blanche and I are heading back to town. Good night."

With a muttered oath, John bent and heaved the other man across his shoulders to lift him into the saddle. Hank didn't make a sound, but the skin around his lips turned white. Blanche made a small, constrained movement.

"Oh, Maddy," she whispered. "What shall I do?"

"We've never turned aside from someone who needs help," Maddy said. "Go to him."

Blanche nodded. Her gaze was fixed on Hank, who had begun to lean sideways in the saddle. She climbed up behind him and put her arms around his waist. Maddy turned toward her own mount, only to find herself staring into John's green-gold eyes.

"What have you done, Maddy?" he asked.

She lifted her chin in mingled surprise and outrage. "Do you think Blanche would be more willing than I to betray our brother?"

"Is it betrayal for her to love Hank Vann?"

"Yes," Maddy said, looking straight into his eyes. "When Hank Vann wants to bring Derek in either to hang or to spend the rest of his life in prison, it is a betrayal."

"It won't work, Maddy."

"What won't work?"

"Putting duty over your feelings. It won't work for Blanche, and it won't work for you. We were made for each other. Maybe in heaven, maybe in hell. And no matter what you say, we're not going to be able to stay away from each other."

Made for each other, Maddy thought. His words stirred her unbearably, because she feared he might be right. No one had ever affected her the way he did. Logic and reason seemed to abandon her when he was near, leaving her only the tempestuous need to touch and be touched.

"You are mistaken," she said.

"Am I?"

"Yes."

John studied her. He might have been concerned if he'd believed what she said. But he preferred to believe her eyes, and the smoky undercurrent of sensuality that lay exposed in those lovely blue depths. Maddy would soon find out that he wasn't quite the fool she thought him.

He'd been looking for something in his life, something that might ease the pain, something to give him a reason to look forward to the future. He'd thought to find it in his job; instead, he'd found it in Maddy. And he intended to have her. He intended to have her despite her brother, her sister, North, or South.

He swept her into his arms and placed her upon her mount. Even that brief contact made his skin tingle. To his intense satisfaction, he saw reaction flood her eyes, and knew that she felt the same.

"You won't be able to keep me away," he said. "And you won't be able to stay away."

Maddy's breath came swift and shallow. "We'll see about that," she retorted.

But her words sounded as empty as they felt, and she had the terrible feeling that they'd come back to haunt her. Then she saw the light of battle flash in John's eyes, and knew she'd just bought herself a world of trouble.

He smiled, a flash of dimples that set her heart to racing. "I suppose we will."

Maddy stood beside the table in Dr. Brennan's office and watched as he cut Hank's shirt away from the wound. The doctor's hand was none too steady, in her opinion, and alarm coiled swiftly up her spine. She glanced at John, who stood at the other side of the table, and saw her concern mirrored in his eyes.

She looked at Blanche next, but her sister's attention was completely focused on Hank. She was obviously useless for any practical purpose.

And as for Dr. Brennan, he seemed completely unconcerned that the scissors he was holding chattered like castanets. He selected a long-handled forceps, his cocks-comb of white hair gleaming in the lamplight, and probed the wound with a ghoulish sort of cheerfulness. Hank held onto Blanche's hand as though he were going over a waterfall and she his only lifeline.

"Caught yourself a good one, didn't you?" the doctor asked.

"It wasn't my . . . Ah!" The groan was wrung from him by a twist of the forceps. "It wasn't my doing," Hank growled after a moment.

"Never is," the doctor replied.

Whiskey tainted the air, and Maddy realized that the doctor had been drinking more than a little. She glanced at John again, but he merely shook his head slightly, then returned his attention to what the doctor was doing.

"Might as well tell y'all," Dr. Brennan said, edging the forceps in further. "I'm going to retire. My eyes are bad and my hands are going—"

"God damn it to hell," Hank snarled.

"—And I figure it's time for me to stop working so hard and start enjoying life," the doctor continued, giving the forceps a tug. "Whoops," he said, pulling a bloody sliver from Hank's wound. "I don't think I got it all."

"Good Gad, Doctor!" Maddy exploded. "Give me those!"

Amiably, he handed the forceps over. "See that knot right there?" he asked.

Maddy nodded, wishing she didn't. It was an ugly wound, and in a bad place. Her stomach lurched as she saw the bullet, a red, angry-looking lump in Hank's body. To get it out, she'd have to hurt him. Badly. But she'd likely hurt him less than Dr. Brennan would.

She looked up at Blanche. "Are you sure you want me to do this?"

Blanche nodded, complete trust in her eyes. The sight steadied Maddy as nothing else could have. Taking a firm hold of the forceps, she slid it into the wound and grasped the bullet.

"Are you ready, Mr. Vann?" she asked.

"Ready . . . as I'm ever gonna be," he replied.

"Brace yourself, then," Maddy said, and started pulling.

Hank's lips skinned back over his teeth, and beads of sweat popped out over his face. Maddy's vision narrowed to the single point of the wound; the sight of his pain was too much to bear. The bullet was lodged against his collarbone, and she had to twist slightly to free it.

"Ah, damn," Hank muttered.

John gripped the other man's arm hard, giving him some distraction. But his gaze remained riveted to Maddy. He saw how hard she'd had to fight to steady herself for the job, and how intensely she hated causing pain. He had the feeling that Maddy Saylor would never flinch from what she perceived as her duty, no matter what the cost to herself. It stirred him. He'd never known a woman like her; she called to everything that made him a man, and his resolve to possess her strengthened.

Some might call him obsessed. Some might simply call him a fool.

She stopped for a moment to shift her grip on the forceps, and he knew she needed time to breathe. He reached over and closed his hand over hers. Her gaze shot up to his, and he saw surprise in her eyes.

"It's all right," he murmured.

He felt her hand flex beneath his and knew she was ready to begin again. Admiration flowed through him, bright and hot as the summer sun.

"You've got it," Dr. Brennan. "Give it a good yank, girl."

Maddy didn't yank. Instead, she exerted a steady pressure, and the bullet finally slid free. Hank groaned once. His body went slack, and for a moment she thought he'd lost consciousness. Then his eyes opened, and he looked up at her.

"Thanks," he said.

"You're welcome," she replied. She glanced up at her sister. Blanche was gazing down at Hank, her heart written all over her face.

Dr. Brennan grabbed a half-empty whiskey bottle from a nearby table. He took a long swig, his Adam's apple bobbing up and down as he drank. Then he sloshed a good draft of the liquor into Hank's wound.

With a howl, the injured man jerked to a sitting position.

He swung at the doctor with his good arm, connecting a solid blow to the other man's jaw.

"I hate when that happens," the doctor said, rubbing his jaw. "Hell, man, you didn't have to get so danged feisty about it. I had to clean that out."

Hank clawed at his side, but John had already taken his gunbelt and set it aside. With another groan, he sank back down. With an effort, Maddy gathered her wits, which had been scattered completely by the doctor's actions. If she hadn't seen this . . . spectacle with her own eyes, she wouldn't have believed it.

She considered several statements, but rejected them all. There were times when silence was the only refuge allowed a lady. So she merely accepted the needle and thread the good doctor held out, and proceeded to sew up Hank's wound. She took small, careful stitches; this would be a terrible beast of a scar, but at least she could try to keep it from affecting the movement of his arm.

"Now that is pretty," Dr. Brennan observed, leaning close to watch her work.

"Thank you," Maddy replied. "I *am* a seamstress, after all." She cleared her throat. "Ah, you said something about retiring, Doctor?"

He nodded. "We're getting a young doctor from back East. Nice fellow, from what I can tell from his letters. Been doctoring a year or so, and knows all the newfangled methods of treatment. This town'll hardly miss old Dr. Brennan."

"Oh, I'm sure they will," Blanche said, her voice hardly audible.

Maddy, who wasn't capable of comment, nodded gratitude toward her sister. Blanche had always hated hurting anyone's feelings, and had a real talent for the social inexactitudes. This one, however, had strained even her abilities.

"There," Maddy said, tying off the last stitch. "I think that will do."

"Looks bad," Hank said, craning his head to look. "I'm gonna need a lot of nursing."

Blanche moved closer to him, an automatic reaction that made Maddy's throat tighten with sympathy. "I . . ."

"We'll stop in every day to check on you," Maddy finished for her.

Hank closed his eyes, looking more disappointed than tired. Maddy made note to watch him very carefully, and not because of his health. It would have been easier if she and Blanche had fallen for less determined men.

Of its own volition, her gaze went to John. He was looking at her with an all-too-easily-read expression on his face.

"So, Doctor," she said, badly needing a distraction, "when is your retirement to be?"

"Oh, a couple of months, I suppose," he said. "It's about time. These old bones just don't work so good anymore. My daughter's up in St. Louis, wants me to go live with her."

Glancing at John, Maddy realized he wasn't the least bit distracted. But the doctor had taken the bull by the horns, so to speak, and was telling the story of how his daughter had married a well-to-do beer baron in St. Louis, and Maddy was able to concentrate on that. More or less.

"Well, it's been a hell of a long night," the doctor said, his story finished. "Take this fellow on out of here so I can clean this place up."

"But Doctor—" Blanche began.

"Don't try to tell me he can't be moved," Dr. Brennan said, rubbing his jaw. "If he's got enough energy to hit me as hard as he did, he's got energy enough to get home."

"There is no home," John said. "He's been camping just outside of town."

Maddy looked at Hank, whose expression had turned guarded, then at Blanche, whose face revealed everything. So, she thought, they'd gone out to his camp intending to consummate their love. And it hadn't happened. Maddy could see that in her sister's face, too. She was suddenly, absurdly grateful to the bushwhacker for rescuing Blanche from herself.

"We can take him to our home," Blanche said.

Slowly, Maddy folded her arms over her chest. "No."

"See here, Maddy—" Blanche began.

"No."

Blanche's jaw firmed. "What do you expect? That he's going to climb back on that horse and ride out to his camp? Who's going to take care of him once he's out there?"

"Blanche—" Maddy began.

"Don't worry about me," Hank protested.

Both sisters swung around to look at him. "This is not your concern," Maddy snapped.

"The hell it isn't!"

"Hank." Blanche's voice was as flat as her eyes. "Kindly shut up."

Maddy had never actually seen someone's jaw drop open. But Hank's did now, with an almost audible click. A grim sort of satisfaction filled her. So, the big, strong bounty hunter had just encountered the steel beneath his ladylove's feminine facade. Good.

She turned back to Blanche. "You must be insane even to consider bringing him into our home. For a number of reasons, all of which you know."

Blanche crossed her arms over her chest, an unconscious imitation of Maddy's gesture of stubbornness. "I know the reasons. But I'm not going to let him sleep on the ground and risk an infection, or worse. If he doesn't come home with us, then I'm going out there to stay with him."

"Absolutely not," Maddy said.

"You're far too bossy, Maddy."

"Hear, hear," John murmured.

Maddy shot him a glance that should have burned him where he stood. But Blanche's words had shocked her out of her anger, and made her look at things with the cool logic on which she prided herself. Blanche had climbed on her high horse, plain and simple, and her determination was fueled by her love for this man. Maddy knew the extent of her sister's determination; without hesitation, Blanche would go to his camp to nurse him.

"All right, Blanche," she said. "He can stay with us until he's strong enough to ride. But not a moment longer."

Her gaze drifted automatically to John. Noting his smile, she felt alarms go off at the back of her mind. She'd fallen into a trap somehow; she could almost hear the bars clanging shut around her.

His eyes remained shuttered and secret, however, and she couldn't discover exactly what kind of trap it was.

"John, could we prevail upon you to help get Hank to our home?" Blanche asked.

"I'd be happy to," he replied, his expression suspiciously innocuous. "Maddy, can you handle his feet?"

She nodded. Moving to the table, she grasped Hank's ankles and waited for John to lift the upper body.

"One, two, three," John murmured. "Now."

They lifted Hank in a smooth, careful motion. Even so, his eyes went wide with pain. Then he passed out.

"Hank," Blanche gasped.

"Don't worry about it," Dr. Brennan offered. He drained the last of the bottle and set it on the table with elaborate, drunken care. "This way he won't be hurtin'."

"Thank you for the reassuring words," Blanche said, her tone arid.

They carried Hank down the quiet street. Dawn had just begun to stain the eastern horizon, washing a pale violet glow across the sky.

"We've got to decide where to put him," Maddy said. "It would hardly be proper to have him in the bedroom."

"We can fix up some sort of cot or something," Blanche replied. She turned to John. "I hate to impose, but couldn't you fix something up for us?"

He smiled, but his gaze remained on Maddy. "It's no imposition at all," he replied. "After all, Hank and I are getting to be real good friends. I'm planning to spend a lot of time with him during his recovery."

That was when Maddy saw the trap. And it was an inescapable one. Damn him. Damn him to bloody hell.

Fifteen

Maddy looked down at Hank, who was sleeping peacefully on the pallet they'd fixed in the front room. Pain had etched deep grooves around his mouth, making him look ten years older.

What if it were John lying there? she wondered. *How would I feel?*

Terrible. Awful. It would twist her heart cruelly to see all that heat and vitality dimmed.

Hank's eyes fluttered open. "Blanche?" he whispered.

Maddy reached for the cup of water she'd set on the table, then knelt on the floor beside him. "Blanche sat with you all night," she said. "Let her sleep."

She slid her hand beneath his head and lifted him so he could drink. Afterward, he lay watching her as she wrung a clean rag out in the basin and laid it on his forehead.

"If it wasn't for your brother—" he began.

"I've seen the way you and Blanche look at each other," she said. "If things were different, I would gladly welcome you into our family."

"Blanche said you would say that."

"Blanche is a smart woman," Maddy replied. "You should listen to her."

He shifted position slightly, and grimaced. "Damn, that hurts. Look, Maddy . . . I don't have education. I don't know how to do anything but bounty hunting. And if I don't get that reward, how am I going to take care of your sister?"

"My sister loves what's inside you," Maddy said. "As far as taking care of her, well, you've got a mind and two strong hands, and a woman who is willing to pull right along with you. That's worth far more than money."

"That's easy for you to say," he muttered. Then he sighed, and his gaze turned inward. "My Ma was twenty-seven when she died. She'd had seven children and a farm to take care of, and it just plain killed her. I watched her get thinner and sicker, and I watched the light slowly die in her eyes. There came a time when she was too tired to smile, and then she just laid down and gave up. I love Blanche too much to do that to her."

Tears welled up in Maddy's eyes. He was a hard man, made so by the hard life he'd led. But he'd just bared a piece of his soul to her, and the raw courage of that act had earned her respect more than any number of notches on his gun could possibly have done.

"You should trust yourself more," she said. "And you should trust Blanche."

He looked away from her for a moment. When his gaze returned to hers, it had become guarded again, as though he regretted his moment of vulnerability.

"I'll think about it," he said. "But I'm not long on trust."

"Now that is one trait we share, Mr. Vann."

"What are you going to do about John Ballard?" he asked.

Maddy's first impulse was to avoid the question. But avoidance sat as poorly as lying just now, and she looked him straight in the eye before answering. "I intend to keep John Ballard away from Derek any way I can."

"And?"

"And what?" She frowned, annoyed that her voice was more heated than she'd intended.

"He ain't going to go away," Hank said. "And it ain't because of your brother."

"My opinion on that particular issue isn't any different from Blanche's," she retorted.

"Yeah," he agreed. "And you've got the same chance of stayin' away that she does."

"You are on your honor, sir," she snapped.

"I got shot in the shoulder, not the head," he retorted. "Blanche made the decision to stay apart. The responsibility to make it work is hers, not mine."

"You are splitting hairs," she said.

"Hairs are all I've got right now."

Maddy studied him for a moment, wondering how and why she and Blanche had fallen in love with two such stubborn men. Ah, well, she thought, they'd get their way eventually. Saylor women could out-stubborn anyone.

Even John Ballard. Especially John Ballard.

Someone knocked at the door. A twinkle came into Hank's eyes, momentarily piercing the fog of pain. "I wonder who that could be," he said, his voice desert-dry.

"You're not very funny, Mr. Vann."

"Maybe not. But since I'm miserable, I'm sure as hell going to enjoy watching you two make each other miserable."

Maddy studied him carefully. "I'll wager he'll be the more miserable of the two of us."

He looked shocked for a moment. Then he started to laugh. With a gasp, he grabbed his injured arm. "Oh, hell, that hurts," he growled, his face taut with pain. "You know, Maddy, I believe you. I ain't never seen anything like you Saylor women, and I doubt anyone else has, either."

"Very good," she said, rising to her feet. "I'm glad you've figured that out."

Blanche came out of the bedroom. Her hair hung in a pale cloud around her shoulders, and she looked sleepy and very beautiful. Raw hunger came into Hank Vann's face, born of a man's soul-deep need for his woman. Maddy's heart turned over with sympathy for him, for he'd denied himself what he wanted most.

"Aren't you going to answer the door, Maddy?" Blanche asked.

"I hadn't planned to, no," she replied.

"Maddy." Blanche put her hands on her hips. "You know John planned to build Hank a bed this morning. Now go answer the door."

Maddy matched her sister's gesture. "You answer the door."

"John doesn't want me to answer the door," Blanche said. "He wants *you* to answer it."

"I'm not going to," Maddy said.

"You'd better come in on your own, Ballard," Hank called. "The ladies can't decide whether to let you in or shoot you."

Something hit the door with a solid thump. It sprang open, and John edged into the room. He carried an armload of boards, which he set down in the middle of the floor.

"Good morning," he called.

The cheeriness of his greeting annoyed Maddy. She didn't want to be cheerful. She didn't want to have John Ballard here at all; he shook her to her soul, and she wanted more than anything to have control over her reactions to him. Instead, she was possessed by an unwelcome, powerful stirring of her being—heart, mind, the slow molten movement of desire through her veins.

She folded her arms over her chest. Ah, she had too little defense against him today. The light slanted across his face, accentuating the hard line of his jaw and the molten green-gold of his eyes. His pupils looked strangely transparent, and she felt that if she only stared long enough, she could see straight through to his soul.

"You didn't say good morning, Maddy," he said softly.

His words broke her strange reverie. Giving herself a stern mental shake, she tore her gaze away from his. Unfortunately, however, her gaze dropped to his mouth. The resulting memories were all too disturbing; she knew how firm that mouth was, how passionate, how demanding.

It took her a couple of tries to get her voice working. "Good morning," she finally managed.

He knew what she was thinking, of course; creases appeared

at the outer corners of his eyes, and that dimple flashed again. Oh, he was a fine rogue, she thought. But her blood had begun to move more swiftly through her veins, testament to the effect he had on her.

"How's the patient today?" he asked.

"Well enough," Hank said. "Considering."

John hooked his thumbs in his gunbelt and regarded the other man. Hank lay on a double thickness of blankets, and was wrapped in what looked like the Saylors' best quilt. Blanche knelt beside him, one hand propped on the floor behind her, the other lying on his chest.

All in all, John didn't think Hank was suffering much.

"Looks like I ought to get myself shot, too," John growled.

"I'm not nearly as gentle a nurse as Blanche is," Maddy retorted.

"I'd take that chance," he replied.

Maddy smiled. "Then please, do go get yourself shot."

"It gets much colder in here, I'm gonna get a chill," Hank complained.

"Had you cooled off last night, you wouldn't be in this predicament," Maddy retorted.

"Cooled off . . ." Hank began. Then his eyes narrowed. "You got that situation all wrong, Maddy."

"Do I?"

"Yeah."

Maddy jammed her fists on her hips. "Then why did you take my sister out unchaperoned?"

"To look at the moon," he said.

Startled beyond words, Maddy stared at the bounty hunter. Did a poet's soul lurk behind that rawhide-tough exterior? It was an incredible notion. But a glance at Blanche told Maddy that it was indeed true.

It was all John could do not to laugh. Maddy had confronted Hank with her direst lady-of-the-manor pose, ready to take him to task for compromising her sister's honor, and Hank had completely disarmed her.

John grinned. A woman of Maddy's passionate nature would never have been content merely to look at the moon, and he didn't think Blanche would, either. He glanced at Blanche, who had the look of a cat on the hunt, and his amusement grew even more. Hank hadn't had a chance.

"I left the tools at the bottom of the stairs," he said. "Mind giving me a hand, Maddy?"

Maddy didn't like the lilt of amusement in his eyes, particularly when she didn't understand the joke. But she couldn't find a reasonably polite reason to refuse. Still, she remained suspicious as she headed toward the door.

John took her arm as she started downstairs. His hand was warm, even through her sleeve, and a wildfire of reaction raced through her body. She tried to control her trembling as he drew her to a halt.

"Do you want me to show you the moon?" he asked. "Is that what you want?"

"I want to be left alone," she replied.

John ran his hand along her forearm, watching goosebumps follow in his wake. She wouldn't want to be worshipped from afar; Maddy was flesh and blood and passion, and she needed to be touched, held, possessed.

By him. Only by him.

"I can't leave you alone," he said.

He stood one step below her, which brought their faces level. Slow heat coiled through her limbs. "Why must you do this?"

"Do what, Maddy?"

"Play games with my emotions only to get to my brother."

His brows contracted. "I'm not playing," he growled. "And what I feel for you has nothing to do with your brother. What I feel for you is . . ." He hesitated, not knowing the words to describe the powerful force that had gripped him the moment he'd first set eyes on her, and had only grown stronger with every kiss, every touch.

"Lust," she finished for him.

"That's not it."

"You don't have to lie to me. At least don't lie to yourself."

He considered that. With any other woman, it might be true. But the feelings he had for her went so far beyond mere lust that he didn't know what to call them, or how to manage them. He only knew that when he walked away from her he felt as though he'd left a part of himself behind.

"I wish it was lust, Maddy," he said. "Lust would be simple."

"All right," she said equably. "Then it's lust and avarice."

"Damn it, Maddy . . ." At a loss for words, he grabbed her by the shoulders. His initial impulse was to shake her until her teeth rattled, but the moment he touched her, that changed to something else entirely. He spread his fingers out over the curve of her shoulders, feeling the smooth muscles, the delicacy of her bones.

So fragile, he thought, surprised by this aspect of Maddy. She seemed so strong in her independence, her rationality, and her stubbornness. It was only in times like this—brief, but incredibly precious times—that he saw the other, more vulnerable, Maddy.

"Why do you have to fight everything?"

Maddy didn't even try to deny the charge; his touch had sent her heart into a gallop, and she knew her feelings were betrayed in her eyes. "Because that is the only way to survive. And I intend to survive."

"Who hurt you, to make you so mistrustful?"

She laughed. "Mistrust? Is this from the man who's vowed to hunt my brother down like a dog?"

"You never let up, do you?" he growled.

"No." Tilting her head back to look directly into his eyes, she smiled. "Never. And I will not allow you to manipulate my emotions in order to get to my brother."

"Derek has nothing to do with this."

"But he does."

The ever-present smolder of desire in his eyes burst into open flame, and she found herself falling helplessly into the heat. Her vision narrowed to one single point: John Ballard. His dark lashes drifted downward, and he slid his hands from her shoulders to her back, bringing her against him. Shock waves of sensation raced through her.

"I can make you forget Derek, if only for a while," he murmured.

"Stop it," she panted, trying to lever some room between them with her arms.

"Yoo-hoo, Maddy!" a female voice called.

No interruption had ever been more welcome.

"That's Dolly Mayhew," Maddy said. "Oh, Lord, I'd forgotten she had a fitting this morning."

"Damn it to hell," John growled.

But he relaxed his grip, prepared to let her go. It was for the best; he'd been so close to the edge of control that he'd actually considered taking her right here on the stairs. Maddy didn't understand the power of this passion. There was nothing gentle in it, nothing restrained. Rather, it was a savage thing, a raging, tempestuous beast that could only be tamed by having her. At least he hoped so; he didn't want to imagine what his life would be like if he had to feel like this forever.

"I'll walk you down," he said.

"That isn't necessary—"

"Maddy. Don't push your luck."

He spun her around, still keeping one hand on her arm, and escorted her around to the front of the shop. Dolly stood on the sidewalk just outside the door, looking more than ever like a man with her lanky frame and wiry grey hair.

"Howdy, Maddy," she said. "Howdy, John."

"Good morning, Dolly," Maddy replied a bit breathlessly. "I'm sorry to make you wait."

Maddy glanced at John, hoping to telegraph the suggestion to leave. But he ignored her deliberately, instead turning that Ballard charm on poor Dolly.

"Maddy tells me you're going to be the most beautiful woman at that party," he said.

Dolly actually blushed. "Wal—"

"Come in and see your gown," Maddy said, unlocking the shop.

John followed them in, as she expected. Maddy studiously ignored him as she took Dolly by the hand and drew her to the worktable, where the gown lay shimmering.

"Oooh," Dolly breathed. "But I'm such an ox. I'll tear it fer sure."

"You will not tear it," Maddy said. "And whoever called you an ox?"

"Honey, I been an ox all my life. Big and square, fit fer carryin' babies and doin' a hard day's work. I ain't foolin' myself."

Maddy picked the gown up. "Well, let's get you into it, and then we'll talk about that."

She glanced over her shoulder at John, willing him to disappear. But he'd already sat down, and propped his long legs out onto the ottoman.

"Weren't you supposed to build a bed or something?" she asked.

He looked up, cocking one eyebrow lazily. "Later. I'm dying to see this gown."

With gritted teeth, Maddy led Dolly into the fitting room and helped her into the gown. "Here," she said, turning the older woman toward the tall, oval mirror in the corner. "Take a look."

Dolly's eyes grew wide. "Holy Jesus," she gasped. "I got an honest-to-God figger! Tits and all."

Maddy lost the capacity to speak for a moment. Even when she regained it, she couldn't think of a reply to that astonishing statement. So she merely reached into her sewing basket and took out the set of tortoiseshell hair combs that had belonged to her mother.

"I want you to borrow these," she said.

Dolly recoiled as if they were rattlesnakes. "I ain't goin' to know what to do with 'em."

Maddy was ready for that. "Let me show you."

She brushed Dolly's hair until it shone, then twisted it into a knot at the back of her head and secured it with the combs. Then she pulled a few tendrils out and smoothed them into curls around her finger.

"There," she said.

Dolly stared at herself for a long time. "That's . . . that's right nice, Maddy. But I cain't do it myself."

"Well, you come to me before the party and I'll do it for you."

"That bitch Janet Taylor's goin' to be green with envy," Dolly said. Pulling her bodice out with thumb and forefinger, she peered into it. "What did you do to give me tits?"

"I, ah . . . tucks," Maddy finally got out.

"Tucks. Oh, them little things sewn in the lining."

"Yes."

"Hmmm. Zeke's goin' to be one randy ole coot after he gits a gander at me."

Maddy had finally passed beyond embarrassment. She didn't think she'd ever be embarrassed again, or shocked. "I'm glad you like it."

"I shorely do." The older woman's bright gaze met Maddy's in the mirror. "I heerd you got Hank Vann at yore place. And I cain't help but notice that John Ballard's hung right tightly on yore skirttail."

"I—"

"Honey, I ain't askin' no questions, and I shore ain't givin' no advice. But if you want a spot of peace, then git yore horse and come back to the ranch with me. Spend some time visitin'."

"Oh, I couldn't impose," Maddy said.

"Ain't no imposition," Dolly replied. She reached up to touch her hair. "You took the time to try and turn this ole sow's ear into a silk purse. That was right nice of you, and I'm grateful. Now, that's one hell of a man you got out there. But I kin tell there's problems between you, and I've had enough problems with my Zeke to know that there are times when a woman jest needs to git away and think. Men don't understand that. So I'm offerin' you the chance to git some time fer yoreself."

Maddy laid her hand on the older woman's shoulder. "You're a wise woman, Dolly Mayhew."

"I ain't lived this long fer nothin', honey. Not that I think fer one second that feller out there's goin' to jest lie back and let you git gone."

She looked at Dolly, pure mischief tugging at the corners of her mouth. "But Dolly, he committed to building a bed for Hank today. He can hardly . . . what's the term you Texans use . . . ?"

"Weasel out."

"Yes. He can hardly weasel out of building a bed for a sick man, can he?"

Dolly chuckled. "Nope."

"I can hardly wait to tell him," Maddy said. "Shall we show him the new Dolly?"

"Shore." Dolly tossed her head, making her curls bounce, then grabbed her skirts and strode out of the room.

John was still sprawled in Maddy's chair, his booted feet planted on the ottoman as though he owned the place. Oh, she was going to enjoy this. His eyes widened when he saw Dolly, and he got to his feet.

"You are stunning, Madame Mayhew," he said.

Dolly's expression grew fierce. "I ain't no madam."

"I meant . . ." He glanced at Maddy. "I meant only that you look beautiful," he amended.

Dolly seemed mollified. "All right, then. I told Maddy it was goin' to drive ole Zeke crazy."

"Undoubtedly," John said, absolutely straight-faced.

"Maddy tells me you're goin' to build a bed for Hank Vann today."

John flicked a glance at Maddy, wondering what she'd cooked up now. "True."

"Then you ain't goin' to mind if I take her out to my ranch

for a visit," Dolly said, not the slightest guile showing in her eyes.

John knew he'd been had. And by whom. He studied Maddy from beneath lowered brows, noting the gleam of self-satisfaction in her eyes.

"I'm sure you'll have fun," he said.

Maddy smiled, thinking about how Blanche was going to keep him doing chores most of the day. Few men had the moral strength to resist Blanche's gentle suggestions or the gratitude in her soft blue eyes.

"Oh, we will," Maddy said with a smile. "We will."

Sixteen

The sun burned straight overhead as Maddy rode up the slope of a ridge overlooking the road from Palatine. Off in the distance, she could see the pale cloud of dust kicked up by the stage.

She adjusted her Stetson, pulling it low over her eyes. Ali Baba shifted beneath her, obviously sensing that something was up. And indeed it was. Maddy glanced down at herself, long-legged and lean in trousers and a man's shirt. A leather vest helped hide her breasts, although she didn't plan to get close enough for that to be a problem.

She had only one goal today: Derek Saylor had to be seen. He had to be seen somewhere he was not.

"Thank you, Dolly," she murmured.

She could see the stage now as a dark blot in the center of the dust cloud. A few moments later the blot resolved itself into more defined images of the vehicle and the horses that drew it. Soon she could see the shape of the driver, and even his whip curling gracefully across the horses' backs.

Sunlight flashed on metal as the driver readied his rifle. Goodness, she thought, *folks certainly are nervous these days*. Obviously, they expected her to go tearing down this hill to chase them.

Now that, she thought, ought to show anyone with half a mind that Derek Saylor hadn't committed those robberies. No Saylor would ever work so sloppily. If she intended to rob that stagecoach, she would have lain in wait for it in one of those spots where the road bent to skirt a hill. Then she'd pop up, gather the booty, then let the crumpled landscape simply swallow her up.

But if they wanted to be chased, then far be it from her to disappoint them. She pulled her kerchief up over her nose and mouth, then dug her heels into Ali's flanks, sending him at a run down the hill that would put her a little behind the coach. The driver worked the whip more vigorously now, urging the team to greater speed.

Of course, she knew better than to put herself either in that choking dustcloud, or in the driver's field of fire. So she rode a bit behind and to the left of the vehicle. She could see the passengers staring out the windows, their mouths dark ovals of surprise and consternation.

She tipped her hat to them. There could be no doubt in their minds as to who had traveled with them for a time today.

But, since she had no intention of actually robbing the stage, it was time to go. A pair of ridges paralleled the road up ahead, one humped close upon the other's side. Perfect. There were enough folds and crannies there to hide a dozen Derek Saylors.

"Come, Ali," she said. "Let's show them that their escape is due only to Derek's lack of interest. Pride, you know."

The bay lengthened his stride, running as though all the joy in the world was held in his heart. He was showing them, well and truly. Maddy laughed, caught up by the sheer delight of it.

She twitched the reins, pulling him more to the left as he overtook the stage. Just then, the road veered right, pulling horse and vehicle apart with dramatic speed. Maddy slid the bay into a slot in the rocks up ahead, knowing it would look as though she and Ali had disappeared into thin air.

But then, disappearing into thin air was the Gray Ghost's specialty.

Maddy stroked the side of Ali's neck absently as she

watched the stagecoach retreat into the distance. The resulting dustcloud hung for a long time upon the horizon.

"Good boy," she murmured. "Let's go home now."

She walked him until he was cool, then dismounted and changed back into the riding habit she'd put in her saddlebag. Then, once more a refined Southern lady, she rode back to Cofield at a leisurely pace.

When she arrived in town, the sun hung like a crimson ball in the sky. It turned all the west-facing windows the color of blood, and even the dusty street took on a ruddy cast. Her vastly-elongated shadow preceded her, a long, drawn-out caricature of a woman on a horse.

A clot of men blocked the sidewalk in front of the sheriff's office. No doubt, she thought, news of Derek's appearance had already arrived. Zachary Marsh and two of his sons held the center of the group. Zachary, of course, did all the talking; Alf and Vince stood like sullen, blond shadows behind him. The Sheriff lounged in the doorway, his long, lanky frame as relaxed as if he hadn't a care in the world.

Maddy eased Ali closer. Sheriff Cooper was the only one who noticed her; he registered her presence with a single, encompassing glance, then returned his attention to Zach Marsh.

"We ought to form a posse," the rancher said. "Hunt that bastard down once and for all."

A murmur went through the group. Maddy knew the news of Derek's latest exploits had reached the town, of course bearing the usual embellishments. She wouldn't have been surprised to find herself described as seven feet tall and foaming at the mouth like a rabid dog.

"Good afternoon, gentlemen," she said.

Marsh twisted around to stare at her, and she knew she'd startled him. Then his brows twitched down, and resentment took the surprise from his eyes.

"Yore brother's been at it agin," he said. "As if you didn't know."

Maddy decided to ignore the latter part of his statement. "At what, Mr. Marsh?"

Sheriff Cooper answered. "Derek robbed the bank over at Victorville, Maddy."

She stared at him in astonishment. "What?"

"You don't understand plain speakin', or what?" Zachary Marsh demanded. "Derek Saylor walked into the bank at Victorville today, big as you please, stuck a gun in the teller's face, and walked off with nigh everythin' they had. Only now he's hooked up with four other bad 'uns. Got him a regular gang."

Sheriff Cooper folded his arms over his chest. "But then he rode all the way out here to chase the stage from Palatine all by hisself. Don't make sense."

"Of course it doesn't," Maddy said. "Because my brother didn't do any of it."

"There's less'n twenty miles between us and Victorville," Marsh said. "He could have made it easily."

Maddy replied, "Don't you think there's something strange going on? Why on earth would Derek come all the way out here to chase a stage, when most robbers would be in their . . . what do you call it, Sheriff?"

"Hideout."

Maddy nodded. "Yes. He'd be in his hideout counting his money rather than swanning around the countryside after stagecoaches."

"He's guilty as sin," Marsh insisted.

"Obviously, I'm wasting my breath," Maddy said, turning her mount toward the stable. "I can only hope that some day common sense will prevail. Good day, sir."

"It'll be a good day when yore brother finally swings from a rope," Marsh snarled.

Slowly, Maddy drew Ali around again. She sat for a moment studying the rancher. His eyes looked like glass beads: cold, hard, unyielding. He'd never heard an opinion other than his own, and obviously didn't expect to. She knew the good Lord had His own reasons for putting people like Zachary Marsh on this earth. Just now, however, she was having trouble understanding them.

"You've got a damned rude way of talking to a lady."

John Ballard's deep voice came from behind Maddy, and she glanced over her shoulder in surprise. He stood a little behind her, one shoulder propped with outward casualness against the wall beside him.

"What did you say?" Zach Marsh snapped.

John pushed away from the wall. "I said you've got a damned rude mouth on you, and I'm tired of it."

"Pa, are you goin' to let him talk to you that way?" Alf demanded.

"You stay out of this, boy," Zachary growled. "He's spoilin' for a fight."

"So let's give it to him."

"Didn't do so well last time," Sheriff Cooper offered.

Maddy wasn't in the mood for this. She especially wasn't in the mood to be beholden to John Ballard for defending her yet again; the price was too high. She wished she could just ride away, leaving him to enjoy the brawl he'd instigated.

But Maddy Saylor wasn't built that way. So, with a sigh, she turned to look at him. "Mr. Ballard, will you please escort me home?"

He studied her, surprise plain in his green-gold eyes. "Now?"

She nodded.

John was torn. Maddy had him so annoyed and frustrated that a good fight seemed damned inviting just now. But only a fool would ignore her request for his company, something that happened far too seldom.

"Let's go," he said.

He turned his back on the Marshes. The skin on the back of his neck crawled, as though waiting for a blow to fall. Damn. His every instinct cried out for caution. He hoped Maddy appreciated the sacrifice he was making.

Her eyes were secretive. Deep pools the color of a stormy summer sky, they revealed nothing.

"Fighting Zachary Marsh is useless," she said. "He never learns his lesson."

"Maybe I didn't want to teach him anything," he replied. "Maybe I just wanted the satisfaction of breaking his nose again."

"That's absurd."

"Where were you all day, Maddy?"

She declined to answer. She rode Ali into the livery stable and dismounted, taking her saddlebags off and setting them aside. She didn't want to forget them; John would be highly intrigued if he found men's clothing hidden away.

Mr. Haverty poked his head out of a nearby stall. "Afternoon, Miss Saylor."

"Good afternoon, Mr. Haverty," she replied, bravely ignoring the wash of whiskey fumes that assailed her nostrils. "How are you today?"

"Jest fine, ma'am. Want for me to take care of yore animal for you?"

"You're most kind, but I prefer to take care of Ali myself."

"All right, ma'am. But if you need advice or anything, you jest come to me."

Maddy, who knew more about horses than Mr. Haverty could begin to forget, smiled sweetly. "Why, thank you, Mr. Haverty. I'll be sure to do that."

John snorted, just loudly enough for her to hear. She shot him a withering glare as she took Ali's tack off and set it aside, then began brushing the dust from the horse's coat. Behind her, she heard Mr. Haverty whistling softly and off-key as he tended his equine charges. To her discomfiture, the whistling grew faint and finally faded away entirely. Haverty had slipped out, no doubt to the saloon.

Alone, she thought. With John. She kept her gaze fixed to her task, although she was overly conscious of him watching her.

"Why don't you go home?" she asked.

"Why, Maddy, you invited me."

"I only did that to keep you from getting in a fight," she retorted.

"Well, I'm here now, and perfectly happy to be. Although," he added, "I'm a bit astonished by the display of hypocrisy I just witnessed."

"That was politeness," she replied.

"You wouldn't take Haverty's advice if you were paralyzed," he said.

"That might be true. But he doesn't have to know that."

"You were protecting his feelings."

John's eyes were completely guileless, a fact that made Maddy instantly suspicious. "Ye-es."

"So regard for another's feelings might be considered a virtue?"

She'd done it now, she was sure. She just didn't know exactly where or how. "Yes," she conceded.

"Then why don't you care about *my* feelings?" he asked.

And there it was: today's trap, perhaps one of the cleverest he'd devised so far. Maddy had no intention of falling into it.

"You have no feelings," she said.

"Ah, Maddy, you know that's not so." Laughter turned his eyes molten. "You ought to give me a chance."

"To do what?" she countered.

He smiled. "Come on, Maddy. When we kiss—"

"I don't want to talk about this."

"When we kiss, it's pretty special. And you're much too honest—"

"Flattery will get you nowhere."

"You're too honest a person to deny that you enjoy it. And that's the problem."

Maddy tried to follow that bit of convoluted logic, and failed. "I don't understand what you mean."

"I mean . . ." He took a deep breath, his gaze as intimate

and warm as a caress. "That I'm always the one who starts the kissing. For once, I'd like you to take the initiative."

She stared at him for a moment, not exactly dumfounded, but definitely confused. "Did it occur to you that I might not *want* to kiss you?"

"Maddy, Maddy. Be honest. Can you really, truly say I've forced you?"

"Not exactly forced. Beguiled . . ." That was when Maddy realized her mistake, and stopped talking.

It was too late, however. She cast one resentful glance over her shoulder, only to see him looking at her with an all-too-easily-read expression.

She was beset by memories of what had happened the last time they'd met here. It would have been better had she been more . . . experienced, for then she might have been able to forget it. But that had been her first—and only—acquaintance with sensual fulfillment, and her flesh remembered what her mind did not.

He had the advantage, of course; obviously, he was no neophyte in such things. And that, more than anything, annoyed her. Actually, annoyance was far too mild a term for what she felt. Simply, she hated the thought of him doing such things with another woman.

That thought pulled her around toward him. She found herself pinned by the naked desire in his eyes. Here, in the unyielding brightness of the late afternoon sun, his passion lay raw, exposed. It wasn't a gentle thing, that desire. No. It was as uncontrollable as wildfire, burning high and hot and hard, and powerful enough to consume them both.

Both. Him and her, and both helpless to do anything about it. He didn't like it any more than she did. On her side, it was love. She hadn't expected love to feel like this, so wild and unwelcome, passionate and yet full of despair.

Maddy crossed her arms over her chest and studied him. No painful memories lurked in those eyes now; he was all male, and predatory.

A sudden, reckless impulse caught her. He wasn't immune to her, any more than she could ignore him. The desire she read in his eyes was not a comfortable thing, the sort a man can push away whenever he wanted.

This, she knew, was a woman's power over a man. *Her* power. She wanted to test that power, to make him, in some small way, acknowledge it. Letting the brush fall to the ground, she walked toward him until she stood directly before him.

"You say you're a man of your word," she said.

"I am."

"Put your hands behind your back. Promise me you'll keep them there."

He cocked his head to one side. "Why?"

"Because I asked you to."

Bemused, he obeyed. Besides, Maddy looked much too delectable standing there in a ray of bright sunlight, dust motes dancing around her, a piece of hay caught in her hair. Her eyes looked like the sea at dawn, and as deep. At this moment, he could deny her nothing.

"All right," he said. "I promise."

Maddy smiled, enjoying her power. For this moment, this tall, broad-shouldered man with the cat's eyes belonged to her. For this moment, there was no Derek, no job, no conflict. Her gaze lowered to his mouth. Tiny hairs sprouted above the well-cut line of his lips, a purely male burgeoning of beard that set her pulse beating faster.

Going up on tiptoe, she slowly eased her arms around his neck. The reaction of his body was instantaneous, and profound. Because he couldn't touch her, she felt safe. And more reckless than ever. She fitted herself to him, aware of his arousal.

They stood there for a long moment, gazes locked. The very air around them seemed almost to congeal with anticipation.

Maddy waited another heartbeat or two, savoring the sensation. The planes of his face had gone taut with desire. She

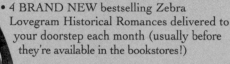

4 FREE BOOKS

These books worth almost $20, are yours without cost or obligation when you fill out and mail this certificate.
(If the certificate is missing below, write to: Zebra Home Subscription Service, Inc., 120 Brighton Road, P.O. Box 5214, Clifton, New Jersey 07015-5214)

Complete and mail this card to receive 4 Free books!

YES! Please send me 4 Zebra Lovegram Historical Romances without cost or obligation. I understand that each month thereafter I will be able to preview 4 new Zebra Lovegram Historical Romances FREE for 10 days. Then if I decide to keep them, I will pay the money-saving preferred publisher's price of just $4.00 each...a total of $16. That's almost $4 less than the regular publisher's price, and there is never any additional charge for shipping and handling. I may return any shipment within 10 days and owe nothing, and I may cancel this subscription at any time. The 4 FREE books will be mine to keep in any case.

Name _____

Address_____ Apt._____

City_____ State_____ Zip_____

Telephone ( )_____

Signature _____ LF1096
(If under 18, parent or guardian must sign.)

Terms, offer and prices subject to change without notice. Subscription subject to acceptance by Zebra Home Subscription Service, Inc.. Zebra Home Subscription Service, Inc. reserves the right to reject any order or cancel any subscription.

A $19.96 value... absolutely FREE with no obligation to buy anything, ever!

knew he wanted to touch her. She knew he wanted to crush her to him, claiming her in the most primitive of ways.

And he couldn't. Bound by his own word, he couldn't. She could do anything she wanted to him, anything at all, and he could only stand here and let her. It was a heady thought. It thrilled her to an astonishing degree.

Slowly, she rotated her hips, using her body to caress the hard shaft trapped between them. Reaction flared in his eyes, an upsurge of desire that might have alarmed her had he been free to take control. But *she* had control now.

John studied her through slitted eyes. He knew what she was thinking, the sexy little minx. She thought she was safe. He couldn't touch her, so there was no danger in this. Amusement ran though him on the wings of his desire. *Ah, Maddy, Maddy. You're playing with fire, my sweet. And you will get burned.*

"Careful, Maddy," he murmured.

"I'll be careful some other time," she replied.

Sinking her fingers into the dark wealth of his hair, she brushed her open mouth across his. It was meant to be a brief, teasing touch, a demonstration of her power. But she found herself unable to disengage.

They stood locked in desire, breaths mingling, hearts pounding in unison. John tilted his head, bringing still more contact between their mouths. Compelled by a force more powerful than her own will, Maddy moved along with him. She thrust her tongue forward, found his waiting.

And then she discovered that he didn't need his hands to make her tremble with desire; he could use his lips, mouth and tongue with devastating effect, and did.

He traced the joining of her lips with his tongue, and without thought, without protest, she opened her mouth to let him in. Still, he didn't rush. Tenderly, he tasted the sensitive insides of her upper lip, then her lower. He nibbled at the corners of her mouth until she moved her head in helpless demand for more. Only then did he claim her as she wanted, thrusting his tongue deep into her warmth. Tasting. Testing. Teasing. She sighed his name. Or perhaps he sighed hers. It didn't matter. Only he mattered in this hot, suspended moment—he and the wonderful things he was making her feel.

She slid her hands deeper into his hair. A small sound escaped him, a soft, thick sound that sent triumph spearing through her. Her knees weakened, and she found herself leaning more fully against him. He shifted position without touching her with his hands, merely leaning back to let the stall take their weight.

He bit softly at her lips, then tilted his head the other way to claim her mouth again. She met his questing tongue with her own, savoring the smooth, slick underside, then tasting the excitingly nubbled upper surface.

"Do you like that?" he whispered.

"Yes," she panted. Mindlessly.

John groaned as Maddy coaxed his tongue back into her mouth. She tasted like heat and honey and mint all rolled together, and he felt as though he'd sunk into Heaven itself. Still more heat burgeoned inside him as she rasped her tongue playfully along his. She didn't know what she was doing to him; like him, she was responding to the irresistible pull of shared desire.

God, he thought, *she is incredible!* His hands ached with the desire to touch her. But, bound by his promise, he kept them behind his back. The limitation forced him to savor other senses: the warmth of her, the fragrance of mingled lilac and woman that was bound to haunt his dreams forever, the unmistakable feel of her nipples against his chest, the heat of her breath as she sighed into his mouth.

He was rocked by the varying sensations, and it was all he could do to keep his promise not to touch her. His manhood was so hard it was actually painful. Damn. A moment more of this, and he wouldn't care where they were or who saw them. He'd lay her down on that floor and plunge into her, filling her, making love to her over and over again until he freed himself from this obsession.

A high-pitched sound speared through the haze of desire that had possessed him. It took him a moment to recognize it as Mr. Haverty's off-key whistle. With a muttered curse, he raised his head. Damn, he thought. Breaking that kiss was more painful than having a sword thrust into his gut.

"Maddy," he whispered.

She gazed up at him with passion-glazed eyes, and he knew she hadn't understood. Her mouth was still parted, giving him a glimpse of the warm, pink-tinted interior. The sight stirred him almost unbearably, and he would have liked nothing more than to dip into those honey-sweet depths again. And more.

But he couldn't. Not now. Damn it to hell.

"Maddy, Haverty's back," he said.

Reality reached Maddy in a stinging flood, and she sprang away from him. Heat raced through her, then cold, then heat again. She reached up with shaking hands to touch her mouth, which was still swollen from his kisses.

"I . . . I . . ." she stammered.

"You see, Maddy?" John asked, smiling in pure male triumph. "It's not I who holds you, but you. Be honest about it—to me and to yourself."

He was right, of course. Maddy hated him for it, hated herself for being so weak. She looked into those green-gold eyes, so infuriatingly self-satisfied and smug, and knew she'd trapped herself neatly.

Ah, but he'd made his own brand of mistake; the Saylors were not so easily manipulated. Dropping her lashes so that they veiled her eyes, she met his gaze levelly.

"Do you think to hold *me* with a kiss or two?" she asked. "If so, you are sadly mistaken. I do not deny the pleasure I feel when we touch. But it's not a binding thing."

His eyes narrowed. "You think it's mere lust," he said, anger blooming hot in his chest.

"Isn't it?"

Her heart screamed no while her stubbornness kept her silent. This was the moment for him to speak the words that would separate her from all the other women in his life.

But he didn't. He merely watched her with those secretive cat's eyes, a half-smile playing at the corners of his mouth. And even now, she wanted to kiss him again. Her body burned for him, her very skin yearning for the touch of his hands. But more than that, her soul ached for a closeness of spirit they could never share.

Then she understood. For him, it was only physical. Passion rather than love, possession rather than cherishing. Perhaps such things were different for a man. Derek had told her many times that for him, love was a matter of opportunity.

She stepped away from John, and even managed a smile. It was a relief to know, finally, how he felt. But she felt strangely empty inside, as though something important had slipped away. But she still had what she'd always had: courage, duty, and always, always, her Saylor pride. It gave her the strength to appear serene as she faced this man who could never return her love.

"Thank you for being a gentleman," she said. "Good day."

"What do you want from me?" he asked.

She lifted her chin with pride. He would never know that he'd hurt her, never know how deeply he'd managed to touch her despite her every effort to stop it.

"Nothing," she said. "Nothing at all."

Seventeen

Maddy took a deep, calming breath as she turned the corner onto Cofield's main street. It simply wouldn't do for her neighbors to see her so agitated.

And she *was* agitated. She'd thought herself in control with John Ballard. She'd thought desire could be bound, like his hands, and thus kept from touching her. She'd been wrong.

John had kept his promise. He'd played her game by her rules. It was *her* passion that had caught her, *her* weakness that had beguiled her. He'd seen her weakness and used it against her, but she was too honest to blame anyone but herself.

"Hellfire and damnation," she muttered. "What am I going to do?"

Do your duty. That is what you do best. There's safety in that, and clarity.

Maddy wanted a return to clarity. Since John had come into her life, everything had become dark and muddled. Now, however, it was time to concentrate on business. Namely, clearing Derek's name. Someone out there was playing a very dirty game, and she had to catch him.

"Hey, Maddy!"

Bill Smith's gruff voice pulled her out of her reverie. She looked up to see him waving from the doorway of his store. "Git over here!" he called. "I got to talk to you."

Maddy had become accustomed to Bill Smith's ways, although she couldn't help but think that her mother would have swooned straight away had anyone summoned her in such a manner. The thought sent amusement rippling through her, and she smiled as she made her way across the street.

He came forward to help her step up onto the sidewalk. His seamed face creased with pleasure at seeing her, and that, she reflected, was his charm. Rough charm, of course, but she'd learned to treasure it.

"Hello, Bill," she said.

He grinned at her, his eyes sparkling with humor. "I got to thank you, Maddy honey. You won me twenty dollars."

"What?" Maddy asked, completely dumfounded.

"Yep. I bet old Zebadiah Mueller that you'd shoot Hank Vann fer courtin' Blanche so hard."

"You did?" she echoed, even more bewildered than before.

"Not that I blame you none, considerin' that the feller ain't got two matches to rub together. Them bounty hunters never do. Might have figured that fine, upstanding ladies like y'all would take care of him after shootin' him." He rubbed his hands together, as gleeful as a small boy. "If I'd thought it through, I'd have bet another twenty that you'd nurse Vann back to health—if he wasn't dead, that is."

Maddy's thought processes had ground to a complete halt. "I didn't shoot Hank Vann," she said when she got her voice working again.

"You didn't?" Bill yelped.

"No. Somebody . . . now, what was the word he used . . . oh, yes, *bushwhacked* him."

"You didn't shoot him?" Bill asked again.

"No."

"Damn it all to hell," he growled. "Now I got to give the twenty back. Ain't that the worst luck?" He looked up at her, hope blooming in his face. "You don't think you could sort of shoot him real quick? It don't have to in anywhere important."

Laughter bubbled up despite her best efforts, washing away her turbulent emotions. She laughed until the tears began to

run down her face. She swiped at the moisture with the back
of her hand, soaking her glove. "Oh, Bill, you are a treasure.
Couldn't I shoot Mr. Ballard instead?"

"Nah. Accordin' to the bet, it got to be Hank Vann. Not
even in the foot?"

"Not even in the foot," she replied. "You really are a bloodthirsty thing, aren't you?"

"Hell, no, I'm a Texan," he said. "And I guess it wouldn't
be right to shoot John Ballard, seein's that he's a war hero and
all. Fer all that he fought on the wrong side. But you cain't
fault a man fer misjedgin' things like that."

"A . . . hero?"

"Yep. Sheriff Cooper did some checkin' when Ballard
showed up here, found out he was awarded the Medal of
Honor. Got hisself all shot up in the doin'." He cocked his
head to one side. "Seems he and his three younger brothers
got caught in the mess at Antietam. Youngest was the standard
bearer, got shot right off. Another brother picked the flag up
and kept on, then he got shot, and the third brother took up
and got kilt doin' it. Ballard found all three of his brothers
practically piled up together. Two of 'em died right there in
front of him. The Union line was crumbling, and Ballard went
howlin' into it, fightin' like a crazy man. Got that line held,
he did. Took six bullets doin' it."

Maddy tried to draw a breath, but it caught in her throat.
Three brothers. Ah, now she understood the raging dark thing
that came into his eyes from time to time. She glanced away
through a shattered kaleidoscope of tears. Yes, she had lost
friends, cousins and cause, and in the end had lost her home.
But she still had Derek.

And perhaps, just perhaps, she had the insight into John
Ballard she'd been looking for all along. She tried to imagine
what it had been like to watch three brothers die and to be
unable to save them. He had fought then, recklessly, hoping
perhaps to die with them.

She'd seen this in her own brother. His comrades had died,

legions of them. As his despair had grown, so had his recklessness. He'd taken more and more chances, deliberately courting death. He'd intended to spend his life as dearly as possible before joining his friends. Only he'd never died. Whether by luck or the grace of God, he'd survived. He'd become the Gray Ghost, bane to the Yankees, and no matter how reckless his exploits, he continued to get away.

They could be friends, if only they had a chance to be. But Derek and John were on opposite sides as surely as if they'd met on the battlefield.

"Maddy, you still in this here world?" Bill asked.

She blinked. "I'm here," she replied. "Did Sheriff Cooper find out anything else?"

"Only that Ballard is real good at what he does, one of Pinkerton's best men."

"That, I expected," she said. "It's only—"

She broke off as she spotted Jim Berry a short way down the street. That in itself wasn't remarkable, but he was talking to Warren Marsh, which was interesting. There was something furtive in their manner that was even more interesting. Warren and Jim Berry, she mused. Rogues, both of them, and trouble for anyone they might consider an enemy. The Saylors would certainly qualify for that honor, and so would John and Hank.

"What's the matter?" Bill asked.

"Do you know anything about Jim Berry?"

"Him?" Bill leaned over and spat on the sidewalk. "He's a hired gun. He'd shoot his own mother if he could make a dollar doin' it."

"He and Warren seem awfully friendly."

"Man like Berry ain't got no friends."

"Ah." Maddy regarded the two men who seemed so involved in conversation. "So you think he's working for Warren?"

Bill regarded Berry with a speculative gaze. "You're thinkin' that Berry might be the one who bushwhacked Hank Vann?"

"Perhaps," she said.

"Is it yore business?"

The blunt question took her aback. Tilting her head to one side, she studied the man who had asked it.

"Blanche loves him," she said.

"Ah." Bill scratched at the grizzle on his jaw. "That do make it yore concern."

Maddy nodded. "My sister has already been widowed once."

He bobbed his head, acknowledging that. "But men die all the time. Cain't get around that nohow, Maddy. And bounty huntin' ain't exactly a safe way to make a livin'. If she's goin' to be with him, she's got to understand the danger."

"But she was with him when he got shot. She might very well have taken the bullet meant for him," Maddy said.

She watched Bill's brows contract. He adored Blanche, and would if she had killed half the town with a rusty axe.

"That so?" he asked.

"That's so," she agreed.

"Hmph. You think Warren's got a grudge agin Vann and paid Berry to even up the score?"

"Remember the fight?" she asked. "John and Hank humiliated the Marshes. I think there's room for a grudge in that."

Bill grunted. "Mebbe. That ain't no reason to bushwhack a feller."

"Not for you," Maddy pointed out.

He let his breath out in a harsh sigh. "Ordinarily, I'd say that Zach Marsh would draw the line at shootin' a man in the back. But those boys of his ain't worth the paper they're printed on. They ain't got the guts to take on fellers like Ballard and Vann."

"Would Jim Berry?"

"Take on John Ballard?" Bill pursed his lips, collapsing the lower part of his face into a mass of wrinkles. "Wal, I think he'd rather shoot Ballard in the back, given the choice. A critter like Berry is like a rat: he'll run if he kin, but he'll fight if you corner him."

"Hmmm." Maddy tapped her foot restlessly, gazing at the two men from the corner of her eye. It might be a perfectly innocent conversation. But her sense of danger had been well honed, and it was shrilling alarms now.

Her nostrils flared as Berry turned away from Marsh with the air of a man who has accomplished his goal. Yes, she thought, something was definitely up. She watched as Berry untied his horse from the hitching post and climbed aboard, then sat looking down at Marsh for a moment. Then he hauled his horse around and jabbed his spurs into the animal's flanks, goosing it into a gallop.

Beast, Maddy thought, hating to see any animal be mistreated. Some men treated their horses with appalling callousness, using them up and discarding them without a thought. She lifted her chin in sudden decision.

"Bill, don't tell anyone I've gone," she said.

Alarm sparked in his eyes, and he grasped her arm hard. "Now, Maddy . . . You ain't fixin' to do what I think yore fixin' to do, are you?"

"Yes, I am," she said, perfectly calm.

"You cain't."

"I can, and I will." She extricated herself gently, then patted him on the hand. "If I'm not back by dawn, you go tell Blanche where I've gone."

"Dawn!" he yelped.

"Now, don't you worry," she soothed. "I'll be perfectly all right."

"You're crazy, that's what. You made Jim Berry look like a fool, and he ain't goin' to fergit it. That's one nasty hombre, and he ain't got no respect fer women. You ought to talk to some of the gals at the saloon, if you want to know how he treats women."

"I'm well aware of Mr. Berry's proclivities," Maddy said. "Nonetheless, I will follow him. Something's up, Bill. I don't intend to lose this chance to find out what it is. And you remember this: if Berry is being paid to take care of grudges, then do you think Blanche and I are safe?"

"Wal—"

"Of course not," she interposed smoothly. "I have to find out what's going on."

"Goddamn it," he growled.

Maddy smiled. "Trust me, Bill."

"Goddamn it to *hell*," he snarled. "You don't got the sense God gave a prairie dog. If you did, you'd go tell John Ballard what's goin' on. He kin handle Berry."

That was exactly the wrong thing to say. Maddy studied Bill for a moment, struggling with the sudden pinwheel of her emotions. She didn't want to go to John Ballard for help. She'd rather be drawn and quartered than ask for his help.

She looked down her nose at Bill. "*I* can handle Mr. Berry, thank you," she said, turning away.

"Yeah," Bill growled. "But kin you handle John Ballard?"

She cast a glare over her shoulder that should have withered him like a plucked daisy. But he merely grinned at her, and she could only fume inside.

Handle John Ballard? Of course she could; she was a Saylor.

She gave Berry enough time to get out of town before following him. She took Blanche's horse this time; Ali had been ridden hard once already today, and she didn't want to risk him.

The setting sun turned the hills scarlet as Maddy followed Jim Berry's trail. She'd been keeping her distance, but the dying light laid long shadows across the land, offering enough cover to narrow the gap between them.

Berry acted as though he didn't have a care in the world; several times, he allowed himself to be silhouetted atop one of the ridges. Watching him, she smiled. This was so much easier than swanning around the Virginia countryside with half a hundred Yankees in pursuit.

The light darkened to magenta, then violet. Soon it was too dark to see either Berry or the trail any longer, and she was forced to stop. Frustration coiled in her belly. She didn't know this area well enough to chance moving now; if Berry did, then she could lose him completely.

"Drat it all," she whispered, sliding down from the saddle to give the horse a rest. The gelding cropped at a clump of nearby grass, then raised his head to nuzzle her shoulder.

Well, she'd been taught never to waste time, so she set about making herself into Derek Saylor. She pinned her hair in a tight coil around her head, then reached up to collect her men's clothing from the saddlebags. But the saddlebags weren't there. She sighed, belatedly remembering how she'd tossed them into the far corner of the stall to keep them from arousing John Ballard's curiosity.

"It takes more than that to foil a Saylor," she muttered.

She slipped off her petticoats and stuffed them into her saddlebags, then twisted her skirts up so that they resembled loose trousers. Crude, but it would do.

"After this is all over, my sweet brother," she muttered, "I hope you find something very good to do with your life."

Light flickered up on the ridge where she'd last seen Berry. She heaved a sigh of relief. Evidently he'd decided to make camp for the night, and all she had to do was wait until he started moving again. She took the horse's saddle off and tethered his reins to a nearby tree so he could reach some grass.

There could be no campfire for her, so she resigned herself to spending a chilly and hungry night. That, too, was something she'd done many times in the past. Somehow, it had seemed more exciting during the war; now, it was merely an inconvenience that had to be borne. Blanche would worry, of course. But she would worry in silence, knowing that there was probably a very good reason for Maddy's absence.

Maddy sat cross-legged on the ground, settling her back against a nearby rock and her pistol in her lap. She didn't mind sleeping in the open as long as her back was covered. That, too, was a spiritual leftover from the war.

The breeze drifted across her face, stirring the wisps of hair that had escaped their pinnings. She lifted her chin, enjoying the cooling touch of the wind. The smell of dust and wood smoke hung in the air, exotically flavored with the scent of bluebonnets. She drew a deep, appreciative breath. Virginia was a green, gentle place. Beautiful, yes. But Texas had a wild beauty all its own.

She loved it here. It was a surprise to her; she'd thought never to recover from the loss of Tallwood and everything else she'd known. But this place caught at the heart like a cyclone, spinning its wild appeal straight to that recklessness that was the bane of her nature.

And the men . . . the men matched the place. They'd come to a land that required guts and grit to tame it, guts and grit to keep it. She didn't know what Montana was like, but if it produced a man like John Ballard, it must be very much like Texas.

Ah, John Ballard . . . he drifted uninvited into her mind as softly and insidiously as the wind. She would have liked to banish him. But just as in real life, he refused to be gone. So he stayed with her, blatantly arrogant, and dared her to throw him out.

And she couldn't. Simply, he was the most man she'd ever met. Her flesh retained the memory of his touch as though it had been burned in. Goosebumps washed along her arms, and a sweet, treacherous burn settled deep in her belly. He'd trained her to this with every touch, every kiss. Unconsciously, she shifted her hips, a primitive feminine response that was as unwelcome as it was irresistible.

She could almost feel the slide of his palms against her skin. He had a magical touch, an uncanny ability to draw from her things she'd never considered giving any man. He didn't even demand them. No, her spirit leaped to obey the desire in his eyes, and she didn't seem to have the strength to keep it from happening.

Her eyes drifted closed. Oh, Lord, she wished she could think about something else. But her desire had come to dominate her world for a while, and desire was inextricably bound to John Ballard. She'd experienced such exquisite pleasure with him. Even now, her nipples tightened into almost painful nubs as she remembered how he'd worshipped them with his hands, his eyes, his mouth. She knew there was more, much more. He'd burn pleasure into her very soul, for his touch was like fire. She'd go up like a torch, and she would never be the same.

Her mother had known this. Every time Papa had touched her a certain way, her eyes would turn starry. Then, Maddy hadn't understood what had been between her parents. But now she did. Oh, she did.

"Why?" she whispered. "Why him?"

Her only answer was the slow stirring of heat in her blood, the aching heaviness in her breasts and her loins. And this was not all of the flesh; she was also possessed by an ache that was heart-deep, soul-deep, that could only be assuaged by the man who'd caused them. She wrapped her arms around herself, a feeble attempt to keep her churning emotions in check.

Relentlessly, she pushed the smoldering desire away. She couldn't—wouldn't—do anything about it in any case, and she was only tormenting herself with wanting things she couldn't have. Her serenity had been hard won, and she wasn't going to allow John Ballard to take it away from her. He wasn't her business tonight; Jim Berry was, and wherever his destination might be.

She opened her eyes and studied the campfire flickering ahead. Berry seemed to have settled in; she didn't expect to have to move again until dark. Pulling her blanket up around her shoulders, she wriggled into a more comfortable position against the rock. Behind her, she could hear her horse cropping contentedly at the grass.

Her discontent faded to a dull ache deep in her chest. Perhaps it would never leave her completely now. *Ah, well, you never expected contentment,* she thought, yawning. *As Derek always said, one could hope for nothing better than a wild ride through life, an honorable death, and a clever epitaph for one's descendants to puzzle over in years to come.*

As her eyes drifted closed again, a single thought shot with incandescent clarity through the sleep-fog that began to shroud her mind: Derek's view was too simple. Too simple by far. He'd played at love, charming his way into women's beds, women's hearts, but always remaining the will-o'-the-wisp. He'd never known this pleasure-pain, this exquisite passion that could make the most timid woman reckless, this terrible stretching of the heart and soul, this need that grew stronger with every passing day.

Derek had been lucky.

Oh, Lord, she didn't want to think anymore. There were too few answers to her thoughts, too few solutions to the problems. So, as sleep pressed more heavily upon her, she let herself drift unprotesting into its lulling arms.

John, a small, treacherous voice whispered deep within her. *John.*

Then someone clamped a hand over her mouth.

Her eyes flew open, and she lunged forward against the restraint. But she was dragged back and slammed against the rock so hard the breath was knocked out of her. Gasping for breath, she still managed to reach for her gun.

But it had either fallen or had been taken from her lap, and her captor held her so tightly she couldn't move. Fear sparked along her nerves like hot quicksilver as she realized just how helpless she was.

"So," Jim Berry growled in her ear, "Here's high-and-mighty Miss Saylor, come to visit me way out here. I guess you jest had to be alone with me, huh?"

Maddy reached up and dragged his hand away from her mouth. But he only shifted his grip to her throat, and she sat very still at the implicit threat in those iron-hard fingers.

Berry laughed, a thick, coarse sound of cruel triumph that sent another wave of fear coursing through her. This man did not understand honor or even mercy. And now, unarmed as she was, she'd put herself completely in his power. He knew it, too; his hand tightened on her throat just enough to hurt. She stiffened her spine, refusing to give him the satisfaction of knowing how thoroughly he frightened her.

"Take your hand from me," she said with icy dignity.

Again, Berry laughed. And again Maddy endured that sweeping rush of fear.

"Oh, lady," he said. "You made a big mistake follerin' me out here, you surely did."

Eighteen

"How . . . ?" Maddy gasped.

"D'you think you could trail *me* without gettin' caught?" he hissed into her ear. "I spotted you right off."

With all the disdain she could muster, she turned her head enough to look at him. Since he didn't loosen his grip on her hair, the movement caused her considerable pain. She wasn't about to show it, however, nor give in to it for one moment.

Berry's eyes looked like hollow pits in the darkness, the moustache a slash of black across his face. It wasn't a reassuring sight. Maddy turned her head a fraction more and stared challengingly into those empty-seeming sockets.

"You couldn't spot a bull in a henhouse," she snapped.

"But *I* can."

The new voice came out of the darkness behind her. A stick popped as the newcomer moved toward her. Finally, he came into her field of view.

She let her breath out with a harsh sound of surprise. Gordon Marsh. Not Warren, she thought, but Gordon. She wouldn't have expected it, for Gordon was the only one of the Marsh boys who'd showed any sort of taste for education.

He seemed the perfect foil for Berry's darkness; his blond hair gleamed in the starlight, and the faint illumination erased the cast of discontent from his features. He seemed almost pretty. But there was nothing pretty about the glitter of excitement in his eyes.

There was something sly in that glitter, something . . . shad-

owy and sick. Maddy felt her stomach lurch, as though it had
suddenly swapped ends.

"Do you always accost women in such a rude way?" she
asked, putting on a bravado she didn't feel.

He smiled at her, a flash of big, square teeth just like his
father's. The sight sent chills crawling up her spine. "We
Marshes always seem to be rude when it comes to the Saylor
women," he said. Still smiling, he surveyed her from head to
toe. His gaze held dislike and a smooth, malicious triumph.

"Now, Miss Saylor, why don't you tell me what you're doing
all the way out here?"

"She was follerin' me," Berry said.

Gordon's pale eyes caught the light oddly. "I'm the one who
told you she was following you."

"So?"

"So keep your mouth shut if you don't know what everyone
else is talking about."

Berry's grip on Maddy's hair tightened, and pain exploded
along her scalp and ran in hot, stinging torrents down her neck.
She came up on her toes in an attempt to ease the strain.

Gordon grinned, crossing his arms over his chest. "See,
Maddy? My good friend Berry don't much care who he hurts,
as long as he hurts somebody." His smile faded. "Now, tell
me why you thought you needed to follow him."

"I'll be happy to," she said, "as soon as you tell me who
tried to bushwhack Hank Vann last night."

Both men started to laugh. Maddy watched Gordon's Adam's
apple bob up and down and wondered exactly what they would
do to her. Whatever it was, she didn't think she'd like it.

"Well, aren't you the clever one," Gordon said, still chuckling. "Sure, I took a couple of shots at Vann. Actually, I paid
Jim here to do it, but he decided to spend his evening at the
saloon instead of earning his money."

"Told you I'd get to him," Berry growled.

Gordon shrugged. "The chance came, and I took it. You
should thank me for doing it, Maddy. For the sake of your

sister's virtue. It looked like things were getting pretty hot between her and Vann when I shot him."

"If I thought Hank Vann needed killing, I'd do it myself," Maddy retorted. "But I'd face him directly instead of shooting him when his back was turned."

Berry used his grip on her hair to drag her to her feet. Maddy, determined not to give them the satisfaction of hearing her scream, gritted her teeth until the pain in her jaw was worse than that in her scalp.

"Bitch," Berry snarled.

"That she is," Gordon agreed. "But now we've got to figure out what to do with her. What do you think we should do with her, Jim?"

With a thick, coarse laugh, Berry pulled Maddy tightly against him. He was aroused, and she strained forward in outrage as his erection pressed into her buttocks. True terror beat frantic black wings in her mind, for she knew that these men enjoyed giving pain.

And they'd see to it that they gave her plenty.

"Mebbe she's one of them women that enjoys bein' hurt," Berry said, licking her ear. "I know plenty of that kind."

Gordon moved closer, so that his chest nearly touched Maddy's. "Is that right, Maddy?" he asked, still more glitter coming into his eyes. "Are you one of those women who like being hurt?"

Maddy knew that any answer would only gain her more pain. These men wanted fear. Beasts, both of them. Gordon was the worst; Berry, at least, was openly a brute. Gordon played the part of dutiful son and good citizen, while all the instincts of an animal raged within him.

They wanted her to cry out, to beg for mercy they didn't intend to give. So she said nothing, knowing that that, too, would cause her pain.

A moment later, however, she learned that there were worse things than pain. Berry wound his hand more tightly into her hair to anchor her in place, then slid his other hand down to her breast.

Gordon Marsh looked right into her eyes and laughed. She held herself stiffly, her body still, her mind shrieking with mingled outrage and disgust. Something very savage roused in her; if she could have, she would have killed them where they stood.

"You like that?" Berry's voice rasped harshly in her ear. "You like that?"

Maddy squeezed her eyes closed to hide an involuntary rush of tears. They would see no weakness in her. No matter what happened, no matter what they did to her, she wasn't going to cry.

But the brave pose was only on the outside. Inside, horror squeezed her chest and sank clammy talons into her guts. Gordon pushed Berry's hand away from her breast, but only so that he could fondle her himself. He kneaded the tender flesh so hard she had to come up on her toes to keep from crying out. And he laughed. He caressed one breast, then the other, always with brutal force, always with pain.

Maddy tried to make herself go away, to shut herself away from what was happening to her body. If she didn't, if she allowed herself to truly feel what he was doing to her, she'd begin to scream.

"My, my, my," Gordon murmured, leaning forward to suck at her bottom lip. "Those are some fine tits you got in there. No wonder Ballard's been following you around like a hound after a bitch in heat."

Berry laughed. "That he is. He must really like what she's been givin' him."

"Is that so, Maddy?" Gordon murmured, pulling at her lip with his teeth. "Well, we're going to get ourselves a taste of what he's been getting. Mmmm. I've got to admit, you're one fine, fine piece of woman once we get that adder's tongue stilled for a change."

This can't be happening, Maddy thought frantically. *Oh, please, this can't be happening!*

But it was. Maddy's spirit rebelled against it, and against her own helplessness. She'd always been able to protect herself. She'd always expected to be able to. Dying didn't frighten her as much as enduring what these brutes would do to her.

"You'll never get away with this," she snapped.

"Sure we will," Gordon said. "Folks in Cofield have known me since I was knee-high to a grasshopper. You tell anybody that I touched you, and I'll just say you wanted it. Hell, after the way you and Ballard have been carrying on, people aren't going to think anything but that you're a hot piece that can't leave the men alone."

"They won't!"

"They will," he said, and his smile was an insult. "People always do. My pa owns half the county, and he's goin' to own a hell of a lot more before he's done."

Berry rubbed himself against her back, and Maddy bucked in a vain attempt to get away. But with Gordon in front and Berry behind her, there was nowhere to go.

"Oh, woman," Gordon muttered, scraping his hands down her breasts. "You sorely need a comeuppance, and I am really going to enjoy giving you yours."

"We're goin' to enjoy it," Berry said.

"Sure," Gordon agreed, his voice thick with arousal. "But I'm first."

"Why should you be first?" Berry demanded.

"Because I'm paying you," Gordon retorted.

"Ain't gonna work, Marsh. After last night, I owe her a taming, and I'm damn well gonna give it to her." With a groan of arousal, Berry pushed Gordon's hands away from Maddy's breasts, then replaced them with his own.

"Hey," Gordon snarled.

He tried to pull Maddy away from the larger man. Berry hauled her back with one arm around her waist, pushing his employer away with the other.

"Wait yore turn," Berry growled.

Gordon surged forward. He threw a punch at Berry that nearly whistled past Maddy's cheek. A solid thump of bone on flesh followed. Berry's grip on her waist eased.

Now! Maddy thought. She thrust her knee straight into Gordon's groin. His eyes rolled upward until there was almost nothing but whites exposed, and then he started to sag. With all her strength, she jammed her elbow back into Berry's solar plexus.

His hands fell away from her as his breath went out with a loud whoosh. She leaped toward her horse, toward freedom. She almost made it. Then Gordon grabbed her by the ankle, bringing her to the ground with a force that drove the air from her lungs.

"No," she gasped, kicking at him with her free foot. Oh, if only she had her pistol!

Gordon swore. Grasping her skirt with one hand, he dragged her toward him. Frantically, Maddy grabbed at the grass, trying for any leverage with which to escape.

Then Jim Berry loomed over her, his face contorted with pain and rage. He backhanded her hard. Pain exploded along her cheekbone, and dark spots jagged across her vision. Her head spun.

Both men bent over her now. Gordon Marsh tore her blouse open, then ripped the chemise from her body.

"Hoo-ee," Berry muttered. "Those are right fine—"

Maddy kicked out again, nearly connecting with Gordon's belly. Cursing, Berry hit her again, this time on the other side. The world spun wildly. But Maddy didn't stop fighting. Couldn't stop. For to stop meant to accept what these beasts were doing to her, and for that they'd have to kill her.

"Damn," Gordon panted, pinning her ankles with his hands. "She is one feisty piece of ass, ain't she?"

Berry grabbed her hair again and slammed her head against the ground. But the pain, instead of cowing her, triggered a wild explosion of anger. This was the Saylor battle-rage, high and hot. She'd heard tell of it, but had never expected to feel it herself.

Pain faded away in a fine red mist of fury, and her vision narrowed to the two men who were tormenting her. Touch her, would they? Hit her? Rape her? No one ever treated a Saylor like this, not and get away with it. Pride and temper, bred into her through a dozen generations, sent a stinging tide of fury through her brain.

She cried out for the first time, but it was the fierce, high call of a falcon. Tearing free of Berry's grip on her hair, she surged to a sitting position and punched Gordon in the nose with all her strength. Blood spattered outward in a most satisfying spray. Howling, he reared backward, clapping both hands over his face.

"She broke my nose," he wailed. "The fucking bitch broke my nose!"

Berry's hard hands closed on Maddy's shoulders so hard she felt her bones creak. He dug his fingers cruelly into her flesh, and jagged shards of pain shot down her arms.

Gordon dropped his hands. Blood streaked the lower part of his face, turning it into a frightening mask. His eyes had turned cold and flat, and much less than human. She knew then that they would kill her, and that by the time they did, she would be very glad to die.

Inexplicably, John's face swam into her memory, and regret tinged the despair that had claimed her heart. There were so many things that might have been. Good things. Perhaps if she'd given it a chance . . .

"You're going to pay, woman," Gordon growled. "You are really going to pay."

"Quit with the talk. Let's git on with—" Berry's voice trailed off in a grunt.

His hands were torn from Maddy so abruptly that she staggered and nearly fell. She saw Gordon's eyes widen, then heard the solid smack of a fist on flesh.

"Bastard," a man growled.

John. Maddy knew that voice better than she knew her own; her heart leaped with hope and something that almost felt like awe. She didn't know how this had happened. Perhaps it had been only an accident, or perhaps a miracle. But he had come when she needed him most, and she would remember this moment for the rest of her life.

Snarling, Berry hit John in the chest with a force Maddy could feel. John didn't even blink. Cold fury darkened his eyes, and Maddy realized with a thrill of dread that he hadn't even felt the blow.

Berry struck at him again. John caught the blow on his forearm, knocking the fist away, then grabbed the other man by the throat with an implacable, white-knuckled grip. Berry's breath constricted to a wheeze. He pummeled John about the head and shoulders, but he might as well have beat his fists against a rock. John didn't waver, didn't even react.

Catching a glimpse of movement from the corner of her eye, Maddy swung around to look at Gordon. Time seemed to wheel into slow motion as he drew his gun and took aim at John. She felt the air rushing into her lungs as she drew breath.

"Look out" she shrieked.

John released Berry and drew his gun in one swift, deadly movement. The shot echoed through the hills, and Maddy's heart rolled with it.

A hole appeared in Gordon's forehead. He held his gun straight for a moment, then slowly, almost carefully, lowered his arm. Then he keeled over onto his side.

Another shot rang out. Maddy whirled to see Berry listing to one side like a ship about to go down. He, too, had drawn his pistol. But he'd been too late; a dark stain marred the front of his shirt and spread rapidly until it covered most of his chest.

John swung around toward Maddy. His gaze was raw, terrible, filled with a rage that matched her own. In this single, staggering moment, they'd become inextricably entwined.

Then her gaze shifted to Jim Berry, who'd managed to remain on his feet. The muzzle of his pistol wavered a bit, but hadn't lowered. Suddenly, her vision clarified to a single point: the flex of his tendons as he tightened his finger on the trigger.

She sprang toward Gordon Marsh's body. Snatching the gun from his lax hand, she raised it and fired. John's pistol roared a heartbeat later.

Blood spattered from Berry's chest as two bullets hit. His arm went up in a convulsive gesture, and his pistol went slinging off into the darkness. Slowly, horribly, he fell, toppling all in a piece like a tree cut down.

John stood watching for a moment, his chest rising and falling as though he'd run a mile. Then he looked at Maddy. For once, his eyes hid nothing from her. She gazed straight into a maelstrom of emotion—feelings as deep and powerful as the sky itself. Pain and despair, anger and outrage . . . he looked like a man who'd almost lost something important, and was just now realizing how precious that something was to him.

It might not be love. But now, in the raging tumult of her own feelings, it was enough.

She took a deep breath, trying to regain her emotional balance. But the wildness in his eyes shattered her, and she seemed to have lost the ability to form words. She began to shake so badly that she had to let the pistol drop to the ground. Then, forced by an urge she didn't bother to reject or repress, she held out her hand to John.

He came to her instantly. Drawing her into his arms, he held her against him with a tenderness that made her breath catch in her throat.

"They were going to . . . going to . . ." she began.

"Shhh. Everything is all right now," he murmured, spreading his hands out across her back.

She nodded, letting her head fall forward until her forehead rested on his shoulder. A deep, shuddering sigh shook her. "How did you come to be here?"

"Bill got worried and came to me," he said. "Maddy, what possessed you to do such a dangerous thing?"

"I thought. . I thought I could find out who bushwhacked Hank," she said. "And I did. It was Gordon."

"To hell with Gordon. To hell with Vann," he growled. "Hank's well able to take care of himself. Now, let's get out of here."

"Back to town?" She was surprised that her voice shook so badly.

"Just away," he said, scooping her into his arms and carrying her toward the flickering glow of Jim Berry's campsite.

The horse whickered behind them. John whistled, short and sharp, and Maddy heard the hoofbeats as he followed them. Maddy sighed and laid her head on John's chest. For the first time in her life, she was content to let someone else take care of things.

"It's going to be all right," John murmured, his voice rough with emotion.

She drifted off to a hazy spot, lulled by the rhythm of his footsteps. It felt good to be safe, good to be with someone she could trust to protect her. For once, she didn't care whether or not he was hunting Derek; he'd come to her when she needed him, and he was with her now. It was enough.

A sudden shifting of position roused her, and she realized they'd reached the camp. A fire burned brightly, warming her chilled skin as John set her on a blanket beside it. She scrubbed her hands over her arms as though to wash away the memory of what had happened.

John studied her for a moment, gauging the emotions in her eyes. Another woman would have been hysterical. But Maddy kept it all inside, for to do otherwise would be to admit weakness.

Damn her. He wanted her to need him. He wanted to know she was *capable* of needing him. He'd never given a damn about such things before, but everything had changed for him the moment he'd met her. Now, he wanted more. If she hadn't been through hell tonight, he'd have been tempted to shake her until her teeth rattled.

But she *had* been through hell. And the violence of his own emotions made him all the gentler with hers, this woman who clutched so tightly to her own strength to keep from admitting, even to herself, that she might need him.

His gaze dropped to her chest. Her breasts were bare beneath the tatters of her blouse, and bruises were beginning to darken upon the pale skin. The sight angered him still further, but also created a deep, abiding tenderness in him.

"Maddy," he said, reaching to cup her cheek in his hand. "Oh, God, Maddy."

He grasped her shoulders. Maddy, who hadn't made a sound of pain in front of her attackers, cried out as he touched her sore flesh.

John pulled her blouse down from her shoulders, drawing in a long, harsh breath when he saw the deep bruises marking her skin.

"Don't," she said, plucking at the fabric in distress.

"Don't what?" he growled. "Don't try to find out how badly you've been injured? Damn, woman."

Ignoring her protests, he stripped the ruined blouse from her so he could assess her injuries. Rage bloomed in his brain, seeping down his arms to make his hands shake.

They'd hurt her. They'd touched her. And they'd intended to do more. "Those bastards," he raged. "Those goddamned bastards!"

Shame, shyness, caution had all been burned out of Maddy. She didn't even try to cover herself as she met his gaze. "They didn't take me," she said. "And if they had, they wouldn't have broken me."

"God, Maddy," he growled. "You don't give an inch, do you?"

That made her lower her gaze. "I can't. Ever."

He let his breath out in a sigh of exasperation. How was he

going to reach her, he wondered. How could he make her *see* how powerful this thing between them was?

Gently, he ran one fingertip over a burgeoning bruise on her cheek. His hand shook, and he slowly closed it into a fist. He felt savage, primitive, uncontrolled, as though all civilization had been stripped away. He felt capable of tearing the hills asunder in his outrage.

"I would have killed them for even looking at you," he growled. "For this . . . I should have killed them slowly, with great pain. I should have—"

"Shhh." Maddy laid her fingers across his mouth. "Then you'd be as much a beast as they, and I wouldn't want that of you."

"What do you want of me, Maddy?" he said, his voice harsh because he knew he would give her whatever she asked for.

So many responses ran through Maddy's mind, things she should ask for, things she would want later. But her assumptions of the world had been shattered tonight. No longer could she think of herself as invulnerable. No longer could she assume that as long as she had her wits and Papa's pistol, she could handle anything or anyone.

Quite a revelation for a Saylor.

She couldn't seem to stop trembling. A wild tumble of emotions raced in a torrent through her, spinning her like a child's top. She felt as though she were flying apart into a million pieces, and had no way of stopping it.

What did she want of him? So many things she didn't understand, so many things she didn't even know the names of. Just now, she had to trust him to know better than she did.

She looked into his eyes. They held the firelight in a dozen tiny, leaping flames that echoed the wild, unnamed emotion within her. He would know. He had to know.

"Hold me," she whispered. "Just hold me."

Nineteen

John drew his breath in sharply as Maddy raised her gaze to his. Tears shrouded her beautiful eyes, turning them indigo. This, at last, was what he wanted from her: to be needed. He didn't want to take her independence or tame her fiery spirit. He simply wanted her to need him.

"Maddy," he said.

Tenderly, he folded her against his chest. The depth of his emotions astonished him. He'd never felt this way about any woman, had never expected to. Gone was the man who'd played at love, banished by Maddy's simple declaration of need. He wanted to keep her safe, he wanted to make her trust him, he wanted to hold her like this forever.

His hands trembled as he spread them over the smooth, silky skin of her back. Her body felt too fragile to house that indomitable spirit. In all his life, he'd never known a woman with such strength of character.

And she needed him. Her vulnerability was a gift he hadn't expected to receive, and he vowed to cherish it.

She began to cry. It began with a tremor, a faint, swift twitch of muscles beneath her skin. He didn't dare move, hardly dared breathe lest he startle her. Moisture soaked the front of his shirt to dampen his skin, hot, silent tears torn from a woman unused to crying. A woman who perceived tears as weakness, and who was less afraid of pain than of being seen as weak.

But still she cried. Helplessly, silently, and for much more than just what had happened tonight. John wondered how long it had been since she'd last had the luxury of tears. A long time, surely. Maddy wasn't one to cry as long as there was a battle to be fought, and she hadn't stopped fighting since the war began.

She took a deep breath, shuddering hard beneath his hands. For a moment he thought she'd finished. Then she half-curled around him, cupping his hip with her legs, her arms going tightly around his waist, and began to cry openly.

It was an admission of vulnerability he hadn't expected, and it affected him powerfully. He felt a great wrench in his chest, as though his heart had leaped from its moorings. He buried his face in the luxuriant hair at her temple, breathing in the scent of lilacs and Maddy as though to imprint them in his soul.

"It's all right, Maddy," he murmured. "Get it out. Get it all out. I'll keep you safe."

Maddy hung on to him as though he were her only anchor. She cried for her mother and father, for the loss of so many friends in the war, for the home she would never see again. She cried for Derek and Blanche—and yes, for herself—and the mess all their lives had become. So much pain came rushing through her, to flow out and away in a hot stinging flood of tears.

Through it all, John held her. He demanded nothing, only held her. And for the first time in a very long while, she did feel safe. Only now did she realize the weight of the burden she'd been carrying since her mother had died. She would have to take it up again, of course. But for now, for this brief, precious interlude, she could lay her burdens down.

It took her a long time to stop. Finally, the sobbing eased, and reason seeped back into her mind. She discovered that John had shifted her somehow during the storm of tears. Now she lay across his lap, her head pillowed on his upper chest so that she could feel the beat of his heart against her cheek.

She became suddenly, painfully aware that she was naked from the waist up, and that she had revealed a part of herself to him that she'd never showed anyone. Even Derek and Blanche thought of their sister as invincible. Practical Maddy. Capable Maddy. The one who fought all the battles, handled all the problems, and never needed anything from anyone.

But oh, she didn't feel practical now. She felt as though she'd been shattered, broken like glass in the terror and pain of the night's events, and had been put back together in a whole new way.

This new Maddy had no defenses against John Ballard. She knew only the warmth of his touch, the solid comfort offered by his arms, the irresistible call of his spirit to hers.

"John—" she began.

"No," he whispered, his voice urgent for all its lack of volume. He didn't think he could stand it if she pulled away from him now. "Please, Maddy. Don't start being rational. Not yet. Just let me hold you a while longer."

The plea sank straight into her soul. Strong, achingly full of his own brand of need, infinitely dangerous in the things it wanted from her, it yet compelled her to stay. She relaxed against him, her cheek against his shoulder as she breathed in the fine musk-and-leather scent she would always associate with him.

For this brief, precious time, he filled all her world. She waited for that part of herself that always rejected this, but it remained silent. Heart, mind, and soul, she wanted him. She wanted to hold him, to be held, and for him to keep the rest of the world at bay. He made her feel cherished, desired, beautiful.

He wanted her. She could feel it in the warmth of his skin, already drying the fabric of his shirt, and in the swift, strong beat of his heart. And that, too, she accepted. Serenity lay softly upon her, and inevitability. This had begun the moment they'd met; now, tonight, she would see where it would go.

"Thank you for coming after me," she said.

He let his breath out, a smooth rise of chest that made her own heart beat faster. "I will always come after you, Maddy."

"No reprimands for being foolish?"

"You weren't foolish, love," he replied. "Only unlucky. Do you think you would have been caught had Gordon not come to complicate things?"

She shook her head.

"Then your original plan was sound," he said.

Maddy sighed. This, then, was validation. He hadn't tried to take from her the independence of which she was so proud. He'd only come to protect her *if* she needed it. It was a generous gesture, one she'd never forget.

"Men like softness in women," she said. "And a certain amount of docility. I've never managed docility. I've never been able—"

"Shhh." Taking her chin, John tilted her face upward. Her lashes were spiky with moisture, and her eyes looked deep enough to drown in. His heart lurched crazily, and he wouldn't have been surprised to find himself floating a foot above the ground.

"I don't give a damn about docility, Maddy. You possess a spirit that's all fire, and I find myself wanting to be burned. I've never felt anything like this."

Of its own volition, his gaze drifted lower. Her breasts looked like white pillows where they pressed against his chest, and they warmed his skin like a brand.

His other hand, forgotten until now, lay on her waist. He could feel the shape of her beneath his palm, from her lower ribs to the sweet, sweet curve of her hip. Of their own accord, his fingers spread to encompass still more. He could no more have kept from doing it than he could have stopped the beating of his heart.

He'd almost lost her tonight. God! He'd stopped caring whether he lived or died, and had lost the capacity to fear. But tonight, seeing Maddy being abused by those two bastards, he'd finally learned what it was like to truly be afraid.

For her. Only for her.

He slid his hand slowly from her waist to her ribs. Then he

waited a moment, ready to stop. After what she'd been through, he expected rejection. But instead of withdrawing, she closed her eyes in a response he felt down to his toes. He leaned down to brush his lips across hers in a butterfly-light caress.

She sighed. It was the most beautiful sound in the world, that sigh, for it meant that his feelings had been right. They'd been shared.

"Maddy," he murmured. "God, Maddy. You feel so good, so incredibly good."

Maddy looked up at him. His eyes looked like pure gold in the firelight. Passion simmered in their depths, but it was tightly controlled. There would come a time, she knew, when it would no longer be controlled. It would flare, and it would consume them both.

And she didn't care.

God help her, she didn't care. Just now, the future seemed too far away to matter. There was only the here, the now, and John.

"You feel good, too," she whispered. "I know I haven't always been . . . nice to you—"

"Honey," he said, smiling down at her. "From the moment we met, you twisted me ten different ways from Sunday. If you'd been a man, I would probably have shot you by now."

"But I'm not a man," she replied.

"And I damn well don't want to shoot you."

His voice was harsh with desire, and a shiver raced up her spine. "What do you want to do with me?" she whispered.

The passion in his eyes flared higher, hotter. "Everything a man can do with a woman," he said.

Such a primitive male response, she thought, even as she registered her own instinctive reaction. Primitive. Female. Powerful. She loved him. She'd fought long and hard and bitterly, and had lost. Perhaps she'd been meant to love him, destined to give her heart to this man since the beginning of time.

Tomorrow would come, of course. Tomorrow always came. Loving him couldn't change the difficulties between them, or the choices she might have to make for the sake of her family. But tonight, she would have this. No matter what happened tomorrow, she would treasure the magic that had, even for a moment, come into her life.

John lowered his head. She lifted hers, welcoming him.

Oh, he kissed her gently, so gently, as though he were afraid of frightening her. But Maddy was not afraid. She had made her decision freely, with her mind and her heart. And she didn't want gentleness from him. She wanted to possess and be possessed, she wanted to fling herself into the bonfire of his passion and for one brief, precious moment, forget that there was anything in the world but him, her, and their passion.

Restlessly, she slid her arm up around his neck and buried her fingers in the warm thickness of his hair. He deepened the kiss then, responding instantly to her unspoken demand. She sighed, and he surged against her in a response that sent a wash of heat coursing through her veins.

Magic, she thought through the drifting haze in her mind. It had to be magic. There could be no other explanation for the explosive passion she felt for him. One kiss, one touch, and the world turned to fire. She knew he felt it, too, by the sudden surge of heat of his skin, the rapid-fire beat of his heart, and most especially in the tender urgency of his hands as they began to caress her.

He moaned as she slid her tongue forward to play with his. The soft, male sound sent another surge of arousal coursing through her body. Unconsciously she turned, cupping her pelvis against his hip.

"Ah, Maddy," he groaned, immeasurably stirred, for that simple movement revealed her passion to him more clearly than words. He slid his hand down her back to her hip, curving his fingers over the soft, delicious flesh of her derriere.

"Oh, Lord," he muttered against her mouth. "Woman, you are more than beautiful, more than passionate, more than anything I could ever have imagined."

Maddy had never felt beautiful before. But now, gazing into

his eyes, she believed him. Moving with a sureness she wouldn't have believed possible, she slid her hand from the back of his head to his face, and stroked the firm line of his mouth with her thumb.

He reacted instantly, his tongue slipping forward to lick the small pad at the tip of her thumb. She froze, breath and movement suspended as arousal whipped through her like a thunderstorm. Ah, such a simple caress to create such a powerful reaction. But she'd passed beyond surprise where John Ballard was concerned; she wouldn't have felt astonished had she burst into flame.

"You like that," he murmured.

"I like that," she replied.

He smiled at her. Then, still gazing into her eyes, he did it again. Taking her hand, he licked his way along her thumb to her fingers, pausing to lave each fingertip before delving into the tender spot where each joined her hand.

It was a simple caress, a touch of tongue-tip to skin that might almost have been innocent in another situation. But there was something incredibly intimate in the caress, something so tender and passionate that her heart ached with the sweetness of it. Nothing could have moved her more.

"You taste so good," he whispered, pausing to look up at her. "So good."

Maddy found herself lost in his eyes. His touch might be gentle, but there was nothing of gentleness in the desire she saw in those molten gold-green depths. No, it was a man's passion she saw, passion as raw and wild and hot as a summer wind.

At another time, it might have frightened her. But not tonight. A conflagration had been lit inside her, and her passion raged as wild and reckless as his. Still gazing into his eyes, she slid her hand around to the back of his neck.

"Kiss me," she said.

John drew his breath in with a hiss of mingled surprise and delight. That had not been a plea; Maddy was not a woman who waited docilely to be claimed. No, Maddy would take, as well as be taken. A very, very, arousing prospect. But there was danger in letting Maddy take too much. Ah, but such a sweet, exciting danger.

Anticipation spurted along his nerves. Slowly, drawing it out as much as he could, he closed the distance between them. Tilting his head, he fitted his mouth to hers. She tasted of heat and woman and passion. Her tongue darted forward to rasp excitingly against his, and he nearly lost control. But he exerted an iron grasp upon his teetering emotions, and set about making her as crazy as she made him.

He was surprised to find that his hand shook as he caressed her spine from neck to waist. She felt hot to the touch, her skin as smooth as fine satin. Arousal surged into his groin as she arched her back in response, and he shifted position to ease the pressure of his jeans.

"You're driving me crazy," he muttered against her open mouth.

Maddy felt the hard length of him against her hip, but there was no shock in her, no reluctance. With deliberate intent, she moved provocatively against it.

His reaction was swift and complete. His arms went hard around her, crushing her against him. She cried out, overcome by this evidence of her power over him. It was a primitive thing, this power, and appealed to her at the most elemental level.

John cupped her chin in his hand, anchoring her to his gaze. "I see what's in your eyes," he growled. "You know exactly what you're doing, don't you?"

Oh, yes, she knew. And oh, yes, she knew he would have to do something about it. Maddy looked straight into his eyes and smiled.

John blinked, astonished by her defiance. Oh, she was one hell of a woman! Slowly, he slid his hand into her hair. It was warm and fragrant, as thick and rich as the finest silk. He clenched a great hank of it in his fingers—not hard enough to hurt, but simply a man's pure, aggressive claim of a woman.

This is mine, that grasp said. *I know it. And by the time I'm finished tonight, she will know it, too. No matter how she denies it later, the prize has already been claimed: she belongs to me.*

He'd never felt like this. He'd never wanted to feel like this. But he did. And she would.

"This is a dangerous game you're playing," he said.

"Should I be frightened?" she asked.

John knew she didn't understand the import of what she'd roused in him. Or the consequences. "Yes," he rasped. "You should be afraid."

"Well, I'm not," she countered.

He laughed softly, sure of his ability to puncture that arrogant self-confidence. Maddy shouldn't have spoken so without knowing more about the ways of men and women.

Still looking into her eyes, he let his hand drift down her body to her waist, then slid it beneath her waistband. Her pupils contracted. Triumph and desire ran hot through his veins, but it had nothing to do with victory. No, this was the simpler pleasure of touching her and seeing her response. He caressed the soft skin of her back, then slid his hand around to her belly. Lord, he was nearly undone by the feel of taut female flesh, then the crisp, curling hair below.

"Oh," she whispered. *"Oh."*

Maddy clenched her hands in his shirt, almost undone by the rioting sensations caused by his touch. Her body remembered that sweet, tumultuous pleasure he'd given her before, remembered it, and craved it. He would give her that again. And more. Oh, and more. Holding her breath in exquisite anticipation, she shifted her legs, helplessly allowing him greater access to the moist secrets of her womanhood.

His breath blew warm against her temple, and then she was surprised by the slick, hot thrust of his tongue into her ear. At the same time, he laid his hand upon her mound, claiming all that made her a woman. It was a primitive, possessive touch, and she stilled beneath it.

He let her wait for a moment. Then, just when the waiting became unbearable, he began exploring the slick, urgent heat of her.

Maddy moaned. Shifting her grip to his shoulders, she held on tightly as a firestorm of sensation buffeted her. She arched beneath his hand as he caressed her swollen flesh. Oh, his hands, she thought. Gentle, urgent, exciting. Her eyes fluttered closed as he began to explore every crevice, every secret spot. Then, as she all but panted with arousal, he slipped one finger deep inside her.

She cried out in surprise and pleasure, digging her nails into his shoulders as he slid his finger nearly out, then back in again. Her hips bucked of their own volition.

"Ah, you like that," he muttered. "There's more, Maddy. Much more."

Her world had turned to chaos, pleasure rocketing higher and higher as he stroked her into quivering arousal. She drew her breath in deeply, let it out again in a soft moan.

John held onto control with iron determination. She was hot, tight, wet, and her response was all he might have imagined. Maddy was made to be loved by him; she'd become all fire and passion, the embodiment of desire made woman. He wanted his loving to be good for her. He wanted her to remember this night as long as she lived. For he would. He would.

Maddy writhed helplessly as her arousal spiraled still higher. A moan escaped her as he slid his finger slowly, oh, so slowly out of her, and she tilted her hips in an attempt to keep him where she needed him.

"Do you want me to stop?" he whispered.

Maddy forced her vision to focus. He hovered close above her, his finger just brushing the outer perimeter of her womanhood. It took an effort of will for her to concentrate on his question, but she managed.

"Could you?" she asked.

"Yes." His eyes darkened, and his fingertip slid deeper into her slick lushness. "Up to a point. But I've got to warn you, Maddy, that I don't know when that point will come. When it does, *you* will have to do the stopping."

Sinking both hands into his hair, she held him still as she gazed into his eyes. She had her answer. If she asked him to, he would stop. No matter what the cost. The knowledge that she had control of the situation made her bolder than ever.

"Then don't stop . . . yet," she whispered.

John smiled. It was always a contest with her, he mused, knowing her thoughts as plainly as if they'd been printed on her forehead. Ah, his Maddy. Always thinking, always pushing the edge. Well, they would see.

Gently, he parted her folds and found the nub that was the center of her desire. He watched her eyes drift to half-mast again as the pleasure overcame her. So beautiful, he thought, as her mouth parted in irrepressible reaction. Touching her was like setting a match to gunpowder: instant, powerful, dangerous.

Maddy thought she'd go mad. Just now, when her own urgency had built to an alarming level, he seemed to have decided he had all the time in the world. She wriggled, trying to urge him on. He remained firmly in control, however, nipping gently at her lips, darting his tongue into her mouth in teasing little forays that left her panting.

And his hand, oh, his hand. He played with her body as he played with her mouth, circling the taut female nub with one fingertip until she thought she would surely scream. She was desperate for him, for the release she knew he could give her. Her hands moved across his back restlessly, clinging one moment, then splaying out to dig nails into the hard muscles.

He groaned, a thick male sound of arousal, and she knew she'd stirred him unbearably. Triumph shot through her, mingling with her passion.

Then something unbelievable happened. He kissed her deeply, aggressively, his tongue delving deep into her mouth. The touch of his hands changed, too. No longer did he tease her. He slid one finger into the swollen, wet delta at the core of her, then two. His thumb strayed upward to stroke the nub rhythmically, causing a shockwave of reaction in her body.

A tremor began deep inside her, grew and spread into a cataclysmic storm that claimed her very being. She clutched John with desperate strength, feeling as though she'd been tossed straight into a whirlwind and that only he could save her.

He held her safe, whispering encouragement. Her eyes flew open, and she looked straight into John's as she cried out his name. Finally the storm abated, although shudders still ran through her body. He held her as she quieted, his hands hot upon her skin.

"I never knew," she panted, undone by the power of the thing that had happened to her. "I never imagined it could be this way between a man and a woman."

"Not just a man and a woman, Maddy," he murmured. "This is you and me. We do this."

Yes, it had to be. Before John Ballard had entered her life, she hadn't known herself capable of such responses. Ah, but her body knew. Had known. It had only taken a certain man . . . John Ballard, and only he, had the power to call forth this primitive, wanton Maddy.

She buried her face in the curve where his neck met his shoulder. Breathing deeply, she inhaled the scent that was so uniquely his. His pulse beat frantically beneath the skin, and she slid her tongue over that pulsepoint. His skin was hot and slightly salty. Male. Aroused. For her. She shivered, pressing herself closer to him.

"You smell good," she whispered.

He made a thick, wordless sound of arousal. Sliding one arm beneath her back and the other beneath her legs, he pulled her against his chest as he levered to his feet. Maddy wound her arms around his neck. She pressed her cheek against his chest as he carried her toward a blanket that had been spread upon the ground nearby.

He laid her down. For a moment he crouched over her, his

shoulders straining the fabric of his shirt, his eyes as deep and hot as molten gold in the firelight. Passion had tautened the planes of his face, making him look more than ever the predator. The sight sent anticipation coursing through her again; for this night, she'd put herself in this man's power.

John wanted her so badly he trembled. She had climaxed so very beautifully, her body shuddering against his, her soft cries the most wonderful thing he'd ever heard. Now he wanted to be inside her more than he'd ever wanted anything; if she denied him now, he was sure he'd die of it.

But Maddy didn't deny him. Honest, straightforward Maddy, as genuine in her passion as she was in anger or defiance or loyalty. She gazed up at him with eyes soft with desire, trusting him to take her as a woman should be taken. And he would. She deserved no less.

In control now, he turned his attention to bringing her to the flashpoint again. Her breasts drew him irresistibly, and he licked his way over every lush, delicious inch. He loved the way she sank her fingers into his hair and held on, and he loved the way she made those soft little moans every time he ran his tongue around her nipples. The scent of lilacs filled his senses, a flesh-memory as seductive as the woman herself.

Settling between her thighs, he framed her breasts with his hands and simply looked at her. Her skin glistened like mother-of-pearl, and her nipples jutted proudly. He lowered his head to run his tongue around each puckered aureole. Then again. And again. She writhed beneath him, demanding more with every sinuous, sexy movement. How could he resist? Slowly, he drew one turgid peak into his mouth and began to suck.

"Oh," she breathed. "John."

Maddy was overwhelmed with sensation. Heat raced from her breasts straight to her groin, bringing her to instant, volcanic arousal. Now she knew how much pleasure she could expect, and had become greedy for more. Boldly, she grasped his head and urged him toward her other breast. He obliged readily, drawing her other nipple deep into his mouth.

But Maddy wasn't content to be a passive partner in this. No, lovemaking should be a shared thing. Besides, she had an abiding curiosity about his big, hard body, and this was the perfect time to assuage it.

"I want to touch you," she whispered.

It wasn't even remotely a request. John raised his head to look at her, and she saw awareness of her demand in his eyes. And acquiescence. A thrill raced through her; now, tonight, he could deny her nothing.

"Touch me all you want," he rasped.

Her boldness both surprised and delighted him. Holding himself above her with braced arms, he gave her free access to his body. He shuddered when she laid hands on his shoulders, more aroused by that simple touch than he would have believed possible.

"Oh, Maddy," he groaned. "Oh, Maddy."

Delight sparkled through her as she explored the hard male planes of his chest. His small nipples peaked beneath her hands, and she drew in her breath, pleased beyond measure that his body responded this way, just as hers did. She slid her hands lower. His belly was taut, ridged with muscle, and iron-hard. But it, too, was subject to her touch, quivering as she caressed that lean expanse.

She paused when she reached his belt buckle, a little intimidated at last. This was the final remaining mystery, that unfathomed territory that was so aggressively male. She knew instinctively that this was the moment of decision, when the option of stopping might be taken from her.

She ought to be afraid. She ought to stop it now, here, before something irrevocable happened. But there was no caution in her, and certainly no modesty. She wanted to feel him, to make him cry out, to take away that control and make him utterly hers.

"Do you want me to . . . touch you?" she whispered.

"God, yes!" he groaned, beyond himself.

The hoarseness of his voice betrayed his ragged control.

Maddy knew he was holding on by his fingernails. She wanted to push him past that point. She wanted to know he'd lost the ability to resist her, for then she would know that for this brief, magical moment, he belonged to her.

Gazing up into his face, she moved her hand down to the long, thick ridge of his arousal. He groaned, and a shudder rippled through his hard-braced arms. Mingled triumph and pleasure made her truly reckless; she rubbed him through the fabric, entranced by the aggressive male power of him.

His eyes slitted nearly closed. With her free hand, she reached up to trace the sensual line of his lips. He captured her fingertip in his mouth, his tongue darting forward to lave the sensitive pad. Boldly, she rubbed his tongue, feeling the varying textures of the skin.

His expression changed. All the cynicism had drained out of his expression, leaving only the look of a man at the extreme of control. She reveled in it, for he was a strong, stubborn man, and she had brought him to this.

Her caresses grew still bolder, more intimate. Beneath her hand, he lengthened still more.

His eyes had completely closed now, and his chest heaved with his labored breaths. Maddy knew she'd begun to tread dangerous ground, and a quicksilver flash of anticipation skittered along her veins.

And then her time ran out.

With a groan, he grasped her hands, pinned them over her head, and claimed her mouth in a torrid kiss. She met him with all the fierceness of her own unbridled passion. There was no reticence, no caution.

He thrust one thigh between her legs, and she arched her back in sheer voluptuous reaction. Supporting her buttocks with one strong hand, he lifted her so that her mound rubbed against his leg. Maddy cried out, mindlessly digging her nails into the hard muscles of his back.

Suddenly he stilled. She opened her eyes to look at him, her breath suspended in shack and dismay. Was he stopping?

Could he do so, leaving her quivering with desire? But no, she thought with a wash of relief. His manhood still lay hard and hot against her, and his eyes still raged with a passion that might have frightened her if she were a more docile woman. Then she realized that this pause had nothing to do with withdrawing; he'd stopped because he wanted to look into her eyes and say something very important to him.

Caught in the intensity of the moment, she waited, breath suspended, for what would happen next.

"Maddy," he said, his voice hoarse, his face showing the strain of the effort it took to speak. "This is your last chance. Tell me to stop, now, this instant, or I'm going to make love to you. I'm going to fill you, possess you, and no power on this earth is going to stop me."

Once again, he'd given her a choice. An honorable act by an honorable man, Maddy thought. But she knew that the choice had been made for her long before now. She had to know the full measure of this exquisitely beautiful thing they'd begun between them.

She would have this. Tomorrow would come, and with it, the consequences. But now, tonight, she would have this. Laying her palm against the hard plane of his cheek, she met his tempestuous gaze squarely.

"Don't stop," she whispered. "Please, don't stop."

Twenty

He gazed down at her for a long, breathless moment. Inevitability lay heavily upon Maddy, beat in a sweet, hot rhythm through her veins as she waited.

She expected him to kiss her. Instead, he slid his other thigh between her legs, spreading her wide. Then he settled slowly upon her. She could feel the long ridge of his manhood against her cleft, and her reaction was instantaneous, a powerful response of flesh, mind, heart, and soul.

Her hips lifted in an unconscious welcoming of him, and his eyes turned slumberous. Bracing on his arms again, he rubbed against her. She gasped. He did it again. Mindlessly, she clasped him to her, her hands sliding down his back to cup his buttocks.

"Do you know what you're doing to me?" he muttered.

"Yes," she whispered.

His eyes slitted further. "I wonder," he said. "If you knew how badly I want you, you wouldn't be so reckless."

"But I am not a docile woman, remember," she replied. "Nor a cautious one."

He shifted down to his elbows and claimed her mouth in a kiss that hadn't the vaguest pretense of civilization. She met him with equal fierceness, clenching her hands in his hair to anchor him close. He tilted his head to one side and feasted upon her. Slowly, as though he weren't aroused, as though there were nothing more important in the world than giving her pleasure.

Maddy had had enough of waiting. Caution no longer existed. Nothing mattered but assuaging this delicious ache, this driving need to possess and be possessed. With desire pooling hot in her belly and breasts, she rubbed herself against him like a cat.

He surged against her, and she knew she'd finally pushed him beyond the limit. Rising to his knees, he moved to one side as he unfastened her skirt and drawers and slid them from her. Then he returned to kneel between her legs, gazing at her with eyes as bright and hot as the fire behind him.

Maddy started to cover herself in a sudden, instinctive rush of modesty. But he trapped her wrists in one big hand and stopped her.

"Don't," he said. "Don't cover yourself."

"But—"

"We are about to do the most beautiful thing a man and woman can share," he said. "There can be no shame, no holding back for either of us."

With his free hand, he moved her legs farther apart. Then he laid gentle fingers upon her mound, making her feel his claim on her. Her breath went out in a long sigh, and she shivered in response. She felt no shame, no reticence. He'd taken over her body, her mind, her world.

"No holding back," she agreed.

John slid his thumb into the nest of curls, seeking the heart of her. She was wet and swollen, more than ready. He explored slick crevices and pouty flesh, spreading her abundant wetness over every surface. She moaned, a soft, tormented sound that sent jolts of pleasure coursing through his body.

John freed her wrists. She made no attempt to cover herself now; her eyes had darkened to indigo, and her hips were beginning to shimmy as he caressed her. He found her small, erect nub and began to work it, then slid one long finger into her. She cried out, and he could feel the sudden increase of heat and wetness. An answering surge of arousal pulsed in his groin.

He'd have to take her soon. He was so hard it was becoming painful. God, she was more woman than he'd ever known—she was hot, and she was his.

"Please," she moaned. "Oh, please!"

There was a lost look in her eyes that bespoke the urgency of her desire. Beneath his hand, John felt her body grow still hotter.

"Yes," he muttered. "I want to please you."

Maddy cried out as his hands left her. But it was only to tug at his own clothes, and she sat up to help him. She unbuttoned his shirt and dragged it impatiently down his arms, wanting only to get to his skin. His chest was thick with muscle, sprinkled with coarse, dark hair. She ran her hand over the swell of his pectorals, feeling the round, raised welts of scars. Three, four, five, six, she thought, caressing them with gentle fingertips. Marks of courage.

She nearly asked him about them. But he took her hand and slid it down to the hardness of his belly. He'd already undone his belt; driven by the desire hammering through her veins, she forgot anything else but the need to touch him. Her hands shook as she unfastened the buttons on his jeans and pushed them down his hips.

His manhood jutted free, and she drew her breath in sharply at the sight of it. She was no expert on such things, but surely he was as much man as a man could hope to be. Fascinated, she reached out to stroke her palm over the springing hardness of him. He was silky to the touch, and hot. She drew her breath in with a hiss as he surged beneath her touch.

He snatched her to him, slashing his mouth down on hers in a kiss that was tempestuous, powerful, primitive. The world tilted as he pulled her up into his arms, then laid her down again so that he lay between her legs. No cloth separated them now; she could feel his skin hot against hers, the exciting brush of his chest hair against her oversensitive breasts, his erection nuzzling the heart of her sex. It was the most intimate caress she'd ever felt or imagined, and the ache between her legs abruptly became unbearable.

"John," she whispered.

"I know," he whispered back.

He looked into her eyes, catching her, claiming her. With an abruptness that nearly made her cry out, she felt her spirit go rushing toward him. It seemed as though everything that made her—mind, body, and soul—went pouring into him. He felt it too; she could tell by the way his body surged against hers.

"Maddy," he groaned.

He came into her then, a smooth, hard thrust that sent waves of pain and pleasure rocketing through her as he breached her maidenhead. Maddy hadn't expected the pain. She clenched around him, her breath going out in a sharp gasp.

"I'm sorry, love," he said, nuzzling the hair at her temple. "But it will only hurt for a moment. Then never again, I promise you. Trust me, Maddy."

How often had he asked her to trust him tonight? she wondered hazily. And how many times had she given him what he'd asked? Perhaps she was a fool to trust him. Had there been risk to another, she wouldn't have considered it. But in this . . . this astonishing experience, she only risked herself, and that she could do. Her choice had been made, by her heart, her spirit, and by desire.

She wasn't capable of speech. So she merely slid her hand into his hair and pulled him down for a kiss, hoping he would understand.

John knew she had given him something much more precious than just her body, although the gift of herself was a most precious one. He lay quiescent within her, content to be patient now that he'd claimed her at last. Stilling the clamor of his own body, he kissed her and caressed her until her breathing grew ragged and her passage glided around him. Only then did he begin to move.

God, she was incredible, he thought. Sleek and hot and responsive. She began to meet his thrusts, her hands moving with deliciously sexy desperation on his back. He'd never felt like this before. She'd touched him, mind, body, and soul, in a way no woman ever had. Or would.

Maddy had forgotten all about the pain. She'd forgotten anything but this wonderful sensation, of being filled, being possessed completely, yet also possessing. Her body had taken over, quickly learning to accommodate his size, contracting around him.

She arched her back as his movements deepened. He thrust into her carefully, drawing out almost completely before plunging deep again in a long, slow glide. Pleasure raced along her nerves, coalescing in a tight, hard knot between her legs. Oh, this was more than she'd expected, more than she'd ever dreamed could exist.

He buried his face in the curve of her neck and shoulder and pressed his open mouth to her skin. She gasped as he sucked heat to the surface. The rhythm of his lower body changed, grew faster, harder. He caressed her breasts with one hand, his touch firm as he slid her nipples between his fingers. She cried out in sheer, wanton pleasure.

Ah, but she was not alone in this exquisite torment; he groaned, a note of boundless male passion, and his hand began to tremble. She knew then that his control had shattered. He was in thrall to her, tuned to her body and soul.

Hers.

A sort of madness claimed her then. Riptides of sensation coursed through her, and she spun helplessly in a web of desire that grew stronger with every moment. Every stroke, every plunge of his manhood into her wet, welcoming depths took her farther, higher.

"Oh, John," she gasped. "Oh, *John!*"

He groaned, grasping her hips in a hard, infinitely possessive grip as he angled her slightly up and forward. Maddy arched her back in pleasure and disbelief as he plunged still deeper into her. She bit at his shoulder, impaled on this incredible passion they shared.

"Yes," he rasped. "Let yourself go, Maddy. I want you completely, everything you have, everything you are."

His words spurred her higher. There was nothing of rationality left in her; she'd become a creature of sensation, wanton, demanding, as primitive as the wild land around her. She soared like an eagle on the wings of her passion, buoyed on this maiden flight by John's strength, John's caring.

She wrapped her legs around his lean, driving hips, letting him take her wherever he wanted to go. This, then, was ultimate trust, a woman's faith in a man on a most primal level. She accepted it, welcomed it. He lunged into her with long, powerful strokes, yet still careful of her. He growled deep in his throat, the wordless, tormented sound of a man in the extremity of desire.

The first tremors caught her, then rolled into a wild, shuddering tidal wave that swept her away. Holding him with slender, strong thighs honed from a lifetime on horseback, she let herself fall into a churning abyss of sensation.

Her vision darkened, and for a moment she thought she might lose consciousness. Then she focused on John, and found him watching her with such tenderness that she nearly cried out.

His eyes closed, his face clenched, and he threw his head back in sheer, male abandon. He drove into her, a powerful thrust she thought went clear to her soul, then she felt him pour himself out into her in a hot flood. The sensation pulled her straight into another climax. This time, she screamed.

"Maddy," he groaned, pumping into her as he shook with release.

Gasping, she held on tightly as he eased down, then rolled onto his back, bringing her with him. He fitted her against him, her cheek on his chest, her legs intertwined with his. It surprised her, both for its tenderness and for its intimacy. She rubbed her cheek against his chest, relishing the prickle of hair against her skin.

"Tell me about these," she said, touching the scars one by one.

He took her hand and brought it to his mouth. "They're nothing."

She hadn't expected him to avoid answering. An unpleasant chill crept into her belly. "I'd really like to know."

"Leave it be, Maddy," he said.

Of course, she should. But they'd just experienced the fullest intimacy a man and woman could share, and she needed this from him.

"I already know," she said.

"What do you know?"

"You received the Medal of Honor after Antietam, and I know your three brothers died there."

John drew his breath in sharply. He felt bare, his soul exposed and vulnerable. He didn't like it. He'd spent years pushing those memories away; now Maddy had brought them rushing back. They hurt too much, too much.

"That's none of your business," he growled, his voice savage and harsh.

His withdrawal hurt Maddy. She'd only wanted to know him, all of him, and to have a bit of his past if she couldn't have any of his future. She watched his eyes change, the focus turning inward, where she couldn't follow. Where she wasn't wanted.

Rebuffed, she pulled her hand free. "Is there anything that is my business . . . other than fulfilling your pleasure?"

His gaze focused on her again. "That isn't what I meant."

"It's what you said."

"Maddy . . ." John sighed. He knew she needed this, but it was the one thing he couldn't give her. He'd never been able to talk about his brothers' deaths, not even with his parents. Eventually, the wound had scabbed over, and he'd been able to convince himself he'd healed.

But he hadn't. For Maddy had torn that wound open now, and he was bleeding.

"I don't want to talk about this," he said.

Maddy glanced away to hide the sudden tears that stung her eyes. This was a good lesson to her; he'd make love to her, he'd take her to the heights of passion and beyond . . . and no further. He wouldn't let her into his heart.

Ah, a very good lesson indeed.

She'd begun to open to him, the fragile flower of her heart unfolding in his hands. It was dangerous to her, and to Derek, and she ought to be grateful to know so soon to protect herself better.

You knew this would happen, chided a rational voice in her mind.

But not yet. She thought she'd have tonight. With a sigh, she moved away from him.

"We should go," she said.

"Why?"

"Well, we're . . . finished."

His brows went up. "Just like that?"

"What do you mean?" she asked.

The remoteness left his eyes, and he reached out to stroke her hair back from her face. "The night's not over yet."

"It is for me."

"Maddy . . ." John pulled her close again, realizing he'd hurt her, yet still unable to give her that injured piece of his soul. "I . . . can't be what you want. But I want you to know that our lovemaking was special, rare, magical. People live their entire lives wishing for something like that, and few ever find it. We're damned lucky."

Maddy tried to think about his words logically and rationally. But the truth of the matter was, she didn't feel lucky.

Yes, the lovemaking had been achingly beautiful, so much more than she could have imagined. For her, it had been love. For John, it had been mere sensuality, the pleasurable joining of two bodies.

Now, she felt cheated. And she had no right; he hadn't promised her anything but the lovemaking, and he'd delivered on that promise. It would be unfair of her to expect anything more than that.

Hellfire and damnation, but she hated being fair.

"I understand my parents now," she said.

Surprise sparked in his eyes. "Yes?"

"Mother and Daddy adored each other. There were times when they would disappear for hours at a time, and when they returned, they had the most, well, cat-that-drank-the-cream expressions on their faces. Until now, I didn't understand."

"So, they had the magic, too," he mused.

Maddy shook her head. "Love makes magic," she corrected. "And that is not what happened here tonight."

"What would you call it?" he asked, lifting one brow.

"Sex."

John blinked. Of all the things she might have said, that was the most astonishing. "How practical of you," he said.

"Of course, it was quite pleasurable," she continued. "The physical sensations were most . . . interesting."

"I see."

Most men would have been pleased to have found a partner who was so practical about the whole thing, John thought. Then why, he wondered, was he so annoyed? Not just annoyed, but furious. He let his breath out slowly, unsure of just how to deal with her. Truly, he shouldn't be feeling like this; he'd enjoyed more than his share of women without his emotions becoming involved. Why, then, should he become angry because Maddy didn't cling? He didn't know. But he *was* angry.

He folded his hands beneath his head and stared up at her. Her face was in shadow now, her hair a bronze halo around her head. Even if he were clear on what he felt, she probably wouldn't believe him.

"So that's what you think," he said. "It was a simple roll in the hay, no more important than . . . a good steak dinner. Such a prosaic event, considering that you were a virgin."

She turned her face away. "Should that be more important to me than it was to you?"

"I suppose not," he said coolly.

Ah, but it was, Maddy thought. There had been nothing simple in it for her; she felt as though she'd been taken apart and put back together a whole new way. Apparently, however, the experience hadn't been quite so profound for him.

She shouldn't care. She *didn't* care. This had been done of her own free will, and she had always taken responsibility for her own actions. She intended to do so now. But an inexplicable ache had settled in her heart, and no amount of rationalization was going to make it go away.

"Are you going to deny that you enjoyed . . . sex?" John asked, unwilling to let her go unscathed.

Heat rushed into her cheeks. "I suppose there is no point in doing so."

"None at all," he replied. "Your response was rather . . . warm." John repressed the urge to comb his fingers through her tumbled hair. He wanted to touch her with tenderness, but that emotion would be wasted between them. "Tell me, my dear, practical Maddy: why tonight?"

"Tonight was . . ." She swallowed hard against the lump that had suddenly risen in her throat. "I don't know if I can explain it properly, but the world sort of . . . went away tonight."

"It went away." His tone was flat, emotionless. "And now it's back?"

"It always comes back."

"And what did you want from me?"

Maddy had wanted to feel cherished. Safe. And in the privacy of her own thoughts, she admitted now that she'd wanted to feel loved, even if only for a moment. John had given her all those things—or had appeared to. She wished he hadn't. She wished he hadn't been kind to her, or made her feel as though she were the most important thing in the world to him.

But she couldn't say those things to him. He would perceive them as weakness, and he would use them against her.

"I don't know," she said.

"You don't know." He let his breath out in a sigh of exasperation. "It's better that we have no illusions about what happened between us tonight. Illusions can be dangerous."

Maddy nodded, feeling like a very great fool. She wished she knew more about these situations. Did one just gather one's clothes and make polite conversation while pretending nothing had happened?

"So, nothing has changed between us," John said.

Everything had changed for Maddy. "Of course not."

"I'm still hunting your brother, and you're still going to do everything in your power to stop me."

"Yes," she said. "That was never in question."

John had had enough of this idiotic, frigid conversation. "Goddamn it, Maddy—"

"Stop," she said, as always falling back on Saylor haughtiness to hide the hurt she felt. "This is obviously a pointless conversation, and there is no reason for either of us to become angry."

"Obviously," he growled.

A strained silence fell. All the intimacy between them had vanished, and Maddy wanted nothing more than to disappear. Hot tears stung the back of her eyelids, but she denied them sternly. She would not cry. Never, never, and never in front of him.

She decided she would retain as much dignity as a woman could retain while reclining naked upon her lover's chest, and as soon as she could manage, she would dress, find her mount, and return to town. Gathering her courage, she started to lever herself up.

John's reaction was swift and instinctive, a hard clamp of both hands on the small of her back. He glared up into her wide, surprised eyes, knowing he ought to let her go but completely unable to do so.

"Where do you think you're going?" he demanded.

"Back to town," she replied.

"No."

"No?"

His voice turned silken, a note of danger she was beginning to recognize. "Are you planning to pretend this never happened, Maddy?"

"I think that would be the easiest all around, don't you?"

"No," he said. "Damn it."

Her temper snapped, spurred by her emotions and his unreasonableness. Furious now, she tried to wriggle away. But he held her with careless strength, not hurting her, but absorbing her struggles against his body.

Suddenly she realized that he had become very aroused beneath her, and that every movement she made only excited him further. She quickly stilled, danger shrilling along every nerve ending.

His eyes had narrowed to gold-green slits. His erection was hard and hot between them, and felt like silk-sheathed steel against her belly. Maddy closed her eyes, fighting the swift, devastating response of her body.

But that battle was lost before it began; roused by his obvious desire and the memory of the beautiful lovemaking they had shared, her body had overcome the directives of her anger. Sweet, liquid heaviness settled in her breasts and loins, and the tenseness ran like water from her limbs.

"No," she whispered. "Oh, no!"

"Oh, yes," he countered. "You said we had tonight, Maddy. I intend to make the most of it."

"But—"

"Don't worry about the rest of the world," he said. "I can make it go away again, I promise you.

He could. She knew he could. Already, her awareness had turned inward, to the sensations he engendered in her. She shivered as he slid his hands down from her back to her buttocks. He stroked her with a firm, knowing touch, making her arch her back on the upstroke and pressing her against his erection on the downstroke.

"Tonight is mine," he growled. "You are mine."

Maddy opened her eyes and gazed down at him. He looked the aroused male animal, his face taut, his eyes almost seeming to glow with desire in the firelight. Her heart lurched. She wanted him, powerfully and primitively.

But as infinitely seductive as he might be, he was also dangerous. He would cost her Derek if he could. She could not pay that price. *Would* not.

And yet, she couldn't seem to find the strength to stop him, or herself. Her body seemed to be on fire, and he was stoking the blaze higher with every caress. Ah, she was weak, weak.

"I am yours," she agreed, but then qualified it by adding, "For tonight."

John studied her closely. She was very aroused; he could see it in her eyes, feel it in the heat and litheness of her body. She didn't want to be aroused; this instant, volcanic passion between them had as firm a hold on her as it did him. Still, she had the gall to look straight at him and set conditions on their lovemaking.

Suddenly, amusement rippled through him, swift, bright rays of sunlight to pierce the clouds of his frustration. Maddy Saylor was in for a big surprise. If she thought they'd be able to stay away from each other after this, she had a hell of a lot to learn.

Damn, he thought, sliding his fingers along the crevice between her buttocks to discover the wet, womanly heat at her core. *She looks like an angel come down from heaven, and she feels as good as sin.*

Lifting her, he positioned himself and slid home. She cried out, but he knew it was in pleasure and not discomfort, for her body was convulsing around him in a most delightful way. Ah, she was made for a man's loving, his Maddy. He held her by the hips, withdrawing almost completely, then entering her in a stroke that went deep and slow. She flung her head back in wanton response, her nails digging into his chest.

"John," she moaned, and it was the sweetest sound he'd ever heard.

"Yes," he agreed. "I'll take tonight, Maddy."

And more, he thought as rationality began to slip away. Much more.

Twenty-one

Maddy lay against John's side and watched as dawn spilled in a golden flood across the hills. Her body was just a little sore, and very much sated. John had taken her to the heights again and again during the night, making love to her with what felt almost like desperation.

She had met him with equal fervor, clinging to the few short hours of escape allowed her. The night had become a dark velvet cloak against reality. She had clung to it, wrapping herself tightly against the intrusion of thought. And no matter what she'd said to John, it *had* been magic. Sensuality as deep and vast as the sea, pleasure so sharp that it almost felt like pain at times, her heart aching with love and despair, passion, shared laughter, and private tears . . . In one night, she'd learned the full reach of emotion possible for a woman.

It was over now. Dawn was coming, and with it, duty. She'd just never expected it to hurt so much. In one blinding moment of weakness, she hated it. She wished, just this once, that she could simply be a woman in love.

The first rays of morning reached her, turning her skin golden and prickling it with a warmth she hadn't known she needed until now. Beside her, John lay on his stomach, his hard male nakedness startlingly pale against the blanket. He'd thrown one arm over her in an unconsciously possessive gesture.

She ought to leave. She needed to leave. But sliding out from beneath his arm without waking him was going to be quite a trick.

Raising her head cautiously, she looked for her mount, half expecting him to have wandered off during the night. But he stood beside John's horse, cropping new leaves from a bush a few hundred yards away.

If only she could reach him . . . Distance would give her the chance for objectivity, something she couldn't seem to find with John naked and warm at her side. She glanced at him, wondering what her chances of success might be, and found him awake and watching her. His eyes had turned hooded. Stare as she might, she couldn't begin to guess at the emotions hidden behind those green-gold irises.

"I must go," she said.

His arm tightened on her, and for a moment she thought he'd refuse. Then he released her suddenly, and rose to his feet with a lithe surge of his body. She had to fight to keep her composure as he stood above her, unself-consciously, magnificently naked. Sleek, lean, hard with muscle, he was as virile and graceful as a cougar.

"You ought to see how you're looking at me," he said.

Maddy knew she should look away. But her gaze dropped down his body, betraying her. His manhood jutted proudly from its nest of dark hair, lengthening and thickening even as she watched. Perhaps her gaze had the power of a touch, she thought a bit dazedly; certainly the effect on her own body was profound.

"I . . . Ah . . ." she began, intending to say something, anything, but words failed her.

John managed to keep from smiling, but only barely. Maddy's eyes had gone heavy-lidded, and her nipples had tightened into luscious, pink-brown nubs that fairly begged for his attention. And last night . . . Last night she had gone to the heights of rapture, and had taken him with her. She'd astonished him, and pleased him beyond anything he'd ever experienced.

But he knew she was also determined to hold them both to the 'one night' limit. Hah, he thought. She'd never be able to do it. His practical darling was nothing if not the sensual female animal; she just hadn't quite realized that fact yet.

"Don't worry about this, sweetheart," he said, waving casually at the throbbing shaft. "It's always like this in the morning. As you said last night, a purely physical reaction."

He stretched with elaborate casualness, and Maddy's throat suddenly went dry. Muscles rippled all over his body, and his skin looked like beaten gold in the sunlight. He seemed elemental, a pure, male force of nature She wanted him all over again, so badly that she had to wrap her arms around herself to keep from touching him. That, she knew, would be complete, utter disaster.

Instead, she rose and looked around for her clothes. But the moment she got to her feet, John caught her by the arm and turned her around. She was astonished to see pure violence in his eyes.

"It didn't look this bad last night," he said, his voice harsh with restrained anger.

She looked down at herself. Bruises marred the skin of her arms, shoulders and breasts, and a throbbing ache in her back told of more damage there. She hadn't felt a thing last night; in John's arms, she had known only passion and gentleness, and had forgotten the hurts of her body.

"It takes a while for bruises to develop," she said, repressing a hiss of pain as she shrugged.

John turned her around so he could see her back. A purple-black bruise covered most of her shoulder blade and ran down along the ribs. The sight of it made him burn with rage.

"Why didn't you tell me it was this bad?" he rasped. "I must have hurt you during—"

"No," she said. "I didn't notice it at all."

He looked down at her. The sweep of her back was extraordinarily lovely above a derriere as smooth and lush as silk. Her skin almost seemed to shimmer in the sunlight, but he thought that the glow came from that fiery warrior's spirit of hers rather than from any external source.

Those bruises were anathema to him, that anyone could lay violent hands upon such a woman. Gently, he laid his hands on her shoulders and turned her toward him. Folding her in his arms, he held her against him. Simply held her. He was surprised by his own tenderness; he held her, not only to comfort, but as a man holds a woman he wants to protect, to cherish, to possess.

Maddy, surprised by his gesture, stood stiffly for a moment. He held her so closely that his manhood was trapped between them, lying hot and hard against her belly. But he made no move to make love to her. No, she realized, this was no attempt at seduction, but the offering of simple, human comfort.

Until this moment, she hadn't realized she needed it, or how badly. Perhaps she couldn't have accepted it from anyone but John Ballard.

Don't question it, a small corner of her brain whispered. *Just accept it.* Just now, that tiny voice sounded more sane than any other part of her. She allowed herself to relax. His skin smelled musky-sweet, tinged with wood smoke from the long-dead fire. Closing her eyes, she focused on the beat of his heart against her cheek.

"I wish I could kill them again," he growled. "Only slower, this time."

She raised her head to look at him. "Dead is good enough," she replied.

John saw a fierceness in her eyes that matched his own. *Damn,* he thought. *This is one hell of a woman. A man could search all his life and not find anything to measure up to her.*

Then rationality raised its head, and he was able to get hold of his teetering emotions. Maddy didn't belong to him, and never would. For he intended to bring Derek Saylor in to face the justice he so richly deserved, and once he did that, Maddy would hate him until the end of time.

Slowly, his body moving with a reluctance at odds with his mind, he dropped his arms and stepped back.

"We'd better get going," he said. "Your blouse is unusable. I'll get you one of my spare shirts."

Maddy nodded. The tender moment had evaporated, for which she was glad. There was great danger in such moments. She'd need all her strength to do what needed to be done.

"What are you going to do about . . . them?" she asked, nodding toward the spot where the dead men lay.

"I ought to leave them for the vultures," he growled "But I'd better haul them back to town. I doubt anyone's going to miss Jim Berry, but Gordon Walsh's family's going to want to take care of burying him."

"Zachary Walsh will want his revenge," she said.

John shrugged. "Better men have tried."

Maddy's hand moved of its own volition to trace the six round spots of scar tissue patterned on his chest. "There are some battles you can't fight with a gun."

"I know that," he said, moving her hand away.

Again, he'd shut her out. Maddy glanced away, the sun refracting off the sudden moisture in her eyes.

"I don't see any need for you to be involved in this," John continued, apparently unaware that he'd hurt her. "I'll take Walsh and Berry back to town—"

"And tell them what?"

"That they jumped me, and I was forced to kill them in self defense."

"I am not ashamed to tell the truth," she said.

"Maddy, you know how people are. Some are bound to believe that Marsh and Berry had their way with you. The gossip will be ugly, and the Marshes will make it uglier. They'll attack your integrity and your reputation, and I don't want you to have to endure that kind of talk."

She let her breath out in a sigh of exasperation. Men! she thought. He'd get himself killed to protect her reputation, and think he was doing something good.

"That's the most idiotic thing I've ever heard," she said. Then she tilted her head back, pinning his gaze with hers. "I no longer have the right to claim an untarnished reputation. It would be unconscionable for me to allow you to put yourself in danger for such a thing."

"I'm not in any danger."

"Yes, you are," she insisted.

John lost patience with her. Couldn't she understand that he was only trying to protect her? And why couldn't she accept at least that from him?

"There's no point in discussing it," he said. "We'll ride together until we're almost to town. Then you're going to go home, and I'll head to the sheriff."

"No."

His brows contracted. "Yes."

"No."

"Maddy." Taking a deep breath, he forced more calmness into his voice. "This isn't negotiable. You will go home, or I'll hog-tie you across your sidle and bring you in like those two bodies over there."

"Fine," she said. "But I'll still go to the sheriff."

He raked one hand through his hair. "God damn it to hell," he snarled.

"I'm glad you're taking this with such grace," she said, loftily. "Now, about that shirt . . ."

Still muttering under his breath—and still naked—he stalked over to the horses and rummaged through his saddlebags. Then he came back to her, a dark blue shirt in one hand.

She smiled.

John registered that smile with a jolt in his guts. She'd won this particular game, he thought, and was enjoying the triumph. It occurred to him that everything they'd shared might just be a ploy in the even bigger game they were playing. She might have been a virgin, but there was nothing naive about Maddy Saylor.

"You look awful damn pleased with yourself," he said.

"I'm always pleased when common sense wins out over idiocy," she replied.

"Your parents should have beaten you with a buggy whip the moment they discovered what you were like," he growled. "It would have saved the rest of the world a lot of grief later on."

"Perhaps," she agreed, meeting his gaze. "But it's too late now."

Maddy glanced at John from the corner of her eye. He rode with his gaze kept determinedly forward, but she knew he knew she was looking at him.

Truly, she thought, he was an insufferable man. Now, *there* was someone who could have benefitted from a good beating early in life. Arrogant, stubborn, convinced that his way was better than anyone else's . . . She was tempted to let him do it his way, and take the consequences.

So she, too, turned her gaze forward and left it there until she saw Cofield squatting on the horizon ahead. Its white-washed buildings almost seemed to glow in the haze of heat that rose from the ground.

John glanced at her out of the corner of his eye, wondering just how much trouble she was going to give him. She didn't understand. All her life, she'd been sheltered by her family's position. She didn't know how cruel gossip could be, and how vicious. There had been many a girl who'd been turned from accuser to accused simply because people were convinced she had somehow seduced a man into attacking her.

He wished he didn't care. But he did. The afternoon sun turned her hair ruddy, like sparks struck off metal. His shirt nearly matched the color of her eyes. Her breasts strained the front of the garment badly, and, combined with the movement of her horse, sustained a gentle bounce that was steadily driving him crazy.

Damn him for a fool, he'd spent the day in torment, wanting to tear that shirt right off her, baring her to his eyes and mouth and hands, yet also painfully aware that there were two dead men behind them, and that the situation was hardly conducive to seduction.

"Maddy, it's time," he said. "Go home. Let me handle this."

"I thought we had this settled."

"Nothing between us is settled," he growled.

She raised her brows. "Ah, but it is."

"Ah, yes. You're a practical woman, as I remember. So you're willing to accept your own responsibility in this, just as you did in the 'purely physical' moments we shared. A fair and rational perspective, as always."

Maddy fought a blush, and failed. "That isn't the issue at hand," she said.

"Yes, it is," he replied. "And if you don't think so, you're more a fool than I think you are."

"Very well," she snapped. "I *am* being rational about this. You see, I grew up with a brother who possessed both charm and an abiding interest in women. So I'm familiar with men's attitudes about . . . that."

"And men seduce without emotions becoming involved."

"Don't they? Judging from your . . ." she blushed again, painfully, almost having said the word *performance*. But oh, it had been wonderful, thrilling, satisfying . . . "And I must point out that *you* didn't seem to mind the lack of emotional involvement."

John grinned, thinking that she was very beautiful with her cheeks flaming and her eyes horrified at her own lascivious thoughts. But her attitude annoyed him just a bit more than her beauty entranced him, and he wanted to make her pay for her assumption of his rapaciousness.

"Don't you consider yourself enough of a woman to inspire me beyond my former capabilities?" he asked, studying her through narrowed eyes.

"I am not a fool," she replied.

"So we shared a tumble in the hay." Tilting his hat so it shadowed his face, he watched dismay spread across hers. "Not a bad tumble, as tumbles go, but nothing to bind us."

Maddy's heart recoiled from that assessment; her mind expected it. That lovemaking had been so much more than physical for her. It had stunned her with its intensity, and it had made her look again at the person she'd thought herself to be. No longer could she think of herself as practical, imperturbable Maddy. The woman in John's arms had been passionate, responsive, and more vulnerable than she would have believed.

As far as being binding, well, men never did understand that it was the heart that bound a man and a woman, not the body. She'd loved him first. Passion had followed, a spark struck by the greater flame.

And that made her angry. No matter that she'd known that men didn't understand such things. She loved him, so he should have understood. True, it was unfair. True, she was being unreasonable. And that only annoyed her more; Maddy Saylor had always prided herself on being fair.

Turning his head, John caught her gaze. He knew she didn't want to be caught, nor see the possibilities in his eyes. Her gaze fluttered and dodged, but he held her, gently but firmly, as a man might hold an injured bird in his hands.

"I want you again, Maddy," he said. "More than you know, more than is safe or sane. If I had my way, I'd put you on the ground right here and now and make love to you until you screamed."

Maddy drew her breath in sharply, mind and spirit frozen by the beauty of the image evoked by his words. He had made love to her gently, totally, and he had made her feel as if she were the most important thing in the world to him. His touch had brought fever and chills, razor-sharp passion and a tenderness so sweet her heart had ached from it. And oh, yes, she had screamed last night, once or twice, as the pleasure became almost too sharp to bear.

If he touched her, if she allowed herself one moment of weakness, they would indeed end up on the ground, right here, right now.

She wanted to. God help her, she wanted to.

If she opened her mouth, she would tell him so. She had to get away from him until she had herself more fully in control. With a flick of her reins, she urged her mount into a canter. She hoped John wouldn't follow, for she didn't trust herself. It was a dratted lot of inconvenience when you couldn't even trust yourself, she thought sourly.

John nearly went after her. But his gut reaction urged him to stay, and that instinct had saved his life too many times for him to ignore it now. Her action had surprised him; he'd never seen Maddy Saylor run from anything, especially an argument.

Whatever the reason, her flight had given him what he'd wanted all along: to keep her from telling what Berry and Marsh had nearly done to her, and suffer the storm of gossip that was bound to follow.

And then he'd also seen the way her eyes had changed when he'd talked about making love to her. Desire had sparked in those stormy blue depths, an awareness of passion shared and remembered.

The little minx had been tempted.

That realization restored his good mood. He would never forget that look in her eyes, and he planned to take full advantage of it. For he had no intention of staying away from her. He didn't know what the hell to call this thing between them: obsession, lust, insanity, or perhaps all three put together. It didn't matter. He and Maddy had been caught up in a bonfire stronger than anything either could have imagined, and it would have them until it burned itself out—or maybe until they were both consumed. Whichever. He didn't care. As long as he was able to keep touching her, the world could end.

Maddy Saylor had a lot to learn about men and women, he thought, not for the first time, *and he was damn well going to enjoy teaching her.*

If they didn't hang him first, that is.

He rode slowly down Main Street toward the sheriff's office. Seeing the burdens carried by the two pack horses, people had followed in his wake until he had a sizable crowd following him.

Damn, he thought, *people surely enjoy any kind of a show, even a gruesome one. Especially a gruesome one.*

Sheriff Cooper came out of his office and stood waiting. His only concession to his injured leg was the shift of weight to the other one. Neither his seamed face nor his eyes showed awareness of pain.

John drew his mount to a halt in front of the sheriff. Dismounting, he went to tie the other horses to the hitching post. Then he untied Jim Berry's corpse and slid it gently to the ground. The crowd surged forward.

"Well, ah'll be," one cowboy said. "Ole Berry finally got his."

"Ain't nobody gonna grieve over that bastard," another man said.

A general murmur of agreement followed. John set his jaw grimly as he untied Gordon's body and lowered it to the ground. The murmuring stopped as shock set in. Then a sibilant whisper went through the crowd.

"Oh, Lawd, mister," someone said. "I hope you wasn't the one who shot him."

"If he did, he's a dead man hisself," the first cowboy said. "Zachary Marsh ain't a man to have as an enemy, and this sure ain't gonna make him feel kindly to whoever did it."

Sheriff Cooper raised that gunmetal gaze to the crowd. "Somebody go git the undertaker. And I reckon I saw Zachary Marsh over at the saloon. You, Shawn Drago, you go on over and tell him I want to see him pronto."

"Shit's gonna fly now," someone muttered.

"Don't you folks have somethin' else to do today?" the sheriff growled.

"Nope," was the consensus.

Cooper shrugged, then crooked his forefinger at John, who followed him into the office. Several cowboys peered in the open doorway. With a wordless growl, the sheriff slammed the door closed.

Easing into the battered chair behind the desk, Cooper pointed to an even more decrepit chair nearby. "Set yoreself down."

"I'll stand, thanks," John said, taking a spot where he could watch from the window.

"Hmmm. Might do the same if'n I was in yore shoes. Did you kill em?"

John nodded. "They jumped me out near Sutter's Ridge last night. I didn't even know who they were until they were dead."

"Anybody with you?"

"No."

"Shit." Cooper reached for a half-empty bottle of whiskey and took a drink. "Nobody gives a tinker's damn about that bastard Berry. He's had it comin' fer a long time. But Zach Marsh is gonna want yore hide real bad." Tilting his chair back against the wall, he fixed John with a not unsympathetic stare. "He's gonna insist that you stand trial. And I'm gonna have to hold you for the circuit judge."

"You know I didn't murder those men."

"Mebbe. But I ain't the one who decides that. Now, not that I wouldn't be inclined to let it go, if it was left up to me. Seein' that you saved my life, I got real sympathy fer yore situation. But if I got to arrest you, I will."

"Is this one of those get-out-of-town-fast kind of warnings?" John asked.

"That would be a sure death warrant, son. The Marshes'll put a higher reward on you than the one on Derek Saylor. These damned bounty hunters are as restless as badgers in a rainstorm, and twice as mean. You'll have half the territory sniffin' yore trail."

John smiled. "That might be interesting. But I don't run from anybody."

The door banged open with a suddenness that made both

men draw their pistols. Zachary Marsh, his face twisted with anger, stood framed in the opening.

"Who killed my boy?" he snarled.

"I did," John said.

Marsh's hand twitched. But since John hadn't yet put his gun away, the twitch didn't develop into anything more. The rancher's eyes were ugly with hate hot enough to burn John where he stood.

The sheriff put his own gun away. "Put up yore weapon, Ballard."

"No," John said, quite amiably.

Cooper dropped the issue of the gun, proving he was a wise man. "We got us a situation here, Zach. Ballard here says it were self defense—Gordon and Jim Berry jumped him out by Sutter's ridge."

"He's lyin'," Marsh said. "Why would my boy do that?"

"Wal . . ." The sheriff scratched at the stubble on his chin, "There's the matter of that fight y'all had awhile ago. You got to admit yore boys carried a lot of hard feelin's away from there."

Marsh snorted. "My boys were taught to stand boot to boot with anybody and spit in his eye. If Gordon wanted Ballard's hide, he'd of got it right here in town."

"Last time I looked," John said, his voice deceptively lazy, "every one of those boys was old enough to be called men."

"Sheriff, I'm an upstandin', church-goin' member of this community," Marsh said. "And a good bit of the money in that there bank is mine. Now, my son is dead by this man's hand. As much as I'd like to take him out and shoot him, I know that's not the way."

Sheriff Cooper's eyes widened. "That's a charitable attitude you got there, Zach."

"I respect the law, always have," the rancher said. "I'm willin' to let the circuit judge decide what to do with him, and it's yore job to see that he gets the chance."

The sheriff sighed. "Since you put it that way, I don't see as I have a choice. Ballard, put the gun down."

"No."

"Listen to me, son. This is the best way."

"No." John didn't take his gaze off Marsh. Give his gun up? Not likely.

Then the click of a hammer being pulled back sent alarm shooting through him. By the time he looked at the sheriff, however, it was too late. Cooper had the scattergun aimed right at his belly, and no man could move fast enough to avoid that wide-angle blast.

"I like you, Ballard," the sheriff said. "I shorely do. But I swore to uphold the law, and I got to do this. Drop the gun or I drop you."

John gave a wordless growl of frustration. But he also knew he had no choice; with a quick flip, he reversed his weapon and tossed it butt-first to the sheriff.

"Thanks," Cooper said. "Now move aside from the door."

The sheriff unlocked the door that separated the jail from the office. Then he stepped aside for John to precede him.

A moment later, John found himself locked in one of the pair of cells that made up Cofield's jail. A cot occupied the wall beneath the tiny barred window, and a bucket sat in the far corner.

"Circuit judge is due first of next week," Cooper said. "Meanwhile, you'll do all right. Meals come from Miz Brodie over at the hotel, and better food there ain't."

John didn't bother to answer. Clamping his hands around the bars, he looked out into the office, where Zachary Marsh still stood in the doorway.

Smiling.

Twenty-two

Maddy rode straight home. The tawdry rooms had never seemed so welcoming as she pelted up the stairs.

She flung the door open, and Blanche sprang away from Hank's cot as though she'd been burned. Her face shone scarlet, and the top two buttons of her blouse were undone. Hank, however, looked perfectly at ease. *More* than perfectly at ease; he had the look of a cat who'd just devoured the canary.

Well, Maddy thought, *I* certainly don't have the right to point any fingers here.

"Maddy, we—" Blanche began.

"You didn't expect me," Maddy finished for her. "That was quite obvious, thank you. I would have knocked, of course, had I known there might be something going on here, but I was under the impression that Mr. Vann was grievously wounded, so grievously, in fact, that he was incapable of returning to his campsite."

She abruptly became aware that both Blanche and Hank were staring at her as though she'd lost her mind. Perhaps she had. Certainly only a madwoman would bed her brother's sworn enemy. Worse, fallen in love with the man! Truly, she and Blanche must both have gone insane.

Something tickled her face, and she reached up to brush it off. Her fingers came away wet. *Tears,* she thought wonderingly. *I didn't even know I was crying.*

"There's nothing to cry about," she said aloud.

Hank's gaze drifted down to her shirt. Or rather, John's shirt.

"Sure, Maddy. Sure. Blanche, maybe you ought to take your sister into the bedroom and have a talk with her."

"I believe you're right," Blanche said, putting her arm around Maddy.

Maddy allowed herself to be led into the other room. The moment the door closed, she sank to her knees upon the rough plank floor. Blanche came down with her, wrapping her arms comfortingly around her.

"Maddy, what happened?" she asked.

"I'm . . . I'm . . ." A wash of tears drowned Maddy's voice for a moment, and she had to swallow hard to go on. "I'm a fallen woman," she whispered.

Blanche's eyes went wide. Consternation and sympathy warred in those soft blue depths, and she pulled Maddy even closer.

"I wondered last night," she murmured. "I knew I shouldn't worry. I told myself that we're both more capable than most men, either on horseback or off, and that you could handle Jim Berry just fine—"

"That's just it," Maddy said. "I couldn't. Berry and Gordon Marsh spotted me, and managed to get the drop on me. They were going to rape me, Blanche, then murder me and leave me for the buzzards. And they would have done it, too, if it hadn't been for John."

"Did he kill them?" Blanche asked.

Maddy nodded.

"Good." Blanche's eyes were no longer soft; for the moment, she looked very much like Papa in the midst of one of his tantrums. "That saves me the trouble of killing them myself."

Maddy scrubbed her tears away with her sleeve. "But I—"

"Made love with the man you love," Blanche said. "So what? Did those two beasts hurt you?"

"John enjoyed a virgin, if that's what you're asking," Maddy said, her tone arid.

"Not that, you twit. Did they *hurt* you?"

"Blanche, sometimes you can be the most stubborn, infuriating—"

"Take that ridiculous shirt off," Blanche ordered.

Interfering with Blanche when she was in this mood was always more trouble than it was worth, so Maddy meekly unbuttoned the shirt and slipped it off.

Blanche drew her breath in sharply. "Oh, Maddy!" She got to her feet and began to pace the room, her jerky movements betraying her agitation.

"They're only bruises," Maddy said. "A few days from now, they'll be gone. But Blanche, what am I going to do about John Ballard?"

Her sister turned incredulous blue eyes at her. "I think you've already done what you needed to do."

"That?" Maddy felt her cheeks go hot. "I was upset, and he'd just saved my life and my honor, and I just got carried away and . . . it was a mistake. The worst mistake of my life. But I'm never going to be weak like that again, and I'm never going to allow myself to be—"

"Stop," Blanche said. "Honey, you're getting upset all over again. Now, this isn't the time to be making decisions like that. You've just been through a horrible experience—"

"John will be glad to hear that," Maddy said. "A horrible experience, indeed!"

She began to laugh, absurdly, uncontrollably. She laughed until her sides hurt, until the tears flowed so copiously that they began to spatter on the floor.

"Slap her face or dose her good with whiskey," Hank called from the other room.

"Mind your own damned business, Hank Vann," Maddy called back.

She didn't even see the slap coming. But it made her ears ring, and stopped the laughter so quickly she forgot to breathe for a moment. Then she drew her breath in with a great, shuddering gasp, and fell forward and buried her face upon her knees.

Blanche laid her hand gently on Maddy's hair. "Sweetheart, I'm sorry."

"Just leave me alone," she said. "Please, just leave me alone!"

She closed her eyes, shutting the world out, shutting herself in. After a moment, she felt Blanche get up. The door opened and closed, and the whisper of skirts faded away.

But Blanche soon returned, and a moment later Maddy heard the clink of glass against glass.

"Maddy, look at me," Blanche ordered.

Stung by her sister's peremptory tone, Maddy raised her head. Blanche handed her a glass with an inch of whiskey in the bottom. The tawny afternoon light cast amber sparks in the liquor.

"Drink it," Blanche said. "The way Papa taught us."

"I don't like whiskey," Maddy complained.

"Drink it."

Scowling, Maddy tossed the liquor to the back of her throat and waited for the burn. It came a heartbeat later, fiery heat starting in her stomach and spreading like a prairie blaze through the rest of her body.

"Ohhhh," she gasped, handing the glass back. "What awful stuff!"

"It's supposed to be awful," Blanche said. "That's why men drink it."

Someone banged on the door, and there was an urgency to the summons that brought Maddy to her feet. By the time she'd donned John's shirt again, Blanche had already hurried out into the front room.

"Don't you dare get up," she hissed at Hank.

The bounty hunter grunted a bit peevishly, but did what he was told. There was, however, a definite, pistol-shaped bulge in the blanket beside him.

Maddy was beginning to like the man. If she weren't so dizzy from exhaustion and the whiskey, she might almost have managed a smile. But she did remember to slip her derringer into her skirt pocket before going out to join Blanche.

Blanche glanced over her shoulder to make sure Maddy was ready, then swung the door open. Maddy's mouth dropped open. Standing on the step was the young woman from the saloon, the one whom Jim Berry had treated so badly.

"I'm here to see Maddy Saylor," she said.

"Why . . . ah . . . Of course," Blanche said, stepping aside.

Black net stockings flashed beneath the girl's too-short skirt as she came into the room, and her face was almost clownish in its heavy covering of cosmetics. But she held her head high, and determination steadied her gaze as she faced Maddy.

"Remember me?" she asked.

"Yes." Maddy scrabbled frantically through her memory. "Ah, Maisie, isn't it?"

"Yes, ma'am. Maisie Griggs."

"This is my sister, Blanche, and that is Mr. Vann over there on the cot."

"Pleased to meet ya, Blanche," the girl said. "How're you doin', Hank?"

"Feelin' better, Maisie," he replied.

They sounded as though they knew each other well, Maddy thought. She didn't dare look at Blanche. She didn't dare think about Hank and Maisie at all. Certainly no Saylor had ever had to deal with a situation quite like this, but manners, fortunately, did not desert her. "Would you like a cup of tea, Maisie?"

"Oh, no, ma'am." Maisie looked shocked, as though Maddy had suggested something wildly improper. "I just came to tell you that Sheriff Cooper arrested Mr. Ballard fer killin' Gordon Marsh. He's sittin' in jail now."

Maddy noticed that Blanche was staring at her, and realized that her sister expected her to rush to do something to help John Ballard. On any other day, she would have. Whether it was the whiskey, or perhaps the devil himself, but she found herself possessed by a veritable demon of mischief.

Serves him right, that nasty little voice whispered in her head. *A night in jail might take the stuffing out of the most arrogant of men.*

She looked back at her sister with wide, innocent eyes, and laid her hand on her bosom. "Oh, the poor man," she cooed. "I should go visit him."

Blanche's eyes widened, then narrowed. Crossing her arms, she studied her sister speculatively. Maddy just smiled.

"Thank you for telling us, Maisie," she said.

"That ain't all," the girl said. She glanced over at Blanche, who was still standing beside the open door. "Mind closing that, Blanche?"

For a moment, Maddy thought her sister had lost her wits. Then Blanche swallowed hard, shut the door, and moved to a spot from which she could see both Hank and Maisie. The gaze she turned on the bounty hunter was less than loverlike.

"What is it, Maisie?" Maddy asked.

"You don't think ole Zachary Marsh is really goin' to wait fer the circuit judge, do you?" the girl asked.

Shock ripped cold through Maddy's chest, and all thoughts of petty revenge flew right out of her mind. "You think he's going to try to take John from the jail and do something to him?"

"Somethin'," Maisie said, her tone dry. "I heard some of his men talkin' about a lynchin' in the saloon a while ago."

"Did they say when?"

"Tonight."

"Tonight," Maddy mused, her thoughts spinning wildly. "I'd better have a talk with Sheriff Cooper; I can prove that John killed those men in self defense."

"You'd better be convincin' Zach Marsh instead of the sheriff," Maisie said.

"Then I shall do so," Maddy said. She cocked her head to one side and regarded the other woman steadily. "I'm grateful that you came to me with this, Maisie, but I can't help but wonder why."

"I know what you're thinkin'." Putting her hands on her hips, Maisie fixed Maddy with a challenging stare. "I'm a whore, so I don't have no principles at all—"

"I don't presume to judge your way of life," Maddy said. *Especially now,* she thought. *Most especially now.*

"It's all right. You're not the only fancy lady who's ever thought *that.*" The girl folded her arms over her chest. "Jim Berry treated me like dirt, and you called him on it. Now, I ain't fool enough to think it was because you thought anything of me. But wrong is wrong, and you stood up for me when not one of those yahoos so much as lifted a finger to help. So I'm beholden to you, whether you like it or not."

Maddy swallowed against a sudden constriction in her throat. She'd been touched by the girl's words, even more by the sight of the gold beneath the dross of the makeup and clothes. And she would be grateful for this lesson about her more unfortunate sisters.

"Thank you, Maisie," she said.

The girl bobbed her head. "Now, you don't have to speak to me if 'n we meet. I'll understand."

"You've acted as a friend today," Maddy said. "And I always speak to my friends."

"Even whores?"

Maddy recoiled, unable to think of Maisie in terms of that ugly word. "I will never think of you as . . . that," she said. "Only as a woman who did me a very good deed. We Saylors never forget such things."

"Fair enough," the girl replied. Her voice was matter-of-fact, but her eyes glowed. "You goin' down to talk to the sheriff now?"

"I think I should."

Maisie nodded. Then she grinned, revealing a chipped front tooth. "Before you do, take some advice from me."

"Yes?"

"Change into something with a higher collar."

"What . . . Oh!" Maddy's cheeks burned as she remem-

bered how John had sucked on her neck, and the resulting
red-brown mark.

"Don't worry about it, honey," Maisie said. "It happens to
the best of us."

"Oh!" Maddy said again, faintly this time.

She watched through a haze of embarrassment as Maisie
went out. Good heavens, what a humiliating situation! Well,
she'd certainly had her dignity well-punctured today.

Fortunately, Blanche and Hank didn't seem to have heard;
they were still glaring at each other. For a moment, Maddy
thought they'd turned to stone, but then Blanche made a sharp,
despairing gesture.

"Exactly how well does she know you, Hank?" Blanche
asked.

"Not *that* well," he protested.

"How well?"

"Well, I had a drink with her," he said, then added defen-
sively, "It was before I met you. Look here, Blanche. I never
pretended to be no angel. But I did promise to be honest with
you, and honest I'm gonna be. If I hadn't been dead broke
after that drink, Maisie and I would have been much better
friends."

"Good Gad," Maddy exclaimed, seeing her sister's stricken
face. "Don't you have better sense than to be honest about
something like that?"

"I'd rather have his honesty," Blanche said, her eyes shining.

Maddy shook her head in exasperation, then went into the
bedroom to change. It was obvious that the Saylor sisters had
truly gone mad somehow, and wouldn't be sane again until
this whole thing was over.

Tonight, however, she had a man to save.

The last rays of sunset slanted in horizontal orange bars
between the buildings as Maddy stepped into Sheriff Cooper's
office. She'd scrubbed and changed clothes, and had pulled

her hair back into a sleek knot at the back of her head. She'd donned her emotional armor, as well, shielding herself with the dignity learned at her mother's knee. It had always served her in good stead; she only hoped it wouldn't fail her now.

The sheriff was sleeping, his chair tipped back against the wall. Maddy cleared her throat. Cooper straightened in a rush that brought the chair legs to the floor with a thump.

His eyes widened when he saw Maddy. He snatched his hat off and unfolded his lanky length from the chair. "What kin I do fer you, ma'am?"

"Sheriff, I have proof that John Ballard killed those men in self-defense," she said.

"Don't matter."

"What do you mean, it doesn't matter?"

He held both hands up in a conciliatory gesture. "Now, don't go gettin' in a swivet, Maddy. See, you sayin' you got proof don't help him none. He admitted to killin' those two fellers. Now, everybody knows Jim Berry needed killin'. But it ain't the same with Gordon Marsh. Ole Zachary is a big man in these here parts, and his say-so holds a lot of weight. He wants Ballard held for the circuit judge. I ain't got no choice but to hold him."

"When does the judge arrive?"

"First of next week."

"Come, Sheriff Cooper, think this through," Maddy said. "You know Zachary Marsh has no intention of letting John live long enough to talk to the judge."

"I don't know that, no, ma'am."

"His men were talking about a lynching in the saloon," she protested.

"Talkin' ain't doin'."

"But you can't take the chance," Maddy said. "You're here all alone—"

"I ain't alone, Miz Saylor," he replied. "I appointed me a deputy today. Insurance."

"One man?"

The sheriff snorted. "Don't you worry none. My jail's built good and strong, and in twenty-four years of bein' a sheriff, nobody's taken a prisoner from me. I ain't about to let anybody start now. I got me a man to watch the back door, and I plan to watch the front."

He scraped his fingernails across his stubbled cheek. "Any way you look at it, this is the safest place for Ballard right now. Out there . . ." he thrust one thumb toward the street. "He's fair game to Marsh or anybody Marsh pays."

Maddy didn't reply. That seemed a very thin premise on which to bet John's life.

And she had a time limit; bruises faded quickly, and by the time the judge came to Cofield, hers might be gone. Then it would be only her word, which would surely be challenged by the Marshes.

So once again, she had to take charge of a situation. Zachary Marsh was an influential man; John was an outsider. Which would be believed? Maddy knew how such things worked; she'd seen them before, in Virginia. Truly, it was simple: the outsider lost. For while it might be hard to believe one's neighbor doing heinous things, it wasn't hard at all to believe that a stranger might.

"Now, you just go on home and stop worryin'," Sheriff Cooper said. "I've got everythin' under control."

My eye, Maddy thought. "I'm sure you're right, Sheriff," she said. "Could I see Mr. Ballard for a moment?"

"Shore, ma'am."

He led her to the barred door separating the office from the jail. She peered past him as he unlocked the door. John paced the length of his cell, looking very much like a tiger in a cage. Back and forth, back and forth he strode, all that vitality penned up inside iron bars. Maddy's heart gave a painful lurch. This was a man who would suffer more than others from being chained. Like Derek, his spirit would wither.

John stopped pacing when he saw her, moving to the front

of the cell to wait. She smoothed her hair back, although it didn't need it, and gazed at Cooper from under her lashes.

"Sheriff, would it be all right if I talk to him privately?"

"Wal . . ." He grinned at her. "You ain't plannin' to slip him a gun or anythin', are you?"

"Sheriff, you wound me," she said.

He left the room, although she noted that he did stay where he could see John's cell. No privacy was going to be allowed, obviously. She gave a ladylike sniff. No such paltry ploy could stop a Saylor.

"John," she said, loudly enough for Sheriff Cooper to hear. "Darling."

John's eyes widened. For a brief moment, he thought that note of tenderness in her voice was real. It went through him like a hot knife through butter.

Then he realized that dear, sweet Maddy was up to something. Not a bad thing under the circumstances, he mused. "Hello, my sweet," he said.

He pressed close against the bars, closing his hands around them at shoulder level. The scent of lilac drifted to his nostrils, and he breathed deeply, savoring it. He wanted to touch her so badly he ached with it.

"You shouldn't have come here," he said.

"You're right," she said, her tone dry. "I should let you rot here for something you didn't do, even though I possess information that can save you. Then I could look at myself in the mirror every morning and know I let a man go to prison— or worse—because I didn't have the courage to take action."

"Maddy—"

"Zachary Marsh is planning to lynch you tonight," she whispered.

John let his breath out sharply. "I'm not surprised. He was much too agreeable when Sheriff Cooper wanted to lock me up for the circuit judge."

"Right." She moved closer, aware that the sheriff was watching them. "I told Sheriff Cooper that I had proof that you killed those men in self-defense."

"I have a feeling I'm not going to like this. I told you—"

"You would stake your life to protect my reputation?" she asked. "That's insane. I shan't ask that price, nor will I pay it."

"Stay out of this, Maddy."

"This is a matter of life or death," she hissed. "Yours, to be exact."

"Go away."

Unobtrusively, she flicked a glance over her shoulder at the sheriff. Cooper had propped one shoulder against the outer door and was cleaning his fingernails with his knife.

John watched the movement of her eyes and wondered what was to come next. One never knew with Maddy. She was truly a vision as she walked toward him, the dark blue of her dress making her eyes look pure indigo and as deep as the sea at night. There were sparks in those storm-blue depths, a glimmering of passion renewed and remembered.

Maddy grasped the bars just below his hands. It was a ploy, nothing more, an attempt to cover their planning under the guise of murmuring romantic nothings.

But John slid his hands down to cover hers, and everything changed. Her flesh became very sensitive, registering the contrast of cold metal and the warmth of his palms. Maddy tried to think only of her purpose. She didn't—absolutely, positively didn't—want to become distracted now. Still, her breathing had become swift and shallow, and her internal temperature went up several degrees.

Oh, Lord, she thought. *Why does this have to be so dratted complicated? Why can't I control the reactions of my own body where this man is concerned?*

"Why are you doing this?" she whispered.

"I'm just making it look good," he said. "Making it look real."

Maddy knew when a man had reached the stage of complete unreasonableness, and John was definitely there.

"You are an idiot," she said.

"And you are an infuriating baggage. I wish that just once, you'd—"

"Do as I was told?" she finished for him.

"Yes!"

She regarded him with narrowed eyes. "And I suppose I should also think that the sun and moon and stars all revolve around John Ballard." Taking a deep breath, she drew a hard rein on her temper. "Well, I've never been long on adoration."

John's peevishness evaporated, to be replaced by amusement. Surely the mold had been broken when Maddy Saylor had been made.

"You're very fierce," he murmured.

"Sometimes," she retorted. "Especially when faced with stupidity."

"Come closer, Maddy."

She saw a familiar glint in his eyes. Desire had roused in those green-gold depths despite his surroundings, a reckless fire that spurred an answering heat in her and drew her forward with irresistible power.

She would save this man. Difficult though he was, dangerous to Derek and to her peace of mind, she would save him.

It *was* real, Maddy thought. Too real. She tried to slide her hands out from under his, but in vain. Finally she gave up, trying to keep her mind rational beneath the sensations that threatened to sweep her away.

"Don't ever think you're less of a woman simply because you've met a few men who didn't appreciate strength," he said. "In my opinion, you're one hell of a woman."

"Well, you're stupid enough to have gotten yourself arrested for murder, so your assessment is suspect," she retorted.

He laughed. "Ah, Maddy, you are truly delicious. A man will never suffer from false ego with you around."

Maddy swallowed against an unaccountable tightness in her

chest. John's eyes held admiration and tenderness, and a deep, abiding passion. He wasn't afraid of her strength; in fact, it excited him. He didn't mind her stubbornness or the rationality of her mind. And in possessing her, he hadn't tried to break her. No, he'd reveled in the woman. Maddy, as she was, as she always would be.

It was thrilling, seductive, infinitely dangerous. For he would cost her her brother, and that was a price she couldn't pay. Not even for John Ballard.

"You know what I want from you," he murmured.

"Yes," she replied. "You want my brother, and you want me to forgive you for wrecking his life. Well, that's something I cannot give you. I'm here because you saved my life, and I owe you. Nothing more."

"Do you really think it's that simple, Maddy?"

She looked him straight in the eyes. "Do you like being in here?"

"Here?" His gaze flicked around the jail for a moment, then returned to her. "Of course not. No one likes to be caged."

"Yet you would cage my brother."

"Your brother has broken the law."

"He didn't."

"Maddy . . ." With a gusty breath, John hunkered closer to the bars. "Are you telling me that letting your brother go is the price of helping me tonight?"

Annoyed by the question, she narrowed her eyes. "Even if I had so little integrity as to propose such a thing, I'm sure you are much too pigheaded to agree. But I owe you, as I said, and we Saylors always pay our debts. Now, we have to distract Sheriff Cooper. I suggest you kiss me—"

John claimed her mouth in a hungry, tempestuous kiss. He'd been taken aback for a moment by her rather clinical demand for a kiss, but his wits had returned with a vengeance. Kiss her? Oh, yeah. He didn't give a damn why.

Maddy was overwhelmed by the power of his embrace. It was made of passion, tenderness, and a need so strong it shook her to her soul. His tongue slid over hers with sensual slowness, tasted the sensitive insides of her lips, the delicate edges of her teeth, then dipped deeper to taste her honeyed depths. He reached up to cup her cheek gently in his hand, his thumb straying to caress the corner of her mouth.

She sighed. Every nerve ending had come to quivering attention. She hadn't expected this. The world dropped away in a wild, chaotic whirl, leaving only John. She clung to the bars with all her strength, sure that she would fall if she let go for a moment. And she clung to him, to his hard, tender mouth that worshiped her, that made the world go away in this driving rush of passion.

She nearly forgot what she'd come here to do. With the last reserves of rationality left to her, she slipped the derringer out of her pocket and into John's.

For a moment his mouth faltered, and she knew she'd surprised him. Then his touch firmed, and he continued the kiss as though nothing had happened. Maddy found herself whirling in a stormwind of desire so hot she thought she surely would catch fire.

"The magic is still there," John muttered against her mouth.

His words brought her back to reality with a rush, and she tore her mouth from his. Her cheeks burned as she remembered Sheriff Cooper, whose eyes must surely be popping right out of his head.

Turning, she saw the sheriff grinning at her. The heat of her blush grew deeper. Strange, because she'd planned all along to use a kiss as a means of getting the derringer to John. But she hadn't planned on this . . . this excess of desire. Her emotions had to be written all over her face, and Cooper wasn't, an unobservant man.

"Sheriff, I'd like to leave now," she said.

"Ma'am."

He unlocked the door to let her out. His expression never changed, but something that looked an awful lot like laughter lurked in the depths of his gunmetal eyes.

Maddy fell back on the few shreds of dignity left to her. "Thank you, Sheriff."

"You're welcome, ma'am."

She left the office quickly, her mind spinning with plans. She only wished she knew what time Zach Marsh planned to come for John; it had to be late, when all the townsfolk were asleep. No matter how rough-and-ready the citizens of Cofield might be, they wouldn't countenance the lynching of an innocent man.

Humming under her breath, she made her way home. She hesitated for a moment outside, gauging the sounds in the room. It seemed utterly silent. Then she heard Blanche sigh sharply once, a sound of passion and fulfillment.

So much for self-control, Maddy thought. *For either of us. God help us both, for this can only end in disaster.*

Still, she didn't have the heart to interrupt. They had so little time. Blanche was in love, deeply and desperately, and deserved these precious few moments with the man she loved. And after her own weakness, Maddy no longer felt she had the right to stand in judgment of anyone.

With a sigh, she turned and went downstairs to the shop. It was time to take stock of their ammunition; there was no way she would allow Zachary Marsh to lynch John.

She might have the urge to shoot him herself at times, but he'd saved her life. A life for a life; she ought to be glad to be given the opportunity to save his so soon. John was the last man on earth to whom she wanted to be beholden.

Humming under her breath, she closed the door behind her and fumbled in the dark for the matches she'd left lying on the worktable. Then she froze.

Someone was in the room with her.

He made no noise, not even the soft noise of breathing. But she could feel him in the shadows, a presence that sent alarm shrilling along her spine.

For a moment, she regretted giving the derringer away. But even as that thought occurred to her, a sinewy hand clamped hard upon her mouth.

Twenty-three

Maddy jabbed back with her elbow and connected with ribs. The intruder's breath went out with a whoosh, and he let go of her abruptly.

"Ouch!" he gasped.

Maddy knew that voice. "Derek!"

"Hello, big sister," he said. "You certainly haven't lost your touch. You used to do that to me when we were kids."

"You deserved it then, and you deserve it now. What madness has possessed you that you came here?"

"I had to see how my lovely sisters are doing, you know," he said.

"Well, I don't have time for you tonight," she said crossly. "I've got to stop a lynching."

"What do you want me to do?"

She marched to draw the curtain, then lit the lamp and turned it down low. Derek looked like a bronze statue in the muted light—if any statue had ever had that Devil-may-care glint in its eye or a smile to charm the rattles off a snake.

"You are not to help," she said. "Half the men in town want to kill you."

"Then I'll make sure I'm not seen," he replied.

"Derek—"

"You're not going to do this alone," he said.

He crossed his arms over his chest. Maddy stared at him in complete exasperation. "Derek, I'm not going to be alone.

Blanche will be with me. Or rather, Blanche will be somewhere close with Papa's Henry."

"Won't work, Maddy. We're in this together, as we always
have been." He grinned at her, and she was no more proof
against it than any other woman in the world. "Now, who are
we saving tonight?"

"John Ballard," she said. "He's the Pinkerton agent who
was sent to bring you to justice."

"Ah, he's the one who's been hugging my trail so hard,"
Derek said. "Good man. He's come close. Give him a little
time, he might even catch me."

She crossed her arms, mimicking both his stance and his
stubbornness. "John was a Yankee scout during the war. He's
good, and he's appallingly stubborn, and he feels it's his duty
to bring you in no matter what."

"So, sister mine, why are you so set on rescuing him?"

"He saved my life." Maddy sighed, knowing she'd just lost
the argument.

"Then we owe him," Derek said.

"You could die."

He shrugged. "We still owe him."

"You're a twit."

"Now that," he said, grinning that rogue's grin, "is hardly
news."

Maddy ran her hands along a bolt of deep gold satin just
the color of Derek's hair. John and Derek were both at stake
tonight; one misstep, one wrong move, and she could lose
them both.

"I'm in love with him," she said, surprising herself. It wasn't
something she'd expected to tell her brother.

Derek chuckled. "Maddy, it's written all over your face. If
you thought to fool anyone, especially me, you were wrong.
At least Blanche has sense enough to give her man a chance."

"Who have you been listening to?" Maddy demanded.

"Blanche. She thinks you're being stubborn."

"Derek, Hank's a bounty hunter. And he's hunting you."

"So let him hunt," he said, shrugging. "As long as he treats my sister right, I'm not going to fault him for what he does for a living."

Maddy closed her eyes, appalled by his recklessness. "I'm afraid that won't work for me, Derek. I can't let myself love a man who might put you in prison. I could never forgive him, nor myself. Love cannot survive that kind of blow."

"Maddy—"

"Prison will kill your soul."

"Come on, Maddy. Maybe I'll be lucky enough to hang instead."

She drew her breath in sharply, then reached out to run her fingertips along the hard curve of his cheek. John, too, was nagged by this deep, dark despair; he, too, courted disaster because he hadn't been able to put it to rest. "Some day, I hope you'll find your peace, Derek. And then you might be able to care whether you live or die."

His eyes darkened for a moment. Then he laughed, and took her hand in both of his. "Fortunately, not tonight."

"Death always wins in the end," she said. "There's no need to court his attention."

"Ah, but I don't," Derek replied. "It's life I court. The more risks I take, the sweeter the living tastes."

Maddy shook her head. Derek had gone smooth and seamless, and she wasn't going to convince him. They'd reached this impasse before. He'd smile that charming, devilish smile of his, look straight into her eyes, and simply not hear her.

"Have you ever been in love?" she asked.

"Many times."

"That isn't love, Derek."

He met her gaze squarely, and for once there was no devilment in his eyes. "I'm not sure I'm capable of love, Maddy. Perhaps I'm destined to spend my life playing at it."

"If so, you may be lucky," she said, surprised at the bitterness in her voice. "Love is not an easy thing."

To her consternation, tears welled up in her eyes. One escaped, trickling warm down her cheek. Derek reached out and caught the crystal drop on his fingertip.

"If he hurts you, I'll kill him," Derek said. "But tonight, we save his life."

The statement was so absurd, so perfectly, completely Saylor that Maddy burst into laughter.

John lay on his cot with one arm flung across his eyes to block the light. The deputy sat just outside his cell, eating his dinner. It smelled like beef and potatoes, and neither prepared well. It wouldn't have been so bad if the deputy didn't eat with such noisy appreciation.

John tried to disengage his mind, to set himself apart from everything around him. Once, he'd known how to do this well. He'd wrapped himself in duty, muffling the memories of men screaming in pain, the hot-copper smell of his brothers' life-blood as it spilled over his hands. But disengaging had been all but impossible since he'd met Maddy. Without even trying, she had pulled his carefully-constructed shroud away from his heart, leaving it naked and vulnerable.

Ah, Maddy, he thought. Beautiful, fiery, seductive. He turned onto his side restlessly as his mind conjured the memory of last night. She'd been everything he'd ever wanted in a woman, everything he'd ever dreamed of. He would remember that night as long as he lived.

He turned over onto his side. The derringer pressed close to his heart, the metal warmed by contact with his skin. One shot only; he'd have to make it count.

He'd never felt like this before. The foundations of his world had been shaken by that beautiful, passionate, bronze-haired woman, and he didn't seem to be able to stop it.

A cynical voice at the back of his mind hooted with laughter. It was too late to worry about that; Zachary Marsh was soon to stop everything at the end of a rope.

Someone came into the jail then, and John rolled off the

bunk. Adrenaline pumped through his veins as he heard Zachary Marsh's voice.

"Evenin', Sheriff," he said.

"Evenin', Zach," Sheriff Cooper replied. "What kin I do fer you?"

"Hand over my boy's killer."

"I'm sorry about yore son, but I cain't help you," the sheriff said. "I tole you I'd hold him fer the circuit judge, and you're jest goin' to have to abide by that."

Marsh laughed, an ugly sound. "I ain't goin' to wait for nothin'," he said. "Ballard's mine."

"Got to kill me first," Cooper said.

"Oh, I don't mind that," Marsh replied.

A noise at the back door brought John's head around with a jerk. He saw the handle turn, and realized with a shock that the door wasn't locked. The deputy. It had to be the deputy.

Turning, he opened his mouth to cry a warning to the sheriff. Then something smacked hard against the back of his head, sending him to his hands and knees in a whirl of pain.

"Git him," someone said.

He saw two pairs of boots in front of him. They seemed to be rotating oddly, and there were times when they multiplied, becoming four pairs, then eight. But he had enough wits left to realize they were all dangerous.

He surged up from the floor, aiming at the center of that confusing jumble of feet. His shoulder connected hard with someone's midsection. The man went down with a whoosh of expelled air, but John didn't stop. He kept moving toward that open door. Then three men came rushing through the doorway, and he found himself staring down the barrels of their guns.

John skidded to a stop. He stood swaying, his head spinning. But a wild rage had bloomed inside him, the same fury that had carried him through so many battles during the war.

And suddenly, he didn't care about the guns. Hell, they were going to kill him anyway. Might as well make them pay. He smiled then, and he saw shock come into the other men's eyes.

They'd come for the sacrificial lamb, and found themselves a wolf instead. His smile broadened.

Someone tackled him from behind. As John went down, however, he drew the derringer, aiming at the man in the center of the group in front of him. A hole appeared in the man's chest, and he flung both arms up with a howl of surprise and pain. Then he went down, and his two companions could only stare in shocked surprise for a moment.

John tried to heave himself free of the tangle of men on top of him. He might almost have done it. Then someone clubbed him again, and dizziness swamped him. His strength ebbed; it was all he could do to hold onto consciousness.

"Don't anyone kill him," Zachary Marsh said from behind him. "At least not yet."

"He shot Buster," one man said.

"What did you expect?" the rancher retorted. "Mebbe fer him to give us all a kiss? Shit. But don't worry, boys. We can hang him for Buster when we hang him for Gordon, and everyone'll be happy."

They hauled John to his feet with brutal force. Someone hit him hard in the belly, and he swayed and nearly went down again. Two men grabbed his arms and held him, and a third man punched him in the face, opening a cut above his eye.

One of the men grabbed John by the hair, anchoring him for another blow. He saw the fist coming, felt it smash into his face just below his cheekbone. Agony sprayed out all along his jaw.

"That's enough," Zachary Marsh snapped. "Let's get him out of town."

They marched John out the back door. The cool night wind revived him somewhat, and he shook his head, slinging the blood out of his eyes. The breeze had been at work; the alley looked as though it had been swept. That bothered him, but he was too groggy to put the feeling into rational thought.

Then one of the cowboys let his breath out gustily. "Where the hell are our horses?" he demanded.

John blinked. Astonishment swept the cobwebs out of his mind, and he began to laugh. Oh, Maddy, he thought. Oh, woman! He could just see her, flitting through the alley and deftly stealing the horses right out from under Marsh's nose.

"Shut up, you," someone growled.

"He'll shut up soon enough once he's swingin' from the end of a rope," Marsh said. "This is good enough right here."

"But the sheriff—"

"It's goin' to be too late by the time the sheriff gits himself untied," Marsh snapped. "Move!"

One of the men tossed a rope over the top of the stairway across the alley. John's captors dragged him toward it, while another cowboy found a small barrel and rolled it beneath the rope. They tied John's arms behind his back, then stood him up on the makeshift platform.

Better hurry, Maddy, if you've got a plan, he thought. He hadn't cared much about living or dying since the war. But now he wanted to hold her again, and he wanted to live.

But he wasn't afraid. That reckless demon that always gripped him in battle had him again, and he stared straight into Zachary Marsh's eyes as the rancher coiled the rope into a noose.

"You killed my boy," Marsh said.

"Your boy needed killing," John replied.

"Damn you," the rancher growled. "Damn your sorry soul to hell."

John smiled. "At least he's there first."

Marsh's face twisted. He lashed out with the rope, striking John on his already-wounded cheek. Pain exploded through John's cheek and jaw, but he didn't stop smiling.

"That's enough, Marsh," someone called.

The rancher whirled. John looked past him to see several people come striding around the corner. At the other end of the alley, more people appeared. John recognized Bill Smith, the portly banker, Dr. Brennan, and even the less-than-sober

Mr. Haverty from the livery stable. Several cowboys from the Double D Ranch had come as well.

The scent of lilacs drifted on the breeze, bringing John's gaze to the jail. Maddy stood in the doorway.

For a moment, John forgot the rest of the world. There was only Maddy and the wild thumping of his heart.

Sheriff Cooper appeared behind her like a grim-eyed guardian angel. "Put the rope down, Marsh," he said.

"It's my right," Marsh raged. "He killed my boy."

"It ain't yore right," Cooper said. "Guilty or innocent is decided by the law."

"The law kin go to hell."

The sheriff stepped to one side, leveling his scattergun at the rancher's chest. "So kin you."

For a moment, John thought Marsh would challenge that double-bore threat. Then, with a curse, the rancher slung the noose aside. The rest of the rope came slithering down to coil in a heap in the dust.

"He's guilty as sin," Marsh snarled. "He admitted he killed my son."

"Yep," Cooper agreed. "Sure did. But we got to find out why, and before he hangs, not after."

"Gordon—"

"Gordon ain't sayin' much," the sheriff said, his gaze full of challenge. "But we got another witness."

"Who?"

"Miss Saylor here. She's got somethin' to say about what happened out there."

Marsh's gaze shifted to Maddy. "What can you know?"

"Everything," she said. "I was there."

She stepped out into the alley. Standing in the wash of light from the doorway, she began taking her gloves off.

Her spirit quailed at what she was about to do. But it was the only way to save John from the noose, and she would do far more than this to protect him. She would have done it even if she hadn't owed him her life; she would have done it out of love—helpless, vain love.

"Maddy, what are you doing?" John asked, and she saw denial in his eyes.

"Making the truth plain to everyone," she replied.

"Maddy—"

"There is no other way."

She read the outrage in his eyes, and knew that had he been free, he would have physically stopped her. He would have died before letting her do this. Well, she thought, he couldn't stop her. He could hate her all he wanted later, but she would save him.

Turning away from him, she unbuttoned her blouse. A shocked gasp went up from the onlookers. Embarrassment lay hot in Maddy's face and cold in her veins, but she locked it away behind a wall of Saylor dignity.

Strangely, the only person she could look at was Zachary Marsh. There was no shock in his eyes, no true grief, only hate. It gave her strength. Marsh was a hard, intolerant man, and he'd raised a brood of nasty, intolerant sons. It was time he learned something new.

Securing her blouse over her breasts with one hand, she let it hang loosely down her back, where the worst of the bruises were. She kept her gaze straight and steady as she turned in a full circle so that everyone could see the ugly purple-black marks upon her back and ribs.

Another gasp went up from the watchers. Maddy's gaze grazed John's face. His jaw was set and hard, and his eyes held pure outrage. The tendons in his neck stood out like wires as he fought his bonds, and for a moment she thought he'd burst the ropes by sheer will.

Taking a deep breath, she returned her attention to Zachary Marsh.

"Gordon did this," she said. "Gordon and Jim Berry."

"No," Marsh growled.

She turned again to show him her back. "Yes," she said.

"Berry and your son attacked me. John intervened. They drew on him, and he killed them."

"Liar," the rancher snarled. But his eyes betrayed him; he believed her. Evidently he knew his son better than he wanted to admit. "What were you doing all the way out at Sutter's Ridge?"

"Riding," she replied. "I purchased a mount specifically for that purpose, you know."

"A woman alone—"

"Has every right to consider herself safe among honorable men," she said. "Unfortunately, I happened to stumble upon two who were not. I hate to think of what might have happened if John Ballard hadn't come along."

Twin spots of dark color appeared in the rancher's cheeks. "So why didn't he say somethin'?"

"He was trying to protect me from . . . speculation," she said, sliding her blouse back up to her shoulders. She glanced at John. He'd fixed his gaze to a point well above her head, and she quailed that he had disengaged so thoroughly.

She tried to tell herself it didn't matter. She tried to tell herself that for the first time since she'd met him, she would be free. After all, if he didn't pursue her, she wouldn't be tempted.

But freedom should have felt better. Perhaps it would in time. Now, however, it just felt like emptiness.

Then John's green-gold gaze locked with hers. The world seemed to spin away as she registered the tumultuous emotions in his eyes. It had been torture for him to watch her bare herself, to make herself vulnerable to gossip. He hated that his life had been the price of that exposure, and most of all, he hated the fact that he'd been helpless to do anything about it.

Truly, it was a shame that he and Derek couldn't get to know each other. They had a great deal in common.

Her hands shook as she fastened her buttons again. Once she finished, she looked at Zachary Marsh again. "Mr. Ballard fought for my honor, as any gentleman would. And as a gentleman, he strove to protect me from any further unpleasantness. I, however, don't care if people talk—either about me or about Gordon. I have done nothing wrong, nor has John Ballard. And I do not intend to allow you to hang the man who saved my life. Fortunately, these good people have come here tonight to make sure that doesn't happen."

She looked at her neighbors. Bill Smith had brought his shotgun and a scowl, and was obviously ready to take on all comers in his defense of the Saylor sisters. The others, however, seemed to want only fairness, and the law.

These were good people. They had built this town with their hands and hearts, and weren't willing to let it become less than what they'd made it.

"You ain't hangin' nobody, Zachary Marsh," Bill Smith said. "This here is civilization, and we got better ways to deal with things."

Marsh's eyes narrowed. "He killed my son."

"And you jest heard why," Bill replied.

"She'd say anything to help him," the rancher snarled.

Bill swung the barrel of his shotgun so that it almost pointed at Marsh's belly. "Maddy don't lie."

"Boys, boys," Sheriff Cooper said, stepping between the two men. Arms akimbo, he faced Zachary Marsh. "Go home, Marsh. Cool off. Yore so damned hotheaded right now that you cain't even understand sense when it's told to you."

"I'm not goin' anywhere," Marsh said.

"Then I'll put yore sorry ass in jail."

Marsh shrugged. "You got no cause to lock me up, Sheriff."

"No cause?" Cooper yelped. "How about hitting a duly sworn sheriff over the head with a bottle of whiskey, or stealin' a prisoner out of my jail?"

"Look here—" Marsh began.

"Git," Cooper hissed, low and deadly. "Yore horses are hitched out in front of the bank."

The rancher studied him for a moment, pure insolence in his eyes. Then he whirled, sending a spurt of dust up from his boots, and stalked toward the end of the alley. His men hurried after him. The townsfolk parted to let them through.

Maddy ran to untie John. He'd already stepped down off the barrel when she reached him, and all she had to do was loosen his bonds. As the ropes fell away, she stepped back.

"I wish you hadn't done that," he said, gazing down into her eyes.

Maddy had passed beyond blushing, and far beyond trying to talk sense into him. She met his gaze levelly, letting him see her defiance. "So?" she drawled.

He opened his mouth to reply, probably something scathing, Maddy thought. Then his gaze shifted to a point above and beyond her, and everything in him shifted to focus on a rooftop across the alley.

Maddy watched as he scanned the top of every building. Her heart thumped away like a mad thing, but she tried her best to keep her expression from giving her away. She searched her mind frantically for the right thing to say.

Then he grinned, and the sight of that smile set her heart to pounding as though she'd run a mile.

He'd spotted Derek.

Twenty-four

Maddy saw a dark shape detach from the shadows on the roof across the alley, and knew that Derek had realized he'd been spotted. He leaped from one building to another, then swiftly moved out of sight.

John started forward. She stepped into his path to block his way, but found herself picked up and set aside before she knew what was happening.

"No," she said, flinging herself into his path again.

This time when he picked her up, she wound her fingers into his shirt, anchoring herself. This time, he'd have to hurt her to get rid of her.

For a moment, she braced herself to be flung down. But John stopped. He stood with his hands clamped on her arms, his chest rapidly rising and falling. Maddy tilted her head back to look into his eyes. He was furious, she knew—with her, but most of all with himself.

Still, her heart soared. In that moment, he'd had a choice: her or Derek. And whether he realized it or not, he'd chosen her.

"That wasn't fair," he growled.

"None of this is fair," she replied.

Her heart pounded wildly as John stood looking at her. His hands slid up to her shoulders, and she could feel the heat of his long fingers through her blouse. Her gaze dropped to his mouth, lingering on the fine-cut, sensual curve of his lips. She wanted him to kiss her. For once, she didn't care if the whole town was watching.

He wanted to kiss her, too; she could see it in the sudden flare of desire in his eyes, and the subtle softening of his mouth. She waited, breath suspended.

John held Maddy still, feeling her fragility between his hands. He was astonished by what had happened. He'd had Derek Saylor spotted, as good as caught. And Maddy—fiery, infuriating Maddy—had forced a choice on him. He hadn't had time to think about it; he'd merely reacted. And he hadn't been able to fling her aside, perhaps hurt her, merely to capture Derek Saylor. *Merely* to capture Derek Saylor!

Damn. She'd really gotten to him. Gently, he set her aside, ruthlessly controlling the tendency of his hands to linger upon her shoulders. Derek hadn't gotten too big a jump on him; this time, Maddy wouldn't have a chance to interfere.

He turned away. But Sheriff Cooper stepped into his path, and he stopped.

"Not so fast," the sheriff said.

John scowled impatiently. "What's the problem, Sheriff?"

"You cain't leave."

"Why not?"

Cooper sighed. "Because I got to hold you until the circuit judge gits here."

Completely dumfounded, John stared at the other man. "What the hell? Didn't you hear what Maddy said tonight?"

"I heared. Now the circuit judge is goin' to hear. You ain't a free man until he says so. This here's a civilized town," he added with obvious relish.

John looked at Maddy. She stood with her arms crossed over her chest, a half-smile on her face, and there was a hint of satisfaction in her eyes that annoyed him badly.

Why, the little . . . he thought. This suited her just fine. It wouldn't have angered him so much if he didn't think she was enjoying his predicament. And there were too many secrets in those beautiful eyes, plans she'd never get away with if he were free.

No wonder she was so pleased to see him locked up again.

He glanced at the sheriff again, gauging his chances of getting away. But Cooper was a canny old bird, and held that scattergun just a bit too ready.

There would be a reckoning, John promised himself. Maddy had been passing herself off as Derek simply to muddy the waters. But she'd played her game a little too long, and now John was going to exact a price.

Sooner rather than later, if he could manage it. And he knew exactly how to get to her.

"I'm all yours, Sheriff," he said, suddenly quite cheerful.

He watched Maddy's eyes narrow. She dropped her hands to her sides, and he knew that she'd start moving back in a moment. Dear Maddy, he thought. Always so quick to catch on.

Before she could get out of his range, he reached out and snagged her wrist. She resisted him, but subtly, and he soon had her hand tucked into the crook of his arm. He smiled down at her, thinking that having to be a lady, and not cause a scene, was more of a burden than she'd ever admit. He knew his Maddy; with her hair-trigger temper, she'd rather kick and scream and make his life hell than go quietly back into that jail.

Ah, but she *was* a lady. And she went quietly, with resentment in her eyes.

"I hate you," she hissed.

He smiled at her. "Your mind hates me. But your body likes me very much, and don't try to deny it."

"Purely—"

"Physical," he finished for her. "But it was one hell of a wild ride, wasn't it, Maddy?"

She didn't reply. Head high, nose in the air, she followed Sheriff Cooper into the jail. A dark stain marred the floor where the dead cowboy had lain, and the deputy's chair and table lay in pieces against the far wall.

"Looks like somebody got slaughtered in here," Cooper said. "Remind me never to let you git inside scattergun range."

John shrugged. "Something left over from the war."

"Yeah." The sheriff scraped his fingernails along his jaw. "Now, I wouldn't worry about this, son. If it weren't that Zach Marsh would run screaming to the judge, I'd have a mind to let you go. But he's goin' to, so I have to."

"I don't blame you, Sheriff," John said, flicking a glance at Maddy.

He grunted. "Plenty of folks saw the bruises those two bastards left on her," he said, jabbing his thumb in Maddy's direction. "There ain't a man who saw that who wouldn't like to have a piece of Gordon Marsh's hide."

"Too late," John said, and didn't even feel guilt. He was glad he'd killed those men, and would do it all over again.

For Maddy. Even now, the thought of their hands on her made his blood run hot and hard. The thought of *any* man touching her for any reason sent outrage boiling through him.

Sheriff Cooper stepped into the jail and waited for them to follow. Once they were in, he slammed the door closed and locked it. Then he pointed to the open cell from which John had been taken.

"In you go, son."

Reluctantly, John went into the cell. The door banged closed behind him with a flat metallic sound that scraped along his nerves. As he watched Maddy turn toward the back door, he had the sudden, uncomfortable feeling that he'd just made the worst mistake of his life.

But instead of leaving, as he expected, she reached up to touch the lock on the back door.

"Marsh's men didn't break in," she said.

"The deputy let them in," John replied.

Cooper's brows contracted. "Marsh must have bribed him, that two-faced son of a . . ." He glanced at Maddy, ". . . gun. I guess we'll never know fer sure; Marsh ain't goin' to tell, and that little bastard Dooley lit out of here like a cat with its tail on fire."

John reached up and felt the lump on the back of his skull. "I had some things I wanted to say to him."

The sheriff chuckled. "Don't worry about it none. You put up one hell of a fight when they took you out of here. That deputy left here missin' all four of his front teeth. He ain't got that pretty smile no more."

"You know, Sheriff, I might actually get to like you some day," John said.

Maddy put her hands on her hips. "Men!"

John studied her for a moment, then looked over at Sheriff Cooper. "Mind if I speak to the lady privately, Sheriff? I want to thank her for saving my life out there."

"Sure. By the way," Cooper said, holding out Maddy's derringer. "Either of you know anything about this here gun?"

"No," John and Maddy said in unison.

"Uh-huh. Y'all know anything about any other guns in this room here—besides the ones I'm carryin'?"

"No," they said in unison again.

Cooper grunted. "Uh-huh. Well, I'll let y'all have yore talk. Ballard, you behave yoreself."

"Always do," John said, all innocence.

Sheriff Cooper closed the back door and locked it. With a wink at John, he went out into the front office. This time, however, he closed the door that separated the jail from his office. Alarm raced in quicksilver spurts up Maddy's spine; even behind bars, John was a dangerous man.

Still, she wasn't about to show him how badly he'd stirred her emotions. Feigning indifference, she crossed her arms over her chest and waited for him to speak first.

"Was it your idea to make me wait for the circuit judge?" he asked.

"Not at all," she replied. "After all, this is a civilized town. They have procedures."

"But you're happy about it."

"Inordinately."

He smiled at her. "Come here, Maddy."

She smiled back. "Absolutely not."

"Please?"

Maddy took a step closer. She knew it was a mistake. A stupid mistake. But his eyes drew her as surely as any chain, and in a moment she found herself standing just outside the cell.

"You saved my life tonight," he said.

"You saved mine. I owed you."

She said it matter-of-factly, as a man might have. But John wasn't feeling matter-of-fact. He raged inside with emotions he didn't know the name of, let alone understand. He only knew that he had to touch her, to claim her in the only way he could.

"And you Saylors always pay your debts."

"Yes."

"Is that why Derek was there?" he asked. "To help you pay your debt?"

"Yes."

"Does he, too, expect me to stop hunting him now?"

Maddy frowned. "Of course not. He's a man, and completely without sense. I think he'd actually be disappointed if you stopped chasing him, as he seemed to think you're the only one who might pose a shred of challenge."

"I'll take that as a compliment"

"You would."

Since Maddy's dramatic scene outside, John had been keeping his temper under control. But that hold was beginning to slip. He knew she'd done the only thing she could under the circumstances. He knew she'd saved his life by doing it. But by damn, he hated it.

He reached through the bars and took her hands to pull her just a bit closer. Still under the spell of his eyes, Maddy allowed it. She didn't realize the danger until it was too late; he slipped one arm around her waist, and all possibility of escape had passed before she realized she needed to.

"Stop it," she said, trying vainly to pull his arm from around her.

Then she saw the depth of the emotion in his eyes, and forgot to struggle. She could only watch, breath suspended, and wait for what would come next.

"Do you have any idea how I felt as I watched you unbutton your blouse out there?" he asked.

Maddy knew the conversation had taken a dangerous turn. "I'd think you would be happy not to hang," she said.

"I wasn't."

Shock washed like ice water through her veins. She could only stare at him, completely dumfounded.

"As I stood there watching you bare yourself," he said, his voice tight and harsh, "I wanted to kill every man in that alley simply because they looked at you."

"That's crazy," she protested. "Showing those bruises was the only way to save you."

"I know it here." He touched his head. "But here," he tapped his chest just over his heart, "I would rather hang than see you expose yourself to the ugliest of gossip."

"That is the most irrational, uncivilized—"

"Yes," he agreed. "But there's nothing civilized in my feelings for you. Nor yours for me."

"Nonsense," she retorted. "We Saylors are most civilized."

He grinned at her, and the sight of that dimple made her knees turn weak. Damn him. No, she wasn't civilized; with him, she was simply a woman. Wanton. Weak.

"You might be able to tell the rest of the world that, Maddy, but not me."

"You don't know me," she replied, feeling strangely sad about it. "You will never know me."

"Don't I?" he murmured, drawing her still closer.

"That's . . . not what I mean," she gasped, resisting.

He slid his hand up her back, leaving shivers in his wake.

Just that touch brought her body to instant attention, almost as though he'd somehow become imprinted in her soul. Ah, she thought, if only she didn't love him. If only he were someone else, or she was.

His hand slipped into her hair, his fingers spreading out to cup the back of her head. Maddy repressed a sigh. Her eyelids started to droop, and it took an act of will to force them open again.

"You took a course of action tonight you knew I didn't want," he said. "I'm not saying I'm not grateful that you saved my life. I'm saying that such a thing will never happen again. You belong to me, Maddy. I'll die before I let another man touch you. I'll die before I let another man *look* at you."

"I belong to no man," she snapped.

"Yes, you do," he said.

He claimed her mouth in a torrid kiss. Maddy tried frantically not to respond, but that battle was lost before it had begun. He swamped her senses, her soul. He took her caution, her conflicts, and her independence, and he cast them to the winds. She couldn't have kept them if she'd wanted to . . . which she didn't, God help her. For now, this sweeping, devastating moment, she only wanted him.

With a sigh, she opened her mouth further, inviting him deeper. He took that invitation, dipping deeply into her moist, eager depths. She moaned when he withdrew, but he came right back, biting softly at her mouth, then running the tip of his tongue along the tender flesh inside her lips.

He slid his hands along her back from waist to shoulders and back again, and she arched like a cat. He made a sound deep in his throat, a hoarse male sound of arousal that sent an answering rush of desire sweeping through her veins. She arched her back again as he caressed the curve where her arm met her side, then spread his hands out upon her ribs so that the weight of her breasts rested upon them.

She waited in aching anticipation for his next touch. It came a heartbeat later, a butterfly-light graze of his thumbs across her nipples.

"God," he muttered. "You're so responsive. It's as though your body turns to fire beneath my hands."

He cupped her breasts then, his touch gentle yet completely possessive. Maddy shuddered in reaction. Her breasts swelled as if to meet his hands, and her nipples tightened into hard points against his palms. Ah, if only she didn't know the pleasure he could give her . . . But she did. Last night, he had taken her to heaven and back again, and the memory was burned forever into her mind.

"If I could, I'd take you here and now," he rasped. "I'd lay you down on that bunk and fill you, and I'd love you until you screamed."

Maddy closed her eyes, almost undone by his words and the sensations rioting through her. He stroked his palms lightly across her nipples, making slow, exquisitely arousing circles until she found herself leaning against the bars to get closer to him.

"Talk to me, Maddy," he whispered, sliding two fingers between the top buttons of her blouse.

"What do you want to talk about?" she asked, dizzy with arousal.

"Tell me what you like. What you want. What you need."

Talk to him? About that? Oh, Lord. The thought of doing so scandalized her just a bit, but it also brought a rush of wetness between her legs.

Maddy's attention focused on those two long fingers that were now tracing the upper curves of her breasts. Her skin registered his touch, turned it into pure desire streaking along her limbs. Molten heaviness settled deep in her core, an ache that she knew he could ease. Her breasts swelled still further, anticipating a deeper touch.

But that touch didn't come. Instead, he continued to caress her chest, warming the skin with his fingers, yet not giving her what she wanted.

"There's nothing wrong about two people sharing passion," he said. "And there's nothing wrong with talking about it. If you want me to touch you, say so."

She shifted restlessly, spurred by her own need. Oh, his touch was pure magic, as it always was, but he wasn't giving her what she craved. It was all she could do to keep from wriggling. But she wouldn't beg. She'd never beg. But oh, she wanted him to touch her breasts.

John looked down at her, marveling at the heat of her, the passion, and the stubbornness. He knew she wanted him to touch her more intimately, and the amount of willpower it took for her to keep from asking.

He wanted her to ask. He wanted her to tell him that she wanted him, that she needed his touch as much as he needed hers. For if she denied him her passion, she denied him everything. He wanted to claim her, and he wanted her to acknowledge his claim. For however long it lasted, he wanted there to be nothing but passion between them.

Her breathing changed dramatically, becoming swift and ragged. John could see her erect nipples through her blouse, and the sight jolted him to his toes. He wondered then if she could keep from asking longer than he could keep from touching her.

"Oh," she sighed, and he knew he had her.

"What do you want, Maddy?"

"Lower," she whispered, her voice strained as though it had been torn from her. "Touch me lower."

"Here?" he asked, slipping his fingers down the deep cleft between her breasts.

She moaned softly, wanting that, wanting more. John took pity on her then. And on himself. The feel of her warm, silken skin, the scent of lilac and Maddy . . . It was almost more than he could bear. He slid his hand beneath her chemise to stroke her smooth, lush flesh.

"There," she breathed "Oh, there."

He circled her nipples with his thumbs, bringing them even

more erect. Bending, he took one of those turgid peaks into his mouth, suckling her through the fabric.

Maddy cried out, arching her back. He tugged lightly at her nipple with his teeth, eliciting another soft cry.

Damn, but he wanted more than his hands on her. He wanted to rip these bars from their moorings so he could gather her in and hold her against him, and bury himself deep in that luscious, incredibly responsive body.

"Maddy," he groaned.

"I . . . This is crazy," she panted.

"Yes, it is," he agreed.

Straightening, he sank both hands into her hair and tilted her face back. Holding her still, he gazed deeply into her eyes. Desire burned there, as scintillant as sunlight on deep water. He didn't know if it would always be like this between them, or if their passion flared so high and hot it would burn itself out some day. He didn't even know which he would prefer; their relationship had been torturous from the beginning, at times as painful as it was pleasurable.

"I know what you've been doing," he said.

Her eyes widened, then narrowed.

"I don't know what you mean."

"Don't you, Maddy?"

She tried to pull away, but he tightened his grip. Not enough to hurt, but enough to communicate his determination to finish the conversation.

"The Gray Ghost had an uncanny ability to travel," he said. "Sometimes he moved so fast it seemed he could be in two places at once. I always wondered about that, being rather a good traveler myself."

"No one is better than Derek."

"Is he good enough to rob the bank at Victorville at noon, then ride nearly twenty miles to chase a stage near Palatine?"

"As I've told you over and over again, Derek didn't rob that bank, and he didn't rob those stages," Maddy said. "My brother is not a thief."

John smiled at her. "Why did you take Blanche's horse when you followed Jim Berry?"

"I . . ." Maddy took a deep breath, cautioning herself to be very careful here. John was too close. Much too close. "Ali didn't look well. I didn't want to strain him."

"Either that, or he'd been ridden hard during the day."

"Oh?" Maddy met his gaze with her most supercilious Saylor look. "Are you suggesting that *I* am the thief?"

John knew Maddy was no thief. She was completely, blindly loyal to her brother, who probably didn't deserve it. But her defiance angered him, and so did her assumption that he would think the worst of her.

"Are you?" he asked.

The heat drained from her eyes. Ice replaced them, and John felt chilled to his very soul. If he could have taken his words back, he would have.

Maddy reached up and disengaged his hands from her hair. She took a step backward, removing herself from his reach, but kept her gaze locked with his.

"I will testify in your behalf in court, for that is the right thing to do," she said. "But other than that, we have nothing to say to each other."

She turned and stalked to the door, waiting with her back to him until Sheriff Cooper came to open the door. Just as she left, however, she glanced over her shoulder at John. Then the door closed behind her, shutting her away from him.

Dread ran cold through his veins. She'd had a look of pure recklessness in her eyes. He'd seen that look in the war, in the faces of men who had lost all fear, all caution. He'd felt that way himself.

Maddy was going to do something rash. And with half the territory hunting her brother, she might get herself killed. And John had lost the ability to protect her.

"Maddy," he whispered.

Grabbing the bars, he shook them viciously. They seemed

to mock him with their immovability. He raised his voice to a shout of pure frustration. "MADDY!"

The door rattled open, and Sheriff Cooper poked his head through the opening. "She's gone, Ballard," he growled. "Madder'n a wet hen, too. I got one thing to say fer you; you shore got a way with women."

He banged the door closed again, leaving John alone with his thoughts. They weren't very good ones.

"Nobody has a way with women," he growled.

Twenty-five

Maddy fought tears as she hurried home. "How *dare* he suggest that I robbed those stages?" she asked herself, her words taking on the same rhythm as her feet. "Would I be living here in those two little rooms? Would I be spending ten hours a day, every day, doing honest work? No. I'd be back in Virginia, using my ill-gotten gains to take Tallwood back!"

"Ma'am?" a man called from behind her. "Miss Saylor?"

She stopped and turned. Three cowboys came riding down the street, having no doubt been visiting the saloon. It was late, it was dark, and she didn't know these men.

"Yes?" she asked.

They rode up to her, the creak of their saddles loud in the quiet street. Maddy held her ground, although she was a little nervous. She hadn't been able to bring a gun to Sheriff Cooper's office, and sorely regretted that now.

The cowboys drew their mounts to a halt. She stood quietly, waiting. Then all three men pulled their hats off.

"I'm Jase Franklin," one said, "and this here's Drew Wilkins and Howie Forbes. We work for the Crooked Rock Ranch."

Maddy inclined her head, inviting more.

The cowboy cleared his throat. "Ah . . . we heard what happened with Berry and Walsh, and just wanted you to know, ah . . ." He ducked his head sheepishly, and Maddy was astonished to see him blush. ". . . We don't hold with that kind of thing, and we don't want you thinkin' that the rest of us fellers is anythin' like those two. If you ever want to go visitin', and need protectin', well, we'll be happy to escort you."

Maddy was truly astonished. She stared at the three for a moment, then smiled. "Why, thank you, gentlemen. That's very nice of you."

"Remember, ma'am," the spokesman said. "You need somethin', you ask us."

"I will remember," she replied, touched by their offer.

They put their hats back on, then eased their mounts away from the sidewalk. Maddy watched them until they disappeared around the corner.

Something more than John's life had been gained tonight, she realized. The residents of Cofield had begun to accept the Saylors. It meant more to Maddy than she expected. For the first time since she'd left Tallwood, she felt as though she'd found a home.

A shadow moved out of a nearby alley. Maddy's heart thumped in alarm, and she moved back into the doorway of the storefront behind her.

"Maddy, it's me."

Blanche's soft whisper sent the tension draining from Maddy's body, and she stepped out into the open again. Blanche wore men's clothing, and she'd tucked her hair up under a dark Stetson. Maddy was struck anew by her resemblance to Derek. She even carried her rifle the same way, cradled in the crook of her arm so she only had to swing it up a few degrees to be at the ready.

"Did you hear what those men said?" Maddy asked.

"Yes, I did. Weren't they sweet?" she asked, smiling. Then her smile faded, and her eyes seemed to turn dark beneath the brim of her hat. "Maddy, I like it here. I like these people. They came with you tonight to stop an injustice, and some of them hardly knew us. And then for those cowboys to offer us their protection . . . Well, rough and rowdy they might be, but they have the hearts of gentlemen."

"Yes," Maddy said. She pressed her fingertips against her

closed eyelids, willing the sudden upsurge of tears to go away. This wasn't the time for tears. "I made a decision tonight. We . . . I can't keep this up any longer."

"I know," Blanche said softly. "Maddy, I know."

Of course she did, Maddy thought, reaching out to take her sister's hands. "We have to convince Derek to hide out in Mexico for a while. Then you and I are going to finish this thing once and for all."

"What do you mean?"

"The thief has gotten greedy—that's why he robbed the bank at Victorville. If we play it right, we ought to be able to lure him into revealing himself."

"You've got a plan, no doubt?"

Maddy nodded. "Tomorrow, I suggest we take Dolly's dress out to her. And we'll teach her how to do her hair. Then we'll have the rest of the day to ourselves. We're going to that place Derek told us about—"

"Miss Penny's House of Pleasure?" Distress creased Blanche's normally placid brow. "Oh, dear."

"Blame our dear brother," Maddy retorted. "Any other man would have a different sort of address, but not Derek."

"No," Blanche murmured. "Not Derek. What if we can't find him today?"

"Then we'll stay out until we do. He's not safe here any longer. He's reckless, Blanche."

"He has always been reckless."

"Yes. But there's a desperation about him now that frightens me. If he doesn't think there's a future waiting for him, he won't care whether he lives or dies."

"Oh, Maddy!"

"I'm afraid for him, Blanche. I really am."

"Then we must get him into Mexico despite himself," Blanche said. "What about John and Hank?"

"John will be locked up at least until the first of next week, and Hank is out of commission for a while. He might object, but he won't be able to do anything about it."

"Mmmm, I'm not altogether sure about that," Blanche mused. "He has recovered remarkably well."

"Can he ride?"

"Perhaps. He's stubborn enough to try it. But he won't ride fast or far, I'm sure of that."

Maddy smiled. "Then we'll just have to make sure we get enough of a head start to leave him behind."

"Well, that's something we're used to, isn't it?" Blanche let her breath out in a long sigh. "Maddy, what if we fail?"

"Then we'll have to join Derek down in Mexico," Maddy said. "We'll take new identities. As long as people know who we are, they will try to use us against our brother."

Blanche looked stricken, and Maddy knew she was thinking about the possibility of never seeing Hank again. Maddy understood. Oh, yes, she understood. Her mind accepted the possibility of never seeing John again; being a rational person, she could do nothing else. But oh, her heart ached at the thought. Oh, she didn't want to face the emptiness that would be her life.

But she had to.

"We have to do this, Blanche," she said softly. "I'm sorry."

"So am I." Tears glittered in Blanche's eyes and made water-jewels on her lashes. "I've become selfish, sister. Selfish and greedy. I want Hank. I want to live with him, be his wife, have his children. I want all those things for myself, for me. So I'll do this. I'll move heaven and earth to clear Derek's name for his sake—and for mine."

"I understand," Maddy whispered.

"Now . . ." With a sharp, impatient gesture, Blanche dashed her tears away. "Tell me something good. Tell me you're sure we can really pull this off."

Maddy glanced down the street at the jail. She'd thought of this thing between her and John as a game, a contest of wills and wits that might almost have been enjoyable. But it had become far more than that. All unwittingly, she'd thrown her heart into the fray, and lost it to her opponent.

"We have to," she said. "We just have to."

* * *

The first pale light of dawn had begun to stain the eastern sky when Maddy woke. Blanche had already gotten up; Maddy could hear her moving quietly around the outer room.

Maddy flung the covers aside and got up. She donned her riding habit, then slid her men's clothing into her saddlebags and lowered them through the trap door into the shop below.

"Hurry up if you want breakfast, Maddy," Blanche called from the other room.

Maddy winced; that call meant that Hank was awake. She had hoped they could slip away without having to offer any explanations.

Hank was sitting up when she walked into the other room. He looked completely at ease, tenderness softening his eyes as he watched Blanche fix a pot of tea.

"Mornin', Maddy," he said, without looking away from Blanche.

"Good morning, Hank. How are you feeling?"

"Well enough to move around some," he replied. "If my nurse will stop hovering like a worried mama cat."

"Someone has to have some sense," Blanche retorted. "And it's certain that you don't. Now you listen to me, Hank Vann. You might think you're feeling better, but it wouldn't take much to break that wound open again. And then you'll be sorry, believe me."

"I'll try to be good," he said.

Blanche's eyes changed then, a glitter of tears drowning them. She turned quickly, putting her back to him, and poured a steaming stream of tea into a cup. Maddy's eyes widened as she watched her sister take a bottle of laudanum out of her pocket and let several drops fall into the hot liquid.

Oh, Blanche, she thought. *That took courage.*

Another woman might have burst into tears and abandoned her resolve. Blanche looked over at her. The tears were gone now, and there was only a hint of despair behind the determination in her eyes.

Maddy held her sister's gaze steadily. They were both risking everything on this single roll of the dice: their brother, their future, the men they loved. And Blanche risked even more; her man returned her love.

It wasn't fair. Blanche didn't have to be involved in this at all. Even as the thought occurred to Maddy, Blanche shook her head. Maddy sighed; Blanche had always seemed to know the drift of her thoughts. And the message was clear: they were in this together to the end. Win or lose, the Saylors stood together.

Blanche stirred a spoonful of sugar into Hank's tea. Taking it to him, she put it in his good hand. "Drink up," she said.

"Tea?" He sniffed at his cup, then wrinkled his nose in distaste. "Smells awful. Come on, Blanche. Take pity on me and brew me a cup of coffee?"

"Never," she said. "Coffee is terrible stuff. Drink your tea. It's good for you."

He took a sip. "That's horrible," he said, making a face.

"Stop being a baby and drink it."

He glared at her for a moment, then dutifully took a sip. Maddy was possessed by an almost uncontrollable urge to laugh, and had to turn her back on him. Afterward, he ate with good appetite, unaware of what was about to befall him.

It took him a half-hour to begin yawning. Maddy set the dishes in the basin to soak, then went into the bedroom to clean and load Papa's revolvers. When she returned, Hank was asleep, still propped in a sitting position.

"Help me lay him down," Blanche said.

They carefully eased him down onto the cot. Blanche tucked the quilt around him, her hands lingering longer than they needed to. Her eyes were soft, full of love and regret and a hundred other things Maddy knew well. Blanche had betrayed him, and only time would tell if he could ever forgive her.

"He's going to be furious when he realizes what we've done," she murmured.

"Well, that won't be until he wakes up," Maddy said. "Besides, don't you remember what Papa used to say? 'A good, flaming fit of temper cleans out the arteries and clears the brain. A man will live years longer if he allows himself to vent his spleen."

Blanche's teeth shone white as she smiled. "And Papa vented it regularly."

"That he did," Maddy said. "That he did."

They collected a package of hairpins and combs, then went down to the shop to collect their saddlebags and Dolly's gown. They carried little else; during the war, they'd learned well to live off the land.

As they walked down the street toward the stable, Maddy noticed that the door to the sheriff's office was open. Caught by a sudden impulse, she decided to pay John a last visit before leaving.

"You go on," she told Blanche. "I have something I need to do."

Blanche laughed. "You're not going to torment the man, are you?"

"Not at all. I just want to talk to him."

"And while you're 'talking' to him, you're going to make sure he knows you're riding out unescorted to do heaven knows what."

"Hmmmph. He suggested that *I* might be the one stealing all that gold."

Blanche's eyes widened. "Did he? You know, Maddy, it has occurred to me more than once that it would be easier to pretend to be Derek if we actually were holding up stages and robbing banks. What do you think?"

"I think John Ballard is an idiot," Maddy retorted. "Now, I have this one chance to get a bit of my own back, and this may be one of the few pleasures I'll ever have in this ridiculous, insane situation."

"Oh, really?" Blanche drawled.

Maddy blushed. "You know what I mean. I would be a complete fool to pass up this opportunity, and I have never been a fool."

"Mmm-hmm."

"Rarely, then." With a toss of her head, Maddy lifted her skirts and crossed the street to the sheriff's office.

The front room was empty. She nearly lost her nerve then and left, but then she heard voices coming from the jail. Holding her breath, she walked silently to the door and put her ear against it.

"Sheriff, you've got to let me go," John said. "There are things going on you don't understand—"

"I understand that the circuit judge'll be here Tuesday. If he says you git let go, then you git let go."

"Tuesday will be too late." A rattle of metal upon metal told Maddy that John had shaken the door to his cell. "Damn it, man! There's a gold shipment coming on the stage from Preston on Monday."

The sheriff grunted. "Anybody else know?"

"Shouldn't be. But Saylor always seems to be in the right place at the right time, doesn't he?" John asked. "We're planning on him being there."

"You got a trap set?"

"Yes. Now if you'll—"

"Uh-uh. Sorry, son. They're gonna have to spring that trap without you. I admit I'd like to help you out, I shorely do. But the stage ain't my business, and until somebody in authority makes it so, I'm holdin' you fer the circuit judge."

"Damn it, Cooper," John raged. "You can't do this!"

"Yes, I kin," the sheriff replied. "Now you jest settle yoreself in until Tuesday, and we'll git along fine."

Hearing footsteps approach the door, Maddy hastily retreated to the desk and sat down in the creaky visitors' chair. Sheriff Cooper gave a start as he came into the room and spotted her.

"Mornin', Maddy," he said, snatching his hat from his head. "You're up early."

"Blanche and I are heading out to the Mayhew ranch today. Are you enjoying having Mr. Ballard as your guest?"

"Hell, no," he growled. "Pardon my French, ma'am, but yore friend is in a foul mood this mornin', and he's makin' sure I know it."

"May I see him?"

"You sure you want to?"

She smiled at him. "Oh, I imagine I can calm him down for you."

"That so?" He clapped his hat back on and regarded her with a speculative gaze. "He's been houndin' me since you left. Hell, he spent the night pacin' his cell like a trapped wild-cat, and I like to never git to sleep."

"You poor man," Maddy cooed, all sweetness.

He grunted peevishly. "Well, I'll let you see him. But you got to promise not to git him any more riled than he is. I'd shorely hate to have to shoot him this mornin'."

"No, you wouldn't," she said.

His eyes widened. Then he grinned, and he opened the door with a flourish. "Ma'am."

"Sir." Maddy swept past him with a regal inclination of her head.

John must have heard her voice; he'd leaned against the bars of his cell, arranging his long body in a casual pose. Of course, he didn't fool her for a moment; his eyes held boiling-hot fury and frustration.

The sight gave Maddy an inordinate amount of satisfaction. She approached the cell, but this time, she made sure she stayed out of arm's reach.

"Hello, John," she said.

"Come to twist the hook?"

"This was not my doing," she replied. "I did everything I could for you."

John knew she was right. But damn it, he wanted out. Even

more now that he'd seen that she still had that reckless look in her eyes.

"Why are you here, Maddy?"

"Couldn't I have just come to see how you were doing?"

"No."

She smiled at him, thinking he looked very much the aggressive male animal this morning. She wouldn't have admitted it to save her life, but she was glad he was on the other side of those bars. He would *not* have been manageable.

"Come here," he growled.

Ah, even caged, he wasn't about to be manageable, she thought, admiring a man who could be arrogant even in a jail cell.

"I'm fine right where I am, thank you," she said.

John studied her with narrowed eyes. "What are you up to, Maddy?"

"Oh, nothing. Blanche and I are taking Dolly Mayhew's gown out to her, and then we're planning to find a nice, shady spot for a picnic."

"All alone, no doubt."

"Of course."

He pushed away from the wall. Clamping his hands on the bars, he locked his gaze with hers in an attempt to make her see how serious this was. "You don't know what you're fooling with. This is dangerous."

"A picnic?"

"Don't play games with me, Maddy."

"Ah, but you started this little contest, didn't you?" she retorted. "And now that it isn't going your way, you don't like it."

"I don't think you stole that gold."

She let her lashes drift downward. "Indeed."

"But I do think your actions are dangerous and ill-considered. Your brother is the famed Gray Ghost. Surely he can take care of himself."

"You've made your own assumptions," she said. "I told you Blanche and I are going on a picnic."

"Yes," he agreed. "A picnic. Come here, Maddy."

She knew better than to let him touch her. He wasn't even trying to hide the danger in his eyes; in his present mood, there was no telling what he might do.

"Are you afraid?" he asked.

"Of what?"

"Of yourself."

Maddy cocked her head to one side. "You're very sure of yourself."

"I have reason to be," he said softly. "Do you remember last night?"

Of course she did; even now, her body was reacting just at the thought of what he'd done with his hands and mouth. Desire raced quicksilver-fast along her limbs to pool in an aching knot at her core.

"You remember well," he said. "I can see it in your eyes. And your body, Maddy. It betrays you."

Surprised, she glanced down at herself. To her humiliation, she saw that her nipples had pouted, and were very evident beneath the fabric of her blouse. He hadn't even touched her; his voice, the desire in his eyes, her memories of touching him and being touched . . . all had conspired against her.

Angry at him for doing this to her, even angrier at herself for letting him, she whirled and strode toward the door. Then she stopped. Turning, she looked straight into his eyes and smiled.

"It's been a profitable visit, even if you weren't very pleasant company," she said. "Not only did I discover that you're a rake and a cad, but I overheard what you told Sheriff Cooper about the gold shipment."

Alarm tightened his shoulders, and he leaned forward against the bars. "Maddy—"

"Don't bother denying it."

"Damn it, Maddy—"

"It must be very frustrating for you. After all, you went to all this trouble, and now you've gone and gotten yourself locked up."

"Will you listen to me?" he hissed.

Maddy lifted her chin. "We've gone around and around and haven't gotten anywhere, and I'm tired of it. You won't be out of here until at least Tuesday. Well, I'm telling you now that this thing will be finished before then."

"What are you going to do?" he asked, his knuckles turning white as he tightened his grip on the bars.

"Finish it," she said, turning away again. "Good day."

John watched her walk out. He had no idea what she had in mind. All he knew was that she was going to put herself and Blanche in danger, and he couldn't do a thing to stop it.

Derek Saylor was going to run into big trouble if he accosted that stagecoach, which he would. It would be carrying twenty thousand dollars in gold and a pair of Pinkerton's most experienced men. The moment Derek showed up, another war was going to start

And Maddy would be right in the middle of it.

John pulled at the bars, putting tension on until his muscles began to burn. With a final yank, he flung himself away and lay down on the narrow cot.

There was only one thing to be done: he had to get out.

Twenty-six

John paced the confines of his cell. Ten paces one way, eight the next. He'd been pacing all day, the savagery of his anger rising as the hours passed. The single window cast a rectangle of sunlight on the floor. As the afternoon waned, the light changed from yellow to gold to orange.

"Got to get out," he muttered, for what must have been the thousandth time that day.

He had to get to Maddy. He clenched his hands into fists. Damn it, he had to get to her. He had to fix this.

For the first time since this thing began, he didn't care about his job. Even the terrible memories from his past had lost their power over him in his concern for Maddy.

He knew the truth now. Fool that he was, he'd looked straight at it and refused to see it for what it was.

He loved her. He'd loved her from the first moment he'd set eyes on her.

Quite a revelation for a man who had wrapped himself in his work, shrouding his heart, his mind, and his soul in order to keep the terrible memories at bay. He'd barricaded himself from the world, and from love. But Maddy had come into his life like a whirlwind, stripping all that away and leaving him open. Wanting. Needing.

She'd touched him, she'd claimed him, she owned him. And if something happened to her, he would die inside. He had to get out. He had to. With a muttered curse, he pressed his forehead against the cool steel of the bars, trying to find some order in the chaos raging inside him.

"Maddy," he whispered. "Damn it, Maddy, you should have trusted me."

He should have trusted her. That night in his arms, she'd given him everything. If he hadn't been so blind, so god-damned stubborn, he would have seen her heart as it really was: loyal, generous, brave. She'd dared give herself to a man who'd sworn to hunt her brother, an act whose courage he hadn't understood until now.

And now, he faced the realization that he might have thrown it all away.

The door to the front office swung open, and John whirled, ready to confront the sheriff. It wasn't Cooper who walked in, however, but Hank Vann.

The bounty hunter's face was pale, and he moved with a carefulness that betrayed his pain. But his jaw was set and hard, and determination blazed in his eyes.

John knew what had brought him here; his own emotions raged in the bounty hunter's eyes. "What happened?" he asked.

"Blanche drugged me," Hank growled.

John nodded. "Where's the sheriff?"

"Sleeping."

"For long?"

"Long enough," Hank said. "Gave him the same thing Blanche gave me. Put it in his whiskey. I was out for more'n seven hours, so we'll have plenty of head start."

"You can't ride like that," John protested.

"Done it before. And there wasn't half the reward at the other end."

"Ten thousand dollars?"

Hank smiled grimly. Taking Sheriff Cooper's ring of keys from his pocket, he bounced it on his open palm. "To hell with the money. I just want to get my hands on my sweet, treacherous lady love."

"I've got some of those notions myself," John agreed. "Let's go."

Maddy tilted her head back to study the facade of Miss Penny's House of Pleasure. It was quiet now during the day, but an air of debauchery seemed to hang about the place. Perhaps it was the pink-painted exterior with the frilly wood fretwork around every window, or perhaps the snoring drunk lying on the porch just in front of the door.

"Do you really think Derek is here?" Blanche asked.

"There's only one way to find out," Maddy said.

She and Blanche had come disguised as men; two ladies visiting a whorehouse would have been as conspicuous as a hot air balloon in a cactus patch. Maddy had to be spokesman—Blanche's voice was too soft and high.

Pulling her hat low over her eyes, she stepped across the sleeping man's legs, then raised the brass knocker and let it fall.

"Go away," a woman called from inside. "Come back during business hours."

"We're not here for . . . business," Maddy called, pitching her voice as low as she could. "We're looking for someone. It's very important. Could we speak to you, please?"

Silence reigned for a moment. Then the door was flung open, framing a tall, voluptuous woman in a pink silk dressing gown. The top gaped open to reveal large white breasts barely contained in a black, lace-trimmed corset. Her hair was an improbable shade of red, and rouge turned her mouth into a crimson slash.

"Miss Penny?" Maddy asked.

'Yep," the woman said, suspicion chilling her light brown eyes. "What do you want?"

"May we talk to you inside?" Maddy said.

The woman stared hard at her for a moment, then nodded. She stepped aside, allowing Maddy entrance. Blanche hovered close behind. The inside matched the outside in garishness: red velvet sofas and chairs, red velvet draperies, gilt and crystal everywhere.

Tawdry, to be sure, but the place was spotlessly clean. She made a decision on the spot. Sweeping her Stetson from her head, she let her hair fall down around her shoulders.

Miss Penny gave a start of surprise. "Well, I'll be damned," she said, the suspicion vanishing from her eyes. "You look jest like your brother, you know. Come in. Make yourselves to home. Can I get you somethin' to eat?"

"Thank you, but we can't stay more than a few minutes." Maddy pulled her gloves off and tossed them into her hat. "I'm Maddy Saylor, and this is my sister Blanche."

"Penny Abbott. Pleased to meet you. Your brother told us an awful lot about you. Now come on in and set."

She turned away. Pink silk rustled around her as she led the way to a room at the far end of the foyer. Maddy might have called it a parlor if it hadn't been for the enormous four-poster that dominated the room. The covers were indigo velvet trimmed with gold, and the walls were festooned with a wealth of gold brocade.

"You've done very well for yourself, Miss Penny," Maddy said, turning to survey the room.

One corner of that crimson mouth went up. "Honey, I know this ain't your kind of place. But I have done well, and I'm right proud of it. After all, men can do without food and water, and they can, in a pinch, do without whiskey. But they cain't do without women, and that's a fact. I keep my place and my girls clean, I don't water the drinks, and we give honest service. The fellers don't have to worry about being robbed or beaten up, so they keep coming back. It's jest good business."

"How do you know our brother?" Blanche asked.

Miss Penny blinked. "Are you kiddin'?"

"My sister is very naive," Maddy said, ignoring Blanche's gasp of outrage.

"This is a whorehouse," Miss Penny said, her voice flat. "You know what sort of business goes on here, and what your brother comes here for."

Maddy knew if she showed one flicker of disapproval, she would lose Penny's trust. As usual, she opted for the direct approach.

"Miss Abbott, what you do for a living is no business of mine. I only care that our brother told us he could be reached through you, and that means he trusts you."

"He's a fool to trust anyone," Miss Penny said. "Ten thousand dollars is a hell of a lot of money."

Maddy looked into the woman's eyes. A month ago, she wouldn't have recognized what she saw there. Now, however, she knew it as well as she knew her own name. "You're in love with him."

Miss Penny's expression changed. The truth stood out like a torch, emotions Maddy had felt deep in her own soul. And Derek played the will-o'-the-wisp in love as he did in everything else.

Impulsively, Maddy reached out and took both of the woman's hands in hers. "I'm sorry," she said.

Tears glinted in Miss Penny's eyes. Then she blinked them away, regaining her composure with a visible effort. "Don't you worry," she said. "Men like Derek Saylor don't fall in love with women like me. He thinks of me as a friend who watches his back and warms his . . . well, you know."

"His trust was not misplaced," Blanche said.

Miss Penny let her breath out in a gusty sigh. "If that man wasn't such an idiot, and so danged . . . sweet, I'd of been tempted to tell him not to show his face here again. But once he turns that smile on, I want to drop one wing and run in circles like a mama bird defendin' her chick."

"That is Derek," Blanche murmured.

"Does he live here?" Maddy asked.

Miss Penny shook her head. "Your brother comes by to visit from time to time. He's got him a woman somewhere—"

"Oh, Miss Abbott!" Blanche gasped.

"As I said, I know the way things work," Miss Penny replied. "And men. One thing for sure: he doesn't love *her,* or he wouldn't be comin' back to me for . . . what he comes for." She sighed. "He's an honorable cuss, anyhow. Almost any of my girls would be tickled to take a tumble with him, paid or not. But since he started with me, he doesn't pay them no mind."

"Good Gad!" Blanche exclaimed.

"Men will be men," Miss Penny replied, a chill in her eyes.

Blanche's cheeks flamed. "Oh, I didn't mean that, Miss Abbott," she said. "I wouldn't offend you that way, please believe me. It's just that our brother is . . . is . . . well, he's just impossible."

"Wild as the wind," Miss Penny agreed.

"Here he is, wanted for just about everything under the sun, and he still finds time to play games with women's hearts. It just makes one want to knock him over the head."

"That would surely be a waste of one hell of a man," Miss Penny said, chuckling so that her big, soft breasts jiggled. "Oh, don't worry about him, honey. He jest needs to find the right woman. Man like that needs a real strong hand on the reins, by a woman smart enough not to let him know she's doin' it."

Maddy laughed, touched by the woman's generosity. "Oh, Miss Abbott, you do know my brother. What shall we do with him?"

"Pray, honey. Pray that he finds that woman soon and gets out of your hair." Miss Penny strolled across the room to her white-and-gilt dressing table. Taking an enormous atomizer, she puffed a cloud of perfume over her neck and shoulders. "Now, what message do you want me to give him?"

"It's extremely important that we talk to him," Maddy said. "Please tell him to meet us. We're going to spend the night at that big, dry wash just east of Rattlesnake Butte."

"I'll do my best to see that he gets your message, but I cain't guarantee you'll see him tonight," Miss Penny said.

"Now, you'd better get on out of here before some of my customers start complainin' that they want daytime visits. I cain't have that; my girls deserve their rest."

"Miss Penny . . ." Maddy had so many things she wanted to say to this woman who had befriended Derek when he'd needed a friend the most. But what could be said when Derek was incapable of giving Miss Penny the one thing she truly wanted? "Thank you. If there's ever anything you need, you call on us, hear?"

The woman smiled. "I hear. You two are jest like your brother, did you know that? But you don't owe me anythin' on his account. He paid his own debt by stoppin' a man who was hittin' one of my girls. Derek beat him bloody, then slung him out the door with the promise to kill him if he ever showed his face again. We haven't had trouble since."

It was so typically Derek that Maddy couldn't help but smile. "Thank you again, Miss Abbott."

"You're welcome."

She didn't see them out. Maddy gathered her hair up and secured it under her hat, then left the whorehouse with Blanche a step behind her. A moment later, they were heading west, toward Rattlesnake Butte.

"Pray that Derek meets us," she said.

"Can you believe this?" Blanche asked. "I wonder how many times he's broken hearts without even knowing it."

"He's an idiot," Maddy said. "He's always been an idiot, and he's always going to be an idiot."

"We have to get him married," Blanche said, determination hardening the line of her jaw. "As soon as possible."

"Let's see that he doesn't hang first."

"So you say. But I for one am keeping a sharp eye out for the right woman."

It was almost dark by the time they reached the spot where they'd set up camp earlier. The light seemed to run from the onrushing shadows, finally to be swallowed up as the sun dipped below the western horizon.

"We'd best not have a fire," Maddy said.

"Then it's biscuits and cold beans for supper," Blanche replied, sliding her saddlebags off her mount.

"Remember that time in Virginia when we went three weeks without eating anything but some sweet potatoes we stumbled across?"

"Mmmm. Lucky for us the Yankees didn't know that sweet potatoes are food, or they would have stolen those like they stole everything else."

Maddy leaned back against a rock, enjoying the retained heat against her shoulder blades. "I wonder how we both ended up falling in love with Yankees," she mused.

"I don't know. I really don't know," Blanche said. "I tried not to. But it was like getting hit from behind, and a . . . a sort of wave washed over me, and there I was."

"Oh, God," Maddy murmured. "That's the way it happened to me. Why does it have to be so hard, Blanche? Couldn't we have fallen in love with men we could actually have?"

"We Saylors never take the easy route, dear sister. You ought to know that by now."

"I wonder what Mexico is like," Maddy said, more to herself than to Blanche.

Dragging her hat off, Blanche shook her hair out in a golden cascade. "I don't know, and I don't care. Without Hank, it's the end of the world."

Maddy studied her sister for a long, thoughtful moment. Blanche needed so much more than she did, and it simply wasn't fair to ask her to give up so much.

"I don't think you should come with us," Maddy said.

"What?" Blanche's eyes went wide.

"You shouldn't come to Mexico," Maddy said again. "Stay here with Hank."

Blanche's face softened as she considered the possibility. Then she shook her head. "I couldn't abandon you."

"It's not abandonment," Maddy said. "It's pure common sense. Derek and I have nothing to bind us to anyone or any place. But you do. Why should you give up the man you love and who loves you desperately?"

"Because he's—"

"Hunting Derek?" Maddy finished for her. "He'll give that up, Blanche. You are the most important thing in the world to him, and in the end, he will choose you."

"How do you know?" Blanche whispered.

"I know because I can see the difference between him and John, who will not, or perhaps cannot, choose me."

Blanche sighed. Oh, Maddy. I wish—"

Something rustled out in the darkness. Shushing Blanche, Maddy strained to discover the source.

Blanche's head came up as she heard it, too. She listened for a moment, then pointed toward a stand of mesquites a short distance away. The shadows were thick there, and pregnant with an unseen presence.

Casually, Blanche rose and walked over to the horses. Hiding her actions from the unseen watcher, she tugged on Ali Baba's bridle, swinging him around so his hindquarters crowded the other horse. Startled, the chestnut neighed.

At that moment, Maddy slipped behind the rock, then melted into the darkness beyond. Drawing her pistol, she stealthily began making her way toward the trees. Blanche had managed to slip away from the horses, and was undoubtedly approaching their quarry from the other side.

Maddy caught a glimmer of movement a short distance away, a spark of starlight on pale hair. Blanche. And careless; a moment later, she moved more fully into the light. Maddy's heart went into a trip-hammer beat.

Blanche, Blanche, get under cover! she thought, cocking her pistol. *Please, Lord, don't let him see her. Don't put her in danger.*

A man stepped out of the shadows and grabbed Blanche. Maddy had a shot, just barely, and not for long. She crouched, holding his heart straight in her sights, and tightened her finger on the trigger.

Then something stopped her. Impulse, perhaps, or an angel come to save her from disaster. Either way, it seemed as though a hand fell on hers, staying her. In the next heartbeat, Blanche had moved into the field of fire and the shot had vanished.

"Hank!" Blanche cried in a high, breathy voice that didn't sound at all like hers.

She turned in the circle of his arms. Their gazes met and locked, as their hearts had locked the first moment they'd met. Hank bent close, his arm going around her waist in a gesture of tenderness that brought a lump to Maddy's throat.

"Don't say anything," Maddy whispered. "Don't do anything but love each other."

Hank pulled Blanche close against his side, then drew her into the veil of darkness.

Maddy blinked against the sudden prickle of tears. Ah, it had been so beautiful. She repressed a surge of wistfulness; Blanche deserved this. Sweet, soft Blanche had been made to be in love, and to be loved.

With a silent prayer of thankfulness for whatever had stayed her hand a moment ago, Maddy eased the hammer back up and slid the pistol back into its holster. That had been too close; she would never have been able to live with the guilt if she'd killed her sister's lover.

She rose, just a little shaky from that close call, and turned back to the camp. It was to be a lonely supper as well as a cold one, she thought. Then she smiled. Blanche had won; Hank had come after her, injured, weak, but determined, and had claimed her for his own. Maddy couldn't help but sigh, wishing she'd had that kind of true magic for herself.

Suddenly, two hard arms came around her, pinning her hands to her sides. Her captor didn't speak, nor did he move other than to immobilize her. But she knew him. She knew his touch, his scent, the inflexible strength of the body pressed so close against her back.

John Ballard.

Twenty-seven

"Hello, Maddy," John said.

His voice slid over her like dark, smoky wine, and it was all she could do to keep from shivering.

"How did you get out?" she whispered.

"Broke out," he said. "Or rather, Hank broke me out. Did you think I was going to let you get away with this? We started this game, Maddy, and I'm in it until the very end."

He unbuckled her gunbelt and tossed it away. Then he turned her toward him, never giving her the slightest chance to pull away. Even if she were free, she wouldn't have been able to run; simply by being here, he bound her.

He was so close that she had to tilt her head back to look at him. His face was half-shadowed in the starlight, all hard-cut lines of jaw and cheek and brow. She couldn't see his eyes; they were hidden in the wedge of shadow cast by his hat brim. But his face might have been cut from granite for all the emotion it showed.

Maddy was possessed by a terrible urge to see something, anything in him, even hate. "I didn't want to see you again," she said, forcing the words through a throat gone tight and dry.

The grim line of his mouth didn't change. "I'm not that easy to get rid of, Maddy."

"I should have shot you when I had the chance."

"Yes," he agreed. "You should have."

With one hand, he pushed her hat off her head. Her hair

came tumbling down around her shoulders. Maddy felt as though he'd stripped her naked. She stood taut and unmoving, every nerve aware of him pressing against her, hips and breasts and thighs. He drew his breath in with a hiss, then sank his hand into the silky bronze mass.

And then she saw his eyes.

Everything in her hung suspended in that moment. His eyes glittered with an anger hot enough to sear her where she stood. Maddy had never been docile, and she had plenty of physical courage. But now, looking into those furious green-gold eyes, she quailed inside.

"Where did you think you were going that I couldn't find you?" he asked.

Somewhere, somehow, she found her outrage again. He had no exclusive right to anger; she, too, had been betrayed. Perhaps only by her own heart, but betrayed nonetheless.

"Anywhere," she said. Heartbreak changed her voice until it didn't sound remotely like her own. She didn't care. All she wanted to do was lash out, to ease this terrible pain in her heart. "I'd run to the ends of the earth to get away from you."

Shocked by the savagery in her voice, John curved his fingers around her neck just below her ear and tilted her face more fully into the light. Her eyes were huge, raging with wildly intertwined emotions it might take him a lifetime to unravel.

A great tenderness swept through him then. It didn't require anything from her; it sprang unexpected and powerful from somewhere in his soul, whether or not he wanted it, whether or not she deserved it.

He slid his hand to the nape of her neck, savoring the silken warmth. She gasped, then tried to pull away. Vainly. He couldn't let her go; at the price of his life, he would hold her.

"Damn you," she said, her eyes rebellious.

"I was damned the moment I met you," he growled. "That's what brought me out here."

"You came for Derek."

"No," he said, "I came for you, Maddy. Only for you."

Lowering his head, he claimed her mouth. The kiss was feather-soft, yet fraught with needs that came straight from his soul. He could only pray that she wouldn't reject it, for rejection now would surely kill something inside him.

So this is love, he thought. Exquisite and dangerous, and with this woman, more challenge than he'd ever faced. He'd risked his life more times than he could count, but he'd never risked his heart.

For a moment, he thought he'd lost. Just as a cold knot of despair formed in his chest, her mouth softened beneath his, flowering into desire. With a low sound of mingled triumph and satisfaction, he deepened the kiss. She went right along with him, parting her mouth wider, taking him in with an eagerness that soon had his hands shaking.

He wanted everything at once. He wanted to kiss her forever, he wanted to lay her down, right here, right now, and take her for his own. He broke the kiss then, pausing to nibble at the corner of her lips, and pressed his open mouth over the throbbing pulsepoint in her throat.

Maddy cried out softly, reaching up to sink her hands into his thick hair. One touch, one kiss, and she'd passed beyond pride, beyond thought, beyond caution. She, Maddy Saylor, had been brought to this by her love of this man.

"I hate this," she whispered, even as she let her head fall back to give him easier access.

"I'll take even that, if it burns so hot," he said against her skin.

Heat raced along her nerves, setting up a burn deep in her core. Her body reacted powerfully. Her nipples hardened, matching the sweet ache between her legs.

John slid one hand down over the lush swell of her breasts. He found her nipples already peaked, and he nearly groaned as his own body responded. She arched her back as he stroked those taut nubs with his thumbs, and he marveled once again at her fiery responsiveness.

"Maddy," he groaned.

"Kiss me," she whispered.

He held his mouth over hers, their breaths mingling. Her mouth was open, wet, ready, and a jolt went through his groin. In one smooth, powerful motion, he swept her into his arms and carried her back to the campsite.

There, he laid her down on the nearest blanket. He crouched over her, just looking at her. She was the very image of desire; passion made Woman. Her eyelids drifted down, shielding her eyes with long brownish-blond lashes.

John didn't want her shielded. He wanted her open, willing, meeting him with equal passion. "Look at me," he said.

Her eyes opened. He gazed deep, deeper, finally seeing what she'd been trying so hard to conceal from him. Love. She loved him. Damn, he'd been so blind, and so had she! How much pain had they caused each other in their unwillingness to recognize their feelings for each other?

"Why did you fight this so hard?" he asked softly.

"Fight what?"

"This," he said. "Us."

"Because I had to," she replied, fighting for rationality amid the rioting sensations of her body. "Because you'll take everything from me if I let you."

"Yes," he agreed. "I will."

He moved so that he knelt straddling her. It was a gesture of protectiveness, and also of possessiveness. She belonged to him. Heart, mind, and soul, she belonged to him. Even if, he added silently, she didn't know yet that she wanted to.

She didn't look away, nor did she protest as he unbuttoned her shirt. Her breathing changed, grew faster and more shallow, betraying her arousal. The last button undone, he grasped the edges of her shirt and spread it open. She moaned softly, arching her back as though he'd touched her.

He didn't move for a moment, only looked at her. She wore no corset, no restraints other than a simple cotton chemise. And she was so beautiful it made his heart ache.

"Maddy," he whispered. "Oh, woman."

Rising to his feet for a moment, he levered her boots off. Then he came down beside her. She looked delicious in jeans, her hips sleek and curved, her legs impossibly long. Looking at her, he couldn't believe that she'd managed to fool him, even in the storm-filled darkness.

Slowly, deliberately, he eased her legs apart to make room for himself between them. Bracing himself on his hands, he fitted his hips into the cradle of her pelvis. He encountered heat and softness, and nearly went over the edge of his control. With iron determination, he pushed his own clamoring desire into abeyance.

Sliding his hand between them, he stroked her beneath the denim. The heat increased, and now he could feel wetness beneath his fingertips.

He leaned down and kissed her, a torrid, searing kiss born of love and longing and desire. Their tongues rubbed and teased, seeking ever more heat. She ran her hands along his arms, his back, until he thought he'd go crazy from the pleasure of it. He slid his erection along her cleft, stroking her, stroking himself through the shielding fabric. She cried out softly.

"You like that?" he murmured, doing it again.

Maddy dug her nails into the hard muscles of his back. Her body had taken over, wanting only to be possessed by him. If she'd had her way, their clothes would have evaporated into thin air, leaving only skin. And possession. Frustrated, she tilted her hips, encouraging even more contact.

He untied the ribbons of her chemise, spreading that garment open with a slow, sure movement. The night air drifted across her skin with a cool touch. Then his mouth closed over her nipple, and everything turned hot.

He drove her crazy with wanting as he caressed first one breast, then the other, tracing with his tongue the lush underneath curves, the sensitive spot just over her ribs, then up toward her nipple again. He licked her aureole, the texture of his tongue an incredibly erotic touch on the swollen flesh.

Maddy held his head to her, wanting, needing . . . She cried out softly as he drew her nipple into his mouth again, suckling her. He raised his head to look at her.

"Is that what you wanted?" he asked.

"Yes," she murmured, moving him toward her nipple again. "Yes."

He suckled her thoroughly, arousing her to a fever pitch. Her hips began to move of their own accord, sliding her pelvis against the rock-hard manhood pressed against her. She wanted to drive him crazy, she wanted to make him forget everything but her and the magic they were making together.

For it was magic. Heart and soul, mind and body, they'd struck a spark together that had flared into a raging bonfire. No matter how hard they'd tried, they hadn't been able to put that fire out.

Now, she wanted only to be burned. Here in his arms, she wanted to go up in flames.

"Hold me," she said. "Hold me tightly."

John lost what little control he still possessed. He rose, easing back onto his heels, and unbuckled her belt. The starlight gleamed on the skin of her breasts; her nipples were a deep pink, and fully erect. He drew his breath in deeply. Leaning forward, he laid his hands upon her shoulders, then slid them downward to cup those sweet, lush mounds.

"You belong to me, Maddy," he said.

She didn't answer; she seemed lost in passion. But he knew she'd avoided the issue, and he wasn't about to allow that. With one hand, he continued to caress her breasts, teasing the swollen flesh of her nipples with his palm. With the other hand, he unbuttoned her jeans, revealing a wedge of creamy skin. The sight aroused him powerfully, and he moved backward, sliding her jeans down as he went.

Her taut belly, the shadowed, inviting depression of her navel, the thatch of curly hair shielding her womanhood from his gaze . . . every inch was beautiful. He slid the jeans down and tossed them away. Then he lifted her and swept the shirt and chemise away to leave her completely naked.

Maddy reached up to unbutton his shirt, but he put her hands from him. "I don't think I could take it if you touched me just now," he said, his voice hoarse.

Maddy watched him as he took his clothes off. Shadows delineated the sculpted muscles of his chest and abdomen and the sharp-cut lines of his face. Her gaze drifted along the line of hair that ran downward from his chest to below his navel. His manhood jutted up from its nest of hair, strong and proud as the man himself. It was a powerful, primitive image, and appealed to the primitive female deep inside her.

Oh, she'd thought herself so civilized, so rational, and she hadn't been at all. She'd been waiting, without even knowing it, for this man. In loving him, she'd been set free of the constraints that had governed her life, and had been cast into the chaos of the heart. It didn't matter what his reasons might have been for coming after her. Anger, desire, ambition, revenge . . . nothing mattered now but being in his arms. She would have him. Now—tomorrow, too, if that was her destiny—but she would have him.

This was pure and true. There were no more games, no tricks, nothing but him and her, and the passion that flamed between them.

Driven by an impulse more powerful than anything she'd ever experienced, she pushed up to a sitting position and kissed him. For a moment, he went very still, and she knew she'd surprised him. But he recovered swiftly, his arm going hard around her waist to pull her against him.

"Do you feel the magic, Maddy?" he whispered, his breath hot against her temple.

"Yes," she said. "I think I always did."

He tucked her close against his body and levered them both down to the blanket. Maddy wrapped her arms around him, her body tingling with anticipation. She felt almost as though she were floating, buoyed by the heat of her desire for him.

"I dreamed about loving you again," he rasped.

"I, too," she replied.

The admission surprised John, and he leaned on one elbow to study her face. Something had changed in her. The recklessness was still there—Maddy would never be tamed—but the conflict was no longer there.

His heart beat so fast he thought it might pound right out of his chest. He loved her. Could it be possible that she loved him, too?

He took a deep breath. And then he took the biggest risk yet.

"I'm in love with you, Maddy."

She went very still. She hadn't expected this, not this. It stunned her; she had barely come to the realization that he had followed her here, not to find Derek, but to claim her. Not revenge, not ambition or anger, but love.

The few defenses she still possessed vanished in a sweeping tide of joy. He loved her. Somehow, in the confusion that had claimed all their lives, he'd come to love her.

Reaching up, she slid her fingers into his hair.

"I love you," she whispered.

John closed his eyes. She had been silent for a long, heart-clenching moment, and he'd been afraid that she wouldn't answer. Before he'd met her, he'd been immune to fear. He'd been immune to a number of other feelings as well, his emotions buried behind the same wall that had insulated his pain.

Now he could bear his past, for he'd discovered his future.

"I wish I hadn't been so blind," he said. "When I think of the time we wasted—"

"Shhh." Maddy ran her fingertip along the sensual curve of his mouth, applying pressure so that the caress strayed to the sensitive flesh inside his lower lip. "You're wasting time now, you know."

He smiled. "So I am."

"And you talk too much."

"So I do."

John hadn't lost the urgency of his desire for her; his manhood lay erect and ready between them, and desire ran like sweet, hot wine through his veins. He'd only held it in abeyance for a time, so they could strip away their last, lingering conflict. Now, he wanted only to hold her, to feel her heart beating against his.

"You feel so good," she whispered. Fascinated with the maleness of his body, she ran her hands along the hard swell of muscle on his chest. "You're so different from me, and yet we fit each other as though we were made for it."

He laughed softly. "Analyzing again, Maddy mine?"

"Well, it's true."

He spread his hands out over her back, savoring her smoothness, the fragility of her bones. "This is the way God meant us to be, love. But we're the ones who make the magic work. Even if," he said as he leaned down to kiss her nose, "one of us insists it's only physical."

"I was a fool," she said.

"And so was I," he said, all humor dropping away. "Or I would never have allowed you to leave my bed."

His fierceness surprised her. "Good Lord, John. You would have had to let me out sometime."

"Would I?"

Maddy framed his face between her hands. All the cynicism had left his mouth, leaving only tenderness. He'd stripped himself bare so she could see who and what he was, and it was a precious thing. For as long as she lived, she would remember this moment.

"John—"

"Now it's you who's talking too much."

"So it is."

She kissed him then, a bold foray of her tongue into his mouth. All thought of restraint left her; she became primitively female, all heat and wanton response. And she didn't care. This was good, this was right, this was the most powerful truth she had ever encountered. So she gave herself up to it, and to him, totally.

She arched her back as his hands slid down to her buttocks, smoothing her rounded flesh, then pressing her pelvis against the rock-hard thrust of his manhood. She moaned into his mouth, rubbing herself against him with complete abandon.

"Maddy," he said. "About—"

"Shhh." She laid her hand over his mouth. "Love me, John. Love me."

His eyes drifted closed, and she knew she'd stirred him unbearably. Then his tongue darted out to taste the sensitive skin of her palm, and it was her turn to be stirred. It was always like this between them, such seemingly simple touches turning their passion white-hot.

He moved over her then, sliding his legs between hers with a gentle aggression that sent her passion hurtling still higher.

But he didn't take her. Instead, he settled down upon her as if he had all the time in the world, his chest against her belly, his head upon her breasts. He caressed her sides, sliding his thumbs along the spot where her breasts met her ribs, then upward to her underarms. She arched her back in delight and surprise; she hadn't expected that to be a sensual touch. But it seemed every part of her was sensual beneath John's expert, loving hands, and she might as well accept that.

He kissed his way along the undercurve of her breasts, then moved lower. She sank her hands into his hair as he licked a heated path down her torso, pausing to delve into her navel with the tip of his tongue.

Reaction poured through her in a molten flood, sending her arousal racing higher and hotter until she thought surely there could be no more.

Ah, but she soon discovered otherwise. He slid lower, laving her skin with his open mouth. She cried out in surprise when he moved lower, kissing the thatch of curly hair that shielded her womanhood.

"What are you doing?" she gasped.

"Loving you," he replied.

"But . . . but . . ."

"There is no shame between us," John said, looking up at her. "Only pleasure."

Slipping his thumbs into the folds of her womanhood, he spread her open. Then he bent, licking her slick flesh, savoring her heat and taste. Ah, she was all woman, and by some miracle, she was his. If it was in his power, he would take her to heaven and back again, and bind her to him forever.

Maddy cried out again in sheer, voluptuous reaction. She'd never felt anything like this; the intimacy of it stunned her even as the sensations rocked her to her very soul. She hadn't known, hadn't imagined, that a man and woman could share something so erotic and yet so beautiful. It felt as though sunlight had bloomed in her body.

She rolled her head from side to side as he moved up to the small, erect nub that was the center of her desire. He claimed it gently, but with expert intent, and Maddy was lost. Her hips bucked in involuntary response, moving in rhythm with his stroking tongue.

Her arousal peaked higher, higher still. She could no longer feel the blanket beneath her; all sensation centered on the incredible pleasure he was bringing to her. And then . . . and then it wasn't enough. She needed more. She needed him.

"Oh," she gasped. "John. I have to—"

"I know," he said, shaking with the need to possess her. "So do I."

He entered her with a deep, hard thrust, and she arched her back in wanton response. This time, there was no pain. Only pleasure. Oh, such pleasure. She let her eyes drift closed as she ran her hands down his back to his buttocks, holding him there. Savoring the incredible sensation of feeling him there inside her, filling her, possessing her completely.

Patient now that he was where he wanted most to be, John let her enjoy him. He held himself still, feeling the tiny tremors inside her, the sweet, almost imperceptible movements of her body, the ragged tempo of her breathing.

But soon, her hands began to stray, sliding up his back and over his shoulders, then down to his chest and lower still to his belly. It was a sure touch, the touch of a woman who was powerfully aroused, and who wanted to put him in the same state. And oh, damn, it was working. He closed his eyes, almost undone by the pleasure of it.

She gasped in protest as he withdrew almost completely, and it was the sweetest sound he'd ever heard. Slowly, he slid back in until he was sheathed completely. Her tight, hot depths clenched around him, and he nearly lost control.

"God, Maddy!" he gasped, burying his face in the sweet curve where her neck joined her shoulders. She smelled of lilacs and desire. He pressed his open mouth against her skin, nibbling, sucking, feeling her response in the subtle movements of her body.

Maddy's passion was spiraling out of control. She could no longer bear patience from him; she wanted to possess him, to be possessed, and she wanted it now. But he seemed determined to hold her here at the edge, aching with desire.

Ah, but she was not a woman to be denied.

She drew his head up so she could look into his eyes. Then she pulled her knees upward, sliding him in that last, precious fraction of an inch. His breath went out in a gasp. A lost, wild look came into his eyes, and she knew she'd won.

He moved in her then, purposeful and sure. She lifted her hips in rhythmic response, giving, taking, pulling him to the heights even as he drove her to the edge of distraction.

They strained together, thrusting, stroking, breathing in unison, his passion stoking hers, hers stoking his. A fine film of moisture sheened their bodies. Maddy lifted her hips, responding to his thrusts, tremors racing along her limbs as she neared the peak.

"Oh," she gasped. "I'm . . . I'm . . ."

"Yes," he whispered. "I feel you."

Maddy had lost the capacity to think. She could only feel, as though she'd become only a creature of passion. Wanton. Aroused. Demanding. She bit gently at his shoulder, sucking heat to the surface as the speed of his thrusts increased.

She moaned as the first, tiny tremors of her climax began. John slid one hand beneath her hips, lifting her for his down-stroke, then called her name over and over as he followed her into completion. Maddy felt consumed with heat and light and shuddering fulfillment.

John held her through the aftershocks of release. Slowly, her body relaxed beneath his. He, too, drifted into the lassitude of satiation, his only ambition to bend his head and kiss her tenderly, a reaffirmation of their love and their passion.

"Ah, Maddy," he murmured against her mouth. "That was heaven."

"Yes," she agreed. "It was."

The sounds of the world drifted back into her consciousness. She lay quietly for a moment, listening to the whisper of the wind playing through the leaves, the skitter of small night creatures in the grass, the soft hoot of a hunting owl.

Her skin prickled at the touch of the breeze, bringing a wash of goosebumps along her limbs. Yes, indeed, the world had returned—as had the thought that Derek might show up at any time, and would not react well to the sight of his sister naked in the arms of a man.

"You're cold," John said.

"Now," she replied.

With a sigh, he sat up, bringing her with him. "Much as I hate to see you cover that beautiful body, I bow to the limitations of comfort and privacy."

Maddy reached for her clothes, but he put his hand on her arm to stop her.

"Providing, of course," he added, "that I get to take them off again as soon as possible."

She leaned close and playfully caught his bottom lip between her teeth. His eyes widened in shock, but she slid away from him before he could react more forcibly.

"That," he said, "could have gotten you in serious trouble again, my sweet."

"What kind of trouble?" she asked.

Then she glanced down, and saw that he was becoming aroused again. She stared at his manhood, watching it lengthen and rise from its nest of hair as though it had a life of its own.

"I see it doesn't take much to gain your interest," she said, tossing his pants toward him.

He grinned at her, that devastating flash of dimple that always sent her nerves tingling. "*You* don't have to do much to gain my interest."

Once they were dressed, he opened his arms to her. She went to him eagerly, laying her head against the warm hardness of his chest. His heartbeat was steady and slow against her cheek.

Then she lifted her head and met his gaze. "Will you tell me about your brothers now?"

John nearly refused. He wanted to tell her. He needed to tell her; this was the last thing he'd held back, and she deserved nothing less than everything he had to give.

They were only words, after all, simple things that would give her the past that had been frozen in his soul. But his throat closed down, and he found himself unable to speak.

For a moment, Maddy thought he'd deny her again. Her heart clenched into a cold knot in her chest. *Not now,* she thought. Not now, when she had made herself completely vulnerable to him. Then she looked into his eyes and saw the struggle there.

Laying her palm against the hard curve of his cheek, she said, "Let it go, John."

He let his breath out in a long sigh, and it felt as though his pain went out with it. And he was free. He framed her face between his hands and kissed her brows, her nose, the lovely double curve of her mouth. No matter what happened, he would always remember this gift she'd given him.

He would tell his story. And he would give her his past. "When my brothers and I left for war," he said, "I made the arrogant promise to my parents that I would watch over them. After all, I was the oldest. I'd always protected them."

He closed his eyes, letting the memories rake through him. Now, however, they were only memories. Hard ones, terrible ones, but they didn't claim his present. "But that day at Antietam, I found that all I could do was close their eyes for them as they died. I went a little crazy that day. I couldn't stand being alive, and did everything I could do to spend my life as dearly as possible."

"And got a medal for your trouble."

"The medal means nothing. Not now, not then. I didn't earn it. That wasn't heroism, Maddy. It was the accidental result of a man lashing out because he couldn't stand his own pain."

He brushed a stray curl back from her forehead. "After the war, when I went home, I could see in my parents' eyes that I'd failed them. And every time I saw it, I wished I'd died in that field with my brothers. My parents didn't live long after that. I sold the farm and never looked back again. Except in my dreams."

Maddy swallowed hard. No wonder he had closed himself off, and fought so hard against opening up again. "And I threw our losses into your face so many times," she said. "How frivolous it must have seemed to you. After all, Tallwood was home, but when held against the lives of people we love, it was only a house and some land. At least Blanche and I still have Derek."

"I didn't think it frivolous," he replied. "I understood you wanting to protect your brother. I admire that. And I was jealous."

The blunt admission surprised Maddy. Yes, he would be envious. Perhaps if he'd had someone to lean on, to understand, he wouldn't have closed himself off from emotion for so long.

"John, what are you going to do about Derek?"

He could give her nothing but the truth. "I don't know, Maddy."

Derek's smooth, lazy voice drifted out of the darkness. "Perhaps the question should be, sister mine, what am I going to do about him."

Twenty-eight

"Derek!" Maddy gasped.

John flung her to one side and snatched his gun from the gunbelt lying on the ground beside him. Light glittered on metal as Derek drew his own weapon.

Maddy hurled herself between them. She stood, arms outstretched, chest heaving, her hair lifting in a shining bronze cloud upon the wind.

"Please," she said. "Don't."

John knew he could make the shot over her shoulder. So could Derek; he could see the knowledge in the outlaw's eyes. But he couldn't do it. Maddy was reckless enough to put herself in the path of a bullet to save him or her brother, and John wasn't willing to risk her.

With a wordless growl, he let the barrel of his weapon drift downward. Derek watched him for a long, frozen moment, then lowered his own gun.

"Hello, sister mine," he said, his mouth grim. "This wasn't exactly the reception I expected."

"Nor did I," she retorted. "If you would walk into a campsite like a normal person, and not scare people half to death with these dramatic entrances, perhaps fewer people would take potshots at you."

"You didn't say hello," he said. "Nor did you ask how long I've been here."

She blushed painfully, and had more than a fleeting urge to

take a potshot or two at him herself. "How long *have* you been here?"

"Long enough to know what's going on," he said. Then he grinned like Satan himself, and it was like sunlight had broken through stormclouds. "But not long enough to be embarrassed. I did find Blanche and her bounty hunter sleeping like angels, and took the liberty of appropriating his gun, just in case."

"What the hell are you doing here, anyway?" John demanded.

Derek's gaze went to him. "I received a message to meet my sisters here," Derek said. "So of course I came. You're the Pinkerton agent."

"Yes."

"My compliments. You came close to catching me a couple of times."

"I know," John said. "What's next?"

Instead of answering him directly, Derek spoke to Maddy. "Maddy, come here."

John expected her to argue. He expected her to insist on remaining between them, protection for them both. But she turned instantly and went to her brother. Shock hit John like a bucketful of cold water. Had be been wrong about her? Had everything been a lie?

Once she stood beside Derek, she turned to look at him. He was struck by the similarity between them. Not only in height and coloring, but in the proud carriage of their bodies and the calm, level courage in their eyes. These two would stand together against the world.

It made him angry. Not because she might have betrayed him in the worst possible way, but because he wanted that kind of loyalty for himself. He wanted Maddy at his side, ready to fight everything and everyone for him.

"So shoot me if you're going to," he growled.

Derek's brows went up. "You're anxious to die, aren't you?"

"I'm just tired of talking. Get it over with."

Derek glanced at Maddy. "Shall I shoot him?"

"I'd prefer not," she said.

"Ah." Gesturing to the pistol in John's hand, Derek said, "You wouldn't consider putting that away, would you?"

"Would you?"

For a moment, Derek didn't answer. Then he grinned, recklessness flashing in his eyes, and slid his pistol back into its holster. Then he crossed his arms over his chest and regarded John cheerfully.

The man is insane, was John's first thought. Then he looked more deeply into his eyes, and recognized the shadow there. Derek didn't care. Life or death, it was all the same to him. John had lived too many years like that. It had taken Maddy to open his eyes and his heart, and set him free.

Damn. This had started out so easy; find an outlaw, bring him to justice. Now, he would have to judge first, and decide himself what to do with this man. With a wordless growl, he put his own weapon away.

"Talking is better than shooting," Derek said. "Maddy, why don't you go fetch Blanche and her bounty hunter? I think it's time that we all had a talk."

John watched as Maddy walked away. She moved in utter silence, slipping into the darkness as though her very flesh had become insubstantial.

When he looked at Derek again, he found the other man smiling openly. "Surprised?"

"Nothing about the Saylors surprises me anymore," John said.

Derek's smile widened. "I see that you don't know us nearly well enough, or you wouldn't have said something so rash."

Maddy reappeared, Blanche and Hank just behind her. Not one of them made a sound. They just walked out of the shadows as though only the starlight gave them substance John was amused in spite of the situation; the refined, ladylike Saylor sisters seemed to have a number of talents beyond using a needle.

Hank Vann's face was inscrutable. But Blanche almost

seemed to glow with happiness; whatever difficulties they might have, it was obvious that Blanche didn't think they would be enough to keep her and Hank apart.

John only wished he could be as sure of Maddy. She'd stopped beside her brother again, looking incredibly sexy in men's clothing.

"I want my gun back," Hank growled.

"Later," Derek said. "I'd rather not get shot before I have a chance to discuss this situation."

Hank glanced at Blanche, then nodded. "First, I want to get a fire started. I like to be able to see a man's face when I'm talking to him."

"Agreed," Derek said.

A short time later, they faced one another over the leaping yellow flames of a campfire. Maddy wasn't sure where to sit; her place was with two men, John and her brother. Blanche had made her choice; she sat in the circle of Hank's arm, her pretty face all but glowing in the flickering firelight.

So Maddy stood at the edge of the illumination, her gaze riveted to John. He didn't seem to notice her; he watched Derek with eyes that were as chill and impenetrable as fog.

Dread ran cold through her veins. Had he gone away from her again? Had he seen this as a betrayal, perhaps, a ploy on her part to allow Derek to rid himself of his most tenacious pursuers? Oh, she hoped not. Surely she and John had shared too much and loved too deeply for him to doubt her now.

She had to know. So she went to him, standing before him as she waited for his reaction. He didn't look away from Derek. Her heart quailed, but she waited still. A heartbeat passed, and another. Then he looked at her, his brows rising as he contemplated her with a speculative gaze. Tears blurred her vision, and she very nearly turned away.

Then he held out his hand. Accepting her, no matter what. Maddy let her breath out in a shuddering sigh. She laid her palm against his, letting him draw her down beside him. He put his arm around her, claiming her.

"Now," he said. "It's time to talk. Derek, if you give yourself up, I'll do everything in my power to help you."

One side of Derek's mouth went up. "That's not what I wanted to talk about, sir," he said. "I want to discuss your and Hank's intentions toward my sisters."

John and Hank glanced at each other, and Maddy knew they were astonished by Derek's question. Evidently they'd expected him to be concerned about his own situation.

They still had a great deal to learn about the Saylors.

And about Derek. He *had* no concern about his situation. She watched her brother carefully, gauging the level of his recklessness.

"Our intentions?" Hank repeated.

"Yes," Derek said.

John met his gaze levely. "Maddy belongs to me."

"And Blanche is mine," Hank said.

"Now, just one moment," Maddy protested. "We aren't some sort of property just because—"

"I accept your claims," Derek said. "And approve your courting my sisters."

"Is he loco?" Hank asked, shooting a glance at John.

"They're all loco," John replied. "And I'm becoming as crazy as they are, because they're starting to make sense."

Hank snorted. "Damn. One thing's for certain, marriage ain't going to be boring. Now that that's settled, what are we going to do about him?" He thrust his thumb toward Derek.

"It would be easier all around to shoot him," John replied, "but it's going to be hard to explain that to Maddy."

Derek laughed. "At least I'll have brothers-in-law with a sense of humor." Then all levity drained from his face. "I don't expect you to believe what I have to say, but for my sisters' sake, I have to try. I didn't rob those stagecoaches, and I didn't rob that bank."

John studied him closely. "Then who did?"

"I don't know," Derek said. "I only know that I didn't."

"Can you prove that? Have you been with anyone who can vouch for you during any of the robberies."

"Yes. But that can't help me."

"Why not?" Hank asked.

Derek slid a glance at his sisters. "I was with a lady."

"But Miss Penny wouldn't mind vouching for you," Blanche said.

Everyone turned to look at her incredulously. Then Derek cleared his throat and said, "I, ah, wasn't with Penny, my dear."

"Not . . ." Blanche took a deep breath, and her eyes narrowed. "Oh, Derek. You *are* an idiot. She's married, I suppose."

"She wanted to come forward, but I wouldn't let her," he protested. "Not only would it destroy her reputation, but her marriage as well. I can't allow her to ruin her life."

John stared at Derek, speech having failed him. He might not have believed such an incredible story from anyone but a Saylor. After his time with Maddy, however; he knew Derek was perfectly capable of letting himself hang rather than compromise a woman's reputation.

Well, so are you, whispered a cynical little voice in his mind. *You very nearly got yourself lynched to protect Maddy.* So, he and Derek were a pair. Idiots both.

John found himself grinning as the absurdity of it all struck him. He'd been teasing Hank when he'd said they were all crazy, but he'd been right. Yet for all its impracticality, the Saylor honor was a fine, shining thing in a world that sometimes seemed to be lacking in luster. There were worse things, then, than being an idiot.

He found a strange sort of kinship toward the man he'd been hunting, and he hadn't felt this way since his brothers had died on that battlefield at Antietam. He didn't want to feel kinship for this man; his duty demanded that he bring Derek in to face the charges that had been made against him.

But he did feel it. And looking into Derek Saylor's eyes; he saw truth. The man was innocent.

"Damn it to hell," John growled. "You're lucky you've got

the sisters you do, or somebody would have shot you long before now."

"You're right," Derek said cheerfully. "Did they tell you the story of how they slipped into the Yankee prisoner of war camp and helped me escape? They even managed to get a dozen or so comrades out with me."

Slowly, John turned to look at Maddy. "No, they didn't."

"They decided they didn't want their baby brother languishing in prison," Derek said "It was quite a shock, I can tell you. My sisters donned men's clothing, and, with inescapable logic, decided it would be easy to slip in. After all, most people want to break *out* of prison."

"That's the general idea," John said. "But they did have to get out again, and bring you with them."

"True," Derek said. "But you've seen how quietly they can move; it's a quality all us Saylors seem to have. Slipping back out was easy, once we overpowered a few of the guards."

It was Hank's turn to look at his ladylove. "You overpowered the guards?"

"It was the only way to get our brother," Blanche replied, as though things like that were done every day. "That was a bit tricky, I must admit. But we had great fun after that, riding out night after night to fool the Yankees."

Derek nodded. "I told them to go home and stay home. But do you think they listened to me?"

"Of course not," John said.

"Without my knowledge, they rode the countryside, pretending to be me," Derek continued. "My reputation swelled, of course, for I couldn't very well lay the deeds at their door."

"Oh, you should have heard him when he found out," Maddy said. "He forbade us most forcefully."

"We know where *that* got him," Hank muttered.

Derek laughed. "Oh, yes, they bruised my male pride considerably, but the truth was, they were very good at it."

"If Derek goes to prison," Blanche said, "we have every intention of breaking him out, just as we did during the war."

A vast silence followed that statement. Maddy knew John was looking at her, but she kept her face resolutely turned toward her brother. Derek was enjoying this, she knew. But beneath the jovial pirate's facade, he watched the men whom his sisters had chosen. Watched and listened and judged.

"Well, gentlemen," he said. "What are we going to do?"

John transferred his gaze from Maddy to her brother. He rose and added more wood to the fire. The flames licked higher, pushing the encroaching darkness back.

"We seem to be at an impasse," he said. "We can't shoot you because we're in love with your sisters, and you can't shoot us for the same reason."

"True," Derek said with a grin.

"And I'm inclined to believe your story. That means we've got to try to fix this thing."

Maddy let her breath out with a sigh. She'd hoped for this, hoped and prayed and waited.

"Me, too," Hank growled. "Damn me for a fool."

Blanche threw her arms around him. "Oh, but a marvelous fool!"

"Did you have something specific in mind, John?" Derek asked.

"Yes," John said, crossing his arms over his chest. "I want to put you in jail."

Maddy gasped, trying to find some balance in a world that had just taken a spin.

"Now don't get upset," John continued. "I'm working on the belief that you're innocent. Until now, you've been playing right into this fellow's hands."

"He had no choice," Maddy said. "If Derek were in jail, the man would have had to stop his thievery. But then people would say that the robberies stopped because Derk was in jail. Even if he left Texas, this man could continue to blame him, for who would really believe Derek was gone?"

"Impeccable logic; as always, my sweet," John said. "But

this time; Derek has an advantage: he has the belief of people who are in a position to help him."

Maddy shot him a glance. "The trap?"

"The trap," John agreed.

"Which trap?" Derek asked.

"I arranged for word to get out that the stage from Preston is carrying a shipment of gold," John said. "I'd planned to shadow that stage and catch you when you tried to rob it."

"Ah." Derek's expression turned thoughtful. "And when is this supposed to happen?"

"Monday," Maddy said.

"Now, my plan is that we sneak you into the Cofield jail," John said. "We'll let the ever-vigilant Sheriff Cooper watch over you while we spring the trap at the stage as planned. Even if we fail to capture our man, no one will be able to blame Derek Saylor, since he was locked up during the attempt."

It was a good plan, Maddy knew. It might be Derek's only chance. But this wasn't her risk, nor her decision. It might be possible that Derek didn't want this to end, that he enjoyed the chase, the risk, and the end that would come when he made that inevitable mistake.

But something new came into Derek's eyes, something she'd never seen before. And then she realized that he was tired. Tired of running, tired of hiding, tired, finally, of playing the game. Warmth bloomed in her heart; perhaps now, like John, Derek had reached the point where he could *choose* life.

"There's one flaw in your plan," Derek said. "If no one comes to rob the stage, then there's no one else to blame, and I'm in jail."

One side of John's mouth went up in a smile, and he spread his hands.

For a moment, Derek looked hard at him. Then he threw back his head and laughed. "So it's a roll of the dice, yes?"

"Yes," John said.

"With my brother's life in the balance," Maddy said "I don't want either of you to forget the stakes."

They turned identical gazes on her, and she knew they had entered a purely male territory of recklessness where no woman could follow.

"Of course we know the stakes, Maddy," Derek said. "This is all to happen on Monday, you say? We'll meet Sunday night, and you can take me in to the jail. You'll discuss this with the sheriff, I trust?"

"I thought I'd surprise him with it," John said. "You see, I had to break out of jail myself to get here."

For the first time since he'd stepped out of the shadows, Derek looked astonished. He stared at John for a long, breathless moment, then started to laugh.

"Oh, Maddy," he gasped, tears running down his face. "You should keep this one, you really should."

Yes, she should. If he survived this, that is.

Derek, gentleman that he was, left once the details had been set. Blanche and Hank had gone off to find their own privacy. Maddy lay on the blanket with John, her back to him, his big, warm body curled protectively around hers.

"Do you think Sheriff Cooper will help us?" she asked.

"I don't know," he said. "He's a smart old bird, but he's not going to be pleased with me for breaking out of his jail."

"Sheriff Cooper is an honorable man. You saved his life; the least he'll do for you is give you a fair hearing."

"I hope so," he said. "If not, he'll lock me and Hank up with Derek, and we'll be stooped and grey by the time we get out again."

Maddy shrugged; she and Blanche were hardly going to allow that to happen. Yankee prison camp, federal prison, simple town jail . . . none had bars strong enough to hold anyone dear to them. Mentioning that fact, of course, would only lead to trouble, so she kept it to herself. "Has it occurred to you that now that you're free, Zachary Marsh and his men will be hunting you?" she asked.

"I've got more important things to worry about besides Zachary Marsh," he said. "Such as why I have this beautiful woman, whom I love to distraction, in my arms, and I'm wasting the little bit of time I have with her."

"Oh, you," she said. "This isn't—"

"This is," he murmured.

He brushed her hair off the bask of her neck and kissed her there, sending shivers of reaction racing all through her body. Then he unbuttoned the top two buttons of her shirt and pulled it down to her shoulder. With his tongue, he traced a hot, wet path along her neck to just under her ear.

Maddy shivered as arousal spiraled through her body. Ah, such a simple touch to have such an effect! But he'd affected her powerfully from the very beginning, and so much more now that she loved him.

"Oh, you feel so good," she sighed.

"It will feel even better soon," he said.

Maddy smiled, feeling the hard length of his manhood against her buttocks. "Yes," she said. "I know."

He laughed softly, his breath stirring the hair at her temple. Then he kissed her ear, a featherlight touch yet intensely erotic. Reaction ran quicksilver-fast through her, and she tilted her head backward to give him greater access. He teased her earlobe with his tongue, then nibbled his way along the delicate outer curve. Slowly, teasingly, he slid his tongue into her ear.

Maddy drew her breath in with a hiss, completely entranced by the sensations he was causing. Her whole body tingled with desire and anticipation, as though her very flesh knew the pleasure he would give her.

"You like that," he whispered.

"I seem to like everything you do," she replied.

"That's good," he said. "Because I plan to do things like

this every day, every night. I'll love you with my mind, my heart, and my body."

Unbearably stirred by the beauty of his words, Maddy had to close her eyes against an upwelling of tears. To be loved like that was a precious thing, and she intended to treasure the gift.

And not waste this beautiful night.

Boldly, she rubbed herself against him, inciting him. His reaction was most gratifying. With a low groan, he grabbed her hips and pressed her still closer.

Then it was her turn to groan as he began to caress her breasts, lifting them, rubbing them, stroking her erect nipples through the fabric. He unbuttoned her shirt and slipped one hand inside to work his devastation more intimately. A soft moan escaped her, and she reached back to grasp his hair in both hands.

"Ah, Maddy," he groaned.

He reached down then to unbutton her pants. Maddy gasped as he slid his hand over her belly, over the crisp, curling hairs, and claimed the core of her. Parting her folds, he explored her slick flesh, stroking her lightly, teasingly, until she bucked against him.

Maddy became lost in a wild cascade of sensation. The night seemed to close around her in a dark-velvet blanket, securing her in a world peopled only by her, John, and their passion.

She wanted to kiss him, to caress him, to feel his chest against her aching breasts. But he kept her where she was, with her back to him, and drove her to quivering need with his fingers.

His touch deepened, pulling her yet farther into a haze of sensation. Suddenly he withdrew, and she cried out in protest. But then he grasped her jeans, pulling them over her hips and down her legs. A moment later he lifted her, seemingly without effort, and divested her of her shirt and chemise.

She was free at last to turn to him, to touch him like he'd been touching her. But her hands shook so badly when she tried to undress him that he brushed them away and did it himself. Maddy could hardly wait for him to finish. She only knew that she wanted him back so badly it hurt.

She crouched beside him, running her hands over him, then leaning down to press her open mouth to the hot skin of his chest. He'd given her so much pleasure. So much. Lost in a shimmering haze of passion, she caressed him with her lips and hands, recklessly, without restraint or inhibition. He arched in wild response, touching her, caressing her, urging her to still more.

And then his control broke. The world tilted around Maddy as he turned, putting her beneath him. She spread her legs to welcome him home. He claimed her mouth, his tongue delving deep just as he plunged into her body.

Maddy wrapped her legs around his lean, driving hips and hung on. They kissed, gasping into each other's mouths as they strove together. Her climax swept through her like a tidal wave, and she cried out in sheer abandon as she was plunged deep into the pleasure. He followed her over the edge, groaning, his face pressed against the side of her neck.

They clung to each other for a long time afterward. Finally, John rolled onto his back, bringing her with him, and pulled a blanket over them both. Safe in the circle of his arms, Maddy laid her cheek on his chest and let herself drift off on a tide of contentment. Beneath her, she felt John's muscles relax as sleep claimed him.

The night pressed around her, warm and fragrant, and as peaceful as anything she'd ever known. It seemed a magical place in the starlight; even the most mundane shapes turned mysterious.

Lulled by John's deep, slow breathing, Maddy found her eyelids growing heavier by the moment. She cuddled closer, and he reacted, even in sleep, by tightening his embrace.

He'd said he would hold her. Forever. Maddy smiled, letting her eyes finally drift closed.

A sudden thought slashed through her mind, jolting her back

to wakefulness. Oh, she'd been sadly distracted to have missed something so important! She'd been so relieved that John finally believed in Derek's innocence that she'd missed the biggest flaw in his plan.

It didn't include the Saylor sisters. And that simply wouldn't do. Wouldn't do at all.

Twenty-nine

Monday dawned clear and warm, but Maddy and Blanche had been up long before the sun. Maddy sat packing their saddlebags while Blanche slipped around to the jail to see if Derek had been brought in yet.

Just as the first lemony light of morning hit the windows, Blanche returned. "He's there," she said. "Evidently Sheriff Cooper believed their story."

"John and Hank?" Maddy asked.

"Gone. Don't worry, Maddy. They didn't see me." Blanche turned to the stove and poured herself a cup from the teapot Maddy had been keeping warm. "I can't believe they expected us to stay here twiddling our thumbs"

"They're men," Maddy replied. "They feel it's their job to protect us."

"Hmmph. And who's going to protect *them?*"

Maddy smiled. "We will, of course. Now, I suggest you wear something light and comfortable, sister dear. The interior of these stagecoaches can get quite hot on a sunny summer day."

"Are you sure taking passage on the coach is the best way?" Blanche asked.

"Definitely," Maddy replied. "There's nothing remarkable about a pair of women taking passage, but two men following the coach is going to make people very nervous. Besides, we can stay hidden from our sweethearts, who will take a very uncharitable view of what we did, and might even do something reckless to take us out of any possible danger."

"Idiots," Blanche said.

"Of course. That's why we love them." Finished with the packing, Maddy stood up. "You'd better get dressed, dear. We have barely enough time to get to Preston before that stage leaves."

A few minutes later, she and Blanche entered the livery stable. Mr. Haverty's snores rolled through the building. Maddy was glad of the noise; she and Blanche could have shot their pistols and not been heard.

Humming under her breath, Maddy went to Ali's stall. She froze, completely astonished.

The stall was empty.

Bridle, reins, saddle, halters . . . and Ali, gone. And she knew who'd done it: John Ballard.

Surprise turned to fury. It didn't matter that he'd done it to protect her. He hadn't trusted her. Of course, he shouldn't have trusted her. After all, she'd already decided to do what he'd stolen her horse to keep her from doing. It was terribly convoluted and completely illogical, but knowing that didn't dim the heat of her anger.

"Blanche?" she called.

"Mine's gone, too," Blanche replied.

"The sneaky, son-of—"

"Maddy!"

With a sigh, Maddy pressed her fingertips to her temples. "Oh, dear, I think I've been in Texas too long."

"What are we going to do?"

"We're going to wake Mr. Haverty and arrange to hire two of his horses, and then we'll go to Preston as planned," Maddy said. "If John Ballard thinks he's stopped a Saylor, he has a rude surprise coming."

John and Hank rode toward Preston, intending to pick up the stage just outside town. A faint haze stained the horizon to the east, but dawn was still some time away yet.

John glanced at his companion, gauging the level of his strength. "Are you all right?"

"Right enough," Hank said. "Hurts like the devil himself, but I ain't about to let it keep me from doin' what I came to do."

"What do you think about Derek?"

Hank let his breath out in a long sigh. "I've known plenty like him. Most of them managed to get themselves killed. The only reason that boy ain't dead is that he's good enough to overcome his own damned foolishness."

"Nobody's good enough to keep that going forever," John said.

"That's why Maddy and Blanche have been helping him. *They* know that if he keeps this up, he's going to ride himself straight into a shallow grave."

"Those are two fine women," John said.

"Yeah," Hank agreed. "If a man can survive 'em."

John laughed, but he wasn't completely sure that Hank had been joking. The Saylor sisters were unique; no matter how much a man might think he knew about women, he could throw all that away when dealing with those two Virginia belles.

"You're sure they're goin' to keep out of this?" Hank asked.

"I'm not sure about anything where those two are concerned," John said. "I stole their horses."

"You stole their horses?"

"And all their tack. I must admit, I never thought I'd end up a horse thief, but I figured it was necessary this time."

Hank's mouth twitched. "Man does what a man has to do."

They rode for a while without speaking, the gentle creak of their saddles the only sound. John wasn't easy in his mind, not easy at all. He'd done the best he could to keep Maddy safe, but she was as wild and ungovernable as a force of nature.

"If I'd thought this all through," he said, "I would have talked Sheriff Cooper into locking them up with their brother."

"Sure. It was all you could do to convince the old boy not

to lock *us* up," Hank growled. "He's still pretty mad about being snookered with the laudanum."

Hank's mouth had turned grim, and there was a worried edge to his voice. John, too was possessed with uneasiness. He told himself that Maddy and Blanche would be sensible with Derek safe in jail. He told himself that there was nothing he could have done in any case—to keep Maddy with him was to bring her into danger. But that nagging feeling kept gnawing at him. Instinct, pure and simple. And that instinct saved him too many times for him to ignore it now.

"I've got a bad feeling about this," he said.

"You, too?" Hank asked.

They turned to look directly at each other. Then, in perfect unison, they slapped the reins against their mounts' necks, urging them into a gallop.

"Could have fallen in love with a preacher's daughter," Hank shouted.

John laughed into the wind. "But that wouldn't have been half so much fun," he shouted back.

Now that the decision had been made, John fretted with every mile, every passing minute, every possible obstacle. He didn't know how or when Maddy would appear to bedevil him, but he was sure she would. And she'd probably get herself killed doing it.

The hills were higher here, piling up in front of them like wrinkles on a giant's skin, and slowed them down even more. John's impatience grew, and he could see the same impatience in Hank's face.

They rode diagonally up the face of a hill, taking the slope faster than was prudent. As they crested the top; John heard a crack, then felt a bullet zing past his ear. He flung himself off his mount, pulling his rifle from the boot as he went.

Hank came down beside him with a grunt of pain. Pain notwithstanding, the bounty hunter had the presence of mind to bring his own rifle with him. They crawled into the lee of a nearby rock. John put his back against the sun-warmed stone while he tried to get his breathing under control. Bullets spanged off the rock, spattering rock chips down on them.

"Friends of yours?" Hank panted.

"Could be," John said. "Since I got involved with the Saylors, it seems that almost everybody wants to kill me."

Hank chuckled. Then he turned, peering over the top of the rock for a moment. "I've got them placed on that ridge due southeast of us. What about you?"

"Let's see." Balancing his hat on the barrel of his rifle, John raised it above the sheltering rock. A hail of bullets struck it, sending it rolling away down the hill. "Yes, they're definitely coming from the southeast."

"What time does that stage leave Preston?"

"Noon," John said, squinting tip at the sun. "Which won't be long. Damn it, we don't have time for this."

More bullets ricocheted off the rocks and went whining off into the distance.

"Why don't you stand up and tell those fellers they're keeping us from an appointment," Hank offered.

"That's a thought," John said, rising to his knees long enough to get off a quick shot. "But they don't seem to be much in a mood for listening. Can you see our horses?"

"Nope. They're probably halfway to Mexico by now."

John cursed under his breath. "Then we've got no choice but to take theirs."

"Yeah," Hank agreed, with a laugh. Then he hissed, easing his good hand underneath his shirt. "You want to cover me or flank 'em?"

"What hurts you less—running or shooting that rifle?"

"Shooting."

"Then I'll do the running. How are you doing on ammunition?"

"I've got enough for this job," Hank said. "Providing you don't take too long."

"You're awful damn cocky," John growled.

Hank smiled a bit grimly "Sure. After all, we've survived Blanche and Maddy so far."

"So far," John echoed. "Goddamn. Ready?"

"Ready."

With a smooth surge of muscles, John hurled himself out from behind the rock.

The stagecoach was crowded, and Maddy found herself crammed in the center of the seat between a portly man with a wide, shiny face, and a thin, hard-faced woman in a black-and-white-striped foulard that made Maddy's vision swim if she stared at it too long.

Blanche sat across from her, but had been lucky enough to get the seat next to the window. Maddy watched in envy as a breeze stirred the golden curls framing her sister's face.

"Hot day, isn't it?" asked the man beside her.

"Indeed it is," she replied.

"Where are y'all headed?"

She turned to look at him, thinking he might be flirting. But honest curiosity lit his eyes, and she relaxed.

"East," she replied. It was the truth; the stagecoach was indeed heading east.

"Ah. You've got family there?"

"Yes," she said. "In Virginia."

"Nice place, Virginia," he said. "I was there once as a boy, and I remember how gracious the people were."

She inclined her head, touched by the compliment. "Why, thank you, sir."

The miles rolled by without incident. An hour passed, then another. Maddy scanned the hills constantly, looking for any sign of pursuit. But the countryside remained empty, and she began to think nothing would happen. Perhaps the robber had seen the guard riding shotgun with the driver, and had decided not to intercept the stage.

Her stomach churned. Of course, she didn't want trouble.

But Derek had risked his freedom on this gamble, and she didn't want to think about the consequences of failure.

Then she glimpsed a shadow flitting across the ridge just ahead. Her spirit soared. She glanced at Blanche, and saw her sister's slight nod of acknowledgment. Maddy craned to look farther ahead. The road took a long curve, disappearing between a pair of long, rocky ridges. As soon as they hit that curve, they'd be blind to what lay ahead.

That's where it's going to happen, she thought. She shot another look at Blanche, then took out her handkerchief and fanned herself.

"Oh, dear," she gasped. "I'm feeling a bit ill."

"Is there anything I can do, ma'am?" the portly man asked solicitously.

"If I could just get a breath of air . . ."

"Of course, of course," he said.

It took some doing to wriggle his bulk out of the seat in the crowded compartment. But he managed, and Maddy slid into his seat beside the window. Now she and Blanche could cover both sides of the stagecoach.

She leaned her head against the side of the coach. "Would you be so kind as to hand me my bag, sir?" she asked her unwitting benefactor

"Certainly," he replied, bending to lift her satchel from the floor under his feet.

Surprise widened his eyes as he felt the weight of it, and it was all Maddy could do to repress a smile. It held two revolvers and a goodly number of bullets; she only hoped it wouldn't clank as he handed it over.

"Thank you, sir," she murmured, opening it just enough to reach in and get a fresh handkerchief, then leaving it unlatched so she could reach her guns quickly.

The stage tilted as the driver headed into the turn. Maddy's heart pounded in anticipation and fear. She was glad she still had the capacity to be afraid; otherwise, she would be just like Derek, seeking danger simply for the thrill of tempting death.

The light inside the coach dimmed as the vehicle entered the shelter of the ridges. Maddy slipped her hand into her bag and gripped one of the revolvers. It wouldn't be long now.

She nearly jumped out of her skin when the driver shouted suddenly to the team. His whip cracked, and a moment later the stagecoach lurched wildly as the horses broke into a gallop. Maddy grabbed the edge of the window with her free hand, bracing herself against the jolts.

Where is John? she wondered, realizing at that moment just how much she'd been counting on him.

"What is it?" the hard-faced woman cried. "What's happening?"

The trap door in the ceiling banged open, and the guard poked his head through the opening. "We got trouble, folks. Jest hang on tight."

"What kind of trouble?" the portly man shouted.

"Looks like Derek—" Shots rang out, and the guard's eyes went wide all of a sudden.

Then he slumped, one arm hanging limply in the coach. Blood pattered down on the floor below him.

"He's dead!" the hard-faced woman screamed. "Oh, Lord, we're going to die, too! We're all going to die!"

Bullets smacked into the stagecoach, one splintering the wood of the window frame not a foot from Maddy's face.

She knew John would never willingly have abandoned her, and fear for him lay a shadow of coldness in her heart. But she didn't—couldn't—allow it to affect her This situation had been laid in her lap, and she and Blanche would just have to deal with it. She glanced again at her sister. Blanche's eyes held no fear; whatever she might be feeling inside, she could be counted on in this.

"Ladies, I think you should get down on the floor," the portly man said, shouting to be heard over the frightened woman's shrieks.

With her free hand, Maddy brushed wood chips from her

bodice. "Thank you, sir," she said, "but I think not. You might, however, try to calm the lady beside you."

He nodded. But before he could speak to the woman, she fell forward in a faint and rolled onto the floor.

"Best place for her," he said. "Ma'am—"

The stagecoach lurched again, and this time Maddy sensed something new. "The driver's gone," she said.

She hoped that the team would stop, but the horses kept running, drawing the coach after them at a dangerous pace. The wheels hit a dip in the road, bouncing the heavy vehicle into the air. It came down again with a tremendous jolt.

Maddy was flung against the wall with enough force to drive the breath from her lungs for a moment. Gasping, she looked to see if the others were all right. Blanche had a cut on her lip and a torn sleeve, and the other passengers seemed shaken but unhurt.

"Get ready to . . ." Maddy began, but the coach gave another tremendous bounce, flinging them all about again. This time, the portly man caught her by the arm, bracing himself and her against the jolt.

"We're going to crash if we don't get this coach slowed soon," he shouted.

Maddy nodded. She pulled the big Colt out of her satchel and thrust it into her waistband. Balancing against the violent sway of the coach, she grabbed the dead guard's arm and hauled him down through the trap door.

"Good Lord!" the portly man exclaimed.

"Help me up," she panted.

"Madam, you can't—"

"Sir." Her tone brooked no interference. "If you please!"

He didn't argue. Bending, he cupped his hands so she could step into them. A moment later, she'd wriggled up onto the top of the coach. The vehicle swayed and swung, and it took every bit of her strength to stay aboard. She had a clear view of the road now. Five horsemen pounded after the stagecoach, sometimes mere shadows in the cloud of pale dust that boiled in the stagecoach's wake.

She swung around toward the front. The driver sat slumped in his seat, the reins still wrapped around his hands. Maddy managed to slide down into the seat beside him. Gunfire cracked behind her, and she went down on her knees, using the back of the seat as a shield. Grabbing the reins from the dead driver, she pulled with all her strength.

The team began to slow. Finally, they drew to a stop, and the dust caught up with the stage, momentarily enveloping it in a choking cloud. Maddy flung herself flat in the floor of the seat as she heard hoofbeats pounding close.

"Everybody out," a man shouted, his voice muffled and harsh. "Now!"

The coach swayed as the passengers disembarked. Maddy was powerfully aware of the strongbox poking against her back, and knew her concealment would soon end. She eased her gun around to the back of her waistband and pulled her blouse out so it would hang down far enough to cover the weapon.

Then she sat up very slowly, keeping her hands where they could be seen. The thieves had stopped their horses beside the stage, dust coating their hats, shoulders, and the bandannas tied over the lower part of their faces. The leader *did* look a bit like Derek, she noted with one swift, encompassing glance at his broad shoulders and dark blond hair.

One of the robbers noticed her, and swung his pistol around to cover her. "There's another one" he said.

The leader swung around to look at her. Their gazes met and locked. Maddy read surprise . . . and, to her astonishment, recognition. He knew her. Which, of course, meant that she knew him.

She knew he wouldn't speak lest he betray his identity. Grim humor turned her mouth upward. He gestured for one of his men to help her down. Maddy climbed down herself, disdaining his outstretched hand.

"You're Derek Saylor, I presume," the portly man said.

The leader swept his hat off, a dramatic gesture worthy of the man he impersonated. It gave everyone a good look at his hair. Then he urged his horse close beside the stage, and swung directly from his mount onto the vehicle. Pushing the dead driver aside, he lifted the strongbox up and handed it to one of his men.

The woman in the foulard began to cry. One of the thieves gave her a shove, sending her stumbling to her knees.

"Shut up," he growled.

Blanche moved quickly to place herself between them. With her arm around the woman's shoulders, she faced the robber defiantly.

"She's just frightened," she said.

"She's gonna be more than that," he said. "If you want to help her, git her to shut her damned mouth."

Maddy joined her sister. They lifted the sobbing woman to her feet, supporting her between them. Then Maddy looked at her sister. Blanche was as calm as ever, but her face seemed abnormally pale, stirring the cold touch of alarm in Maddy's chest.

"I'll take care of her, Blanche," she said. "Go on."

The beginnings of protest lit Blanche's eyes. Maddy held her gaze steadily, trying to send the warning that was screaming in her brain.

Something was wrong here. Maddy had had much experience with desperate men, and had been desperate herself more than once. And these men were nervous, much more nervous than professional thieves ought to be. The danger was much greater than she'd anticipated.

The woman beside her drew a deep, gasping breath, and Maddy feared she'd begin to scream again. And that might get them all killed. Quickly, she put her arm around the other woman's shoulders, holding her tightly.

"Tell me your name," she said.

"E-Ella Ella Weatherston," the woman stuttered.

"You must listen to me, Ella," Maddy said, speaking slowly and calmly. "Do exactly what I tell you. Now, take a deep breath—it will calm you. Very good. That's very good. Now, take another."

Ella nodded, but there was a glitter in her eyes that Maddy didn't trust. So she kept hold of the woman's hand, hoping that the contact would keep her calm.

A sudden flash of light caught Maddy's gaze. She looked up, seeking its source, and saw another flash on the ridge opposite. Sunlight on metal, she thought, or perhaps glass. Her heart swelled with joy—and hope. It had to be John.

She knew he'd never be so careless as to let the sun reflect off his gear like that, so it had to be a deliberate attempt to tell her that he'd come. But even he couldn't approach the stage without being seen. He needed a distraction.

"Hey, what are you waitin' fer?" one of the thieves called. "Open the box. I got to get me a look at that gold."

The leader nodded. The robbers dismounted and gathered around the strongbox. One man drew his pistol, aiming at the heavy padlock securing the top.

The moment the shot rang out, Ella tore out of Maddy's grasp and ran, shrieking, back toward town. One of the thieves raised his rifle and snapped off a shot. The woman flung her arms straight out to the sides, as though she were flying, then fell face dawn in the dust.

Maddy took a step toward her, but the man swung his weapon so it pointed straight at her chest. She froze, her chest heaving.

"Let me help her," she said.

"You jest stay there," he snapped.

Maddy met his gaze for a long, heart-pounding moment, gauging the extent of the danger. Peripherally, she noted a slight tremor in the rifle barrel, as though the man holding it had trembled for a moment. Ah, he'd given himself away; that shot had been instinctive, not planned.

Deliberately, she turned and started walking toward the fallen woman.

A gunshot seemed to split the quiet, dusty air. Maddy stopped and glanced down, expecting to see blood on her blouse, expecting to die. She was completely stunned when she didn't.

Turning, she looked back at the others. The man who'd shot Ella stood with his eyes wide with shock, blood pouring from a wound in his throat. Then he fell.

The thieves started shooting in all directions, and everyone scattered. One of the robbers managed to get to his horse, but a bullet caught him before he could do more than get his boots into the stirrups. He fell backward, and his panicked mount dragged him as it bolted down the road.

Maddy searched for her sister in the melee, her heart pounding with fear. "Blanche!" she screamed "Blanche!"

"Here, Maddy!"

Turning in the direction of the cry, Maddy saw that the passengers had taken cover beneath the stage. Blanche had drawn her revolver, ready to protect the group.

The thieves had retreated into a cluster of rocks at the side of the road. They returned fire, shooting wildly at the hillside around them. Bullets flew everywhere, forcing Maddy to take cover behind a rock of her own.

It was tempting, so tempting, to add her fire to John and Hank's. But instinct and hard-won experience made her wait until her six shots could do the most good. And it seemed that John and Hank might not need her help at all; two of the robbers were down, and another seemed to be wounded.

A loud whinny pulled her attention back to the stagecoach. The team was reacting to the chaos around them, stamping and pawing in the traces. The stagecoach shivered like a live thing. If it moved, it would crush the people beneath it.

Even as that thought seared through her mind, one of the

lead horses threw up its head and neighed. Then the whole team lunged forward.

Maddy flung herself toward the stage, her heart clenching because she knew she wasn't going to be in time.

Thirty

Maddy cried out in protest as the stage started to lurch forward. Then a man leaped into the driver's seat, grabbing the reins just as they slithered toward the ground.

John. No one else moved with that catlike grace, that economical power. He hauled back on the reins, holding the panicky team by sheer strength and will.

"Get out of there!" he shouted to the passengers.

They scrambled out from beneath the stagecoach and took shelter in a fold of rock on the side of the hill. Bullets spattered all around John, sending bits of wood flying into the air.

Maddy opened fire on the robbers then, keeping the thieves at bay as John struggled with the stagecoach team. And she prayed for his safety, this man she loved more than life itself, like she'd never prayed before. If something happened to him . . . she rejected the thought, as she rejected the wasteland her life would become without him.

He held them a moment longer, glancing over his shoulder to see if the passengers were safe. Then he leaped from the stage, rolling across the road to clear the dangerous wheels.

A bullet struck one of the horses, sending it lunging forward with a scream. The stagecoach tilted and veered as the frightened team bolted with its injured mate. Dust boiled up into the air as the vehicle bounced into the air once, twice, then gave a mighty leap and turned onto its side. The horses dragged it forward, churning up still more dust, and finally disappeared around the curve.

John rose to his feet, staggering slightly from the jolt he'd taken. The breeze whipped the dust into a cloud around him, nearly obscuring him from view.

"Maddy!" he shouted.

"Here," she cried.

He turned toward her. The breeze died then, and she realized that no shot had been fired in the past few seconds. It seemed as though a blanket had fallen over them all; she could almost hear the grains of dust settling back to earth.

John's expression made her knees tremble. He'd been angry with her for interfering, she knew. He'd be angry again later. But now, his eyes blazed with love as raw and powerful as a summer storm. She felt as though the wind had swept her up and away, leaving her nothing but the man striding toward her.

He belonged to her. And she to him, forever.

Then, suddenly, her vision shifted, refocusing to a point behind him. And she saw the spurious Derek Saylor rise from the rocks in which the robbers had taken refuge. Blood made a startling bright banner across his shirt, and he swayed like a reed in the wind. But he still had his gun.

Even as she registered his presence, he aimed at John's back. There was no time to cry a warning.

With one swift, instinctive motion, she raised the Colt and fired over John's shoulder. Red bloomed in the center of the robber's chest. He stood for a moment, his gun wobbling from side to side as he tried to hold his aim. Then he fell forward across the rocks.

Maddy's gaze shifted back to John. Through it all, he hadn't looked away from her. He hadn't moved, hadn't even flinched, and it had to seem as though she'd fired straight at him. Her chest ached with emotion almost too great to bear. He'd trusted her completely, even to his life. It was a gift beyond price; for as long as she lived, she would remember this.

John went to her. He didn't touch her, not yet. He only wanted to look. Her soul seemed to blaze in her eyes, and all for him. Truly, she was everything he'd ever need, everything he could ever want.

"Maddy," he said, his voice harsh with emotion. "I love you. I love you so much . . . There aren't words strong enough to say—"

"So show me," she said, sliding her arms up around his neck.

Maddy sighed as he pulled her to him, his hands spreading out over her back with tender possessiveness. But he didn't kiss her; instead he gazed into her eyes, letting her see into the depths of his soul. Her heart began to race. Here was a man who loved her beyond reason, beyond caution, beyond limit.

It wasn't only trust that had kept him from flinching when she'd fired a moment ago. Yes, the trust was there. But it went far beyond that. He loved her so much that he would have stood there, unmoving, even if she'd meant to kill him. For to live, knowing that she could have done such a thing, would have been more than he could bear.

"John," she whispered.

He kissed her then, a wild, tempestuous kiss that burned hotter than the sun overhead. She held to him with all her strength, feeling as though the earth had dropped out from beneath her feet. She had no concept of time; they could have been kissing for an instant, or a century.

Someone cleared his throat nearby, bringing reality back to her with a rush. John lifted his head, gazing into her eyes for a moment. Then he sighed and let her go. She turned, and saw the portly man who had sat beside her in the stagecoach.

"What?" John growled.

"Forgive me for interrupting," the man said, reaching out to shake John's hand. "I want to thank you for your timely intervention. Although," he added, laughter twinkling in his eyes, "this lovely lady and her sister were most—"

"Foolish," John said.

"—Courageous," the portly man continued smoothly. "I

don't know what would have happened if it weren't for them."
He smiled at Maddy. "I must admit, I thought you were a bit
reckless when you climbed up onto the top of the coach to
stop the team before we crashed—"

"WHAT?" John yelped.

"—But you did not underestimate your abilities, dear lady,
not a bit." He tried to brush the dust from his clothing, but
soon gave it up. "Let me introduce myself. I'm Gabriel Polk,
owner of this stage line."

"John Ballard. Pinkerton's. And this is Maddy Saylor."

Polk blinked. "Maddy . . ."

"Saylor," she finished for him.

"But my dear young lady—"

"We'll explain everything soon enough," John said. "Mr.
Polk, you weren't supposed to be here. You *shouldn't* have
been here. And there weren't supposed to be any passengers
on this coach. I arranged it all with your man in Preston."

"Arranged what?"

John stared at him in astonishment. "You didn't know?"
Giving himself a stern mental shake, he went on. "When word
slipped out that there was gold on this stage, I decided to set
up a trap for the thieves. The agent in Preston agreed to put
Pinkerton agents in place of the regular driver and guard, and
to make sure there were no passengers. He told me he'd sent
a telegraph informing the company about this, and that he had
full authorization."

Mr. Polk's genial expression hardened, and Maddy got a
glimpse of the man who'd built and run a successful stagecoach business.

"He never told anyone," Polk said. "I found him intoxicated
on the job, and discharged him immediately. Someone told me
he was a regular and enthusiastic patron of the bottle. I
wouldn't be surprised if he was the one who divulged the information about the gold in the first place."

His brow furrowed, and a shadow darkened his eyes "And
as far as the passengers being on the stage . . . I . . . I'm

afraid I took things over myself, and was most upset to find my stage leaving without passengers. So I hired someone else on the spot and instructed him to fill the vehicle. That poor woman," he whispered. "That poor woman."

Maddy reached out and laid her hand on his arm. "It wasn't your fault. You can't take responsibility for the actions of either the agent or the robber."

He looked away for a moment. Then he turned back to her and lifted her hand to his lips in a gallant gesture. "Thank you. And now kindly tell me how you came to bait the trap for your own brother."

"I didn't," Maddy said. "That isn't Derek Saylor."

Polk's eyes widened. "What?"

"Saylor is in jail in Cofield," John said.

"Then who is the thief?" the other man demanded.

"Let's find out," John said.

He took Maddy's hand as they walked toward the man who'd impersonated Derek. His hat had fallen off, letting his blond hair trail in the dust. John crouched beside him and reached toward the bandanna shielding his face.

"Wait," Maddy said, gesturing for Blanche and Hank to join them.

Maddy smiled at them both. Lightning had struck twice in one spot, giving both Saylor sisters so much happiness.

"Ready?" John asked.

"Do it," Hank said.

John pulled the bandanna free. He let his breath out in a grunt of astonishment as the dead man's features were revealed. A glance up at his companions told him they were as surprised as he.

"Alf Marsh," Hank said. "Well, I'll be damned. Who the hell else do we have?"

John went to unmask the other robbers. One man still lived; a bullet had only creased his skull. John pulled his bandanna off, then glanced over at Hank.

"Vince Marsh," the bounty hunter said. "I can't wait to tell that holier-than-thou son of a—"

"Hank," Blanche exclaimed.

"—Bitch," he continued with relish.

"You should he kinder," Blanche said.

"I'd be damned sympathetic," Hank growled, "if he hadn't tried to hit you. And for all you know, he was involved up to his eyeballs. You're too soft, Blanche."

"Soft!" Polk exclaimed. "She shot that one over there," he said, pointing to Vince.

Hank's pale predator's gaze turned tender as he regarded his ladylove. "I said she was too soft in feelin' sorry for a cold-hearted snake. I never said she didn't shoot people."

Polk's eyes widened. "I . . . ah . . ."

"Don't worry, Mr. Polk," Maddy said taking pity on him. "He's teasing you."

She didn't address the fact that Blanche had, indeed, shot people. But since Polk didn't bring up that particular issue, she didn't either. He stared at her for what seemed a very long time. Finally, he burst out laughing, and she knew he'd become a friend some day.

"Come on, folks," he said, wiping tears from his eyes. "We have work to do."

John turned to Maddy. Slipping his arm around her waist, he pulled her against him. "And a future to begin. Marry me, Maddy."

"Oh, yes," she murmured. "Oh, yes."

Epilogue

August, 1868

"It was so nice of Mr. Polk to insist on paying the reward even though it wasn't Derek who was robbing the stages," Blanche said. "It gave us the chance to buy those adjoining parcels of land, and to build two sturdy houses in which to raise our families"

"Gabriel is a nice man," Maddy replied. "Besides, it was John and Hank who found all that gold hidden in a line shack on Zachary Marsh's ranch."

Blanche sighed. "Aren't we lucky?"

"Indeed we are. And we're especially lucky to have married men who don't object to our having our own business." Maddy took another neat stitch on the bodice of Dolly Mayhew's new gown. She held it up "What do you think?"

"I think Dolly is becoming a regular peacock," Blanche replied. "And if she continues sashaying . . . That *is* the word, isn't it?"

"Yes," Maddy said.

"If she keeps sashaying around the way she is, we might expect another addition to the Mayhew brood."

"Her youngest is nearly thirteen," Maddy said. Then she laughed. "But then, she'd hardly be the first woman to be given a . . . late surprise."

Blanche laid her hands upon her own stomach, which had

become quite round. "If she is, I hope she's half as happy as I am."

"And I," Maddy said.

John came striding into the shop, and it seemed as though he brought the sunlight with him. Maddy smiled. Marriage hadn't dimmed what she felt for him; her heart still raced whenever she looked at him, and when he kissed her, he still made the world go away.

"Hello, lover," she said.

He swept her up in one arm and kissed her soundly. When the kiss ended, she was breathless, trembling with desire. If they'd been alone . . . She glanced at Blanche, who smiled a very knowing smile. Life was good indeed for the Saylor sisters.

"How are you feeling?" John asked.

"As well as the other hundred times you've asked," she teased.

His eyes held a fierce tenderness that made her heart beat faster still. "I can't help it," he murmured. "I love you hard and hot and helplessly, and you're carrying my child. Let me be an idiot about it if I want to."

"Idiocy is one of your most endearing traits," she said. "Now, tell my why you're here instead of out . . . what was the term Hank used? Oh, yes. Punching cows."

"The cows are all punched, my darling. I came to ride home with my lovely wife."

Maddy knew that meant a leisurely picnic somewhere shady and private, and then an even more leisurely lovemaking. Anticipation ran sweet and hot through her veins.

"Just let me fetch my parasol," she said.

The bell tinkled as someone came into the shop. Maddy turned, her interest quickening when she saw the girl who'd entered.

She was petite and very pretty, and quite fragile-looking with her oval face framed by a riot of red-brown curls. But Maddy noted the firm line of her jaw and the determination in her long-lashed brown eyes, and knew that this was a woman to be reckoned with.

"Hello," the girl said in a rich, liquid accent that seemed to fill the room with music. "I'm Melina Antonini. My aunt and uncle bought a ranch—"

"Oh, the Marsh place," Blanche exclaimed "I'd heard someone had bought it." She hurried forward to offer her hand. "Welcome to Cofield, Miss Antonini."

The girl studied Blanche for a moment, then gave Maddy and John the same intent perusal. Then she smiled, and became startlingly beautiful. "Please, call me Melina. I have been told that you make very beautiful dresses."

"Yes, we do," Blanche agreed. "Is there something we can help you with?"

Melina nodded. "You see, the ship I took from Italy sank, and I was left with only the clothes I was wearing. Now, I must have all new things."

"A shipwreck!" Blanche said. "Such a tragedy."

The girl's eyes darkened. "Yes. But such are the things of life, are they not? One goes on."

"Yes," Blanche said. "One does."

Blanche glanced at Maddy over her shoulder, and there was such a look of calculation in her eyes that Maddy nearly laughed. But she couldn't disagree; this girl was perfect. Absolutely perfect. She smiled.

"Yes, we do make beautiful dresses," Blanche said, returning her attention to the visitor. "Why don't you come sit and have some tea, Melina?"

"I would like that very much," the girl said.

Then, with a sly look at Maddy, Blanche walked into the back room and knocked at the trap door leading upstairs.

"Oh, Derek," she called. "We've got company."

Maddy looked at her love, her lover, her husband, and saw the rueful look that came into his eyes when he realized what had happened. For it had happened. Derek just didn't know it yet.

"He'll have to teach her how to shoot," she murmured.

John shot her a look. "I think she has more than enough weapons," he growled. "Well, Derek's on his own. Now I want my picnic, and I want my wife."

"Always," she whispered. "Forever."

TODAY'S HOTTEST READS
ARE TOMORROW'S SUPERSTARS

VICTORY'S WOMAN (4484, $4.50)
by Gretchen Genet

Andrew—the carefree soldier who sought glory on the battlefield, and returned a shattered man . . . Niall—the legandary frontiersman and a former Shawnee captive, tormented by his past . . . Roger—the troubled youth, who would rise up to claim a shocking legacy . . . and Clarice—the passionate beauty bound by one man, and hopelessly in love with another. Set against the backdrop of the American revolution, three men fight for their heritage—and one woman is destined to change all their lives forever!

FORBIDDEN (4488, $4.99)
by Jo Beverley

While fleeing from her brothers, who are attempting to sell her into a loveless marriage, Serena Riverton accepts a carriage ride from a stranger—who is the handsomest man she has ever seen. Lord Middlethorpe, himself, is actually contemplating marriage to a dull daughter of the aristocracy, when he encounters the breathtaking Serena. She arouses him as no woman ever has. And after a night of thrilling intimacy—a forbidden liaison—Serena must choose between a lady's place and a woman's passion!

WINDS OF DESTINY (4489, $4.99)
by Victoria Thompson

Becky Tate is a half-breed outcast—branded by her Comanche heritage. Then she meets a rugged stranger who awakens her heart to the magic and mystery of passion. Hiding a desperate past, Texas Ranger Clint Masterson has ridden into cattle country to bring peace to a divided land. But a greater battle rages inside him when he dares to desire the beautiful Becky!

WILDEST HEART (4456, $4.99)
by Virginia Brown

Maggie Malone had come to cattle country to forge her future as a healer. Now she was faced by Devon Conrad, an outlaw wounded body and soul by his shadowy past . . . whose eyes blazed with fury even as his burning caress sent her spiraling with desire. They came together in a Texas town about to explode in sin and scandal. Danger was their destiny—and there was nothing they wouldn't dare for love!